Dark & Day
The Angels' Masquerade

3

A
Israel Grey

⚘ Visit ⚘

www.**DarkandDay**.com

Become a Fan and Like the book on Facebook
http://www.facebook.com/pages/Dark-and-Day-book/102844399757795

See artwork at DeviantArt.com
http://jono-wyer.deviantart.com/favourites/#Dark-and-Day-art

Also by Israel Grey

DARK & DAY (series)

Dark & Day 1

Dark & Day 2: The Withering Mark

Dark & Day 3: The Angels' Masquerade

With more to come!

For Nick and Mikel

The world of Dark & Day
is better for having you two
in it

By

Israel Grey

Cover Art by Andrew Hou, Tyler Edlin, Israel Grey
Interior Art by Andrew Hou, Tyler Edlin

The truth about stories is,

that is all we are.

Thomas King

CONTENTS

Dr. Pengull's Book of Classical Fairy Tales

The Parable of

The Angels' Masquerade

By

Hana Xavier Vilhiem

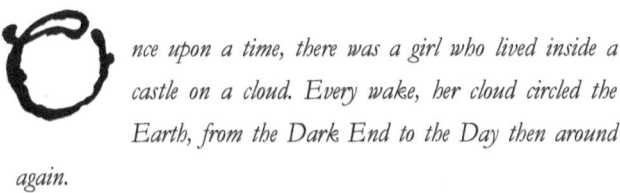 nce upon a time, there was a girl who lived inside a castle on a cloud. Every wake, her cloud circled the Earth, from the Dark End to the Day then around again.

When the castle was beneath the blue skies of the Day, the girl would play with water wisps that glistened as they frolicked together. The Day was a bright and happy place in the warmth of the young, new sun.

Under the Dark sky, however, her cloud grew cold and gray. The girl was afraid of the Dark. She hid inside her castle and curled up in her bed to sleep.

With her last thought every wake, she sent a wish to the Angels.

"Please bring me a friend," she asked. "I don't want to be alone."

Every wake, the girl crawled out of bed, just as her cloud was nearing the Dawn. She searched the castle for the answer to her wish, and every wake the castle remained empty. The halls would be hollow, the other bedrooms barren. The girl was sad and yet as the sky turned bright and the sun approached, she gained the strength to enjoy another wake.

Except on one wake, when the time of Dawn grew near, the atmosphere remained black and full of stars. The cloud had floated into the endless void, and the Earth grew smaller below.

"Dear Angels," the girl cried out, "don't send me away! Please, I don't want to be alone."

As her tears hit the castle floor, the cloud itself began to cry. Huge tears rained down, pulling her toward the Earth. Her castle descended slowly, until it landed beside a small town.

The girl wiped away her tears as the castle doors opened to the warm light of Day casting a woman's silhouette in the middle of the doorway. The woman's wings spread wide through the rays of light.

"Come with me," the angel said. "I have heard your cries and brought you to a land where you will be loved."

The girl approached the door, but the brilliant light was too much for her to see anything. She shielded her eyes with her hands.

The angel offered her an ivory mask. "Hold this to your face and you will be able to see this world."

The girl placed the mask on her face and saw a beautiful mountain village, bustling with smiling people. Wood houses lined cobblestone streets with trees cresting the rooftops. A baker waved as he passed by with a cart of bread. Children squealed as they splashed in puddles of her cloud's tears. Birds sang a welcoming tune from signposts. A cat nuzzled against her leg and purred.

The world below the clouds was full of wonder, games, and friendly faces. In such a place, she would never have to be alone again!

For many years, the girl lived happily in the village with the townsfolk. She gained many friendships and found adventure and love with the families in the town. She celebrated their joys and comforted them in sorrow.

She never removed the mask, but no one noticed it.

Life had become everything she dreamed it could be.

One shiny wake, a tall mirror caught her eye. It reminded her of a mirror in her castle. She approached, expecting to see the reflection of a little girl, but instead it was the angel that looked back at her. When she moved, the angel moved. When she spoke, the angel spoke.

She was the angel she imagined that wake so long ago. She had brought herself to the town, making a life of friendships and happiness.

She had given herself the ivory mask.

In a moment of curiosity, the girl lowered the mask from her face. Instantly, the town disappeared.

The girl stood alone in her castle with an infinite array of stars filling the depths of space outside. She held the mask to her face again, and peering through one eye, she could see the town, but this time she reached out to touch a friend, and her hand faded through them.

Everything she had wanted paraded in front of her, a living dream, hollow and beautiful.

She pulled the mask from her eyes and gazed at the angel in the mirror.

"Is anything real?" she asked.

"Aren't you?" the angel in the mirror replied.

The girl looked at the castle around her. The stone was cold, the stars so very far away.

The back of the ivory mask felt of the town's warmth. To return to that land of friendship and joy, all she needed to do was close her eyes.

"What should I do?"

The angel smiled and said nothing.

After so many years away, the girl grew weary being back in the castle. Her hands were wrinkled and her body frail. Her legs shook as she clamored to her bed.

Beyond the window, the castle floated in an endless sea of black. Distant stars twinkled, always present yet forever out of reach.

The girl collapsed on her bed, exhausted. Her trembling hands lifted the ivory mask to her face. Her body shivered, and the mask fell with a thud against her face.

Her eyes cracked open against the blinding light. Noise and life surrounded her again in that tiny mountain village in her mind.

Her breathing eased. She stood on the cobbled street beyond the gate, the frail girl in the castle gasping for air so far behind her.

The ivory mask smiled, as the woman smiled beneath it, forevermore continuing the masquerade.

Chapter One

The Things We Leave Behind

"Tell me another story," said a boy.

"It's late," a woman replied. "You should get some sleep."

"But I'm not tired."

The woman smiled and held back a tear on the edge of her eye. "Once upon a time, the gods shone brightly across the globe. The seas and sky were calm, the fields grew fat with food, and the people were happy and at peace. A great kingdom spread across the stars, and people of distant planets joined the kingdom as friends. The people there were good and wanted everyone on every planet to be happy and safe, but the gods knew life would always be filled with danger, so the Great Father and Burning Mother created a plan. Above all planets, they loved Earth the most, so they asked seven of their must trusted angels to be bound to our planet, to watch over all life and guide every child along the Narrow Path."

Static flickered over a small room, distorting the candlelight into horizontal strips of orange. A young boy lay in a bed, tucked under covers that looked purple in the dim twilight. A woman sat beside him, brushing his messy brown hair with her fingers.

"Is that why there are so many aliens on Earth?" the boy asked.

"That's right. They all flocked here to be close to the love of the Mother and Father. Whenever people would get scared or lost, the gods and angels would send whispers to the quietest parts of their minds. They would remind them about the beauty of the world and joys that person had known. The whispers would give people strength and hope, and with them, they could get through anything."

"What if someone couldn't hear them?" the boy asked.

"That is a problem," the woman said. "The whispers are very quiet, so most people don't hear them. Most people get so busy with their lives that the noise of everything else drowns the whispers out. They get distracted by the world and can fall off the Narrow Path. They can end up in terrible places, but the angels are smart. They know how lost people can get, so when a person is most in need, the angels would soar down from the stars to leave clues to guide them back on the right path."

"What types of clues?"

"Oh, they could be anywhere or anything. They could be a comment you overhear at school, or the color of a lilac petal that catches the corner of your eye. They could be the croak of a woolly frog or light shimmering off the wings of a pixiefly. You'll know them when the gears of your mind start clicking and for no reason at all you feel a weight lifted off your heart."

The boy smiled. "Mom, are angels real?"

The woman smiled and touched the tip of his nose. "What do you think, widget?"

"I want them to be."

"Me too, Jono." She kissed his forehead. "Me too."

Static flickered and the scene in the video cut to black.

End of Memory Watch recording number BW132.

No activity detected. Sleep mode activated. Time code: 08:43

Motion activated. Time code: 15:07

Video begins

The cozy house's front door swung open, and Dahlia rushed inside the living room, her curly blond hair bouncing as she waved with a glowing green cast on her arm.

"Guess who made their grades?" she squealed.

"Don't spoil his surprise. Why don't you wait outside for your brother?" said their father, Charles Wyer while cleaning a machine that looked like an octopus made of exhaust pipes. "I'm sure he could use your encouragement."

Charles watched his daughter through the distorted glass windows. She swung on the rocking bench until a brown haired boy crept up over the curve of the hill.

They sat together on the porch before coming inside and gathering the family to eat cold, spicy noodles for dinner.

"That is truly fantastic news, Jono. I'm proud of you," their mother, Beky Wyer said.

"I knew you could do it," Charles added. "How do you want to celebrate?"

"We could go to Jupiter Gorge," Dahlia said. "They added a new ride down the canyon."

"We can't forget the shrine," Beky said. "It would be good if you consulted the angels before you leave, Jono. You may not get another chance."

"I'm tired already," Jono said slowly. "I may just go to bed and read."

"I like that idea," Beky replied. "We don't have to do anything exciting. It's nice to just savor a quiet evening at home."

"Not many of those left," Dahlia said before receiving a swift kick to her shin from her father. "Ow. Sorry."

Jono disappeared up the stairs. Dahlia's friend came to the door and they both ran outside to play. Their parents sipped tea in silence, curled next to each other on an old brown couch. Charles began to cry, and Beky did as well. They comforted each other, sobbing as quietly as they could.

Eventually, Charles cleared the dishes and washed them. Beky baked a chocolate corn cake. Once the dishes were cleaned and stored and the cake baked, iced, and placed in the reizofridge, the two sat on the couch again and watched a screen on the wall with the volume at the lowest setting.

After two point four hours, they turned off the screen and entered the downstairs bedroom.

No activity detected. Sleep mode activated. Time code: 19:27

Motion activated. Time code: 20:03

Dahlia returned home, entering quietly then ascended squeaky steps to the second bedroom on the top floor.

The video ended.

Begin video file carnival-18071311a.vid

A row of trees surrounded a wide field full of colorful, striped tents and rickety steel rides. Balloons were tied to every post, and smoke wafted up from barbeques. Muskcows snorted to each other as they carried children around a circular track. Children's screams of joy echoed through the grassy valley.

The memory watch's camera focused on a garish tent with shiny baubles and plush drapes of cloth and beads surrounding its opening. A woman's hand brushed aside the beads, and the camera peered inside the dimly lit tent.

A weathered frostlet woman sat behind a table. Her pale blue skin was trimmed with icy crust. She wore many layers of colorful shawls. Her brow was decorated in twirling vines that had small mauve blossoms growing off them like jewels in a wooden crown.

On the other side of the table sat Jono and Dahlia, a year younger than before. A crystal ball dominated the center of the table and glowed in a prism of colors from the light of a candle below it. Animated cards were carefully laid on either side of the wooden stand. One set for Dahlia, the other for Jono.

The frostlet woman moved her hands about the crystal ball, invoking its apparent powers. "Now watch the scrying light as it reflects against the cards you've chosen. Deep inside the light and shadows, it holds the secrets of your fortunes!"

"What do you see?" Dahlia whispered with reverence.

The fortune teller waved her hands around the crystal, making beams and shadows dance on the table. "Your futures are filled with wonder and wandering. Love won and lost and won again. Great and terrible deeds call to you through the distance of time! As siblings, your paths will split, your journeys will be your own, but destiny will bring you together again. Whelps no more, but far from settled you will be. You will find yourselves in the middle of a winding path, searching for your place in the ether with little but the thread of family to tie you together still."

Dahlia nudged Jono. "Ask a question."

The ten-year-old Jono blushed and looked to the swirling colors inside the crystal. "What will I be like when I'm grown up?"

"A wise question, my child," the fortune teller said. She made a show of manipulating the crystal, her rings reflecting light and blocking the side of the crystal where the girl's cards were placed. "For you, I see many challenges ahead. Broken shards and swirls explore far and wide. Full of endless wonder, you are! Your luminous spark flitters on the edge of a deep chasm. Your cards cut between the light and shadow. The upside down Researcher says you will travel far across places and ideas. The Beggar King speaks of riches and loss. The Barren Queen tells of separation from family, yet new kindred found in those that will follow you. You will not have an easy road, but the path of greatness is never easy. A summit of peaks rises before you, but the greater the pinnacle, the farther the fall. You will find what your heart hungers for, although it may not be what you think it is. Whether you can hold on to it, is foggy in the ether."

Dahlia and Jono stared at her in awe.

"Who will I be?" Dahlia asked.

The fortune teller stared into her side of the crystal. "Strong, yet weak. Beautiful in scars. Bold, but astray. You too will traverse arduous times, yet your vigor will see you through them. The world will be astonished at your accomplishments. See here, your card, the Queen of Nine Blades—see how it cavorts in the crystal's light, from red to blue. You will be torn, my fiery darling, between two paths, both tremendous in their own way, but it is up to you to decide which one to take."

Dahlia sat back in her chair to let the mystery of her future sink in deep.

Jono leaned forward. "Do I have two paths to choose from?"

The fortune teller's eyes twinkled. "No, my child. You have already chosen."

The video stopped and was replaced by small square pictures that scrolled by until they ended on the final video entry.

Charles Wyer stared directly at the camera. His hair waved over his eyes in a soft breeze. It was longer than the earlier video. Over his shoulder was a grassy hill leading to a crooked two-story home.

"Remember the walk up this hill?" Charles said. "I bet you could leap up it now with all your installs. I'm sure you're busy at the academy, but I was cleaning up my desk at work this wake—oh, I got a promotion! Did your mother tell you? Assistant regional engineering manager! I even got a window office on the third floor of the EC plant. Anyway, I was cleaning up my old desk for the move and guess what I found?"

The image rustled until it settled on a cartoonish drawing of a boy sitting on a man's shoulders on the bridge of a sailboat. Blue lines of wind pushed the red sails outward while triangle waves crash up and down. The boy and man wore wide smiles shaped like circles with the top halfs cut off. Charles laughed. "You must have been six or seven when you drew it. You played Illius, and I was your first mate, sailing around the liquid seas. It's been a while since we talked, and well, I just wanted to share what I found. Maybe some wake, when you are graduated and have some free time, and with the world becoming more peaceful, we can all make a trip to the Day. We'll find some beach town to charter a boat tour and get that sailing in you always wanted. I'm saving my credits now, so in a few years we may be able make it happen.

"Anyway, I hope Windom is treating you well. Take care, Jono. Say hi to Keiko and Isaac for us. I'm so proud of you, son. Goodbye."

End of video.

Chapter Two

Where the Heart Is

J'onothon Wyer sat alone on the curb of Main Street in Polari, at the edge of the town's square and central park. He kept his eyes closed as he slowly breathed in and out, just like he'd learned to do to calm his heart a lifetime and another world ago.

He could feel the town all around him; the bricks and lamp posts were alive and humming. He listened to distant sounds, a grunt and then the rattle of a bell—it was the portly banker entering old Sheriff Burt's restaurant for an early wake coffee. Across the street in the town square's park, leaves rustled in the breeze. Everyone wore thick coats. The snow was just beginning to be melted by the town's steam pipes. A young girl in a red tweed coat near the corner of Groandring Elementary complained to her mother about not having the right style of boots for school.

A twitch on Jono's lips betrayed a grin. He'd been like that at her age, so delicate, so worried about how to fit in and be liked by the other children. In those wakes simple worries felt like they took up the whole world, but Jono was fifteen now, and he wasn't the same boy that slunk down that long street, alone and afraid of bullies.

The soft twinkling of stars over the twilight-crested town made that wake appear in no way dissimilar to every known wake before it.

It was quiet.

Peaceful.

Ker pop

Jono opened his eyes. He knew what had come.

In that moment, Polari was everything he remembered: the simple joys of a crisp breeze sprinkled with the scent of spiced crapple cider. It was innocent. It was home.

In a blink, that world came to an end.

KER POW

Blocks of air, metal, cement, and brick were sucked into nothing. All around him, the world imploded in violent spots. The town square's park lost trees to massive round bites from invisible jaws. The ground quaked and crumbled as broken shards of earth jutted into the air. The elementary school's sign lost its pole and crashed onto the sidewalk. Specks of red dust filled the air in billowing clouds as the pox swallowed Polari citizens whole.

This place of happy children seeped in the innocent squabbles of life transformed into a chaotic purgatory.

Green spheres of light popped like lightning all around the town's square. Flashes of emerald peppered the Twilight canopy above them. Cement streets rippled like angry waves and buildings collapsed into the vast mining tunnels below the town. In seconds Polari was scarred in a litany of harsh, melted marks.

Jono turned his gaze to the hill just outside of town. A crooked two-story home remained unaffected by the turmoil below. A gentle breeze stirred tall grass over the distant, muted screams.

KER POP! KER POW! KER POP! KER POW!

Jono stood and moved through the rubble at a calm pace. Gas fires and gnashing metal rollicked around him as he strolled through the disaster and hopped over newly formed chasms. Bloody specks of the dead littered the street.

He held up his hand, and with a thought, the fires and tumbling debris froze in mid-air.

Across the abyss that used to be the park now stood an island of fragile dirt, an earthen tube with a patch of grass and a picnic blanket flailing in the plumes of smoke. A child was curled up crying on the island of crumbling soil.

Behind Jonothon floated a pale green woman draped in robes and rings. Her long, green hair floated weightless around her.

"What is it that you are looking for?" the holographic professor, Persephone Wishe asked.

Jono shook his head. "I'm just looking."

It was a simple question, spoken kindly, but still it grated against every inch of his body. He clenched his fist and buried the urge to smash something.

Wish observed the scene with him. "All video logs have

been scoured for any evidence. The search was thorough down to every last drop of DNA. There is no trace of your family, and that could very well mean they are alive."

"Are you certain everything here is accurate? There was nothing changed in the video?" Jono stared at the scared child in the park, frozen in time. Her eyes betrayed an innocence that had never imaged the horror that was consuming everything she held dear. They glistened with the knowledge that there was nothing she could do to stop it.

"It is one hundred percent original as catalogued by the Eyes of the Empress," Wishe replied. The holographic professor floated by as Jonothon explored the devastation in progress. "Would you like me to highlight the viewpoints that you have spent the most time on in the past? That may help you to learn about how your subconscious is trying to process this trauma."

"Maybe later."

The flagpole of Groandring Elementary was tilted at a forty five degree angle, ready to be swallowed into the pit below.

"How do you feel when you see this?" Professor Wishe asked.

Jonothon shrugged. He hadn't felt anything in months. He floated through each wake, numb and uneasy. Feelings weren't useful anyway. Feelings wouldn't stop the pox or bring any of them back.

"You've taken me back to this scene for thirty seven of your sessions thus far. Tell me truly, Jono, why are we here?"

Jono clenched his jaw and winced. "You're the therapy expert, Professor. You tell me."

"Both the answers and the questions are inside you. I am merely a guide."

Jono squinted in silence at an unmoving red balloon that waited patiently to fulfill its trivial destiny. "Clues," he finally replied.

"A clue implies a mystery," Wishe said. "What is it that you are trying to solve?"

"The mystery of everything." Jonothon looked up at the digital image of Professor Wishe, who had a tired sadness in her eyes.

How could she not understand? The pox was bigger than him, bigger than one family. He could barely imagine their faces anyway. His stomach ached inside, like he was starving and no food existed to fill him.

"It must be devastating to lose your hometown," she said.

Jono glared at her and struggled to keep from yelling. How could she be so concerned with his feelings when real danger lurked in the chasm between atoms?

"It's bigger than Polari. It's not just the Tombs and the pox. There's something wrong all around us. Like the world is lying and a sliver of our minds knows it, but we are already charmed by its siren's song, eager to sail into the embrace of those rocky cliffs to our death."

"Now you're the one talking in mysteries." Wishe gave him a sad smile. "What do you mean by that?"

Jono pointed to a steam vent on the side of the street. "Do you see that? In the Dark, we're able to change the whole valley in the steam seasons without a sun to warm us. The Day has mastered magic that can conjure demons and there must be ships somewhere in the world that could still travel to the stars, if the Terralunans would just let us off the planet. But this? This pox?" He pointed to a petrified green fissure of burning air above the girl with the red coat. "Why don't any of us know what it is?"

Though Wishe nodded, Jono knew she didn't understand his line of thinking. "Perhaps there is blame to serve all around," she said. "We haven't learned enough, but be careful on that path, Jono. History is always a puzzle to those in the middle of it."

"If we're in the middle of this, then it's not over." Jono shook his head. "The historian once showed me people all over the world cheering for war. In that moment they looked proud of what they were doing. And they were wrong." A thought followed his words: *Were they wrong because of what I did? Or would they always connect the stars to see what they wanted?* He swallowed the idea and continued. "And then we blamed it all on the Tombs. What good did that do? Blame is not a useful thing. It's cause and effect that tracks the signs that truth leaves behind. This place is where the clues have to be."

Wishe tried to reach out to him, but Jono moved on. "You want read the future as though it is a calculation of infinite variables, but Jono, no one can predict every factor and every outcome."

"Not *me*, but all of us. Everyone that ever lived. Isn't there a finite amount of things that can be known?"

"Are you really expecting that we should have learned all there is to know by now? Certainly, the universe still has mysteries for us to explore."

"The pox isn't a mystery. The Tombs set it off, and it happened in Eve's Dale before that."

"Would you trust any answer the Tombs gave you?"

Jono clenched his hands and turned away. "No. But someone out there knows exactly what is going on. It's only a mystery to *us*."

Jono released the video, and the carnage resumed in a roar of clacking cement and fiery moans. He let the pox devour his hometown as he let slip a whisper. "I need to know why."

Satisfied with his masochistic escapade, Jono turned his back on the familiar scene, tore a hole in the code world around him, and marched through the black code hall of consciousness and toward the real world.

The island in the middle of the park crumbled, and for the thirty-seventh time, its tiny inhabitant was lost to the fire and rock below.

Wishe bowed her head in reverence as Jonothon disappeared back into the material world.

"That's all for this session," she said. "Same time next week."

Chapter Three

Strangers in the Dark

tatic lines cut across the Twilight horizon above periwinkle mountaintops. An unshaven, brown head panned into view with wide smile.

"Good wake, world," the man chuckled. "And hello from Pox-Chaser Team Seventeen."

"We're not here for some cheap thrill, Javon. We're field researchers," a voice grumbled from out of view. "Please don't minimize our work in front of the world."

Javon pointed the camera at their camp, which included six bright red tents, two large terrain bots, and boxes of scientific and magical equipment along with a snoring basilisk, whose collar identified her as Snarly. "Doctor Lamb, as your mountain guide and expert photographer, I can assure you that *nothing* can make pox chasing sound like a cheap thrill." Javon turned the camera back toward himself and the distant peaks. "We're here on Faragloo ridge following up on a scientific lead. We thought monitoring this exact spot may just confirm the secret to—"

"You're getting it all wrong," Lamb said. "Put that down and let's do this properly."

The image cut and now Doctor Lamb stood in front of a stable camera. She wore a thick orange coat. Her face sparkled from a fresh cleanse but retained hints of the dirt that had built up over weeks in the field. Her eyes were weary from the rugged life, and streaks of silver cut through her black hair—a few more than before she started on the expedition.

"My name is Doctor Shai Li Lamb, lead researcher for field team seventeen, funded by the Pox Explanation program jointly funded by both the Dark and the Day. We are here in sector one-eight-three in the Ullr Mountains with the hope of recording pox activity.

"We were led to this location following the hypothesis of pox modeling known as the quantum elasticity theory developed by Doctor Binstead's team at Shimmerlake University. The data we have collected from recent pox sightings has led us here in hopes of validating quantum elasticity and understanding how the pox moves, and where it will appear. If we can find supporting evidence for this model, then we should see some pox activity somewhere in the sector you see behind me. We've been in various locations along this ridge for the past six weeks and had nothing to show for it."

"But!" Javon's voice cut in.

Doctor Lamb grinned politely. "But, at o-four-three-seven this wake, the cameras pick up a green flash just above peak kay-twelve."

Lamb pointed toward a distant ridge, and the image switched to a previously recorded close up of the mountains. For an instant a flash of green sparked over the edge of the mountains.

"Then again at o-five-twelve there were three consecutive poxes in the same sector. And again at o-six-two-two, same sector, there were seven pox spots of varying intensity and length. It is now o-seven-o-three, and we expect to see a—"

Kerpop

"Was that one?" another researcher asked.

Kerpop kerpow

"Get the cameras on the ridge!"

"It's spreading out across the valley. Set them at a wide angle."

Green flashes speckled in and out of existence along the jagged peaks like glistening emeralds adorning a crown.

"Holy Mother, this is big one!"

"Are we getting this?"

Kerpop kerpow kerpop kerpow

The sound of rock and wood crushing into oblivion sung a ghastly chorus with the shrieks of birds and beasts caught in the chaos.

"All four cameras are scanning and grabbing. Greasy gears, this is unbelievable!"

Kerpop kerpow kerpop kerpow

"The pox is going gizmos!" A camper said with a nervous laugh.

Kerpop kerpow kerpop kerpow

The camera panned to catch larger and larger swells of hungry pox massing with rings of green, burning air bursting along the ridge. The pox lingered for eternal seconds, growing and feeding on the smaller poxes around them as they devoured the mountainside.

KERPOP KERPOW KERPOP KERPOW KERPOP

The mountain bellowed in landslides as the growing pox devoured the entire ridge in mammoth bites. The mountain wailed a death cry that thundered through the valley. Winds thrust trees from their roots. A tsunami of dirt rushed to wrap the sky in a shroud of death.

Doctor Lamb hung onto the nearest tree to keep her balance as the cloud roared over the camp.

"Get back from the cliffs!" she yelled over the wind.

Flashes of green cut through the terrible veil of dust.

Kerpop kerpow

A sprinkle of pox followed the behemoth ones as a lingering warning after the outbreak subsided. The camp was drowned in the mountain's pulverized remains. Screeches of the terrified and dying wildlife haunted the devastated valley.

"Holy Mother of light," Javon cried as he curled his knees into chest and rocked madly back and forth. "Holy Mother of light."

As cracks in the dust began to clear, the husk of the decimated mountain arched upward in a barbed skeleton of rock and trees. Fragments of the horizon beyond the mountains now pierced through the clouds. An orange thread of Dawn peeked over the edge of the earth where the range had once stood a sentry against the light.

Kerpop

"Bloody burnin' stars." Keiko Kirin gasped with tears of horror in her eyes.

The image hovered against the stone-textured ceiling as she lay, looking up at it. Her heavy blanket was damp with sweat. She looked around the small apartment to remind herself where she was. She was lying on the top bunk of a bed where her uncle Cid would normally be snoring loudly below her. Jono was sprawled on the couch with his blanket half on the floor.

Keiko exhaled. She should feel safe in the heart of the Dark city, but she could feel the pox tingle at the back of her neck. Her muscles tensed around her mechanically enforced skeleton, as unwanted memories of being trapped below a wall of stone crashed like storming waves against the levee of her mind. All of the installed strength her body could handle would do nothing to hold off the hunger of the pox.

She looked at the gray brick panels which covered the walls with robotic boxes stacked against them. A light flickered on the corner of each box as they waited patiently to be instructed where to deposit their contents. It was all so fragile.

The summer had passed quickly since Cid Kirin had moved to Eies to be the replacement mechanix instructor at Windom. Professor Helios had taken a position at the Pathaganon to work on a research project. Cid being close did make Keiko feel more at ease, but it could only help so much.

Together with Jono and Cid's werepup, Forge, they had managed to visit nearly every corner of the city but somehow never made the time to move boxes into the storage below the floor. Keiko figured her uncle liked all the clutter around him; the chaos made it feel more like his old shop in Dollup.

Keiko rubbed her head as the city lights sparkled behind a blurry pane of glass beside her. Muted roars of flying cars and trams zipped above a narrow alley that opened to a view of the depths and heights of the sprawling city. Keiko blew on the glass window then rubbed it with a corner of her blanket. The apartment was in the middle heights of Eies. Heavy greenhouse clouds lingered far above them, and bright, colorful lights reflected off the greasy sheen that emanated from the mech district below. Across a maze of towering buildings, one of the gates into caverns of the Windom

Academy stood as a vigilant reminder of why she'd come here.

A plate of cheesy eggs and bacon slid on her lap.

"You really shouldn't watch those vids," Cid said as his bearded face peered over the bunk's railing. "It's no good worrying about what you can't control."

Keiko shook her head. "Ignoring doesn't help either. What is there to stop that from happening in Eies? Or maybe there's something we could learn so we are prepared."

Cid looked out of the foggy window. "The Empress has the smartest people on the planet working on this. You need to stop worrying."

"My first year at Windom, the Tombs hijacked the mechyard and sent our own mechs storming through the academy. The next year I almost died on a school trip. No, *two* school trips! There are plenty of things the Empress won't see coming. More eyes is more armor."

Cid sighed. "Maybe we should move to a city that won't crumble in on itself if even a small pox hits."

Keiko shook her head. "You're always saying how much you love it here, and I'm *not* leaving Windom. Besides, no one can predict where the pox will show up next, so moving won't help."

She looked at Jono asleep on the couch. His hand shook as hidden fears tormented his dreams. Keiko slid from her bed and knelt beside him at the couch. She held his quivering hand until it stopped shaking. She pulled his blanket up and tucked him in. His breath slowed again. She smiled.

"Sweet sleeps, Jono," she said.

Cid filled another plate and nudged Jono with his foot. "Time to power up, Wyer." He then shot a look to Forge, who'd curled up at Jono's feet. "You too, Forgikins."

Jono yawned at Keiko's face smiling down at him. "Thanks, Cid."

Forge yawned as well. The tiny werepup stretched his gray and white fur body. The pup's smiling muzzle made it look like a plush child's toy.

"Did I ever tell you how Forge scared away a pack of pungrusses on our way to Eies?" Cid said as he handed Jono breakfast.

A grin cracked on Keiko's face. "Only about forty times."

"He is impressive, even for a werepup," Cid said with pride. "Aren't you, Forge?"

Keiko wrapped an arm around her uncle, and Cid kissed the top of her head.

"It's good to have you close, kid," Cid said. "You too, Wyer. I can't believe it has been five years since you first snuck into my shop and whisked my niece away to the big city." Cid wrapped an arm around Jono and pulled him into a three-way hug.

"It'll be nice to have you at Windom," Keiko said. "What monstrosity should I build this year?"

"Just because I'm taking over mechgineering doesn't mean you're getting an easy time of it." Cid winked at his niece.

"Please," Keiko said with a rising laugh. "I dare you to be as tough as you can! At least then class will stay interesting."

"You asked for it, sprocket! I heard about that little side project you built last year. If you are going to use scrap parts to build a squad of mech-raptors to storm your rival globall team's hall, you're at least going to be graded on it."

Keiko lifted her hands in joking defense. "Andromeda Aisle was asking for it! They were boasting that they could sleep through anything before a game wake. Besides, they made our doorknockers malfunction all sleeps. The lion heads were singing the Gear Golem's Anthem until four o'clock."

Cid frowned. "I'm adding an updated doorknocker encryption to my to-do list. While we're on the subject, who won that match?"

Keiko held a fist into the air. "Me and the Roariers— sixty eight to forty three. I defended three bases solo against two siegers and a charger."

"That's my girl," Cid laughed. "I may last until Hollow's Eve before getting fired for your antics."

"I love how you always put my creative development first," Keiko said, winking at Jono. She did what she could to make him feel at home, both of them did.

"Listen," Cid said as he grabbed his old tech-embedded coat from the hook by the door. "School doesn't start for another two wakes and with all our exploring we've yet to catch an Explorers game. They're playing the Ice Kings at fourteen o'clock."

"How are you going to get seats?" Keiko asked. The Champion's Cup playoffs start in two weeks, which meant the only people with seats were season holders or those with enough money to buy them from scalpers. "It's gonna be totally gizmos at Starchester."

Cid had a hand balled into a fist, holding it out for Keiko and Jono to see. He blinked and opened his hand, revealing a set of holographic tickets. "Commander Grail shared his season pass with all the new teachers this year. We've got four seats on the third row on the home side of the globe."

"No burn'em way!" Keiko hugged her uncle.

Jono beamed. "Welded."

Cid grabbed his long coat. "I hear that all the true Explorers fans are going to rally at the stadium for the pre-game show. I wonder what that makes us?"

"Fans to the end and back again!" Keiko and Jonothon chanted in unison.

Forge yapped and spun in a circle.

Cid cheered. "Let's rocket!"

The tips of two spy wires dangled dangerously close to Jonothon's eyes. With a thought, his goggles zoomed in on the strange metal snakes that had inhabited his body ever since he took that shot of pixels years ago. The wires peeled away their metal sheathing and small spark blades poked out. He'd finally been approved for an assault upgrade to his cloak installs, but he found himself spending more time mesmerized by the blue blades than using them to cut through his enemies.

The goggles' microscopic view grew more focused, until the miniscule pixels appeared as they healed the scratches in his installs. The army of mechanized microbes looked like gray amoebas swarming to polish a vast metal wasteland.

"Do you think pixels have thoughts of their own?"

"No," Isaac Ohm replied dryly from below Jono's perch.

Jono slid the goggles onto his forehead. He was hanging upside down from a tree in Gearmany Pet Park. Across the field, Keiko goaded Forge into chasing her. Whenever his paw touched her leg, she spun around and chased after him while Forge sprinted away in delight.

Sitting in the tall grass below him, Isaac watched three hovering screens at once while he played a planet explorer game with one hand. He had dyed his orange head tendrils purple, which brought out a darker tone to his scaly green skin.

"Pixels are bionetically engineered to complete specific tasks based on instructions from their network," Isaac explained without turning from his screens. "Their thinking is nothing like what we do."

Jono rested his head on a tree branch. "Maybe it's more like an ant. Pixels do have to create things infinitely more complex than ant tunnels, and they need to communicate with millions of other pixels to be efficient. Isn't there some creativity in that? What if pixels had a society with different roles filling different needs? Food distribution pixels, mayor pixels, entertainment pixels . . ."

Isaac shrugged. "Of course they are specialized."

"More to my point, what if *we're* like that? Tiny specks being controlled by the impulses in our specialized parts, guided by the triggers from our environments. All the subtleties of our genetics and how we are conditioned in life is leading us to a destiny that some person could predict or manipulate, if only they knew everything about everything."

Isaac took a moment before responding. "It is possible to statistically predict trends of populations based on their inputs, but for individuals there are too many wild cards to factor in."

"Unless the puppet masters controlled the wild cards or at least observed them more closely than the others. They could twist the world like one dynamic puzzle."

"And who would *they* be?" Isaac replied. "The angels the Day makes statues of? Or a supercomputer on Terralunis? Jono, there is no one moving all the pieces of the world around like a tri-chess board. There is us and what we choose to do."

"You don't think we are chemical machines inclined to patterns?"

Isaac sighed and looked up at his upside down friend. "Certainly, nature and nurture set us on a path, but as pilots of our own brains, we can inflict nurture on ourselves. We can choose what shows to watch, what to read, who to talk to. We can experiment on ourselves and change our own thought models if we wanted to."

"But *why* would we want to do that if not because of the nature and nurture that came before, making us want to change something?"

Isaac paused the screens. He scrunched his face to one side, deep in thought. Then he shrugged.

"Wild cards."

Isaac started the screens playing again.

Cid scooped up Keiko in his arms and ran as fast as he could with Forge bounding behind them. Jono mumbled, "We are shadows dancing on a wall, three dimensional beings in a deca-dimensional universe."

A new ping flashed in the back of Jonothon's mind. *The Empress will make a surprise announcement in one minute. Stay linked!*

All over the park, people stopped what they were doing to catch the news.

"Did your parents know anything about this?" Jono asked Isaac.

"Not like they would tell me."

With a wordless thought of approval, Jono allowed a news feed to project in front of his eyes. Through the mechanix installed in his brain he could hear the news anchor, Cheryl Chongwas describe the video hovering in front of him. A golden airship descended into the city, surrounded by six sundrakes.

"We have breaking news of a Day convoy arriving in Eies. Smeltport Station is on high security alert. Could this be the Windom exchange program that was rumored over the summer? It looks as though the first passengers are disembarking now."

"It's the Sage of Ages!" said a chubby man next to them in the park.

The Sage's large, tree-like body was the first to leave the golden train. He waved his wooden staff as golden light swirled around him. A few people dressed in fine clothes followed him, likely some of the lords Jono saw at his short time in Caer Midus. Knights and mages followed after them and then . . .

"Suriana," Jono said.

The young princess' blond hair was braided down her back. A crowd of Day students flowed out of the train behind her. Jono recognized two as Suri's friend, Marissa Haljeers and the pyrebran, Freya Faisal. Behind them came two human boys, two scaldios, three wood dryads, four elvayns, a pyrebran boy, two feli'yins, and three rock golem kids.

"Is that Murphy Wumples?" Jono squinted at the image.

Looks like we'll have some new friends this year, Keiko pinged Jono through TeamThink.

Cheryl continued on the news feed. "We are getting word the Empress will be officially recognizing the start of the student exchange program between the Dark and the Day at a ceremony at the Crown castle later this wake. The official press release states there will be an ongoing cultural exchange, including students and teachers from the Day, celebrations of Day holidays, and regular historical and cultural seminars hosted at Saint Newton's Science Cathedral. Stay linked for more details as this stunning news unfolds!"

And here I was hoping for an uneventful year, Isaac thought back.

I can see the firehead girl! I wonder if she remembers me, Oscar thought gleefully.

Some thoughts aren't meant for Team Think, Bohrs, Isaac replied.

Everyone in the park was fixed to the images as more people from the Day disembarked from the train. Wood dryads and elvayns in flowing garments looked starkly out of place in the middle of the metallic city. White-robed Fellowship clerics gathered in a crowd, but only one wore an optimistic smile on his short, bearded face; Jono expected Alexsayter Aquinas was the only one of them actually happy to be in the Dark.

Chapter Four

Magic versus Machine

R umors about the Day Enders spread across Windom in a blink of the Line. The welcoming ceremony had tried to keep them anonymous, except for Suriana, who represented the transfer students in a well-rehearsed speech. She praised the ingenuity of the Dark and implored the cadets to make the squires from the Day feel welcome.

On the first wake of school, any image of a Day Ender walking nervously down a hallway or gawking at the gargoyles was circulated over the student network so many times that the professors began complaining about losing their students' attention. Ms. Drudge added a filter to block any image of a squire and snarled over the academy chat that any cadet caught stalking a squire would have to run laps around the outside walls of the city.

Even without the squires, Windom was in a fit of chaos with all the new cadets. David Kepler's twin siblings Ulysses and Rex were finally old enough to enlist, and the troublemakers wasted no time in breaking any rule they came across. During the distracted clamoring around an elvayn boy, Rex had climbed up to a gargoyle roost and attempted to ride on ones' back while Uly carved her name into the stone wall. Their parents, Percival and Fiona, were summoned to Commander Grail's office before the bell rang for the first class of the wake.

Oscar's younger sister, Esmeralda, had enlisted as well, but she was so terrified of catching an illness from the Day that she spent the first three classes crying in the Lionoh Loop bathroom.

Jonothon escaped the chaos of the first wake of school, arriving at the front of Advanced Applicable Mathometry eighteen minutes before the bell would ring. He waited for the rotund Professor Lumph to arrive. While he had begun his time at Wimdon in a terse relationship with Lumph lasting his first two years, he'd eventually won over the professor's favor by being the best mathometry student in any of Lumph's classes.

Instead of the large, grumpy professor, a skinny human man with brown hair and blue eyes entered the classroom carrying a robotic briefcase. He wore a top hat to cover his messy hair; stubble textured his cheeks and chin while a delicate mustache stuck out like two curled tails beneath his nose. Small, round tech glasses rested on the brim on his nose. The man took off his long, brown coat and placed it on the back of the chair at the teacher's desk at the front of the room. He wore a brown and copper vest underneath with gears for buttons. Before taking a seat, he rolled up the sleeves of his tan, striped shirt, revealing a bionetic left arm and a flesh right arm.

The man set his briefcase on the desk, and it scurried to one side on robotic legs and opened itself up. He looked at Jonothon and smiled. "You're early."

"You're not Lumph," Jono replied.

The skin around the man's eyes made long creases when he smiled. "You've caught me." The man took a small card from his vest pocket and with a snap, the front board lit up with information. A flowing image of a biography appeared for Professor Johan Fourier, Emeritus of the Eies Pathaganon research facility, Doctor of Atomology, Quantum Chemix, and Theoretical Mathometry.

"What happened to Professor Lumph?" Jono asked. He'd finally worked up a serviceable relationship with his last mathometry teacher, and the idea of starting over made him feel exhausted already.

Fourier frowned. "Not impressed? I think what my bio needs are explosions . . ." Fourier cleared his throat. "The Day happened to Lumph, as a matter of fact. I trust you've seen our guests from the lighter side of life? That academic exchange goes both ways. Our esteemed friend is teaching students at the First Order Shivan Monastery near Systine. He is probably soaking in their hot springs and getting foot massages all wake, lucky clunker."

"Why have I never heard about any offers for an exchange to the Day?"

"Would you have been interested in going if you had?" Fourier asked.

Jono thought for a moment. He was sure he wouldn't have been allowed to leave Eies after everything he'd done. He shrugged.

"Perhaps, that is your answer then."

As the classroom filled up, Jonothon realized Fredrick Finley wasn't there. Fred was the only cadet in his class that bothered to talk to him. Surely he wasn't soaking in the sunlight without saying goodbye? Jono wondered who else would be missing from Windom, off to explore the odd cultures in the Day.

Four Day squires entered the room and huddled together in the back row. They looked out of place wearing bright, loose robes.

Fourier waved at the murmuring cadets to be quiet. "Welcome, everyone! And a special welcome to our esteemed guests from across the Dawn! How about a round of applause for these intrepid travelers? Come on. Let's make them feel welcome."

The clapping was timid at best and only served to make the four squires blush with embarrassment.

"Please sit and let's begin." Fourier motioned to his bio on the board. "As those of you looking forward can tell, I am Professor Johan Fourier. I will be your mathometry teacher this year."

In the back of the room, an elvayn girl opened a small container of fairies. The tiny creatures looked like a humanoid mice with butterfly wings. They giggled and glowed as they recorded every word Fourier said.

"As you look over the syllabus, you'll see we will be warming up with a review of stochastic processes like Maarkov chains and Brownian motion before we ramp up to mechanix stress probability for a bit of fun and then onward to predictive probability in dynamic social systems."

The elvayn girl raised her hand, but Fourier wasn't looking. The cadets in front of her couldn't stop staring. She nodded and the fairies began to hum loudly.

Fourier frowned and turned around. "Yes, Miss—" A twitch of his eye, familiar to anyone from the Dark, indicated an info pull from the Line, "Laika Zaveen, is it? Whatever can I do for you?"

"Professor, what does stochastic mean?"

Fourier arched his eyebrows. Then he sighed and cleaned his tech glasses and explained. "Well, in probability theory, it is a system whose state is non-deterministic so that the following state of the system is determined probabilistically."

Laika's jaw dropped, and all the Day student's looked at each other in confused horror.

"Did all of you take a placement test before school started?" Fourier asked cautiously.

The squires nodded. "Yes. In the Day."

Fourier's face sagged with worry. "Perhaps there are some terminology issues I wasn't aware of. Let's all meet after class to discuss your previous mathometry studies, shall we?"

"We have another class after this," Laika said.

"Correct, how about after the school hours then?"

"We have an exchange student meeting."

"Okay," Fourier said, pinching the bridge of his nose and closing his eyes. "You four. At any time that you are available, ask the gargoyles where I am and I will make the time to work this out with you, yes?"

The fairies convened in high-pitched chirps then returned to Laika's shoulder. "Yes, that will work."

"Excellent." Fourier looked over the rest of the students, stopping when he found Jonothon's encouraging face.

This was going to be an interesting year.

With that problem out of the way, Fourier straightened and returned to teaching. "Now, if you will activate the screens on your desks, we will go through a quick refresher of your lessons from last year."

Laika took out a wand from her sleeve and with a whisper and a wave, blue dust clouded in front of her face. All four Day students breathed it in through their noses and then smiled with full attention to the professor.

Fourier cleared his throat. "My apologies, but what was that you just did there?"

"A studious spell," Laika replied, quite proud of herself. "Everything you teach will be absorbed into my subconscious and during sleeps I'll dream through it again. These spells have shown a three hundred percent increase in information recollection. It's quite useful. If anyone else is interested, I'm more than happy to cast it on anyone who would like it."

Chairs screeched as the Dark students moved away from her.

"It's a simple spell, and I'm a perfect caster, I assure you," she insisted.

"I'm terribly sorry, but all this magic is distracting the other students." Fourier tried to be delicate, but Jono recognized the professor's own misgivings in his tone—he had more experience with the Dark's prejudice than just about anyone. "Would you mind keeping any creatures or performing any spells out in the hallway, please?"

The Day students begrudgingly shuffled their bags and scooted their sparkling fairies out the door. A burp of fire breath erupted out of Laika's satchel.

Fourier frowned. "That too."

Ever since Professor Talmage died in the ruins of Lailet Dem, Windom had struggled to find a suitable replacement teacher for Geo Studies. At the beginning of Jonothon's fourth year at Windom, they hired a grudgon from Aires named Yunglan Ong, but every creak and pop from the machines that filled Windom's caverns made him shriek in fear of a pox attack. By that Giftmas, they replaced him with a yeton, Dominica Laplas, but she was caught sleeping during class hours one too many times.

Along with the student exchange came the newest Geo Studies teacher, a dryad from the Day named Solinser Moss. He arrived to class as the students sent whispered pings of cautious interest. Moss looked down his aspen bark nose at the cadets. He wore a thick, enchanted coat that repelled anything coming into contact with his skin.

He also wore gloves and refused to shake hands or come into any physical contact with someone from the Dark. He said his bark was particularly sensitive, but rumors spread that he despised the Dark End and had only taken that position at Windom to learn more things to hate about Dark Enders.

Moss waved a wand over his desk and his name appeared above it.

"As you can tell," Moss began, "I'm not from around these parts."

Moss twirled his wand and images of sunny woodlands pranced around the classroom. "I was born in a dryad glen near a small town on the Morning Ring. Whilst I am your class minister you will be gifted with a firsthand education on the miraculous lands of the Day. I anticipate that your knowledge of our histories is, how to put it . . . limited? As such, you will be partnered with a student from the Day as group leader. They will guide you on the various processes for your studies. Do treat them with the deference fitting of their expertise, will you?"

The Day students smirked proudly at their advantage over the class, while the rest of the cadets recoiled at the idea of magic being in front of them.

Moss waved his wand again and a mauve mist spread out to every desk, placing a small crystal in front of each student.

"We will begin by introducing you to the great regions of the Day, from the fields of Ma Haila to the islands of the Ankor Flox. Now, please pick up your crystals and summon a map of the Day."

Jono raised his hand. "None of us have used crystals before." Jono was lying about himself; he'd studied crystal hacking in his cloaks class for years, but he wasn't about to give any Day Ender that information. It was true for the other cadets, and Jono found it useful to bring it up on their behalf.

Moss answered with a condescending smile. "Ah, yes. I shouldn't expect *that* much of you. Crystal commands are quite infantile, really. Simply grasp the crystal and think the words 'Day. Map.' Does everyone feel capable of conquering that ordeal?"

The Day students giggled.

"I am not touching that thing," Clarissa Bauer grumbled from the back of the class.

Moss wasted no time in giving a harrumph. "This is my class and you will learn in the manner that I will teach. Is that understood?" The bark on his nose had begun to crack in the dry air. "This wretched climate is making my bark peel." He peeled a shred of bark and flicked it onto the ground. "How do you creatures stand it?"

The rest of the classes were no more accommodating to magic and enchanted creatures. By the time Jono and his friends sat down together for lunch on the fifth year's balcony, wild stories about the Day had made their way through Windom the old fashioned way.

"I heard the rock golem boy wet himself during Stone's Chemix class," Oscar whispered as he leaned over the table. "Stone startled him with that transform trick he does and the lad thought the machines were coming to rise up against their biological masters!"

"That's terrible!" Keiko replied.

"Terribly funny!" Oscar said. "The kid wouldn't come out from under the desk for five minutes!"

Isaac used his fork to point at a table of Day students on the first floor. "Roger Hyland told me one of the feli'yin girls got in a fight with Clarissa Bauer in the dorms. Something about hair clogging the showers. I don't think they know how to use the tech in the simplest things. They probably have water fairies wash their exhaust holes in the Day."

Oscar chuckled. "Water fairies. Good one."

"Did any of you hear about invites to transfer to the Day?" Jono asked.

"Why would anyone want to spend more time in the light?" Oscar asked, giving Jono a quizzical look. "I had my fill at the World's Faire. No, thank you."

"I got an invite," Isaac said. "But I turned it down, obviously. I'd much rather apprentice at the Pathaganon."

Keiko slapped Isaac's arm. "I can't believe you waited all this time to say something! What was the invite for?"

"It was to study in a Systine monastery. That's just past the Dawn along the Calm Coast. One full school year with the option to come back for holidays or stay there to learn whatever it is the Day does for Giftmas."

"What an adventure you're missing!" Keiko sighed. "I wonder if they'd teach you magic. You could'a been the world's first master chemix magician!"

"I think boys are called wizards," Jono said. "And girls

are witches."

Keiko gawked. "Different names for boy and girl things? So gizmos. I love it!"

Isaac sneered. "I don't need magic polluting my veins when I have perfectly good machines in there already."

"I doubt they'd teach you any of the best spells," Oscar said. "Do you think they'd trust a Dark Ender with the power of Blizzagarama?"

"I'm sure magic comes after the brainwashing," Isaac said. "And I just can't see spending a second on angelic doctrine when there is real science to research. Besides, there are plenty of other Dark Enders going. You all know Frederick Finley? And Kirstin Orbit is there as well."

They all looked down from the fifth year balcony at the Day students' lonely gathering of colorful clothes in a sea of dark blue and silver suits. The Windom dining hall roared as the twenty Day students and Professor Moss sat in whispers at the center table on the floor. The tables around them were barren, forcing the Dark cadets to squish together.

"They look so sad," Keiko said.

Jono waved at Suriana, who waved back as though everything were perfectly fine. She was the only one smiling, while Professor Moss actively grumbled about the cadets that mulled around them. Jono couldn't help but assume their first wake at Windom was going worse than they might have hoped.

Down at the squires' table, a short dryad girl named Riley Shrub pulled out a wand. A few Dark Enders took notice as she waved it at a jar of sweet salts on the empty table next to them. A golden wisp of dust floated out of the wand, snatched up the jar, and then began carrying it back the Day's table.

The jar landed with a thud. The Day students barely noticed, as wand play was as natural to them as breathing, but the dining hall grew noticeably quieter and people began to stare.

Riley was about to dip a spoon into the salt jar when the jar began to shake. It darted through the air and landed in Kain Etheredge's glowing metal hand two tables away.

He smirked at them.

"Just ignore them," Suriana said with a smile. "Isn't this food interesting?"

Freya Faisal, a fiery pyrebran girl who wore a purple gown, pulled out a spoonful of squirming mugaluk from her bowl. "*Interesting* is more polite than the word I was thinking."

A caramel-skinned human boy named Ammer O'Nasser opened up a blue bottle and a drop of liquid floated up. He clapped his hands around the hovering drop to wash them and then passed the bottle along to the other squires. Freya accidentally dropped the bottle and it rolled along the stone floor.

"I'll get it." Riley waved her wand, and the bottle

floated back toward them. It was directly over Ammer's head when the wand was snatched from her grip and the bottle smacked onto his head, pouring its contents onto his plate.

Elise snapped the wand in half and tossed it on the table.

"Machines crush magic, burnt brains," she boasted.

"Is that so, greaser?" Ammer touched a blue gem on his ring and then pointed it at Elise, who was flung into the air. She crashed on top of the table full of food.

Elise's brother Kain growled as his broken plate splattered on the floor. "You smashed my chicken crisps! I love chicken crisps!"

"You're dead, Blue Skies!" Elise stood as plates of sticky food fell off of her.

Dark Enders stood up from their tables all around them.

Suriana stood first. "Everyone, please calm down. We just want to eat our lunch in peace."

Freya laughed. "You haven't tasted real magic, oil blood."

"You want to educate me on your bag of tricks?" Kain said.

Ammer stood up and opened the satchel slung over his shoulder. "You greasy cogs are not ready for magic, but we're ready for you!" He pulled out a fiery orange orb that seethed with power.

"Everyone relax!" Jono called down from the balcony.

"You about to join the Day, Wyer?" Kain shouted back. "I always knew you wanted to be a mage knight instead of a soldier."

"No, Wyer's just wetting himself 'cause he thinks magic is so scary," Elise said. "Get ahold of yourself and act like a Dark Ender for once. Gears crush spells. Everyone knows that."

"You want to try to crush the Dragon's Cough?" Freya said, pulling an orange vial out of her sleeve. "Be my guest."

"You're helpless without your trinkets!" Elise said. "No wands, potions or crystals means no magic."

"Pyrebrans don't need spells to burn your metal hide," Freya said.

"Doesn't matter. The Dark is smarter."

"Why must it always be a competition?" Suriana said, fuming. "Both are good. Both Ends are powerful. Let's just—"

A loud thump came from behind the crowd of Dark Enders that had surrounded their table. Everyone stopped to watch drills instructor Boargrin Krust push his way through the crowd. The fuglian was covered in fur and horns. His tusk-filled smile stretched wide.

"Did I hear that someone was eager for a challenge?" he roared.

Kain and Elise smiled at each other. Ammer and Freya nodded bravely.

"Then let's do this proper!" Krust bellowed to a crowd of cheers. "Contest of the century! Machines versus magic! Head to head! May the strongest survive!"

Boargrin Krust was known for making the most elaborate drills courses in the Dark, but this time he'd outdone himself. The woods in the chasm outside of the city were snarling with dangerous creatures and simulated magic-slinging robots. A crowd of students and teachers had filled the drills stands on the edge of the woods.

"Pick your team, bold munchkins." Krust said. "Who will join the test?"

Elise and Kain looked around. "Who's with us? Wyer?"

Jono turned to Suri and raised his hands. "I'm out."

"Come on, Twig," Elise said. "You're on our cloaks squad. We would slaughter them together!"

"Where's Knox?" asked Kain.

"Probably out polishing his cannon," Elise growled.

"I'll do it," Isaac said, stepping forward with a hand raised.

"Alright, a chemix master!" Kain cheered.

Jono glared at Isaac, who shrugged. "What? This will be an educational test of their skills. We do drills all the time. I want to see how the Day is trained for combat."

"I'll join too," Keiko said. "Like Isaac said, it will be an education." She grinned when Jono glarred at her. "Don't worry. I won't break any of their bones."

"Don't go easy on them, Kirin," Elise said with a slap on her shoulder. "Like Ohm said, let's crank their shaft and see how they tick."

Boargrin waved to the crowd and the eight contestants.

"The rules are simple! Here in the Windom woods are arrows to three hidden keys—the earth key, the air key and the water key. Two keys are in each chamber. It will take one of each type unlock the one and only Victor's Flag! First team to get all three keys, unlock the flag, and bring it back—" He stomped on the ground. "—across this line, are the champions."

Krust looked directly at the four cadets and four squires.

"You can use any manner of magic or tech, but, hear me clear now, nothing lethal or permanently scarring. Any of you dat breaks des rules will get my fist in your chomper. Now let's have it out!"

The crowd roared and Jono looked worriedly at Suriana. She had an arm wrapped around Riley Shrub who was shaking with anxiety in the stands. The crowd of Dark Enders cheering around them was less than a comforting welcome.

Solinser Moss had the Day students huddled together. His sneering aspen face was gleeful at the chance for magic to beat their less than gracious hosts.

"The players are set then," Moss said. "Ammer, Freya, Marissa, and . . . Mister Wumples, are you certain you are prepared for this?"

Murphy nodded bravely and held a fist to his chest. "I will defend the Day's honor."

"Excellent," Moss replied. "Now, remember to use the flaws of the Dark against them. They have big egos and are quick to pride."

"Which will come right before they fall," Freya said.

Moss whispered, "Each of you have enchantments and spells. Don't use your most powerful magic first. Let them think they have the upper hand then catch them off guard. The rules never said you couldn't take the keys from the other side, so try to get two first and then surround the third to get their key."

"That's little conniving," Marissa said, eyes on the ground as she fiddled with her wand.

"That could work," Murphy said with a new sense of hope.

"They will use whatever tricks they can to win and so must we," Moss said. "Let's humiliate these nasty Dark Enders and make the Day proud, eh?" He put his hand into the circle they'd formed and they rested their hand on his.

"For the light of Day!" they all cheered.

Kain waved at the instructor. "Hey, Krust. Is this just

like last year's course? Are we going to be digging out Day limbs from the paranamole's teeth?"

Boargrin growled. "This ain't nothin' like the courses you've ever seen, you sparkin' cog. You'll get no clues from me. Watch your own limbs while you're out there. Players at your marks!"

The eight contestants stood at the line.

"We should all split up for the keys," Kain whispered. "I'll take the air key, Elise gets earth. Ohm, you take Kirin with you and get water."

"Teams of two," Freya said to the Day students. "Ammer and Murphy go for the air. Marissa and I will get water and we meet near the Earth key for the . . . exchange. Then it's on to the flag."

The rest nodded.

Boargrin raised a handcannon to the sky. "Three, two—"

The cannon boomed and echoed through the chasm.

The two teams were off running. In a second, Kain and Elise had activated their cloaking skin and disappeared.

Moss gasped. "Can they do that?"

Keiko's eyes switched through light spectrums until she could see the trail of dim green key arrows. "This way."

Isaac ran after her. "You lead and I'll deal with our competition."

Ammer leapt over a fallen tree with a white arrow on it. He was midair when his chest hit an invisible arm. He flipped and thudded on the ground.

Ammer moaned. "Dirty, underhanded Dark Enders…"

"Winning is winning, sunbeam." Kain yelled, and the leaves rustled as he ran away.

Ammer climbed to his feet and pulled out a green box from his satchel. He whispered at the top of it, "Wings of virtue hear my plea and make the hidden home in trees."

When he opened the lid, a flurry of green pixies flew out in a cloud of sparkling light. They soared through the forest, and as soon as one landed on Kain's invisible skin, the rest of the flock followed, covering Kain in green lights. The swarm of wings lifted him into the trees as he swatted frantically at them.

"Call off your bugs!" Kain yelled.

"What's that?" Ammer said, cupping a hand to his ear. "I can't hear you through all the winning I'm doing."

Murphy ran past him and was already half way through the trees when he shouted back, pointing toward the cliffs. "I see the air arrows! This way."

Isaac fell behind Keiko as he flung orange elixirs on the trees as they passed. The elixirs stuck to the bark as blobs, wobbling with any movement near them, itching to explode.

Marissa was running right behind them. As she passed one of the blobs, Freya leapt onto her back. They slammed onto the forest floor just as an explosion of sticky goo shot out from the elixir like a net.

"You're going to have to do better than that!" Freya shouted, a grin on her face.

"Look." Marissa pointed at Keiko. "She's way out

ahead."

"Climb on my back and hold on," Freya said. She held a wand in either hand and pulled her arms to her sides. "I summon the Winds of Wonder!"

A gust of wind swept them over the forest floor and whisked them through the maze of trees. In seconds they had passed Keiko.

Keiko stopped as the massive gust rushed past her. "Ok, that one is impressive."

Isaac was huffing when he caught up to her. "Let's try a little less admiration, a little more beating them, huh?"

Kain clung to a treetop and sent a shock over his cloaked skin, not enough to short-out the invisibility casters, but enough to burn the pixies off him. He hung to a branch and looked out across the woods. He scanned for the sky key arrows and followed their path to an outcropping on the cliff wall.

He smiled. "Thanks for the lift, guys."

Kain's spy wire's swung him through the tree tops toward the key.

Freya and Marissa followed the green arrows to a murky cave alongside the chasm's wall.

Freya peered inside to find it flooded with foul-smelling water. "Do they expect us to swim in that? It'll clog up my flame follicles."

"The ugly guy did say it was the water key," Marissa said. "And I am not losing to those oil blooded maniacs for the cost of a shower." She dove into the water. The cave had enough room for her head to breach the surface.

"It's too dark in there. I can't see anything."

"Pyrebran to the rescue." Freya knelt then pulled a lock of her fiery yellow hair and cut it with a knife from her pouch. Freya then sprinkled her hair on the water.

As Marissa swam, the floating hair gleamed with a bright yellow light that cut through the mire. At the bottom of the cave was a lockbox. She opened it to find two green keys.

Elise grumbled as she crawled through a maze of tree roots and dirt. Dimly glowing mushrups lined the narrow path under the roots. At the end sat a lockbox with the earth keys inside.

"Good luck unlocking the flag," she said as she took both keys and put them in her pocket.

Murphy had climbed the rocky path to where the starry sky met icy stone. Just below the glowing Terralunan moon a black box glistened in the light. He snatched a key just as a wire darted from behind him and grabbed the other one.

Murphy spun around to see Kain reaching across the

piney tree tops. "Hah! I've seen rock snails move faster than you two! See you at the finish line!"

"Not before us!" Ammer's orb blasted through the tree trunk and sent Kain flailing into the air. Ammer turned to Murphy. "Toss me the key!"

"No. I'm faster, trust me." Murphy curled into a ball and rolled down the hill, into the forest.

Isaac's head burst from murky green water. "We're too late. They took both keys!"

"Those burn'em, sunburnt thieves!" Keiko said, clenching her hands into fists. "Come on. We'll cut them off at the flag."

A two-story fort stood in the middle of the woods with a red flag flapping in the wind on its roof. Murphy rolled to the edge of the fort and stood, dizzy, but first. He looked over the grounds with suspicion. A quiet growling sound came from somewhere, but he couldn't place it. He picked up a handful of rocks and tossed them around the perimeter of the fort.

One rock went right through the ground and a pointy pair of sharp teeth covered in whiskers chomped up from the hole.

Murphy gulped. "That's interesting."

Elise could see the flag on the fort's roof through the trees as well as Murphy's cautious experiment. She grinned. "Fearful hearts and sand for brains," she said to herself. "That's why you're going to lose—"

One moment she was running at full speed, and the next she was falling through the air with the leafy ground about to greet her face.

After smacking into the ground, she spat out dirt and found that she'd stepped on a stone mushrup that was slowly covering her left leg with a rocky shell. It had grown past her knee and made its way to her waist. She tried to peel it off, but it grew over her hands.

"A cog being reckless?" Marissa said, smirking as she stepped from behind a tree. "Who could have possibly predicted?"

Murphy waved back at the other three as they surround Elise from their hiding spots.

"This burn 'em rock better not suffocate me, or this contest will be the least of your problems," Elise said.

Ammer laughed. "Don't worry, gear head. It's breathe-through. Just another bit of magic that your tech can't handle."

They held her arms down as Freya dug through her pockets. "Now look at that. Both Earth keys. I guess you aren't completely unclever. One for us . . ." She placed her dove necklace on the other key. It came to life and flew off with it. "And one for the woods."

They left Elise on the ground to struggle with her stony cocoon.

"Just use the installs that negates entrapment charms," Ammer chuckled. "What? You don't have one? Pity."

As they arrived at the fort, Marissa held out a pink wand as wisp dust spread out over the ground. It pooled over the hidden holes, and when the paranamoles poked their heads up, the dust flashed in front of their eyes.

"Let's go!" Marissa shouted.

They ran inside and up a stairwell to the flag on the roof. With the Air, Earth, and Water keys they unlocked it from the clamp at its base.

"We did it!" Murphy cheered.

Marissa put a hand on his shoulder. "We still need to get to the finish line."

A soaking wet Isaac arrived, crouching beside Keiko and Kain who hid in the woods out of view of the fort.

"Where's Elise?" Kain whispered.

Keiko pointed at his no-longer-struggling sister a few meters away. "They're turning her into a boulder."

Kain scowled. "Rottin' magic! What's the plan?"

"Let them unlock the flag," Keiko said. "You sneak over to your sister and break her free."

"How?"

Keiko shrugged. "I don't know."

Kain shot a glance at Isaac. "Ohm, do you have a solvent that could eat that rock off?"

"I could come up with one, but I don't know what the rock is made of. I'd need time we don't have. Keiko how's your aim?"

"Just about perfect," Keiko said. "Why?"

"Throw me," Isaac replied.

"What?"

"You have super strength and enhanced sight." He smiled. "Throw me."

Freya grabbed the flag from its unlocked housing on the fort's rooftop, just as they were about to climb down the stairs, an explosion of orange goo bombarded them from every side. The goo covered their bodies and stuck them to the roof. Isaac's scaly hand snatched the flag as he smiled and flew over them. One more elixir landed in front of him like a giant bubble bag, and Isaac landed safely in its center.

Ammer growled as Isaac waved from below with the flag in his hands.

"What the shard just happened?" Marissa said in shock.

"We just lost," Murphy replied.

"Not yet we didn't." Ammer's orb seared through his coat pocket and cut their sticky bindings. The hole from the orb's blast spilled the rest of the contents of his pocket out. The potions and hexes bounced onto the roof's ledge then rolled off of the fort to the ground below.

"No!" Ammer looked back at the others. "Quick, what do you have? We need to catch them!"

Murphy dug through his pockets and pulled out a

confusion charm. Ammer snatched it from his hand and tossed it at Isaac as he ran. It landed ahead of Isaac, and he avoided it with ease.

"Shimmerin' pixies!" Ammer cursed. "What else?"

Freya was already holding an orange gem whose light curved into the shape of a bow. She pulled back on its ethereal drawstring. "Flames of Calla, hit my mark true!"

A blast of fire rocketed past the trees, sending a shockwave through their branches. It hit Isaac square in the back and flung him into the air and into the dirt. The flag landed out of his reach.

Below them came a loud rumbling.

"Ammer," Freya said with more than a hint of worry in her voice, "what else did you have in your pocket?"

Ammer shrugged. "A little of everything. You never know what you're going to need."

The ground below the fort erupted, tilting the building to one side. From a massive cloud of soil burst an enormous paranamole. The beast roared with newfound fiery breath! It smashed its head against the fort.

"Run!" Freya yelled.

The four squires leapt off the roof just as the giant paranamole's foot came crashing down behind them.

The paranamole fumed, flashes of fire coming out of its nose. The smaller paranamoles squealed and ran away from their enormous cousin. One massive furry foot crushed the confusion charm and the green twinkling spell soaked into the beast's skin.

"That's not good," Murphy said.

Another foot swept down at the four students. A second before they were crushed Keiko dashed to them, holding up her arms and letting her mechanical skeleton take the weight of the blow.

"Go! I can't hold this thing off forever," Keiko groaned. The weight of the beast was already pushing her into the soft ground.

The giant paranamole roared and swung its paw, sending Keiko flying into the trees.

The four Day students ran in different directions. Freya charged toward the flag.

"What are you doing?" Marissa asked.

"I'm going to win," Freya replied.

The paranamole stomped around wildly, edging closer to Elise, who still lay stuck in the rocky shell that had grown up to her neck.

"A little help!" Elise yelled.

Kain's wires yanked her away just as the paranamole's fiery breath ignited the leaves around her. Without anything in its immediate vicinity, the creature seemed content to burrow into the ground.

"Don't ever say I don't do anything for you," Kain said.

"You're stars deep in debt to me already," Elise said. "Now get me out of this stuff."

Kain looked her over. "How'd this start?"

"I stepped on something."

Kain noticed a part of the rocky mushrup still stuck to her foot. "Watch your toes!" Out of one of his wires opened into a blade that sparked with blue light. He chopped the stump off of her foot and the rocks stopped growing.

Kain lifted Elise over her shoulders. "Now let's go win this thing."

Freya had made it half way to the finish line before a flying rock cocoon smashed into the back of her knees and pinned her to the ground.

Elise smiled. "Miss me, ashbreath?"

Keiko was right behind her and picked up the flag.

"Finish this, Kirin!" Elise cheered.

Keiko burst through the woods, with the crowd in the stands cheering. The rest of the contestants were right behind her as the ground rumbled and the giant paranamole breached the surface once more. The audience screamed as the beast sent an eruption of earth and rock into the air. The ground above the tunnel began to collapse. Keiko dropped the flag as she scrambled to get to solid ground.

The paranamole shot plumes of dragon's breath into the air, as the crowd scrambled to escape. But another giant emerged from the crowd, striding toward the beast with a pair of massive mechanical arms.

Commander Grail cocked his head to either side, his stern gaze squarely on the paranamole. The giant paranamole flared its nostrils and charged. With one swift punch to the jaw, Grail sent the beast crashing through the woods. With a thud, it landed in a cloud of dust and did not stir further.

The crowd calmed in the silence.

In the last moment of chaos, Murphy Wumples picked up the flag that had landed at his feet and, with a single step over the finish-line, he brought the competition to an end.

Everyone was is too much shock to react, but Murphy smiled as he held the flag above his head in pride.

Chapter Five

The Mentor Quest

"This is not working."

Commander Grail looked down at Jono and Suriana from across the desk in his office. Beside the young princess stood a red-haired knight who seethed with fury.

"I should say that is putting it lightly, Commander," the knight said. She wore gleaming armor of the Day that held a familiar reverence for Jono, who still had fond memories of his brief time in Caer Midus even if it had been bookended by fights with the Tombs. "I leave my charge for one wake to your school and you release monsters to eat your students."

Grail clamped his massive hands together in a pose resembling contemplation; Jono saw it more as careful restraint. "It was magic that escalated the situation, Sir Brigid, but yes, the responsibility is mine."

"Why are we here?" Jono asked. "We tried to stop them."

"That is precisely why I've asked you here," Grail replied. "You two are responsible students with close ties to the offenders." He unclasped his hands and sighed. "I need your help."

"Anything, Commander," Suri said, sitting as straight as she could in her chair.

The images of the nineteen squires appeared above the desk.

Grail took a deep breath before continuing. "We Dark Enders are not like you, and you are not like us. The Tombs want us to fail. Your fellow squires and my cadets would rather fight against each other than build with each other, and the world is watching this experiment. Every mind out there is on the precipice. For them, for all of us, we need this to work."

Sir Brigid grumbled. "You are the commander. Order your cadets to comply, and they will—"

"And what happens when they leave my command? What does that say to the world watching us? That the Dark can only build peace under an iron fist?" He held up one of his hands and clenched it. "Both sides need to choose peace. They need to do it down in their gears. And it doesn't help when the teaching staff is encouraging this behavior."

He was referring to Moss and Krust—Jono was used to the prejudice of kids around his age, but seeing the same behavior in those meant to instruct them made things seem almost hopeless.

Suriana stood, her eyes now level with Grail's. "They need to become friends. Have shared troubles and shared joys. The only way to get over the past is to get to know each other for who we really are."

Grail nodded his approval. "Are you up to the task?"

Suriana held her chin high, and Jono caught a glimpse of the generations of political leaders that had come before her. "I was born for this, Commander."

Grail's silver eyes turned to the boy that was born to have his heart collapse and lungs implode. "Wyer?"

Jono nodded. He'd made a habit of taking on vastly more than he knew how to manage. Why stop now?

"Good," Grail said with certainty. "Work together to come up with a plan. Lead them. If there is anything you need, send your request through Mrs. Drudge."

"And what of the teaching staff involved?" Sir Brigid asked.

"Also my responsibility, but I cannot undo a lifetime of prejudice with a reprimand. It would not do to suspend them as much as it would help the students under their tutelage." Grail sat in silent contemplation for a moment before continuing. "I will need to speak to both Krust and Moss further, but in the meantime I'll be keeping them under close watch. This trouble is working against both the students and faculty."

"I agree." Suri turned to Jono. "Will you meet me at my Father's apartment in the Crown after school? We can work on a strategy."

"Yeah, see you then."

"Excellent." Suriana went to leave but stopped at the door, turned, and bowed. "And thank you, Commander, for saving us all from that beast. Magic is powerful, but it can get out of hand."

Grail stood. He was an imposing figure whose metal arms dominated any room he was in. His eyes were fixed on Sir Brigid's. "I will always protect my students, no matter where they are from. Dismissed."

Suriana and Brigid left the room, but Jono stopped and let the door close. He turned back to face the commander.

"You let them do it," Jono said.

"I did what?" Grail replied.

Jono approached the desk. "I don't believe for one second that you don't see everything that goes on at Windom. You have the Eyes of the Empress looking everywhere."

Grail raised an eyebrow. "And why would I do that?"

"You must have thought it was best," Jono said. "Maybe a fight was coming, one way or another, and this way they could purge it from their system. Maybe a good fight is one way to get to know somebody better. To see their face up close, instead of a dot on a screen. With everything that has happened over the past few years, maybe people need to blow off some steam."

Grail retook his seat and leaned back in his chair. "I can't protect any of you forever. All of my students must learn that their choices to fight or cooperate have consequences. We can only hope they gathered a drop of respect for each other in the Drills woods and that the nightmares of that giant beast will make them think twice before doing something brash again. The world beyond these walls will hit you all sooner than you know. Be ready for it."

The Crown's lower level apartments filled the walls like a towering metal canyon. Trolleys sped along rails built into the walls, carrying passengers to doors that glittered like tiles in a mosaic.

Jono sat alone on a curved couch in a trolley car, tapping his fingers against a metal armrest, nervous for the awkward reunion that awaited him.

Each apartment had a balcony decorated to bring a little personality to the grey cavern. Bright white lights beamed down at one porch covered in exotic, flowering plants. Above the door hung a mauve banner trimmed in gold. In the center was a symbol of a white tower surrounded by sunrise waves.

With a thought, Jono linked the image on the Line to the symbol of the Systine sheikdom in the Day. Suriana's lineage had ruled that country along the Calm Coast for the past thirty generations. The elected sheiks ruled over the quaint country just beyond the Dawn and boasted of the treasured warm springs that lined its coast.

Just as Jono's trolley arrived, the front door slid open. Sir Brigid held her sword out of its scabbard, its blade sparking with purple light. Her delicately engraved silver armor and thick blue and white tunic shouted that she was from the Day. The six-winged dove, the symbol of the angel Shiva, was embossed across her chest.

Brigid glared at Jono. "Are you Dark Enders always late?" she growled, her hands gripping the hilt of her spell blade.

Jono cleared his throat. "Sorry. Is Suriana still here?"

"That's for me!" Suri called as she came to the door from another room.

Sir Brigid stepped aside, and Suri hugged Jono; he noted a glower from the knight as he entered the apartment.

"Come in!" Suri said. She always kept to a professional demeanor when dealing in politics, but now that they were in a more casual space, she was able to drop into her natural enthusiasm. "It's so great to have a free moment with you. Everything's been so busy since we arrived. I barely have had any time to settle in."

The knight waited patiently, glaring beside the door.

"Oh, don't worry about Maergann," Suri said. "She's just here to protect me since all you Dark Enders are so terrible and threatening." Suri said as they entered her living room. "Sit down." She motioned to a red leather couch. "Can I get you anything?" Suri disappeared into another room without waiting for an answer.

"Something fizzy to drink," Jono called after her. He sat on the couch in the center of the room facing a wide window screen that opened to a spectacular view of the city. They were just under the greenhouse cloud line and could see far into the maze of buildings and elevated roads below.

The walls of the apartment were already covered with moving pictures of Alistair, Suri, and a second man with a twirly goatee, who Jono didn't recognize. There were serious pictures at formal events and shots of the three of them making silly faces near a beach resort in front of a sun-rising horizon. Despite a few remaining enchanted crates, the apartment felt comfortable and settled in.

"How about this?" Suri returned with a tray of two sparkling drinks and a pile of green cookies. She set the tray on a carved wood table in front of the couch then took a seat next to Jono.

Jono pointed to the pictures. "You're family looks happy."

Suri glanced back at the image of Alistair swinging her six-year-old self and the twirly goateed man about to catch her.

"We were," she said and then caught herself. "We are. Papa used to say that his spirit would live on through Dad and me. I think that's true. I still feel him around me every wake."

"He's . . .? I'm sorry."

She turned back to Jono before he could mention his own family. She hid the sadness from her eyes with wide smile. "It is so good to see you! How have you been?"

Jono opened his mouth to speak, but nothing came out. To fill the awkward moment, he reached for one of the drinks and took a few sips. He had no idea if Suriana was aware of the fate that befell Polari, and he was happy enough to avoid it.

"It's been good," Jono finally managed. "Just more school and training."

"Are you still majoring in Cloaks?"

"That's right. It's been . . ." Jono thought back to how Grail had to force Professor Goest to keep him in. ". . . fun," he lied. "How does it work with all of you Solans not having any bionetics installed?"

"It's different for each of us. Some people still believe any installs would be used against us. Others have religious objections to it. They say it makes the body impure."

"What do you think?"

"Take a look!" Suri turned around to show off a tiny metal circle on the back of her neck.

"Nice!" Jono said. "You got a linker!"

Suri gave him a proud smile. "And a brain computer, but my father doesn't want people to know about it. He is starting to trust the Empress, but you can never be too careful about how other people might react."

"Do they have you scheduled for a track at Windom?"

"No. They're letting all of us survey each track then choose one if we decide to stay next year."

"Choose?" Jono thought back to his first year when he had no choice. "That's a luxury. So, you may be sticking around more than a one year?"

Suri smiled. "If we want to, we can finish our knight training while at Windom."

"And four years ago the world was at war. Times really are changing."

"They are. I may get to see this Jupiter Gorge of yours yet!"

"Jupiter?" Jono had forgotten that he'd once offered to take her there if peace ever happened between Dark and Day. It was close to Polari. Too close. He hadn't thought about it since that wake long ago in Caer Midus. He didn't even know if it was damaged by the Pox. "Right." He forced a smile. "Just say when."

"Maybe next summer when the winds are warmer and the starlilies are in bloom."

"That would be perfect," Jono said, relieved he didn't have to bring up Polari's fate.

Suri looked down, her hands on top of one another in her lap. "I do have an important question for you."

"Oh?" Jono sipped his bubbly fizz.

"How many friends do you have?"

Jono found himself making a weird face. "Enough?" He shrugged.

"Friends you can truly trust. Remember, we are putting the lives of my squires and the fate of the world in their hands. We need one for every squire . . . dedicated mentors that will help them feel comfortable in your city, and someone that won't be intimidated by magic."

"Magic is a tough sell here," Jono said. "Everyone has spent their whole lives thinking magic was going to kill them and everyone they loved."

"And now we all have the pox to fill that fear," Suri said. "We are Day Enders, Jono. We can no sooner live without magic than you can without that metal you need to keep your heart beating. It's who we are. And it's the power we've come to share with the Dark."

"Twenty cadets clicking with magic users? It'll be tough, but I can find them." The entire idea sounded as preposterous as manufacturing a family. Jono didn't even grasp how he'd made his own friends and certainly didn't have a strategy for others.

Jono could count his real friends on one hand, but Keiko? She knew everybody! She could convince enough people to join.

"Perfect!" Suri lit up once more. "I've already started planning activities for us to do together. There will be a buffet social, tours around the city, and we can pair up your friends with squires that have similar hobbies. If both sides can find a common root, then a forest could grow from it. Don't you think?"

Jono nodded despite thinking it was more likely going to cause another fight. "We'll make this work."

Suriana hugged him. "Bless you, Jono! You're the best!"

"Not a clunkers chance in orbit!" Oscar chortled from his bunk in their room. "You do remember what they were like in Al Jebra? They'll probably try to convert us all to their spooky angel club."

"Sorry mate. I don't really think so," Isaac said. "I mean, I'm so busy already. I start my apprenticeship at the Pathaganon next week. I bet David would do it, though, and the twins are at Windom now. They could join too."

"Can you imagine Uly and Rex trying to be mentors?" Oscar said with a snorting laugh. "They'd get those Day Enders arrested within a wake!"

"Good point." Jono leered at the memory watch that sat, untouched, on his end table. He'd gathered a group of trustworthy cadets to discuss Suri's plan, but things weren't looking good. If Oscar and Isaac weren't onboard, then his other, more distant friends wouldn't be a good bet. "Isn't your sister at Windom?"

"Esmerelda?" Oscar asked. "She almost went AWOL when she heard Day Enders were coming to Windom. You'd be lucky if she doesn't start crying if she sees one of them across the cavern. There's no chance of her locking gears with one."

Jono rolled his head back in despair. "Come on, this is important! I need you. Make the time to be a part of history!"

"Sorry, I think Oscar is right about this. You're asking for trouble," Bastion Bittle said. The pulisaur boy's mucus-green skin routinely put him on the outside of group activities, but this was one that he would have enjoyed avoiding. "My mum made me watch one of those new shows the burnt brains have going on at Saint Newton's—where the little hairy guy stands up and talks about how the angels could save us from the pox and all that? Dreadfully dull. They said the angels are just whisking away all the very best people first, before the whole world goes to the Pit. I wager they're all just dead, though."

Clive slapped Bastion's foot and gave him a nasty glare.

When Bastion realized what he said, he began stuttering. "I mean . . . probably not your family, though."

"They're not dead, clunker," Oscar said. "They're just missing. Right, Jono?"

His family was gone and when he had the chance to change the course of the world, it came down to not having enough friends.

"I'm sure they're fine, somewhere, and the Day folk aren't that bad," said Clive Van Der Scant. Clive was a rare feli'yin raised in the Dark. In Jono's experience, people who knew what it was like to be an outsider were more likely to give outsiders a chance. "Sign me up, Jono."

"I'm glad one of you is clicking into this idea, because there's more," Jono said. "I don't know if you've noticed, but we've gone years with two open bunks . . ."

Oscar looked at the two bunks, one covered in piles of unwashed uniforms and the other hidden below stacks of random mechanical gadgets. "You're not serious. Those are our storage bunks! Where are going to leave our dirty clothes?"

"This is straight from the commander," Jono said. "The world is watching and so are the Tombs. We've got to give them a chance."

⚙

Jono slumped from his toes to feet as he waited in the hallway outside of the codiestics classroom. He only had four volunteers, including himself, and fifteen more people to find. He hoped Keiko had convinced more of her dorm's corridor to sign up.

He stepped back with the uncomfortable thought of asking random strangers to participate but was interrupted by colliding with an unsuspecting passerby. Jono tripped over his foot and almost fell, but a hand sprung out to grab his shoulder.

"Are you alright, Mister Wyer?"

A thick book slid out of the large stack in Professor Fourier's arms. His hand darted again and snatched the book just before it hit Jonothon's head.

"Would you mind lending a hand?" Fourier asked with a smile.

"Sure." Jono held his arms out and wires snaked out to wrap around the stack of books.

Fourier gave him an appreciative nod then said, "Aren't you supposed to be in class?"

"Yeah, well . . ." Jono had just ended a therapy session with Professor Wishe but recoiled at the thought of talking about it. He looked at the book on the top of the stack.

"Launch of the Aurora?" Jono raised his eyebrows.

"What?" Fourier scoffed. "I'm not supposed to read history?"

Jono shrugged. "Read what you want."

"That one does have a lot to do with mathometry."

"Does it?"

"The entire conflict was initiated by the application of the Achlisian principal with the invention of the Starskipper drive."

"I guess so."

"It just goes to show how mathometry provides the building blocks of modern civilization."

They made it to Fourier's classroom and set the books on his desk.

"So . . ." Professor Fourier started cautiously, "How's your school year coming along thus far?"

Jono nodded. "It's fine."

"You were a bit early for codeistics. I hear that's a pretty difficult course. Update or freeze, isn't it?"

Jonothon nodded again.

In codeistics, Professor Curia Ism had been moving through each lesson faster than his other classes, but Jono worked hard to keep up. The dennou installed in his brain, like every other student's, made it easy to remember the different patterns and manipulate the code so far, although there were always grumblings from the others as they left the class.

"I like codeistics," Jono said. "It's like mathometry, you know, like, formulas and stuff, so, I don't know, I guess I do pretty well. I just log the formulas. The trick is really in understanding how everything works together. It's like how dynamic code layers with specialized code, like how nothing is really all by itself, it works together, that sort of thing."

"Absolutely right. You know——" Fourier said before he stopped himself. "Well, of course you don't, but what I meant to say was that when I was your age, I had the notion that I had to be the best at everything. My step-brother was in the gunners track, always very athletic. He went on to play Globall for the Quarington Quasars for a few years, but never mind. The point is that I thought I had to be good at sports and drills and all the rest. And when that didn't turn out, and of course it didn't, I took it hard. It wasn't until my fifth year that I grasped how valuable it is to let myself be who I wanted to be. Don't try to do everything. Specialization is the key to progress."

Jono looked at his Professor with a controlled expression to mask his confusion with passive agreement.

Fourier smiled awkwardly. "Sorry. . . Before I started at Windom this term, I taught advance mathometry applications at the Pathaganon——that's a research office at the Crown. The whole mentor aspect of teaching young minds such as yours is still new to me. I only wished to share a bit of the lessons I've learned in my long wakes. Maybe save a fellow Windom cadet a little heartache."

"Yeah, it's okay." Jono scratched his chest. His fingers hit the metal container that protected his heart. He smiled. "I don't think that will be a problem."

"Alright then, I'll see you in class next wake. You did complete the assignment on Treacle's Equation?"

Jonothon grinned. "An equation for controlled rocket trajectories that accounts for gravity, air resistance, and varying propulsion? How could I not?"

"I appreciate your time, Sage." Commander Grail shook the Sage of Age's barky hand with his metallic one.

"It is I who am grateful for yours," the Sage of Ages replied. "I am merely an advisor to the Lords of the Republics of the Day. You, sir, have an entire academy to manage."

"I am honored to be given that responsibility."

The Sage of Ages' entourage of clerics, knights, and mages filed through the elevated cobblestone streets like mice lost in a maze. Grail recognized only one of them: Cassindra Viscariot, the Day's head representative to the Peace Council. Commander Grail's enormous metal arms provoked a number of harsh whispers from her and the others, but he noticed that the Sage kept a gentle smile on his brown, wooden face.

"There are less than three hundred dryads living in Eies," Grail said. "As you can imagine, your kind isn't drawn to cold and stars quite like others are, but we do maintain a sapling grove in a section of Middle Night Gardens."

Grail led them through the door of a building that, on

the outside, appeared to be just like any other brick and metal tower in Eies. The inside was filled by a grove of trees four stories high. Glowing flower lamps warmed the air all around them.

"The Dark has been very accommodating to our visit, Commander." The Sage's eyes always creased pleasantly when he smiled. He patted the Commander's metal shoulder lightly as his followers attempted to hide their gasps. "On behalf of my species and my people of the Day, I thank you."

"The truth is, Sage," Commander Grail said, pointing to a distant dryad dressed in grubby mechanics jeans, "here, they are our people, too. One and the same. Even if they are a rare sight in the Dark End."

"With leaders like you, I believe this peace will hold."

"Likewise. If I may have a moment with you in private?"

The Sage nodded just as Viscariot approached to protest.

"O Wise Sage," Viscariot said, "surely we humble counselors would benefit from observing your diplomacy?"

"Not all topics are a matter for wide world to hear them, Chancelor Viscariot," the Sage replied patiently.

Viscariot forced a smile. "Unfortunately, protocol prohibits dignitaries such as you from being alone in the city." She looked at Grail. "Not that we expect any risk of mechanical infection, please don't be insulted. We are obliged to take precautions. You do understand, of course?"

The Sage stepped between the chancellor and the commander. He rested his weight on his large wooden staff and looked back at Viscariot. "Friendships are grown in a soil of trust. If we spoil the seed now, how do we expect to bare anything but rotten fruit?"

Viscariot raised a finger to reiterate her protest, but the Sage's raised brow advised her to concede.

"As you will it, Sage." She bowed and led the others out of the garden.

As the doors shut behind them, the Sage bowed in apology. "I'm afraid that where I am from, zeal is often mistaken for virtue," the Sage said with a sigh.

Grail waved it away. "We all have much to overcome before we can build a future together."

"Viscariot's intent is pure, but she can be *indelicate*. There is a saying in the Day that she is one that looks at saplings and sees a forest."

They strolled slowly through the shadowy garden, surrounded by hanging branches covered in thick leaves. Grail could feel the Sage's patient nature was at odds with his own urge for expediency.

"I am ashamed that we were at each other's throats not too many years ago," Commander Grail said. "I did not have the chance to apologize for that in person before."

"I regret that as well," the Sage replied. "But the river's water has cleared. Best to let fetid pools wash out to sea and drink of fresh water up stream. Together we have healed more of the wounds than I once thought possible.

Regarding the true instigators of that disaster, how do you feel about our current efforts?"

"Overall, our partnerships remain strong. It is to be expected that some of us will have a harder time than others adopting to the new world schematic."

"And despite betrayal and madness, here we remain. On the verge of yet a new pressure demanding change of both our people. I hear that the squires are having a difficult time acclimating."

Grail knew better than to assume the Sage wasn't aware of everything that was going on. The Empress herself could have been granting him eyes on the squires.

"We are taking efforts to integrate them as naturally and positively as we can," Grail said. "These are good people—teachers and students working on making them feel at home. It will take time."

The Sage brushed his hand against a purple flower that was moist with simulated dew drops. Its edge was wilted. It wouldn't last another wake. "Oh, they will never feel at home in the Dark, I'm afraid. I pray they feel accepted, at best. I take it our mutual friend is a part of the welcoming committee? His unique experience makes him most qualified to assist in their transition."

"He is on the mission now. Wyer has a good heart. I trust he will meet our expectations, although he's been prone to exceeding them in the past."

"I am delighted to hear it," the Sage said. "As a token of the pact we made, the Empress granted me access to our young friend's progress throughout his education. I can see his loss plagues him greatly."

"My orders are to be far more delicate in this case than we would for anyone else. The path may be slower, but the results will be more secure."

The Sage cupped the dangling mauve flower in his hand and smelled deep of its fragrance. "A wise choice. The mind is a fragile vessel. I do not doubt your machines hold great power to mend, but I fear taking risks with this one. He is not simply a wounded soldier in need of repair."

"Our friend has great talents, but discipline is coming slowly for him," Grail replied. "He gets caught up in his passions and loses himself in thought. He has a hard time clicking on many things at once."

"Many tasks that are assigned, but he has no problem with juggling many ideas at once, does he?"

"No, in the realm of ideas he is an advanced juggler. But where will that get him?"

"Ideas are the true currency of the world, Commander. It is what separates the living from the dead."

Among the vines wrapping around a large willow tree, a flower began to bloom with pink light.

"Ah, an Osiris flower!" The Sage brushed the glowing bloom with the tips of his fingers. "A remarkable moment."

Grail leaned down to get a better look at its bumpy petals. "I'm sorry but I'm not familiar with the botany of your kind. What does it mean?"

"A sad yet hopeful sign. A seedling that was planted has

been lost to the nature of the soil and the tree," the Sage said with a tear in his eye. "Yet the flower blooms with the genetic life the seed imparted. And with it, the grove is stronger and the other dryad seedlings may stand a better chance to be born."

Keiko watched patiently as Cid pointed the class toward a pile of mech parts stacked behind him.

"This wake we're going to put your instincts and mech knowledge to the test! Behind me you'll find all the parts to build a small mech. On the far side of the room—" Cid pointed to an odd setup of boards, ladders, rope, and tunnels. "—is an obstacle course. You'll form into teams and have one hour to design and assemble a mech from any of the parts you can find here. The fastest mech to pass all four red flags wins. Any questions?"

Four students from the Day sat quietly in the back, Laika among them. She raised her hand high.

"We don't have teams," Laika said. "And we've never made a mech before."

Cid smiled. "You've nothing to fear. My class assistant, Keiko, will lead your team and teach you the basics of mech design in no time."

Keiko stood up from her chair and saluted the Day students. "I'm on it, boss."

"That's no fair," a cadet replied. "Kirin's two years older than us and basically a mech genius!"

Keiko chuckled. "Don't tell me that a Dark Ender cadet of the Windom Academy is worried about losing to some squires who don't know a camshaft from a piston?"

"What's a piston?" Riley Shrub asked.

"What are they going to learn if Kirin builds it for them?" the young cadet said.

"We're all here to learn. I'm not building on my own, but we're not about setting up fresh widgets for failure, either."

"I still think you put the odds against us."

"Good. I guess you'll have to level up your effort then," Keiko replied.

"Enough debate. Cadet Kirin will coach the least experienced team," Cid said. "Are you all ready?" Cid started a timer display at the front of the room. "Go!"

The students lurched from their desks and dove into the piles of parts. Transistors, joints, and power cores flew into the air as they dug for the best pieces.

The Day students looked at the chaos, as lost as a fish in a space suit.

Keiko huddled them around without even bringing any parts. "The trick to good mech design is having a clear idea of what you're trying to achieve before you go too far with the building," she whispered in the center of the rambunctious storm. "See that course? We need to hit two places up high, one in a narrow tunnel, and one far away."

"Can we make a mech that flies?" Riley asked. Her puffy bush of leafy hair made her barky face look all the more narrow.

"That's a clever idea," Keiko said. "If we had more time, flying would be perfect. The problem is that flight design can be tricky, especially to make it through that tunnel. What we need is something that can move long distances, crawl through tight spaces, and would be easy to aim."

"What about a frog?" Laika asked.

"You have woolly frogs in the Day?"

"No, but my village has forest frogs in all the branch ponds. They're green and squishy but can leap from tree to tree. They also dig into the tree bark."

"Or desert frogs," Riley said. "We have those too, although they mostly dig into the ground and don't move much."

"Forest frogs sound like a perfect model," Keiko said. "Riley, you go to that pile and look for a little cylinder that glows pale blue. That will be a mech brain with a default program for ground moment. You! Get two skinny legs from that pile. You! Get a narrow body, and I'll find some claws!"

By the time the buzzer rang, they had a mech frog the size of a Keiko's fist. The smiling mech frog flipped backward on their work table as the Day students cheered.

The first mech to take to the obstacle course was from another team. It looked like a spider, a compact body and eight legs with tiny hands on their ends. Cid started a new timer for the course, and the spider locked onto its four targets. It climbed up a haphazard tower and touched the first flag in seconds. Then it pointed one of its legs at the next tower and shot a grappling hook out. The hook almost touched the next flag but missed it by a decimeter. The team groaned, but the spider pulled itself over to the tower. It hit the rest of the flags with a consistent but slow pace. Team Spider ended up with a time of ninety-three seconds.

The class clapped in support. Every team had come up with their own creative design that fared better and worse. An ape mech swung to the first two flags but got stuck in the tunnel. A rocket fly hit the first three flags in record time, but it overshot the final one and obliterated itself against the wall. With only the frog mech left, the best time was set by a gliding bird mech at forty-two-point-seven seconds.

"Remember," Keiko said to her team as they prepared the frog. "What matters is that we learned a lot and we had fun doing it, you click?"

The Day students nodded, but in their eyes there was hope for the sweet taste of victory and fear of the humiliation of defeat.

Riley placed the frog at the starting line and Cid started the timer.

With one leap upward, the frog was half way up the tower. Its clawed hands gripped the wall as it dragged itself to a platform. Another leap and it was at the first flag!

Riley had both her hands curled into fists and watched

with an enthusiasm that reminded Keiko of when she'd built her first mech.

The mech frog dangled from the first tower, aiming for the second spire.

"It's not going to make it!" Riley gasped.

"It's gonna make it," Keiko said.

The frog leapt, its long legs thrust backward and its hands clawing the air for any ground. It started to fall just when a claw grabbed below the next flag. Its legs kicked upward, and it touched the flag.

Above the class, the timer ticked away in bright red numbers. *Twenty-eight seconds*

Team Frog cheered as their mech pushed off the second tower. It landed by the tunnel, kept its legs back, and rolled through the tunnel on small wheels built into its belly—a suggestion Laika had come up with . . . with a bit of prompting by Keiko.

Thirty-four seconds

The frog hopped to its feet and turned toward the final flag. Its legs got into position before it leapt into the air. A joint had come loose, and one leg dangled with less power than before.

Thirty-seven seconds

Two more jumps and it would be there.

Thirty-nine seconds

The frog made the final leap as the clock ticked. The frog mech landed directly on the flag, and the clock stopped.

Forty one point nine seconds

The entire class room exploded with applause. The squires blushed and nodded to the pats of congratulations from the other teams.

Keiko hugged them all as they exhaled a collective sigh of relief. The worry their eyes was replaced by a glow of pride.

In that instant, Keiko believed that their mission wasn't nearly as impossible as everyone thought—even she'd had her doubts. In that cheering crowd of students, it didn't matter what side of the Dawn anyone was born.

And then Laika sneezed. The doors of the classroom slammed shut and red lights blared over the students. A gargoyle that had sat in the corner of the ceiling like a stone came to life and swooped down. He slammed Laika against the wall and covered both of them in a metal mesh dome.

The mirth turned to fright as Day Enders screamed, and the cadets looked around in confusion.

The Empress' face appeared on a screen at the front of the class.

"Hello everyone," the Emrpess said in a graceful tone. "I sincerely apologize for the harsh quarantine procedures. However, we have detected a trace amount of flutterbee flu in the air of this classroom. Unfortunately, the dormant version of this virus was not caught during the Day student's transition review, but an active flu can put others at a terrible risk. The carrier is being isolated, and all of you must undergo a purification process before you will be allowed to exit the room.

Please, be patient with us as we work through this uncomfortable circumstance. Thank you."

Ammer and Murphy examined the empty bunk beds after Oscar led them into twenty nine Capricorn corridor.

"One of you can bunk under Kohai and the other could sleep below Clive," Oscar said, pointing to their new beds.

"They're both on the bottom," Ammer said with disappointment.

Oscar shrugged. "That's the luck of a transfer. First come, first served."

"I'll take Clive's bunk," Murphy said. "I don't mind the fur."

"I think I'd rather sleep in the woods," Ammer said.

Oscar snickered at the idea. "Sleep in the Drills woods? I did that once. The paranamoles snuck up and ate all our marshmallows, clever clunkers."

Ammer dug out a glass vial from his bag and poured a drop of luminescent liquid on the bed. The liquid's light spread into a pearl-like gloss over the bed then faded.

"What's that?" Oscar stepped away cautiously. "The others are really not going to like you casting spells in here. They'll get second hand magic on them. You should really never do that again."

"Relax, oil-veins," Ammer said with a scowl. "It's just a purity potion. I'm not sleeping on anything that's been touched by Dark Enders."

Ammer smelled the bed again then promptly added three more drops of purity potion to the thick blankets.

The door of eighteen Lionoh Loop cracked open as Keiko led Riley and Marissa inside. It was late in the sleep hours when they were finally released from quarantine. Every inch of their bodies tingled from the decontamination process.

The rest of the girls were long asleep, which was for the best, since they couldn't protest their new bunk mates if they weren't aware of them.

"Welcome to your new home," Keiko said with a weary smile.

The two empty beds were covered in mech parts.

"Sorry about the clutter. You can set your things in the dresser there."

"Are you certain that we cannot go back to the Day-only dorms?" Marissa asked. "Not to be rude, but I think we would all be happier if we gave each other a little more space."

"Commander's orders," Keiko said. "And besides, you don't want to miss out on all the culture you'll get to learn by living with us."

"What about Laika?" Riley asked. "Are they going to send her back home just for a little flu?"

Keiko winced. "Cid says so, yeah. We can't be too

cautious with bugs from the Day."

"Surely your Empress must have thought this through," Marissa said. "She invited us all here."

Riley agreed. "I heard the Empress has so many machines in her brain that she could predict the future."

"Good thing she's not our enemy anymore," Marissa replied snidely.

Keiko collapsed on her bed and shut her eyes. "Don't ramp up your hopes or fears about her. All the biggest heroes and villains live with the tallest of tales. She's already juggling a trillion eyes watching half the planet in one brain. I wouldn't put too much faith in her ability to predict finding the flu in one student. Everyone and everything has their limits, even if it's scarier or safer to think of them as all-powerful."

"All the same, I think it's going to be alright," Riley said, clutching her stomach. "Flutterbee flu is such a little thing. I've had it three times already."

"Not to the Dark Enders it isn't," Marissa said. "They have probably never been exposed to it. Who knows how it would attack their untrained bodies. Not to mention all the mech things you have installed. The wrong flu could clog your wires and cause massive damage or even death." She motioned toward the dorm's window. "You all live so tightly stuck together in this city that it could spread faster than any plague ever in the Day. That's why the Empress took it so seriously. One sneeze could kill more people than all of the spell casting knights in the world. There'd be no stopping it."

Riley nodded. "It's a good thing tragedy has been averted then, isn't it? Still, too bad about Laika." Riley pulled out a wooden wand and waved it at the piles of metal parts on the bed. A blue cloud of pixels glimmered over to the bed and began organizing the mech parts onto nearby shelves.

Keiko smiled at Riley. "I think that's going to come in very handy. It's is going to be fun having you squires in Lionoh Loop."

Marissa looked at the other girls that slept around them. All three of them knew that despite Keiko's friendliness, the others would be much more wary. "Yes. Fun."

Chapter Six

The Seeds of Friendship

aer Midus glimmered in the sunlight, its golden walls glowing against the rolling green hills like a kiss from the sun. The town below was still sleeping. Shivan doves chirped as they shared worms with their chicks. A patrolling basilisk tasted the soft pollen in the air with its thick, purple tongue.

Jono dropped silently from a rooftop just as the basilisk turned a corner. He tapped his finger on the stone-paved ground in front of a sturdy wooden door, and two taps replied. He switched the connector inside his spywire into a purple gem he used for crystal hacking.

Be clicked with it, Wyer, Elise thought through TeamThink as she flickered into view.

Gem hacking is an art, Jono thought. *Don't rush me.*

Jono's wires pried off a stone panel near the door. Below it was a network of mineral lines running through the inner workings of the castle.

Everything is gems, mirrors and mineral light paths, Jono thought. *What I wouldn't give for a good old box of wires and circuits.*

Jono shut his eyes as his mind stepped into the code world in the Day. It was a psychedelic wonderland of information, constantly morphing around itself in bridges and forests of changing light. Jono switched through filtered masks to views the gem code by its various patterns. The world changed its hue with each filter until the world had turned pale, and a golden path trickled from the crystal spires toward a distant castle. With only a thought, Jono sped toward the castle, flying over the path until he found his way to the treasure room inside the code castle. In the center of the room sat a golden box on a pedestal.

Jono took snapshots of the room and then created a tunnel toward the pedestal that looked exactly like the room itself. He snuck through the tunnel, past the code crystals that watched over the room. The tunnel stretched over the pedestal, replacing it with the image it was covering.

Jono huddled in the shaded tunnel, and as he stared at the box, an exact replica constructed itself in his hands.

Processing lock controls now.

Hurry up, Wyer.

Jono copied the box then switched the original for his fake one. He opened the original box and flipped a green gem inside. It turned red.

We're clear.

The rest of the cloaks team darted from their hiding spots in shaded bushes and behind ivory statues around Caer Midus. Their invisible bodies filed through the opens doors, windows, and gem-crusted grates. They silently spread across the castle. Every few steps they would pull a seed from their pockets and hide it wherever they could. Seeds were shoved into the dirt around topiaries, patted into flower pots, and stuck into the nooks between golden bricks. They hid them in vines and flowers, along shaded arches and in babbling streams.

How goes the sowing, team? Elise thought.

The guard's square is most complete, Clarissa replied.

The Lord's Assembly is clicked, Kain thought.

The masks over the crystal sentinels show zero cracks, Jono thought. *Patrols are closing in. Let's weld it up.*

Five invisible figures shuffled into the corners of the Sage of Age's throne garden. They spread their last seeds in a grid pattern before Suman placed the last seed in the carved ivory throne.

The Lord's Assembly is clicked, Suman thought. *Time to fade. All spy seeds are planted.*

All signals are responding, Elise thought. *Good work, team.*

The extraction path is now activated in your eyes, Elise thought. *Keep it clicking.*

Elise led the squad through a gemmed gate and into a narrow stream that tunneled through the mountains. The stream was designed to allow the water to cool down in the depths of the mountains before returning to the castle to share its refreshing chill. *Keep your body straight. The techsuit will carry you over the current.*

The light of the burning sun faded behind them as they each slid through the tunnel and into darkness. The stream of warm water cooled as they moved through the narrow path.

Ow! Suman thought.

Keep your head down until I say so, Elise thought.

I wanted to see where I'm going, Suman replied.

Theses tunnels aren't meant for bodies. Just hold your oil until I flag the gate.

They wound through the mountain for what seemed like an hour, the rough, carved tunnel bumping against their water flow suits.

I'm at the gate, Elise thought. *Stick your right arm out when I say, and I'll catch you before you fall over the cliff. Kain.*

A moment went by.

Wyer.

Jono stuck his right arm out just as Elise grabbed it and swung him to a ledge where the twins stood. The tunnel expanded down a sudden drop in order to mix the water with the cool air.

Chak.

Bauer.

Elise tapped the stone wall where they had entered. The wall cracked open to the sun's blinding light on the other side of the Epoch Mountains. A steep cliff and vast desert greeted them.

"One side fertile, the other barren," Suman said with amazement.

"The Day is a terribly odd place," Clarissa added.

"Let's not clunker around," Elise said. Despite her attitude around the academy, Jono understood why she was the leader; she cut through the chatter and got things done. He wished someone would do the same with the Firewall.

With a commanding thought, a door opened in an invisible mech that clung to the side of the mountain. It spread its metal bat wings over the gate.

Elise put her hand on the side of the mech and motioned for the others to get inside. "All aboard the cloaks train!"

Or at least, she kept the chatter down when it mattered.

The interior of the bat mech was a tight fit for the five of them, but its small size helped make it stealthy.

They watched a set of monitors for any signs of danger as they soared over the sunny desert.

"Extraction complete," said a friendly voice from beyond the mech.

The world around them returned to the cold, stone classroom. The image of desert and mountains slid to the wall, and scores rating their individual and team performance began popping up over the clouds.

Of the two hundred seedlings, one hundred percent were placed in the target zones of the castle's grounds. Equally high ratings appeared for team planning, codeistics, overall stealth, and the speed of the mission.

Kain slapped Jono on the back as the others clapped. "Good mission, everyone."

"Let's wait for the first score before we celebrate, shall we?" Elise said.

The program's voice began summarizing their mission. "Odds of a single spy seed discovery due to placement and growth patterns and location security . . . ninety eight percent."

"Four," Professor Goest growled from the back of the class.

The celebration was over.

"What is the most important metric of your mission?" Goest asked as he stepped toward his students.

As the squad captain, Elise stepped forward to respond. "Do not get caught. We got out of there with no eyes on us."

"Evidence is capture!" Goest yelled back. "Four of your seeds are almost guaranteed to be discovered!"

"Out of two hundred, though," Suman said.

Goest shot Suman a glare that could have unsettled the Commander himself. "Does it matter if you have one spellblade cut through your head? Or two hundred?"

Suman seemed to shrink under Goest's scrutiny, as Elise continued. "We did get in and out without being spotted."

"The *mission* is to have perfectly hidden eyes in the heart of Caer Midus, not to announce to everyone under Sol that the Dark End is spying on our new partner, isn't it?"

"Why are we training for this scenario in the first place?" Jono asked.

Suman nodded. "Yeah, aren't we supposed to be friends with the Day?"

"Being partners does not mean allowing ourselves to be vulnerable to attack," Goest said. "We will be prepared for every contingency, including the very likely possibility that this peace will not last. What we will learn about the fortresses in the Day, including Caer Midus, may prove critical if this fragile peace were to evaporate like water under their sun."

"Speaking of keeping the peace," Jono said, "the Solar system is watching what happens here at Windom. The Day exchange students are looking for mentors to help them get used to living in the Dark. There are events and outings planned. Mostly they need a local to show them the way we do things here."

For the first time Jono had seen, Professor Goest smiled in class. It was unsettling. "Clever thinking, Wyer. You may have a brain in you yet. It's time for the rest of you to join Wyer's little mentor club."

"All of us?" Suman asked.

"No, not all of you," Goest growled. "That would be suspicious, wouldn't it? A few of you join the club, the rest of you need to start being exceptionally nice to our new Day guests. Sit with them at lunch. Ask them how their classes are going. How do they like our food, our Global teams? Learn who their parents are, what towns they come from. Be as friendly as possible to get them to open up."

The class groaned in unison—except Jono. It was obvious to him Goest just wanted more information, more spying on the Day, but perhaps his paranoid plotting would benefit Jono and Suri's plans anyway.

Goest snapped his fingers, and the students quieted in an instant. "This is an unprecedented opportunity to practice your strategic lying and cover story skills. It must not be wasted. And remember—" Goest stretched his lips apart in a way that made them all feel nauseous. "—to smile."

Few things in Eies took Isaac Ohm's breath away. The Pathaganon was one of them. The research facility was a part of the crown castle that wrapped around the city at the peak of the mountains. The most brilliant minds of the Dark End gathered under that one roof to study the stars, look for signals from ancient planets, and analyze the mystical rhythm of the universe at their fingertips. If Isaac could keep his mental gears clicking, one wake he could be one of them.

The facility's foyer displayed a celebration of science throughout known history. Ornately-framed moving pictures hung on the walls of the domed-room, epic moments of exploration and discovery. A jubilant, and slightly intoxicated, Kansas Hawkling danced awkwardly in front of her first successful test of the Star Skipper drive. Bertrand Bolz cheered in front of a crowd as he presented his validation of the Muirian Equation.

Scattered across the indigo domed-celiing were chemixists, atomologists, mechanixists, and other scientists in various states of professional success, personal expression, or simple moments of joy.

There was nowhere on Earth that made Isaac feel more at inspired.

The director of the Pathaganon, Wendy MacZhao, stood in front of the sixteen new apprentices, wearing the most earnest smile Isaac had ever seen. Every other apprentice was a graduate of Windom, D'Arrow, or Crossridge. Isaac was the only active cadet in the bunch.

"This is the wake *you* change the world," said Director MacZhao. "It starts here. You may not know it yet, but the projects you will be assigned to this year will help us understand more about how the universe works than ever before! Together, we will explore, build, and learn in ways that improve life for everyone that can hear our signals. You are a soldier in this army of knowledge. Each wake, you move one step, one idea, and one null hypothesis further! Are you ready for the challenge?"

The apprentices and crowd of scientists cheered together. One by one, the apprentices were assigned to their projects and mentors. When Evanine Fluff, a yeton girl who kept glancing at Isaac and smiling, was assigned to Doctor Shen Kritters to study quantum energy manipulation, Isaac knew he would be the last assigned. But as the room quickly emptied, and Isaac found himself standing alone.

For an instant, he wondered if his age-exception request

had been denied. Isaac raised his hand. "Pardon me, Director, but I don't seem to have an assignment."

Director MacZhao stepped off the stage and approached him. "You, Mister Ohm, are the youngest apprentice I have had the pleasure of inviting to the Pathaganon in my tenure here. Your application ranked higher than seventy-eight percent of the graduates this year. For you, we have reserved a special puzzle. It is a challenge, I hope, that you will find rewarding, as well as healing." MacZhao pointed to a man sitting on a plush red chair in the shadow of a replica of the squid-shaped Thrallinger space station on the other side of the foyer. "Best effort, Mister Ohm."

One of Professor Fourier's eyes wore a tech monocle, but both stared from below the shadow of the brim of his top hat. "I retired from research, you do realize that?"

Isaac sat across from him on an orange ottoman. "I know that for some mad reason you're teaching mathometry at Windom. I read your paper on irrational quantum phenomenon. It was brilliant. And everything that Copersky accomplished would have never happened without it. You had everything here. I don't know why you would ever leave."

Fourier sighed. "The brain requires a cornucopia of stimuli to do its best work. There comes a time when new surroundings are required to make progress. And, as you may have noticed, the previous mathometry teacher, Mister Lumph, is now warming his toes in lava-heated pools in the Day." His face curled into a complex smile.

"I can think of worse ways to contribute to our new world peace. I do love this place, but burnin' stars, I needed a change of scenery."

Isaac frowned. "So if teaching is your path to an easy wake on warm beaches, why are you back?"

"Why?" Fourier chuckled. "I love that question. But you know it is not needed here. The answer is in your own head. Sort it out, Mister Ohm."

Isaac crossed his legs, leaned on his scaly tail, and rested his chin on his fist. "They already assigned Colin to Doctor Loorp to study the quantum quasar effect, which is really popular right now, so that can't be it. No one mentioned a project on neutrino echoes, which I know you were passionate about when you studied at Windom, but I don't think you'd reverse course just to dig through the past. It would have to be something new."

"No, for you, we have something much more compelling."

"Actually, for *you*, they have something more compelling," Isaac reasoned. "You're the brilliant mind they're trying to pull back in. But why now? And why . . . it's me. That's the connection. I'm why you're back."

Fourier nodded. "Isaac, I needed new eyes to see an old problem. Your mind has been clicking away at it since you saw it first come to life."

Isaac gasped. "The pox!"

Fourier gave him a sly grin. "Are you ready to crack the mystery on the greatest threat of our lifetime?"

Isaac had found his purpose. "When do we start?"

❂

"It's been weeks," Aquinas said as he poured two cups of Elbrish Garden tea. "One might get the impression that you were avoiding me."

The tumnkin chuckled as his handed Jonothon a cup. He sat across from the boy, who sat awkwardly in a twisted wooden chair. The apartments that had been prepared for the Day diplomats had all been decorated to make them feel more at home. Brightly colored drapes covered drab stone walls and potted plants filled with flowers sent whiffs of perfume through the air. Even the electronic windows were set to display the Day, instead of the humming glow of the city's artificial light. It brightened the room as though they were still under the burning sun.

"Sorry. I've been busy," Jono said. He sipped his tea and grimaced at the potent spices.

It had been so long since those lost wakes in Polari that Aquinas couldn't recall which tea the boy preferred. It must have been Dahlia who enjoyed the stronger flavors. Aquinas' heart ached for him, but the years had made them distant. He was only a child when they fled from Polari, and now, here he sat, half-way to a man, raised without parents or fateriarchs to guide him.

Aquinas smiled sadly. "Haven't we all."

They were all *too* busy. Even the provincial life in the Day had been sparked up since this peace was born.

There was not enough time made for dear old friends, until it was long too late.

Aquinas struggled to find the right words. "I know you've received my letters after what happened to Polari, but I never heard back from you. I hope that the Dark is helping you through this difficult time."

"I'm fine. Really."

Jono's face looked calm. He was more distracted by the interesting selection of decorations that spotted the room—old swords and thick cloth tapestries with emblems from the various provinces of the Day.

"It's all so terrible, but I want you to know that they are in a better place and—"

"No one knows where they are. They're missing. No bodies were found."

"Truly? Then that is . . . auspicious indeed. One may never know what secrets the angels hide from us. Yet even if the worst is to be revealed, please know that you will see them again."

Jono scowled but said nothing. It was as Aquinas suspected, growing up in the Dark had torn him away from the faith of his parents. Those seeds planted long ago had withered in the Dark without the nurturing light they needed. He said a silent prayer that he did not return too late to melt metal hearts.

Ever since Aquinas had led that boy out of his quiet mining town, his life had been filled with turmoil. It was *his* fault that so many things happened the way they did. It was his actions that led Jason Wheat to assume the role of hero in Jonothon's stead. Jason had died to keep that truth secret. Jono deserved more than to be lost to the lightless ways of the Dark. Yet try as he would, Aquinas would never be strong enough to set all things right. But, angels be praised, he didn't have to battle alone.

Aquinas glanced back at gold trimmed mirror on the wall. He knew she was watching. He'd asked for her help. Cassindra Viscariot would know what to do. She always did. She was watching them through the magic of the mirror where she could assess the boy's condition in private and council him on the ways to open the boy's heart again to the whispers of angels. Together, somehow, they would bring him back on the Narrow Path.

"I heard that the pox hit a town in the Day. How are they doing?" Jono asked.

"You refer to the Diremarc? By their grace, it was just scarred outside a small village. Only a few beasts and pens were lost. The villagers count themselves blessed, and the last I heard, they rest easy with the idea that the pox won't mark the same place twice. Angels willing, this pox won't curse the land for long."

Jono looked out the false window at a green field of trees swaying in the wind. "How can we stop the pox if we don't even know what it is?"

"There are many powers in the world beyond our knowledge, and some of them work in our favor. When the angels will it, they—"

"So we just wait for some pixiewitch to wave a wand and end the pox?" Jono slurped his tea in disgust. "I hate waiting."

Aquinas set his cup down on the end table. "I hear you are helping the squires find their footing at Windom. That is a nobly kind of you."

"Suriana is really the one making it click. I'm just trying to help."

"I'm sure you *are* helping those brave children. Have faith in that, even if you can't see the results right away."

They sat in awkward silence, letting the ticks of the mechanical clock echo loudly in the room.

Jono perked up. "Did you bring Celeste back with you?"

"No, my new position has me traveling to all corners of the globe. She wasn't happy. I left her with a friend near the Dawn. It's a large farm with a forest nearby. She's quite enjoying it there, but I do miss her."

"What about you? How long are you going to stay here?"

"I don't know." He truly didn't. The future was a veil too thick for him to see through. "As long as my mission demands of me, I suppose. The fateriarchs of the Fellowship are attempting something unprecedented, bringing the words of angels to Eies, and it all rests on my shoulders to make it fly."

"It sounds like you're going to busy. I don't want to keep you."

Aquinas blinked at the slight he'd accidentally implied. He leaped up from his chair, walked over to Jono, and rested a hand on his shoulder. "I will never be too busy for you. I promise. Jonothon Wyer, I have known you since you were as tall as my knee. I know that this is unbearably hard and that you were but a child when your parents raised you with the words of angels. You may feel that those words, those feelings are long lost. You didn't choose to be raised for the Narrow Path, but believe me when I say that those gates are always open, just waiting for you to choose it."

Jonothon stood and set his tea on the end table.

"I've already chosen."

Aquinas held his breath for the boy to say something more, but his eyes were as unreadable as the future.

Jono forced a grin and patted Aquinas on the shoulder. "Thanks for the tea."

"It would fill my heart to see you at sermon sometime at Saint Newtons. The schedule is on the Line."

Jonothon shrugged. "I'll try."

Jono walked to the door and swung it behind him.

"Bring your friends!" Aquinas called after him in a cheerful tone, just as the door shut behind Jonothon. "We could use all the guests we can get."

Ammer O'Nasser tore a poster from a brick wall along the elevated cobble streets in Eies's central district. He sneered at it with disgust.

The poster was one of the many anti-magic reminders that had been so prolific across the Dark only a few years earlier. This one was reprogrammed to have the Freedom Defenders logo rotating at the top. It read:

Remember the old ways! Magic is a poison, and peace is the needle. Don't let the Day corrupt Dark Ender culture! Brought to you by the Freedom Defenders!

Ammer tore the digitized poster into pieces as four squires huddled around him. "Bunch of oil-skulled husks."

"That's the sixth poster on our way here," said Murphy Wumples.

"I bet these Freedom Defenders have never actually seen magic close up, let alone used it themselves," said Freya.

"They's too scared to try magic. That's why the Dark is so depressed all the time. Nothin' but fear and grease in their veins," said a rock golem boy named Paegor Bron.

When the five squires arrived at the gate of Copernicus Plaza, their mouths fell open. Before them stood one hundred floors of shops crowded with Dark Enders of every species.

"It's all so greasy," said Ammer. "Let's see what disgusting curses the Dark End has to offer."

"Ammer, are you sure it's okay that we go into the city alone?" said Murphy Wumples. "There could be Freedom Defenders around."

"I hope so!" Ammer said. "I'd love to give those cogs a

swift lesson in how to treat your guests."

"My wand's humming to show them how magic really works," Freya said with a smile.

"I heard that scaldio hide is a delicacy in the Dark End," Murphy said.

"We are in their biggest city, not a dirty, iced-up village. Besides, I'm sure their Empress is spying on us at every second. It is the Dark End, remember? Her eyes are everywhere. No true freedom." Ammer snarled.

"Ammer's right," said Freya. "I bet they have metal guards lurking in the shadows ready to pounce if anything goes wrong. We are political puppets. Just frosting, so the rulers of both Ends can show us off and make the world feel good about us being all nice-as-gnomes, right?"

"I suppose so," said Murphy.

"Good. Now put some confidence on your face," said Ammer. "Everyone is looking at us."

It was true, although the Dark Enders tried to be subtle about it. All around them the corners of eyes strained in their direction.

Murphy rubbed his pointy face and lifted his head.

"Its fine, Murphy," said Freya. "No one here has seen a scaldio in their lives. They can't tell your scared face from your brave one."

The group marched through the promenade as a horde of shoppers moved out of their way. At the center of the circle of shops, a man with a wide, black mustache and excessively tall hat stood on a box of small bottles with green liquid glowing inside. Behind him a banner read,

Professor Exquelsor's Pox-Off Elixir.

"Gather 'round my friends for I have good tidings to share! I know what keeps you up at sleeps, and I know what you fear for your family. But I say to you now, this wake is the wake it all changes!" Exquelsor waved a green bottle around and dabbed some of its contents onto his neck. "You may finally rest at sleeps with my new, patented formula made from the scars of pox contaminated soil! Yes, your home, your children, your beloved spouse can now slumber safely with Pox Guard! This one of a kind, scientifically proven elixir sends a signal to the pox that it has already scarred wherever you are, and therefore it will not strike again! With Pox Guard, you will have a five meter barrier against the pox per teaspoon you use! No other pox repellant can guarantee the same level of satisfaction as Pox Guard! Our reviews on the Line are countless and all positive!"

"Where's your peer review, mate?" a human girl called out from the crowd.

Exquelsor scoffed. "I dare not reveal my methods, madam, lest I have you lot steal my science? I think not, and for your own good, my friend. Pox Guard is a delicate concoction that, if made improperly, could very well summon the plague of pox upon you! No, no, this perfected recipe can only be produced and sold by officially licensed Pox Guard distributors! This golden seal is all you need to seal the deal!" He tapped the bottle label.

"If it's not reproducible," came another voice from the

crowd. "How do we know it works?"

"How would you even test a pox preventer?" said an ayleen woman. "No one knows where the pox will strike next!"

Exquelsor leaned in, as though it made his words more serious. "This pox preventer is made and warehoused right here in Eies. Now tell me, my hearty skeptics, with such volume in this vicinity, have you, have any of you, heard tale of even *one* appearance of the pox in our dear city? One spot of green devastation? One chirp of the dreaded kerpop? But don't take my word for it. Test it for yourself! Fleginald, share with these wise people a sample of Pox Guard."

The crowd was silent except for a few scoffing watchers. Fleginald, a short and furry mustecrat dressed in a purple suit two sizes too big for him, scurried around the crowd, handing out small green vials of the elixer.

Exquelsor gestured for people to touch a floating checkout screen with their orders. "Each sample will be enough to protect you for one full week, but what of your home? What of your children? One touch and Pox Guard will be sent to your homes and reapplied on a weekly basis. You will never lose another wink of sleep now that Pox Guard is here! I say to you now, that as long as I live to produce this powerful protectant, I will do my best to protect our city."

Most people laughed at him, but a few bought bottles and hid them away in their pockets.

"Maybe we should get some," said Murphy.

"I wouldn't trust anything in the Dark to prevent the pox," said Freya. "The Dark thinks everything can be solved with science, but they don't even know what the pox is."

Ammer growled. "It is abysmal magic! Everyone in the Day has already figured that out and it's only angelic magic that counteracts it." He pulled out a green emerald that hung on a lemon-twine string around his neck and had a small dove carved onto its surface. "I got this back in Al Jebra. I personally witnessed its blessing by Fellowship grand fateriachs. If anything, it's the fact that people from the Day are now in this city that's protecting it."

"That must be why they invited the Day for an exchange in the first place!" Freya blurted. "They couldn't figure out how to stop the pox, so they bring in the Day to keep them safe! It all makes sense now!"

The rest nodded and returned to exploring the plaza.

They arrived at garden courtyard looking over fifty floors of city below them. Night flowers and trees poked through the edges between shops, and a stream crept through the rocks and ferns and ran in covered channels and flowed down a circular path, over a waterfall, and into the city. Statues of carved rock stood at each end of the patio.

Beside the patio, a cupcake and pie shop glowed with green and gold signs. Murphy pressed his snout against the storefront glass.

"We should stop and try some of this out." Murphy

turned to find that his fellow squires were nowhere in sight. "Freya?" he called out. "Ammer?"

Murphy climbed a path by the waterfall to get a better look over the crowd. He spotted Ammer's blue hood in the distance.

"You're from the Day," growled a cranky voice behind him.

An old man sat alone beside the waterfall with a half-eaten doughnut on his plate. He had a few mechanical parts installed in his body, including a gear arm and a set of vents on his shoulder and back. "What are you doing in the White City? Your type can't stand the stars."

Murphy didn't know what to say. "I . . . I'm—I'm here as a student. At the Windom Academy."

"Scaldios have no place in the halls of Windom," the old man snarled. "You didn't think I knew what you are, did you? Oh, I know all about scaldios. Your tunnels and your searing sunbeam guns. I lost three of my best friends to your people. I was in the War of Wet Sands!"

"I d-don't know what that is," Murphy stuttered.

"I was young then. We all were." The old man's eyes glazed over, and his stare went years beyond the young squire. "For one hundred wakes we crawled through your desert, searching for what your people stole from the Dark. While politicians tried to negotiate with you sand cracks, my squad had to repair the wind regulators that would have destroyed whole the coast of the Tail! Forty-million people lived in those villages, but you couldn't trust us, so we had to go in covertly to save you from yourselves! But it didn't go as planned. Halfway up the Tail we were caught in a landslide in one of your dusty caverns. You dirt diggers know all about caverns, don't ya?"

The old man's gear arms clicked away, and red steam from his vents glowed hot. He lunged forward and grabbed Murphy by the jacket.

"Do you know what your people do to prisoners?"

Murphy shook his head.

"Chained in the sun for wakes." The old man glared at Murphy, his eyes mad with anger. "Your people do fine in the sun, but we Dark Enders melted like butter. Nolan took a sand nap first. Then Wilma. All to save your sandy holes. I should like to see how a scaldio takes to being chained up in our wasteland, eh? See how long your shell protects you from the ice and cold."

A large stone hand grabbed the old man's arm and lifted him into the air. Murphy spun around to see the walls and cobblestone ground come to life, transformed into a massive robot. Its eyes glowed red and bright.

"Citizen Walter Cranbles," the robotic city guard bellowed, "you will be fined for aggressive behavior and set to level three observation status. Make sure you rectify your behavior and treat our Day guests with respect."

The stone guard set the man down. "Do not violate civil ordinances again. Good wake."

Cranbles stumbled as his feet touched the ground. He glared at Murphy one more time then slunk into the crowd.

The guard bot kneeled in front of Murphy. "On behalf of the Eies City Guard authority, please accept my apologies for your unpleasant experience, Mister Don . The city is adding a credit to your account for one hundred Dark Dollars."

Murphy was still catching his breath from the shock. "How many cupcakes can I buy with that?"

The robot smiled. Murphy hadn't known robots could smile. "You can now afford sixty seven cupcakes, but I advise that you don't eat them all at once."

Suriana's eyes ached at the sight of the screen in front of her. Calendars hovered around her head like bees investigating a picnic. The door behind her slid open and her father walked in.

"Dad, you're home!" Suri waved at him. "I'm trying to schedule the exchange student events. Do you know anyone that manages the city defense shield? I heard Freya and Ammer talking about the city like it was prison. Maybe seeing the defense system up close and meeting the people that work there would make all of them feel a little less hostile to our hosts."

"No one comes to mind," Alistair Vahlor said, moving into the living room with a few long steps. "I'm sure that the Sage could arrange for a tour with the Empress." Alistair clenched a purple crystal on his sleeve, and mumbled a few silent words. "Your request is on the wind." He rested his hands on his daughter's shoulders and surveyed her schedules. "City tours, study groups, and performing an opera? My tired soul, child. You barely leave any time for these kids to breathe."

"You've seen the city out there. The Dark End is far stranger than they imagined. It's cold and smells and you never quite know when wake or sleep hours are. The people are more insular than in the Day and it's affecting everyone. I've heard of four squires crying themselves to sleep. The more I can help them get used to the ways of the Dark, the sooner they can start to enjoy it." She huffed. "Or at least not despise it."

Alistair frowned. "I think you missed scheduling your childhood. Oh, yes, we can fit it in on a Greenwake the third week of Felbriar."

Suri glared at the lack of seriousness he was giving her work.

Alistair sighed. "I know you want this exchange to be a success and for your friends to give the Dark all the chances that you do, but sometimes it is from hardships we learn the most. This will be a time, for good or ill, that will shape the rest of their lives. You can't always control the outcome, my little sprout."

"But the outcome is so *important*. We can't leave peace to chance."

Alistair kneeled and faced his daughter. "I see so much of your Papa in your vigor. He must be so proud of you, watching from behind the veil. It is you that gives me hope, your conviction that Dark Enders can be brought to the Narrow Path. Hold to your faith in them. I pray you always believe that you can change hearts and guide their whispers with your own. Have patience. A garden doesn't grow in one wake. Take care of yourself, slow down, and savor your travels, my girl, lest the wake arrives when you get to where you are going, only to realize you don't know where you've been."

Chapter Seven

A Warm Wind Rises

"Did you know that pungruses are really blind?" Isaac said as he flipped through screens about the wild nature of the Eiesan region of the Dark End. He stood in front of Doctor Stone's classroom with the squires and mentoring cadets watching him.

"What are you taking about? A pungrus can spot a flark a kilem away!" Keiko replied.

"They can track a flark in flight, that's true. At birth pungrus fetuses contract a parasite that lives inside their mother. This parasite, thembero doxicus gremal, or commonly known as the lumatwix worm, attaches to the inner lining of baby pungrus' eyes and converts all the light into super detailed signals to their brains! The parasite can only survive in the unique liquid of their eye, and the pungrus gets incredible sight, allowing them to be ferocious predators in the wilds of the Dark."

Keiko blinked, and her true sight eyes turned green. "Do you think they used that worm in me? Gross."

"That's welded!" Isaac said. "Your eyes are a marvel."

The Day squires squirmed as Isaac finished his presentation on the oddities of Dark End animals.

"Any questions?" Isaac asked.

"Isaac, is it?" Ammer asked. "Are we going to see any of these creatures in real life and not just in your floating images? In the Day, we are accustomed to dealing with the real thing and not illusions."

"The Crown's zooseum does have some of the animals we talked about, but if you ever make it to Eckleclypse, which is my home town by the way, they have the greatest zooseum on the planet!"

"I've been to the animal gardens in Lay'Aal," Freya interrupted, "and they had over sixty-thousand species from both Ends of Earth."

"It's not a competition," Suri said. "Are there any other questions?"

When no one spoke up, Suriana turned to Isaac.

"Thank you for you very insightful presentation." Suri began clapping and the other Day students followed with significantly less enthusiasm. "Cadet Keiko Kirin is next."

A blocky animation floated in front of room as Keiko approached the podium.

"My presentation is about the founding of Eies. Long long ago, the Dark End was a frozen wasteland, barren of life. A meteor hit the Earth and the devastation left survivors across the globe fearful and depressed. The first Empress wanted to remind everyone that they were smart and creative and could overcome anything, so she found the impact site and laid the first foundations of the center of the city."

"Is that what they teach you in the Dark End?" Ammer scoffed. "That tale is orc spit! It isn't ture. There were people living in the Dark End long before the first Empress showed up. She wasn't some great explorer or hero out to inspire the world. There were other powerful people in the Dark, and she wanted to remove her competition. The Empress was the one that summoned the meteor in the first place. The blast killed every living thing in the Dark. All so she could start over and rule it with the infinite eyes of a dictator."

Keiko clenched her teeth and tried to be polite after such an outrageous insult. "That's an interesting interpretation of history. And just how does one summon a meteor?"

Ammer scowled at her condescension. "There is magic in the depths of the abyss. It is the same power the fuels the pox and fel shades."

A few of the Dark End students snickered at the idea of magic being the source of the pox. And everyone knew that fel shades were made up of fel pixels.

"Actually, you could adjust the trajectory of a meteor toward a target using a variety of means," Isaac said. "Robotic propulsion engines could easily have guided the object's velocity of—"

"You're not helping!" Keiko cut him off. "Listen my dear, sun-kissed friends, if you are going to live here with us in the Dark End, it would make things a megaton easier if you *try* to understand where we are coming from. These stories of our past—" Ammer opened his mouth, but Keiko pointed at him to keep silent. "—whether they are one hundred percent true or not, still tell you a lot about the values we hold dear. Our stories tell you how we see ourselves and the type of people we aspire to be. The Empress in the wilderness is a story every Dark Ender has heard a trillion times. It's who we are. We value facing incredible challenges with ingenuity and intellect. We want to be that person that can figure out how things work when the odds are against us. We want to create things that inspire and make the world better. We may not always live up to that ideal. Every story may not be literal history, but it is illustrative of how we view the world. If we can't learn to understand each other, then this peace is a ticking time bomb."

A tense silence hung in the air.

Suriana began clapping, and soon the class followed.

"That is a very important lesson," Suri said. "Thank you, Keiko. I hope that we *all* remember it. Now please everyone, find the partner listed on your name tag and introduce yourself. Get to know each other. I'm certain there is much you have in common, if you just give them a chance."

Between Jono's cloaks class and Keiko's ability to convince strangers to do anything, the group of mentors had enough volunteers to befriend each of the Day students. They even had to turn a few volunteers away.

Keiko met Freya at a drink machine.

"It's Freya, right? I remember you from Al Jebra. You were welded out there in the drills wood."

Freya sipped her bubbly drink suspiciously. "Thank you for recognizing my prowess. You held your spirit up as well."

"You should try out for my globall team. You'd be a welded sieger, and the Roariors are struggling with our siege game."

"Is that so?" Freya replied with a wry smile. "I could get used to bashing Dark Enders around."

"That the spirit!" Keiko cheered.

Jono's partner-badge read 'Riley Shrub'. He searched the classroom crowded with students uncomfortably trying to introduce themselves until the crowd spread and he spotted the nervous dryad girl sitting quietly in the corner. Her green, leafy hair was braided down her back. She wore a blue Windom jacket over a flowing white gown.

Jono walked over to her then knelt down and smiled. "Are you Riley?"

The girl nodded.

"My name is Jono Wyer and I am very happy to have you at the Windom Academy."

Riley smiled. "Thanks. I'm, uh . . . happy to be here."

The group of students spent the next hour eating and mingling. Jono and Riley talked about their lives on either End of the world, but as soon as they got on the topic of their favorite stories, Riley was shocked that Jono had heard of the Adventures of Illius.

"Have you read the secret fifth volume?" Riley asked.

"You mean the Conquest of Illius?"

"No, that was intended to be the sixth volume, but the original publication was lost after the author's death. The first release didn't even include it in the series at all! That didn't make any sense, because the references in Conquest, like Illius' new friend Jareth and what happened at the Sand Sea races, were completely missing!"

"I do remember that!" Jono said. "But all of that was explained in the Trials of Illius. I read them out of order the first time through because I couldn't find the entire set."

"They are in the correct order. It wasn't until one hundred and sixty years later that they found the old manuscript for the Realms of Illius in the author's lost cabin. Then they re-released the series with the new books including the new fifth volume and the histories of the Land of Seas."

The whole afternoon had gone far better than expected until, as they were leaving, Jono noticed Suriana had spent the entire time chatting with pairs of partners but didn't have one of her own.

Jono excused himself from Riley and approached Suri. "Hey, Suriana. Who's your partner?"

Suri's hair and dress were both a bit flustered from hosting the meet up. "He said he was going to be late, but

I didn't expect him to miss the whole meeting—oh! There he is now."

The door had cracked open, and Nicklus Knox stepped through. He carried a bundle of anti-magic posters rolled up in his arms. The fire bomb chambers on his shoulders steamed hot in the cool air. Jono noticed that his arms had been upgraded with more bomb chambers, in his palms and on his forearms.

"I told you I wouldn't miss this for all the sun in the Day." Nick said as he strolled into the middle of the room. He waved at the Day students as though he knew them all personally, but they only looked back with confusion.

"Sorry about my timing," Nick said with an air of heroism. "I kept finding these nasty posters all over town and couldn't leave this filth for people to see. These Freedom Defenders? They just don't get it. Magic isn't the enemy and neither is the Day."

Jono scowled. "You were a leader in the Defenders, Knox."

Suri glared. "Jono, don't be rude. Nick is helping."

Nick grinned viciously at Jono as he dropped the pile of posters on the stone floor. "That's right, Twig. I'm here to help our new friends feel more comfortable in our, admittedly, harsh End of the world. And that starts by cleaning up this bilge."

Nick shot a firebomb at the posters. They sparked and flared and slowly wrinkled into black husks.

"We wouldn't want you folks to think we Dark Enders are like that. Anti-magic may have been in our past, but it can't be our future."

"I'm glad you could join us," Suri said. "Jono, this is—"

"We've met," Jono said, cutting her off.

"That's right." Nick smiled. "The kid and I go way back, don't we?"

"That's fantastic!" Suri said. "We can really use all the friends we can get."

"As I've always said," Nick said with a smirk, "we must extend the fig leaf of peace to our fellow Earthkin across the Dawn. Peace is the only path to the future. Don't you agree?"

"I couldn't have said it better myself." Suri smiled.

Jono glared at them both, questioning whether or not he'd slipped into an alternate dimension.

"What, you don't know?"

Ammer O'Nasser sat at the largest table in the den, surrounded by orcs, ancient elvayns, and other magical creatures that faintly resembled Jono, Murphy, Oscar, Isaac, Clive, Bastion, and Paegor Bron. Shadowy woodlands covered the table as the holographic scene lit up only the areas the party of characters could see based on their sight statistics. Songbirds chirped through the woods as narrow shafts of light cut through the thick canopy to illuminate the ruins scattered across the map.

Ammer shook his head. "The pox is a curse. Everyone in the Day knows that."

Isaac scowled from across the table. "You're telling me that every researcher across the Dark and Day are wasting their time studying the pox because the good word from a preachy fateriarch is that it's just a curse? What's the cure then? Drink purple bog water and wear a skinned toad on your head?"

"It's your move, Isaacial the Paladin," Murphy cut in and pointed to the board.

"Let's try to stay in the game," Jono said from beneath his gray, wizardly beard. "There are voidlocks lurking in the ruins."

"I don't think it's a curse," muttered Paegor.

Isaac perked up. "See, a thoughtful Day Ender. Miracles can happen. What do you think it is?"

Paegor set down his character cards delicately and met eyes with others around the table with a grave look on his stony and orc-illusioned face. "What if we are trapped in the code world while machines harvest us for minerals? And the pox is a sign that the code around us is finally deteriorating. The only life any of us ever knew will eventually collapse, and we'll wake up plugged into some machine. We may not even be who we think we are."

The table was quite.

Isaac frowned. "It's unlikely, but possible."

"I bet its aliens," Murphy said. "Some new species found their way to Sol and is using the pox to teleport their invisible army all over the Earth. Until one wake and

BOOM! We're invaded and we didn't even know it."

Oscar nodded. "I like how he thinks."

"That would account for the pox being targeted around Earth . . ." Isaac mused.

"A demon's curse makes the most sense," Ammer said. "They've been lurking in the Pit for eons waiting for the veil to wear down enough for their abysmal spells to get through. The pox is what happens when the Pit casts itself into our world. What's so hexed about that?"

"I read a story where a time machine exploded right at the Big Bang and it caused the fabric of reality to start crumbling in on itself," Clive said. "The pox could be spacetime collapsing."

Oscar shook his head. "I'm going with Paegor's robot uprising idea. Bots are sneaky and pretend to be boring all the time, but I think they are hiding something."

Jono looked at the game board. The tiny figures rested at a campsite, waiting for commands on what to do next. "What if we are the pawns?" Jono asked. "Little pieces on a board and in some dimension beyond are gods playing us. What if the world is an illusion? How do you break free from a puppet master when you can't see the strings?"

A loud thud from above them shook the den, and dust trickled down from the ceiling. The boys screamed and half of them ducked under the table.

They caught their breaths as they looked over the table. Jono hit a red button on the table, and the deep, mysterious voice of the Quest Master spoke from the table.

"Verily did the bard Oscathar's enchanted lute glow red with a dire warning of encroaching enemies!"

"Voidwraths!" Murphy said.

"Get ready!" Oscar said, picking up his cards, which had scattered across the table. "They're coming!"

"You hid this, *this*, from me?" Cassindra Viscariot was shocked, excited, and terrified all at once.

She paced around Aquinas's apartment, holding one arm and fiddling with her long, silver hair. She was filled with the nervous energy of one who possessed a secret that could change the entire world for good or bad, depending on how it was used.

"No . . . I didn't . . . how did you know?" Aquinas gasped.

"The whispers washed over me when you spoke to the boy," Viscariot said proudly as she strode around his leather couch for the sixth time. "Like a light it was made clear. I already knew you were released from the Dark after the Sage negotiated a peace *and* that you presented information about Attrayer's Key to the Lords of the Day. But to think you personally knew the truth about Jason Wheat, and your friend is . . . and you—"

"Quiet now," Aquinas implored. "I only meant for you to help me guide the boy through this tragedy and back to the Narrow Path. We shouldn't even be speaking about of this!"

Viscariot stopped and glared at him with wonder in her eyes. "This is all we should speak of. This changes everything! The world will have hope again!"

Aquinas frowned at the thought. "The world will feel betrayed. Exposing lies won't help to heal their hearts."

Viscariot calmed her eagerness and nodded. "A wise consideration, my friend. Truth must be revealed only to those ready to embrace it. This must be treated delicately, but if your friend is *who* you say he is, then he is the right person for this calling. We just need to get him into the right position."

If the world could only have a savior again, she thought, then all of their struggles would be made so much easier.

Aquinas gasped. "You can't be serious. That position killed Jason Wheat."

Viscariot stopped pacing. Pangs of guilt coiled around her heart like a serpent. She was still haunted by that boy's death, the many wakes of sleepless visions about his future and the fate of the world that lay at the foggy crossroads of their two fractured paths.

She turned and knelt to face Aquinas. Tears came quickly in a marriage of sorrow and joy. "Alexsayter, my friend, the whispers have never been clearer in my life. This moment is ours to define. The pox has thrust the world toward a precipice. We have this chance to set not just your friend, but the entire world, all under Sol, back on the Narrow Path. You did say he was a follower, did you not?"

Aquinas scratched the tussled auburn hair among the short horns on his head as he pondered the situation. "He was raised with the whispers, but he has trod a difficult path since then. His family, his whole home town was lost to the pox."

Viscariot clasped his shoulder. "It is a sign. The pox is a poison of abysmal magic that attacked him to deter him from his destiny. This child is meant to be a hero. He has no choice but to embrace his fate and seek his higher purpose. This is not by my words or yours. We are all pawns to the powers that guide the stars and whisper in our hearts. It is they that are fighting over the boy's fate. The angels call to us through this dark land to set him on his way to meet them. Imagine the good he will do? This is the angels' will. Envision the true child that saved the world telling his fellow Dark Enders the words of angels, and tell me that this moment is not ordained? They may actually listen!"

Aquinas winced in fear for Jonothon. "He is not one to speak as such. Whatever remains of his faith is not a banner waving in the light."

Viscariot's face grew dark and cold, as though the life drained out from her. "Has the Dark spoiled it out of him? Those vile machines have no place for faith. Can his be rekindled?"

"I pray that is so, yes."

She curled her legs beneath her and sat in meditation. Aquinas joined her as they prayed for the whispers of angels to speak to them through the silence.

Viscariot's purple eyes burst open.

"What if we got him out of the Dark?" she joyfully declared. "Brought him to the Day to bask in our light? Seeing our End for the glory that it is would spark the flame again?"

Aquinas frowned. "There is no word or wish that could make the Empress allow it."

"No." Viscariot slumped against the couch. After a moment she rose and marched to the window. She turned off the screen projecting a golden field of wheat and stared at the greenhouse clouds that hung over the city. "Unless, we gave her something she wants more."

"What could that possibly be?"

Viscariot turned with smile of triumphant glee. "A hole in the blockade. The Day has leverage over our Terralunan lords. Food, soil, and more. If enough of them can be convinced to align with us, we could negotiate an opportunity in the Empress' favor that she would dare not reject."

Aquinas scratched the tuft of hair on his chin. "In exchange for the chance to set the lad on the right road?"

Viscariot hugged him. "The whispers speak loudly, do they not?"

Aquinas stared back at her. "Jono can know nothing about this."

"He will not. Trust me, he is more precious than our limited minds could know. By my blood, he will be kept safe."

"Are we going to get in trouble?" Marissa said, walking so close behind Keiko that she kept stepping on her heels.

Keiko led a group of Day girls through harshly carved tunnels high into the mountain. The halls led to the Crown Castle, where rotund metal guards stood a silent watch at every corner.

"We're not. Trust me on this. I've come here a thousand times." Keiko's voice carried an echo through the empty tunnel.

"That can't be true."

"It's a turn of phrase. Stars! I didn't think you Day Enders were so literal."

"Are invisibility spells supposed to tingle this much?" Keiko scratched her skin beneath the long, invisible blanket her companions had supplied.

"Magic always has a cost," Marissa replied.

"I've heard that but I never thought it meant itching."

"Hush! Someone's coming."

Orange light flittered across the rocky hallway, invading the blue glow from the distant moonlight. Professor Goest marched through the corridor with a lamp bot floating over his shoulder. He was about to pass Keiko's group when he stopped. The light from his lamp bot followed as he turned his head, looking around the tunnel. But, seeing nothing more than his own impatient shadow, he moved on.

As the bot's orange light disappeared through the hall, the girls simultaneously exhaled their held breaths.

"We shouldn't be here," Marissa said. "Why did we let you talk us into this?"

"We have to try new things, remember?" Suriana said. "That's why we are in the Dark in the first place."

"Remind me to cast a cleansing spell on my mind then," Marissa replied. "I hate being cold, I hate the thick air, and I can't stand how depressing the Dark End is."

"I miss home too. And my glen mothers," Riley said.

"You're looking at it from the Day looking in," Keiko said. "To love the Dark, you have to see it the way we do. Come on, we're almost there. This way."

The chain of invisible girls holding invisible hands snuck through the tunnels to a glass door with a metal frame that looked out at the vast night north of the Crown. Crisp white stars twinkled across the endless void above them.

Riley gasped. "The night sky? That's terrifying."

"It's inspiring to us. It reminds us of the challenge of mind versus nature." Keiko pulled off the invisible blanket. "Only a few steps more. Did you all bring your coats?"

"We are going outside?" Marissa asked.

Keiko cracked open the door. "Be quick. Someone will

notice the cold air creeping in."

Keiko snuck out the door and around the edge of the cliff. One by one, the squires followed her into the freezing air. They climbed up a metal ladder to the highest peak of the mountain range that circled the city.

White light burst in front of them. The city was a glowing star shining against its distant siblings in the blackness above. The air on the city side was warm and welcoming. The air from the icy wasteland behind them collided in a veil of hot and cold. The warmth rose up to wash over their faces while the cold slunk down their backs to chill their toes.

"I get it now," Suriana said. "This is what the Dark is about. Life and death crashing against each other. Clinging to the edge of what is possible. Like the world itself is daring you to give in, the Dark lives to defy its call."

Keiko smiled. "See. Now you're thinking like one of us."

"It's sad. Always fighting for every inch," Riley said. "You must feel so alone."

"But we're not alone," Keiko answered, taking a seat on a precipice. "Look up. Every one of those stars could be just like us. Spinning around those stars is family we haven't met yet. We just need to dare to take the leap to say hello. The gulf of space and the mystery of new worlds. That is the greatest challenge any brain sparkin' person could hope to test their metal on. And with the blockade we can't even visit Jupiter. The engines of who we are need us to move forward, to explore . . . and we can't. We're trapped on-planet and it kills us to the core."

Suriana sat next to Keiko with the warm heat of the city on her back and the chill of the stars in her eyes. "I never thought of that. The Day is so satisfied with the moment that we don't think about the future."

"The truth is, I'm scared too," Keiko said with honest hesitation. "There are people I care about, people I don't want to live without. We're in this together. We're family too. I have a team, the Firewall. We look after each other, fight together, and defend each other. When things get their worst, you can rely on your team. We're all we got."

"But what do we have?" Riley said. "We're not real knights yet, just squires."

"The Firewall will look out for you, too."

"Promise?"

Keiko made a circle over her chest and then thumped the center with her fist. "Steel my heart and weld it true."

The girls clustered together in silent awe of the feeling of two worlds crashing around them.

"Alright, Kirin, you win," Marissa said. Even her compliments had the stain of sarcasm. "This is a shimmering sight. What other gems is this coal heap of an End hiding?"

Keiko's smile was both delightful and daring. "If you are ready to see the Dark, just say the word and I'll show you places you never dreamed of!"

Riley gazed at the distant icy mountains.

"But it all looks the same out there. Nothing but ice

and rock."

Keiko smirked. "You have to look at it up close to see life's little wonders. Just wait till we take you camping!"

Chapter Eight

The Frostbitten Toes

of Nobody Knows

Kieko's head was in the metal guts of a mech. She contorted herself awkwardly as she peeled off the lid of a small container, and three gnashing beetle worm heads popped up. She placed the little beasts delicately on the metal innards then slipped out.

Keiko had managed to convince her uncle to lend her a handy mech for their biochemix study trip. The rotund mech was slightly larger than Dr. Stone, with four hands for versatile gripping and maneuvering and a massive cargo bag strapped to its back. At fifteen, she was one of the youngest people to get licensed to drive a mech, and though she would never admit it, she was excited to show off.

Keiko stepped into the pilot's chamber in the belly of the mech.

"Now I'm ready to rocket," she said.

Jono stood in front of her and pointed to the spot of grease on her nose. "Your mech left you a present."

Keiko wiped her nose with a rag. "Glad to see the Firewall taking a stand against poor hygiene. Do you think they're ready for this?"

Jono looked at the crowd of squires that had been herded into the Windom cargo bay. They were wrapped in their thickest coats, with travel packs sitting beside them. Two B.O.A.R. carrier mechs had been filled with camping gear, cases of food, laboratory equipment, and heaters.

"Not a chance," Jono said.

Doctor Zacharias Stone approached through the cargo bay, followed closely by a soldier that seemed to keep popping up around them, Ramsus Ramaadi. The doctor's cumbersome mechanical body stomped loudly. He had a brown hat on his metal head and a leather satchel with dozens of vials strapped over his shoulder.

"Who's ready for an adventure?" Dr. Stone cheered.

The cadets replied with tepid applause, while the squires mumbled their dire hesitation at the entire notion of camping in the frozen mountains of the Dark End.

The thick cargo doors opened with a rusty groan, and a rush of freezing air gushed in. The Dark Enders pretended to embrace the cold cheerfully, while the Solans stared at each other in horror. Sir Maergann Brigid held Suri's shoulder with one hand and clenched her sheathed blade with the other.

"This is a terrible idea," Maergann said.

"There's probably lawless night pirates roaming the ice cliffs out there," Riley said, her hands gripping her pack. "We're all likely to be murdered in our sleeps."

"We are here to embrace their way of life," Suriana said. "I think camping in the snow sounds fun! You never know what we may find."

Marissa looked out at the snowy mountain canyon as the doors opened wider. "Yeah, we're going die."

Murphy Wumples nodded in nervous agreement beside her.

"You are in safe hands, sun children." Ramsus Ramaadi had an infectious smile that could win over anyone. He held out his gauntlet-covered hands. "See these?" One gauntlet flared hot and red, while the other pulsed with a smoky black aura. "I could fend off an entire armada of night pirates with these two power gauntlets. You'll be safer out there with me chaperoning you than you'd be back in the city alone."

"Are you saying the streets of Eies are not safe?" Maergann asked.

Ramsus grinned. "If you ever have the need of a chaperone in the city, my darling knight, you have but to say when and where."

Maergann glared at him and said nothing.

"Everyone aboard the B.O.A.R.'s," Dr. Stone said with a cheer. "It's a few hours to the campsite, and we will be making a couple stops to gather samples along the way."

"Perfect," Marissa said as she bundled herself tightly in her thick coat. "More chances to freeze to death."

Maergann grunted in agreement. She strapped her sheathed spellblade to her back.

"You're a woman of few words, Maergann Brigid, of where in the Day exactly?" Ramsus asked with a smile.

"As a knight, I have led a life of action and personal reflection," Maergann replied, never taking her eyes off of the icy terrain that, in her eyes, could conceal hidden dangers. "Do soldiers of the Dark End always prattle so much?"

"Have you met many soldiers of the Dark End?" Ramsus asked.

"I've met battalions of them, but none were in such a conversational mood at the time."

Maergann joined Suriana inside the troop carrier, leaving Ramsus's question unanswered.

"It's a pity your father allowed this escapade, my lady," Maergann said. "Such a strange way to see the advanced city of Eies, by crawling through its unkempt back end."

The mech door shut behind them, and the metal beast lurched onto the snowy path. The two B.O.A.R.'s rolled along the snow-covered road, with Keiko in her handy mech following Doctor Stone in the lead. They edged away from the glowing metropolis and into the shadowy wilderness. They crossed through sheer rock canyons, deeper than the buildings in Eies were tall.

Thickets of thorny trees grew in the sparse cracks in the stone. Ice and snow covered the narrow floor of the massive crevasse. The road wove through the narrow, jagged canyon and cut through many short tunnels.

After an hour, they passed an outlook across a wide valley. The squires peered at the display port holes,

amazed by the stark night and how brightly the light from Terralunis lit up the frozen white ice.

Inside the cabin, students chatted or shut their eyes to watch videos or listen to music projected into their brains. Isaac and Oscar were playing a holographic game of globall that hovered inbetween them.

Jono tried to think of conversations to have with the Day students, but nothing came to mind. Suriana was in deep conversation with Nick about the political structure of the Day. Nick took every chance she wasn't looking to sneer at Jono. Even if he was being earnest about his change of heart concerning the Day, he hadn't become any less cruel to Jono.

After another hour, they entered a narrow valley where rugged trees still survived. An icy, melting waterfall spilled down a cliff into a creek that flowed through the valley before being lost in the narrow cracks in the mountain.

Beneath a patch of leafy trees were delicate, multicolored flowers.

"Stop the caravan," Dr. Stone called from the front. "Everyone disembark. There is *science* to be done!"

The students put on their heated coats and gloves and filed out the door. Dr. Stone headed into the gnarled woods with a row of nervous students behind him.

Jono passed Keiko in her mech and tapped on its metal leg. When Dr. Stone wasn't looking, Keiko made the handy mech wave its four arms in a little dance as its body shook from side to side.

The forest spread across the valley as the trees seemed to claw their way up the stark rock walls.

"Alright, everyone. Gather around!" Dr. Stone said as he stood beneath a thin canopy of snowy leaves and purple flowers. "Here is one of the wonders of the Dark End! Even in this icy wasteland, life continues to find a way to grow. These are *belamcanda hydrochloridansus*, more commonly known as the ice iris. As you can see, they grow from vines that have wrapped themselves around, and in fact, inside the bark of the aspen tree. This is a remarkable example of the symbiotic survival techniques that evolved from nature. In the coldest seasons, the iris' vines can freeze off completely, but hidden beneath the bark, the roots and seeds can grow again when the warm steam rolls in and the radiation from our old mother above returns in force."

Jono turned his head. There was a strange yet familiar sound coming from the woods. At first he thought it could be the wind, but it was getting louder.

"Keiko, do you hear—?"

Jono couldn't finish before an explosion of snow and icy fur erupted from the treeline. Keiko spun around in her mech just as the enormous force collided with her. She tumbled to her side, but the mech's arms moved swiftly to fling her assailant through the trees.

A massive white beast thudded onto the snowy ground. It lifted its head, stunned for a moment, before shaking its woolly body.

"Click my gears!" Dr. Stone gasped. "It's a full-grown woolly frog! Children, stay back, it looks injured."

A trail of blood followed from the trees and led to the woolly frog's belly.

In an instant, Ramsus and Maergann were between the children and the bulky monster. Ramsus tried to sooth it with open hands and comforting words, but the woolly frog huffed at him to back off.

"Doctor, is this beast a danger to the children?" Maergann's blade roared with purple lightning.

"No, I don't think so," replied Stone. "But when hurt, all life can be unpredictable."

"I didn't mean to hurt it," Keiko said as her mech climbed to its feet. "It jumped out at me."

"It wasn't you," Jono said. "Look. The blood started back in the forest. It was attacked. The woolly frog was running from something."

The forest seemed to growl from one direction, and then from two. Then three.

"What is that?" Riley asked.

"Pungrus," Ramsus said, his attention turning to the unseen threat.

In a burst of shattered branches and snow, three pungruses charged out of the forest and after their prey. The woolly frog tried to escape, but it was weak from running. The frog smashed two of the pungruses away with a powerful hind kick, but two more leapt out of the forest in front of it. The frog was trapped. The pungruses circled it, clacking their jaws and shaking their horned heads.

"Can't we help it?" Suri asked.

"It's too late, I'm afraid," Dr. Stone said with a sad, knowing compassion. "You see, this too is a part of nature."

The frog chomped back at them but exposed the wound in its belly. The pungruses seized their chance and attacked. After a fit of useless kicks, the woolly beast went limp and the predators had their dinner.

The students stared in horror. Green and purple organs joined red blood in the feast upon melting snow. Wisps of steam rose from the heat that had been inside the creature.

Issac nudged Ammer. "Is that real enough for you?"

Ammer looked away, disgusted.

"That's the inside of a woolly frog?" Riley said with a gulp.

"That is putrid," Marissa said, pinching her nose shut with gloved fingers.

Doctor Stone rested a hand on the young squire's shoulder. "My dear, life does not work despite the gross parts. It works because of them. Now, everyone back on board the B.O.A.R.'s. Let's leave these carnivores to their dinner."

"Wait," Jono said. "Do you hear that?"

"All I hear is chomping," Nick said with sick delight.

"Back here in the forest." Jono turned away from the bloody meal and toward the woods. "Keiko, look around for any heat."

Keiko's eyes turned red. "Over there! It's small. It's not moving."

The group charged through the snowy woods to Stone and Maergann's protests. Keiko's mech smashed a path through the icy trees. She stopped at a thicket of bramble thorns covered in a thick layer of snow.

"Quiet," Keiko whispered. "You might scare it off."

The mech leaned down gently. Keiko's infrared eyes instantly spotted a patch of white fur curled up in a brown lump of dirt.

"Reeello?"

The tiny woolly frog was snuggled in the warmth of the sheltered dirt. It cowered in the corner and looked up in confused fright at the monstrous machine at the mouth of its den.

"Reeello?" the woolly frog said again.

"She had a baby," Suri said, the hurt in her voice apparent.

"If we found it, the pungruses would too," Jono said.

"It won't survive here," Keiko said.

The students, knight, and soldier all looked at the professor, who'd caught up with them at his ponderous pace.

Doctor Stone sighed. "I do suppose I could use some company around my lab . . ."

They all cheered as Stone delicately scooped up the woolly frog and placed it in his satchel.

After another two hours on the snowy road, the convoy arrived at a valley where the jagged mountains surrounding the city had faded into sweeping hills that sloped toward plains leading to the frozen end of the Earth. The stars sparkled perfect and bright in the black canvas of night above them.

The convoy found a wooded alcove to protect them from the harsh winds that frequented the ice plains beyond the forest. Keiko helped to set up the camp using her mech to lift the metal crates on the backs of the B.O.A.R.'s. With a press of a button, the crates stretched their robotic limbs then crawled upward and unfurled a heat shield canvas between each metal spine. In a moment, they had formed tents full of bunkbeds clicking together and mattresses automatically inflating.

Doctor Stone began building a bonfire while the students and their protectors huddled in the warm tents and ate food from self-heating cans.

"Is that a heater?" Suri peered into the glowing orange center of a tent.

"You don't think we'd camp out here near the ice plains without heated tents, do you?" Keiko said with a laugh.

The sight of the fallen woolly frog had left their minds, as the baby woolly frog slowly crawled out of Stone's satchel and crept nervously across the warm carpet warming the tent floors.

Isaac scanned through the Line with an image of floating text projected in front of him.

"It says here that woolly frogs are omnivores, surviving on whatever they can find across the harsh wilderness of the Dark End. They often eat pixieflies, mushrups, or even lick moss that grows on trees or rocks."

Suri looked at the ingredients of her can of mushrup stew. "Do you think it could eat this?"

"Let me check." Isaac looked over the ingredients. "Woolly frogs are not often kept as pets, but there is a series of specialty pet foods that meet their nutritional needs. Yeah, this would work. They just can't have sapseed oil or cantling root. That would be bad for their livers."

Suri held out a spoon of warm mushrup soup, and the tiny white frog hopped cautiously toward it. It looked up at Suri. Its purple tongue reached out, delicately touching the brown broth to taste the stew. It licked its woolly lips, and the students held their breaths. The frog then hopped, spun in a happy circle, and began lapping up the stew.

Suri laughed. "I think he likes it."

"Actually, it's a girl," Keiko said. The others looked at her, confused. "Super vision, remember?"

"What should we name her?" Oscar asked as he sipped at spoonfuls of his own stew.

"How about Bouncy?" Ammer said.

"I like Princess Fluffy," Riley said.

"Looks more like an Ice Ball to me," Nick said with his normal, petulant tone, but somehow there was a shard of sincerity in his voice. Perhaps he'd been acting like a belligerent clunker so long, he'd forgotten how to be nice.

Suri leaned down to be eye level with the confused, young woolly frog. It lashed out its tongue and just missed her nose. "There is a common phrase in the ancient language of Systine. Zuun mu ja sheng. It means 'I honor the mother for my life.'"

Everyone nodded.

"Zuun Mu." Riley smiled. "Here, Zuun Mu. Do you want to try lentil dumpling soup?"

Soon Zuun Mu was hoping gleefully around the circle of students that not long ago were strangers and enemies. The ice melted from its fur, and it shook off the water before snuggling into a fuzzy coat in Suriana's lap. Somehow, in the warmth of the tent and in the presences of the survivor, they had all become friends.

"Woolly frogs grow slowly but can live to be over four hundred years old. They don't reach mature size until around one hundred and thirty," Isaac read.

"You hear that, Zuun Mu? You're going to outlive us all," Jono said.

"Rive. Rive." croaked the frog.

The bonfire was roaring as they toasted s'mores decorated their lips with marshmallow, chocolate, and graham cracker crumbs. Heavy clouds settled low between the mountains, making the crackling fire's orange glow a stark and flickering contrast to the blue darkness of the frozen forests around them.

"And that's when he heard it again!" Nick said. "Thump, scrape! Thump, scrape!"

Nick waved his hands over the fire, creating terrifying shadows against his face.

"The man ran deeper and deeper into the pitch-black darkness of the caves beneath this very campground. He couldn't see. He didn't know how to get out, and still the sound was getting closer!"

The squires huddled together, their faces full of terror.

Nick's voice was deep and foreboding. "The man reached out in every direction, but all he could feel was the cold, jagged rock around him. He was trapped as the rock grew tighter and tighter. He closed his eyes and could feel the rock close in and start to crush his body. And that was when he saw it . . . a crack in the rock let in the dim moonlight just enough to see the dead bodies of his fellow campers, with all of their heads missing.

"Thump, scrape! Thump, scrape!

"The crack in the rock grew larger until he could see the lumpy, bloody bag of heads come down right in front of him! THUMP! He looked up to see the same vagabond they'd passed on the road, but his covered arm was revealed to be a huge metal blade! He SCRAPED it against the rock. The man couldn't move, and the rock opened up to the cold air and the blade came swooshing down! In one blow his head tumbled off his shoulders and into that bag to join his friends!

"For weeks, the Empress sent soldiers out to find the students, but the only thing they discovered were patterns of blood frozen in the ice in the shape of bodies. They say the vagabond was a geomancer. He controlled stone to move at his will. He disappeared into the mountains, never to be found. But during cloudy sleeps, if you listen closely, you can still hear the sounds he makes as he haunts these mountains . . ."

The camp was deathly silent.

Nick whispered. "Thump. Scrape."

The campfire popped just at that moment, and half of the students screamed. Riley tumbled backward and pulled the heat cloak over her head.

Nick burst out laughing.

"You're terrible," Suri said in an attempt to calm everyone's nerves. "We're in a strange place as it is."

"I'm not getting any sleep," Marissa said, helping Riley back up.

"That's the whole point of camping!" Nick replied. "Alright, Goldilocks, what horrifying tales from the Day do you have?"

"We don't tell stories about murder and monsters when we camp in the Day," Suri replied.

"Oh, come on! What *do* you do over the campfire?"

"At the monastery in Systine, we recite the ancient tales of how the world came to be. It's educational and has a moral lesson to go with it. Like, the lesson of when the Old Mother left the seven angels in charge of the world, but new creatures claiming to be gods arose and contested them for the rule of the stars. These were the Titans! The Star Hydra, Manturin the turtle island, and so many more. There are tales of Leviathan and its children, ancient gods that receded to the Dark End, at the middle of Night."

"Boring," Nick moaned.

Maergann used her sword to poke at the fire. "You Dark Enders can keep your terror and fright, but what you are really missing is the wonders of the Day, a tale of liquid seas and adventures across the misty isles."

The cadets grew quiet and listened.

Maergann waved her sword in a slow arc and ignited the purple flame on the blade. The fire rippled down the blade until it waltzed with the orange campfire in captivating swirls.

"In the wakes of my youth," she said as the fire swayed in front of her face, "long before I took the sigil of knighthood, I worked as a sea hand aboard a roaming long ship called the Jolly Squall!"

Jono felt the heat of the sun against his neck. A turquoise dome glowed magically above him. At the helm of the Jolly Squall, Illius guided them through crashing white waves. All of the students were huddled around a campfire at the bottom of the mast. The sky above them grew dark with thick gray clouds that engulfed the world. A crack of lightning illuminated the shadow of a Star Hydra soaring above the clouds, just as it struck the deck of the Jolly Squall, shattering it in half. On one side, the Dark End cadets clung to the rails, and on the other, the Day squires screamed for help. The ship tilted inward and they all fell into the murky blue sea.

Jono held his breath as he and his friends were pulled under the surface. The Star Hydra's many heads and tails fill the sea like distant, faded snakes. He saw his parents in the water, sinking in the glimmering blue. He reached out to them, but they were too far away. He tried to swim, just like he had read about in the Illius books, kicking and waving his arms, but he couldn't move any closer. His parents called out to him, but he couldn't hear what they were saying.

His sister Dahlia sunk beside him. Her blonde curls floated outward like a mane. Bubbles escaped her smiling mouth. She was cackling at him as the depths of the blue sea grew darker still.

Jono's eyes burst open, and he gasped for breathe. The dim light of the heater bot reflected over their sleeping bags. Oscar snored in his sleep while Isaac muttered equations to himself. Jono forced himself to do his old breathing ritual. Deep breath in, deep breath out. Everything would be fine if he could just keep breathing.

The world was quiet. Murphy was wrapped in a mountain of blankets. Jono was certain that Suri and Marissa were similarly covered in their tents, even though the sleek, heated bags were perfect enough inside the tent. Jono cracked his sore neck and wondered what his dream meant, if anything. That was when he saw Keiko sitting by the door. She had parted the external flap so she could see out while keeping the insulated layer sealed tight. Jono crawled out of his bunk and sat next to her.

"What are you doing?" he whispered.

"Listening," Keiko replied without moving.

"What's out there?"

Keiko squinted. "I heard more woolly frogs barking, and a flock of flarks chirping from the cliff side, but there was something else. Something I can't see yet. The crags in the rock are too thick and some minerals hide better than others."

Jono closed his eyes and strained to hear the wooded world outside their tent. A light flurry of snow fell to the ground like specks of ash, but it wasn't like the manufactured snow inside of Eies. This was pure and simple nature. A woolly frog called out as though it were dreaming of a warmer season.

And then he heard it—an odd laugh.

Jono and Keiko looked at each other.

"It's not Knox, up to some trouble?" Jono asked.

Keiko shook her head. Her eyes shifted color. "I can see in the other tent. Everyone is accounted for. The knight is with the mostly Day tent, and Dr. Stone is keeping an eye on Knox in their tent."

Ramsus snored loudly behind them, as the distant sound of laughter echoed softly through the woods.

Jono shivered. "It's freezing out there." Even though he'd lived in the Dark End his whole life, he still had a harder time with the cold than anyone he knew.

"Why would they be laughing?" Keiko squinted.

Jono grabbed his hat and scarf. "Only one way to find out."

They both bundled up then quietly slipped out of the tent, careful to exit one door layer at a time so no cold air would seep in and wake their tent mates.

The Terralunan moon was in full glow through a haze of clouds that rolled down the mountainside toward the valley below. Both the lights of Terralunis and the reflection of the old sun's dim blue glow made the forest bright and clear, gaving the fallen snow an eerie blue glow.

They snuck out of the campground and followed the sound of cracking branches and crunching snow. Keiko's eyes flicked through various spectrums in search of any heat signatures, unnatural metal shapes, or anything else out of place.

"There." She pointed past a thick growth of trees.

She climbed onto Jono's back. He held onto her with his spy wires and delicately carried them over the snow, his wires swinging them along tree branches until they found a secluded vale. They peered through the trees to see a half-clothed man wandering amongst the woods with a wide, half-toothed smile. He wore a tight, dirty shirt and a pair of torn shorts. His gnarly dark hair met a wild beard that had never been introduced to the word *grooming*. His bare feet and hands were covered in dirt, and patches of his pale skin were black, blue, and dead white.

The man sniffed at tree bark and cackled to himself with joy. "Precious pause for this world of wonders! It survives!"

The man spotted a purple ice iris on a nearby tree and darted over to it with glee. He dipped his tongue to taste the flower and his eyes lit up. "It's real and true and not a lie at all! Not at all!"

He curled around the flower and petted it gently like he would a kitten. Jono thought he looked more like an escaped mental patient than a woodland hermit, but where could he have come from?

The man's head curled inward. "I can hear you," the man said without making a move. "I can hear you breathing."

Jono and Keiko looked at each other.

"Breathe," the man whispered. "The breath of life. The soul comes in—" He inhaled. "And fleeting, it goes out." He exhaled.

"Who are you?" Keiko asked from their safe distance in the trees.

The man murmured to himself as though alone and distant. "What is a man, if his chief good and market of his time be but to sleep and feed? A beast, no more."

"I know that," Jono said. "That's from an old story."

The man's eyes twitched as he turned to them. "They knew me as a man with no eyes, and yet I saw all. But no one listened."

"What's your name?" Jono asked.

The man scowled for moment only to giggle madly at a joke only he heard. "My name is Edgar Niles, but they called me Edgar No Eyes!"

He fell onto his back in the snow. "That's what it is! I finally remembered!"

He made patterns by sweeping his arms and legs across the snow.

"Look at me!" He cheered as snowflakes flittered down from the billowing clouds. "I'm an angel!"

Chapter Nine

Knights in the Night

"Edgar No Eyes is dead."

Commander Grail sat at his office desk, where he, Jono, and Keiko stared at a floating image of the man they'd found covered in frostbite. "This man is not the mech custodian that used to work at Windom and yet that is who he claims to be."

"It can't be true," Keiko said, almost pleading. "We saw No Eyes fall off the Crown tower. There was a funeral, wasn't there?"

"We did lay the old man to rest, yes," Commander Grail said with bureaucratic sympathy. "His body was recorded at his cremation. Edgar was always a recluse. I searched our records—he was never admitted for a health checkup, not even when he joined the academy sixty eight years ago. He almost never went out, and there are no images of him when he was younger. Whoever this person is, the Edgar No Eyes that worked here is deceased."

"Remember when No Eyes fought the Tombs on the Crown's balcony? Our first year here?" Jono said. "He seemed to know something about them already. Maybe *they* are behind it somehow. Maybe this Edgar is a clone? Could he get access to the Crown with Edgar No Eye's old access keys?"

Grail shook his head. "I checked that, but Edgar's access was revoked when he was registered as dead. Still, we can't take any chances if Chaucer is behind this." Grail pulled from his desk five bracelets covered with small containers. "These are anti-animancer pixels. One pill will protect you for twenty minutes, but don't take more than four at a time. It could overwhelm your regular installs. Make sure you and your team carry them with you at all times."

On the screen floating by them, Jono watched as Edgar Niles examined the new mechanical parts that had replaced his frostbitten arm and leg. A doctor moved into view and attempted to show him how to use them, but Edgar waved his new limbs around as though they were out of control.

"If the Tombs are trying to use this person as an undercover agent in Eies, they didn't do a good job keeping him alive," Grail said. "Doctor Shenzo had to take off one foot and a hand due to the frost bite. A few more hours and he would have been dead. You two saved his life."

"Maybe he's a relative of Edgar's." Keiko said. "Edgar No Eyes junior?"

Grail shook his head. "Under normal circumstances, we would know familial lineage, but No Eyes was a strange case. We don't have records of any genetic relatives."

"Whoever he is, why was he outside of the city?" Keiko asked. "We didn't see any ship wreckage. So where was he coming from? Or going to?"

"How does someone get lost out there?" Jono wondered. "He didn't even ask for help. It was almost like he didn't think he was in any trouble."

Grail pondered the odd man in the screen. "Some illnesses of the mind can lead a person to do the most absurd things. If he wandered out of the city, he knew how to escape without the city's defenses detecting him."

"There's nothing but icy wasteland until the North Pole," Keiko said.

"He had some clothes on, shorts and a shirt. Maybe the materials could give a clue about where he came from?" Jono asked.

"We are looking in to it, but we have found no unique identifiers so far. Trust me, Wyer. As soon as I know anything, I will let you know. You've earned it. Until then, we'll keep our eyes on the supposedly resurrected Edgar Niles."

Suriana poured a flask of water onto wide leaves. The water trickled down the venations and dripped onto soil, seeping toward the tree's roots. She clasped her hands, shut her eyes, and let her quiet words swell her spirit and meld between the world that existed deep inside her with the world that was all around.

The Quartzden Grotto inside of Middle Night Gardens was silent. Thick stone and soundproof doors kept the noise of the city at bay. The only light came from the dimly glowing plants around her. Large lampdelions grew up the side of a quartz wall and emitted a soft, yellow bioluminescence. Tiny mauve blossoms called Thesia's Kiss sprouted on vines that crawled over the cavern.

"What did you pray for, child?" the Sage of Ages said reverently behind her. He was nearly invisible as he sat in meditation beneath the cover of willow branches.

"I asked Miraphel for courage," Suri replied.

The Sage smiled but kept his eyes shut. "The angel of art and inspiration likes to deliver her whispers on subtle instruments. The rhythm of rain drops or the purr of a kitten. It is the music of life we often shut our ears and eyes to. Listen for you answer to come in a song. Will you sit with me and breathe?"

Suri sat next to the Sage and closed her eyes. They breathed in the smells of the garden. Rosemary, pine, and lavender made the calming corner the perfect place to listen for the whispers of angels. They breathed in deeply through their noses and gently out their mouths.

"Almost feels like home," the Sage whispered. "As long as you keep your eyes shut."

"I miss the smell of lemon weed in the fields outside Systine," Suri said with a sigh. "And the warmth of the Dawn sun."

"It is good to miss things," replied the Sage. "The yearning brings them closer to our hearts and fights against the atrophy of indifference. Treasure your time apart. It will make your time together all the more sweet."

Suriana nodded.

Tranquility didn't come often in the city of Eies, but in the garden, surrounded by the twinkle of flowers and pixie flies, the wider world faded and the comfort of silence brought stillness to their hearts.

And yet, a question lurked inside of her.

"There is a man in the city. He claims to be an angel."

The Sage breathed slowly in and slowly out, not rushing to reply. "I have heard. What do you think of this news?"

"He doesn't seem very angelic to me."

The Sage chuckled. "The history of Earth is full of charlatans looking to steal coin in exchange for cryptic rabbles, and yet, the angels are rarely predictable. Keep a cautious mind, an open heart, and let the whispers lead the way."

"You don't think he is real?"

"Oh, he is most certainly real. But an angel? I'm not certain it matters. If his words and deeds stir goodness into the world? Then that is a wisdom I would follow."

Maergann Brigid stood in the drills woods, glaring at nineteen squires as they silently stared back at her. She hated waiting. She also hated being disappointed.

Suriana came running up the trail, panting.

"I'm . . . sorry . . ." she gasped. "I was working on another project with the Sage, and—"

Maergann raised a hand, and Suriana stopped speaking, instead hanging her head in shame before joining the ranks of squires. The knight drew her sword from its sheath and held it up to the stars.

"This is Brang'thal. A knight's weapon is a vessel of your will. It is your fiery heart, your cunning mind, carved into this world. The wisps listen to your bond and when you speak as one, they will let the world feel your might! It will guide you when the path is lost. And it will remind you of your power when you feel weak."

Maergann thrust the sword toward the ground. "Basil's Fire!"

The blade burst with purple light, creating a thick ring of glowing plasma that shot out around her. The ring met the student's faces—careful not to singe a single hair—and then quickly withdrew back into the sword.

"This power is your birthright, but only if you rise to claim it," Maergann said. "You have had enough time to acclimate to your new grounds. This wake, your true training begins!"

"Does this mean we can drop another class?" Ammer said with a smirk.

"Sign me up for that," Freya added.

"Did you come here to *be* Dark Enders?" Maergann replied. "Is that why you joined this academy? To soak in their oil and savor the smell? Will you ask of yourself only as much as them? Or will you live for more than the minimum? Will you stand for something greater? Will you carve your own destiny or let it be written for you?"

The students looked back at her in terrified silence. Maergann marched along the line of squires and pointed her sword at them.

"This is your chance to learn from our ancient adversary, to become the first lords of the Day in eons with a wealth of insight into the workings of machines that none before you dreamed of having."

Again, their eyes responded in silence. Their timidity stung at Maergann's heart.

"Will you be knights?" she bellowed.

"I swear my spirit to the Light!" Every student replied the motto in unison.

"Good." Maergann smiled. She liked squires. They possessed an abundance of energy and they believed they could do anything without even trying. She liked showing them that they were wrong.

The squire's classical weapons training began with the sword, shield, axe, halberd, and mace. They broke into pairs, swiping and dodging each other while Maergann shouted commands.

"Defenders use the Kendo Stone form. Aggressors practice your Tiger Tsu stance."

The students posed, hacked, and parried. Riley's mace smashed into Murphy's face, but instead of crushing his skull, the silver mace's head squished back like gel and left a purple mark to remind Murphy of his wound.

"Trickle it down, Shrub," Murphy complained. "This mark won't wash out for wakes."

"Wear your practice scars with honor, squire," Maergann said from across the training ground. "It is only when we push ourselves to our limits that we learn who they truly are."

Ammer leaned on his axe. "We practiced this all last year. How much more basic weapons training do we need before we can start enchanting them?"

Maergann smiled at the naivety. "Back in Systine, how much training would Master Hemlock have told you?"

Ammer groaned. "As much as is needed."

Maergann nodded. "Then again."

Suriana blocked Freya's sword with her shield then lunged at her, landing a hit with her own training blade.

"You could have blocked that," Suri said through her heavy breathing. "You let me have that hit."

Freya shrugged. "You started the training exhausted. I didn't want to take any easy hits."

"Training is only useful if it is serious. Don't hold back," Suri insisted. "Come at me!"

For hours they practiced battle patterns. Even in the chill of the Dark, they'd worked up a heavy sweat under their training armor.

"Squires hold," Maergann shouted. She surveyed the crowd of the exhausted students.

Suriana leaned over her buckling knees. Ammer dropped his axe and let his arms shake from the fatigue.

"Meet me here again, every Red and Greenwake. Next time we will start properly with the recitation of the Knight's Oath, and if you get a syllable wrong you will be learning about fighting off ten enemies at once. Squires dismissed."

Murphy thudded as he collapsed on his back.

"Two wakes a week?" Freya said. "I can manage that."

"Good, because that's just me," Maergann replied. "Blue and Purplewakes you will be here for Sir Moss' spell training."

The students groaned.

"The road to knighthood is paved with sores and bruises," Maergann said with a grin. "Savor this time, for *now* is the easy part."

"What's this?" Oscar asked as he looked at a blue piece of paper he'd just been handed. "'Join the theatrical production of the century, *The Ides of Decsomber?*'"

"I've never heard of it," Isaac said.

Suriana stood among the row of stone statues that lined the front of Windom's central city gate with a stack of flyers in her arms. Nearby, nervous squires tried to hand out the flyers as the Dark Enders avoided eye contact.

"Can't we just leave them here in a pile?" Ammer asked. "We're going to be late for Moss' training."

"We have an hour until spell training starts," Suriana reminded them.

"I'm still sore from yesterwake," Murphy moaned, stretching to crack his back.

"I think we may have prep work for spells too," Freya said, a clear attempt to find another excuse for stopping their humiliation.

"Then start handing out flyers and make it flitter." Suriana waved a flyer at the passing Dark Ender cadets. "Be a part of history! The Windom theater department is putting on its first ever opera, and as part of our cultural exchange, they have decided to produce the most famous Giftmas story in the Day, the Ides of Decsomber!"

Oscar examined the flyer as if it were a blueprint, rotating and turning it, trying to understand. "So, it's an opera, like, with singing?"

"Yes," Suri said, a bit flustered between trying to converse with them and hand out flyers at the same time. "It's a love story with epic battles, shocking betrayal, and a moral message set in the era of lost myths! Tryouts start at the end of Oktavian, sign up now!"

The horde of students passed by, ignoring the flyers the best they could.

"You may want to try posting your auditions on the Line," Isaac suggested. "Windom has an events calendar, just plug it in there."

Suri sighed and let her shoulders shrug. "That's a good idea."

"Here, I'll do it for you." Isaac scanned the image with his goggles, and in a blink, the invitation was shared across the school.

"I'm still getting used to how things work here," Suri said with a sad smile. "Of course we have the Line in the Day, but people still like to actually talk to each other, face to face."

The rest of the Day students scowled at Suriana and praised Isaac for his easy escape.

"Face to face?" Isaac chuckled. "That's so inefficient."

Chapter Ten

A Dance in the Shadows

"This is what you call a classy restaurant?" Maergann sat her spellblade against an open table in the Burly Belch pub.

"I didn't say upper class." Ramsus laughed as he sat down. "Besides, you don't really want all that polish and shine. I can tell. You get plenty of that with your royal guard duty. No, what you want is to see how we Dark Enders really tick tock. You want a good hard gaze at the guts below the mech gear. No better place to do that than here at the Burly Belch."

Maergann glared. He was right. It irked her that he could tell so much about her and they barely knew each other.

"I expect the beer and meat to be more than adequate then," she replied as she sat.

"As a fan of the brew, you're in for a special treat. The top six-hundred craft brews from across the Dark are here on draft. We're going to get a true sampling of Dark End ingenuity."

"I didn't realize it was going to be that type of evening."

"There's no shame in a refined lady of the shimmering blue skies avoiding a challenge." Ramsus smirked.

Maergann surrendered a faint grin. "You don't know me as well as you think you do."

"I think I'm going to enjoy learning all the things I'm wrong about."

The Burly Belch was crowded, but it was a manageable chaos. The unlikely pair was half way through their first pint and their steaming plates of muscow burgers arrived when a call pinged the back of Ramsus' mind.

Ramsus frowned. "Sorry, one tick. I have to take a call. Duty summons."

He closed his eyes and in an instant he was connected to the code world. A green-armored feli'yin sat at table in the middle of an empty black room.

"I rang three times," Aramis said sternly. "I hope I'm not interrupting something important."

"No, you don't hope that," Ramsus replied. "And, yes you were. Make it click."

"Two wakes ago, one of our joint operatives went missing in sector twenty one of the Sunrise Ring. He was tracking a lead on the Tombs. Chaucer, specifically."

"How the burning stars was I not informed until now?" Ramsus growled.

"It was a tier one covert op managed by your End's Mactor Hardigan. He attempted to get his team into the zone for a rescue before escalating the incident. They were caught in a distortion field for seventeen hours. When they got to the last known point of contact, the target building was destroyed. No evidence was collected."

"Hardy," Ramsus growled. "I'm going to snap his piston!"

"That's not everything. Ten minutes ago that same operative's contact key went live."

"Where?"

"Two kilems from your location inside Eies."

Ramsus gritted his teeth. "I'm on it. Who's the operative?"

"Sergeant Dougal Bearing."

"Burnin' stars. Send me the tracker."

"You have it now, and Ramaadi?" Aramis scowled. "Bearing may only have moments. Make it flitter."

Ramsus opened his red eyes. They glowed hot with anger.

"Who was that?" Maergann asked.

"A royal feli'yin with some bad news."

"A knight from the Day? What could you possibly be working on?"

Ramsus leaned forward as he slid his plate away. "That info is locked."

Maergann leaned in and glared. "Anything that puts my ward at risk in your greasy city, I must know about."

"This is not something I can take a date on."

"This is not something I can allow you to keep me from. My duty demands it."

Ramsus blinked and paid their bill. He sneered. "I need to track this lead while it's hot. If you are going to follow me, you better be fast."

Maergann chugged the last of her beer and slammed the glass on the table. "Just don't get in my way if we run into any Tombs."

Ramsus grinned. "I think I'm in love."

The streets of the Eies's Mech District were silent in the late sleep hours. Ramsus cut around a corner and ducked into an alleyway with Maergann right behind him. He unlocked a circular cover in the center of the ally, and both of them slipped beneath the city streets into the dark intestines of the mechanized metropolis.

The vast tunnels were dimly lit from mechanical glow bugs that crawled through the cracks and ate the various plant life that grew in the moist air. Sterile tubes of wires carried electricity in near-perfect efficiency across the city.

Beneath their careful footsteps was tons of delicately managed compost. Simple-minded bots treated the biological material, churning it with the soil and armies of worms that prepared it for use again in the farms, gardens, and parks above them.

A small bot popped out of the murky soil and scurried over to the bot station to be cleansed and recharged for another wake's mindless toil.

Maergann pinched her nose shut. "I have to admit, soldier, this wins the crown for smelliest first date ever."

"Just wait until I get us surrounded by Tombs agents with no greater wish than to die bringing chaos into the world," Ramsus said. "My lady friends can't get enough of near-death experiences."

"Remind me to not be one of your lady friends."

The tunnels fell deep below the city. The noise of gears and pipes was a distant hum in these depths.

"We're close to the signal."

They arrived at a mammoth nexus of pipes. Even in the shadowed light, they could see the body hanging from the ceiling, caught in a mess of wires.

"Is that him?"

"Stay back." Ramsus' eyes scanned through the body, looking for signs of a bomb or microscopic poisons.

"He's clean. Dougal, you poor clunker," Ramsus said with a sigh. "He must have activated his tracker before he died."

"Or it was activated for him," Maergann said. "How did he get up there?"

Ramsus approached the hanging body, inspecting every inch in seconds. "There're cuts all over his hands and bits of the pipes are under his fingernails. He tore open the wire pipes. Dougal put himself up there."

"Why would one of your soldiers do such a thing?"

"They wouldn't. Can you see through his skin?"

"I don't have installs like you Dark Enders. Our gems have power, but we don't contaminate the body with them."

Ramsus' eyes changed to yellow. "There are still traces of the tracks in the blood. Pixels. They disintegrated themselves to hide their presence, but the tracers are still there since the body isn't alive to cover them up."

"Someone forced him to do this?"

"Someone expert at animancy," Ramsus said.

Maergann glared. "Vincent Chaucer is in Eies."

Ramsus nodded.

Ever since the apparent leader of the Tombs had escaped from the collapse of the ruins of Lailet Dem, the world had been searching for him with no sign of his whereabouts.

"There's a trail. Dougal was bleeding before he hung himself in the wires. Where did it start?"

Maergan clasped the hilt of her spellblade. "We are not alone."

Ramsus looked around. "I don't see any—"

Before he could finish, oily shadows poured through the cracks in the walls. They swept over the soldier and knight in a wave. Heads popped, cackled and roared as the shadow wrapped around Ramsus' arms and pulled them both behind his back. "Fel shades!"

Maergann flung her crystal-studded fist at the shadow, but the fel was swift and swirled away. Fel material reached out at them like tentacles, bringing the tunnel itself to life. They gripped her ankles and tore at her coat.

A black mouth grew out of the shadow on the ground and snapped viciously at them.

Ramsus ignited his power gauntlets, but the shadow material stretched to avoid each blast. The fel squid flung him into the wall. Its tentacles twisted him around and slammed him against opposite the wall, stone crumbling around his battered face.

Maergann reached for her blade, but the tentacles caught her arms and thrust her against the ceiling.

The shadows yanked Ramsus from the wall and smashed his face into the thick soil. Ramsus struggled— he couldn't breathe. His gauntlets charged to overload and exploded, shattering a hole in the tunnel above them, but missing the grasp of the tentacles that pinned him down from all sides. The tunnel shook with the blast of fiery light. The tremor was just enough to weaken the fel squid's grip on Maergann's hand. She grabbed the hilt of her spellsword and called for it to ignite.

"Vandal's Spark!" Maergann yelled.

The blade burst into a brilliant purple fire, sparking all around her. She thrust the blade into the fel shade's mouth. Purple sparks blitzed across the oily shadow, cutting through its microscopic felcells, and with a ripple of light it turned the shadowy monster into sparking dust.

Ramsus lifted his head and gasped deep as the footsteps of the city guard came clanking down the tunnel.

"You saved my life," Ramsus said, incredulous and thankful in the same tone.

Maergann collapsed beside him. "And your date didn't bore me."

"Well then, stick around, widget," Ramsus said, pointing to the trail of Dougal's blood. "This city is going to be anything but dull."

They gazed up at the remains of the fel beast as lingering sparks illuminated markings scrawled upon the wall with Dougal's own blood. It was the message he was forced to leave behind as last testament, though not his own. The words were the call from the mad man they hunted.

When the mask leaves your mind
The lies will all fade.
As demons awaken,
Your debt will be paid.
And Angels will mourn for
Their lost Masquerade!

Chapter Eleven

Sermon on a Gear Stack

A drop of sweat trickled down Alexsayter Aquinas' forehead. The sight of St. Newton's Cathedral quickly filling with more attendees made him chuckle nervously. The stadium seats were scattered with curious attendees.

"Our biggest crowd thus far and here I am sweating in the city surrounded by ice."

Cassindra Viscariot stood behind him, smiling. She placed a comforting hand on his shoulder. "You're doing a good deed here. Even in the Dark, people are responding to the message. Could you have ever imaged this?"

"I spent my career on the fringes of the Dark, but here in the heart of their machine?" Aquinas chuckled and wiped his forehead with the back of his hand. "I doubt any metal will melt, but still . . . Do you think the whispers are reaching them?"

"You tell me," Viscariot replied. "After your many years sharing the Narrow Path across the Dark, when everyone else hid in the Day to friendly ears, I don't think there is a member in the Fellowship as qualified to lead this work as you."

"Now, you are the one being modest," Aquinas said. "Cassindra Viscariot, the first chancellor of the World Peace Council, youngest prayarch of the Fellowship, and seer of prophetic visions that will heal a broken world. If you're not careful, the Day may start rumors of *your* angelic embodiment!"

"Blasphemy!" Viscariot grinned. "Both kind and cruel of you to say. I wouldn't want to be an angel for all the power in the world. To sit in judgment at the gates of the veil, with the fate of every follower in your hands? To watch over every corner of this broken world and struggle to aid every wayward soul? That burden would be far too great to bear."

The bells of Saint Newton's began to ring loudly above them. Viscariot smiled at the excitement. "It's time. You shouldn't keep your flock waiting."

"Pray for luck," Aquinas said.

"You won't need it," Viscariot said. "I know how loudly the angels whisper to you."

Viscariot snuck out from behind the stage to join the crowd just as Aquinas stepped out from behind a white curtain on the stage at Saint Newton's Cathedral to a crowd of half-full seats. She sat in the front row as Aquinas took a deep breath.

"It's our best turnout yet," Aquinas whispered to himself. Beyond his nerves was excitement, encouragement in his continued mission in the Dark.

He cleared his throat and it echoed through the stadium seating.

"Hello friends and thank you for coming. Earlier this week, I prepared for you a sermon about the lessons I had learned during my many years living in the Twilight Ring, but new rumors have been spreading across the city and as the visiting fateriarch of the Seraphic Fellowship, I wish to share my humble thoughts on the events of the wake.

"The Tombs are in Eies, the rumors say. Those terrorist cowards wrote a threatening poem in a weak attempt at prophecy, and we wake to a world trying to understand what the Tombs mean by their cryptic words. But I say unto you, *do not try*. Do not ponder the ravings of madness. Do not follow a path down the empty reaches of the mind. The Tombs offer us a path only toward oblivion. All you need to know about them is their intent. They want to use fear to infect us, to divide us. They wish to use the mysterious divinity of the angels that whisper in our hearts, to use this strength, our salvation, and corrupt it against us.

"The pox is terrifying, that is true. But I do not wake in fear for I know that the angels watch over me, over us all! The pox sows fear in our hearts, but the Old Book tells us the hands of angels can stop it in its tracks! The hand of the angels can and will end this blight! The angels have protected this city thus far, and with faith and fortitude, they will save us from this cancer.

"Yet, I know my friends here are a questioning lot. Wisely so. You will say to me, the angels are gone, or the angels are sleeping, or some even . . ." Aquinas chuckled. "That the angels don't exist at all. And I say unto you, *no*. They are always watching, they are the whispers on the wind, they are here! Now! Among us! Masquerading in our midst as the friend we needed at the right moment when we did not have the strength to ask for help. Masquerading as the reminder on the news to choose tolerance and understanding over discrimination and hatred."

Viscariot leaned to one side to watch the crowd from the corner of her eye. Some sneered, while others looked bored, but most were listening to Aquinas in earnest. People with metal body parts were opening their hearts to ideas that could have gotten them ostracized not so long ago. There was a magic in his words—no, a magic flowing through him. She felt blessed to bear witness to this moment.

"You may ask, 'Why not now?', when the pox is at our gates. Perhaps we don't need them yet. Perhaps they know that our joint mechanix and magic will see us through these terrible times. Perhaps they wait for the moment when all our strength is lost. As the Testament of Athuliandros teaches us, 'Ye who have given all of yourself, worry not, for it is when you are weakest that the wings of the angels will wake to whisk you safely home.

"You may ask, 'If angels are real, why has no one seen them?' But tell me, friends, would you believe the tale if you did not see it for yourselves? One wake, you will see. You will witness the true power of an angel and it will cause the air around them to hold still. It will stir a part of you that lies dormant. The mask of what you think is reality will fall and for that instant you will look upon a face as familiar to you as your own in the mirror, but you will know an angel resides behind those eyes."

A swell of pride rose up in Viscariot's chest that made her eyes tear up. It was brave work that the tumnkin was doing, and in that moment she felt the stir of an angel inside of her. It whispered to trust the path they were on. It whispered that all would be well.

"I say to you now that the angels of the Old Book are real and alive and they are here with us now, even as they masquerade as something we do not know is the work of an angel. Take solace in that, my friends. Take hope in that. And have restful sleeps knowing you are being watched over. The angels are watching. And you are safe.

"Knowing all this splendor, I encourage you to ask yourself, in the quiet of your heart, in the still of your mind, do you believe in angels? Perhaps the answer may surprise you."

Aquinas closed his eyes, bowed his head, and breathed slowly in and then slowly out.

"In faith of the angels, the Old Mother and Aged Father, amen."

A quiet murmur from the audience repeated those words, *amen*. Viscariot felt the word wash over her like a ray of sunlight. It was barely audible, but its presence at all was powerful. Even in the capital city of the Dark End, there were believers, or at least people who wanted to believe.

Even here, she marveled that the faithful were not alone.

"Look, I'm not anti-Day or anything," Isaac said, "but that was the stupidest bilge I've ever heard!"

Jono, Isaac, and Keiko sat on one of the stone benches just outside of the gates of Saint Newton's cathedral. By the time the crowd of sermon attendees had trickled out, Isaac couldn't contain his criticisms any longer.

"And the question and answer session at the end was so polite I wanted to melt my ear holes! Nothing that little tumnkin said made sense, but everyone just smiled and nodded." Isaac crossed his arms and shook his head. "I bet once the novelty of the Day's myths wears off, no one is going to go to these sermons."

"I thought the Cottage Builder's Parable was a sweet story," Keiko said. "Family looking out for each other, getting lost, and remembering what really matters. What's so clunky about that?"

"Sure. Nice story," Isaac said with a scoff. "The angels though? He thinks they are *literally* real. And why is it that all of these angels are human? Ayleens have been on Earth for over twelve-thousand years! And grudgon have been here much longer than that. Stars! This planet has more non-humans than humans."

"I never thought of that, but it is gizmos," Jono said.

Isaac pointed at both of them. "It is speciesist. They have non-humans all over the Day too, but still they believe this bilge?"

"It's not that bad," Keiko said.

"Oh, it is," Isaac said. "Dangerous idiocy, that."

"It's probably because Earth is the native human planet and it's an old story, from before aliens arrived and magical creatures revealed themselves," Keiko said. "It's just a metaphor to get people to think about each other and empathize more."

"If they were trying to create a metaphor to help improve their people, than why would they not change it to reflect what their people look like in the world now? Be more inclusive? I'm not saying they need a patron angel for every species, but if you can't give up one angel to make non-humans feel included, then they don't really care about them."

Keiko shrugged. "Maybe they think the angels are real and they don't want to change it."

"That's even worse!" Isaac bellowed. "You can't treat mythology as if it is true without terrible consequences. I don't have a problem with them believing crazy things as long as it doesn't hurt anyone, but the thing is, it is hurting people. Remember the Keeper! And now the Day is advertising its craziness all over the Dark End! Every new show has a Day character that's all friendly and preachy. They are trying to insert their culture into ours. Maybe the new Freedom Defenders are right about this one. Keep indoctrination separate and keep Dark culture clean of this madness."

Keiko sighed. "What do you think, Jono?"

Jono watched the bustle of the city waltz around them. Clouds covered the stars, even as light erupted from every direction.

"Isaac is right," Jono finally replied. "It is a speciesist story. I grew up with all the angel stories and shrines and all that. Non-humans have long been just as Earthkin as humans are. There's no utility in leaving them out."

Isaac grinned proudly as Jono continued.

"Stories are as real as we make them. Keiko is right that they are just stories to make the Day people feel closer to each other. Good people want something to belong to and they don't mean anything bad by them."

"Always the diplomat, aren't you, Wyer?" Keiko said with a smirk.

"You're always giving both sides an even hand despite knowing it's not an even argument," Isaac said. "Can't you pick a side for once?"

Jono scowled. "Picking sides is what killed two-thousand people at the Keeper. It's what the Tombs want to use against us. More than one person can be right about the same thing, but in different ways. Taking myths literally is dangerous, but most people in the Day still know the difference between stories and reality, even if they go to sermons like that, and even if they pray to angels. We need to be right about what matters most. We have a real enemy trying to turn us against each other. If we can't keep that in mind, then the Tombs will slit our throats while we're busy bickering with each other."

The brutal truth in Jono's words created a moment of silence as Keiko and Isaac both recalled the Keeper and their personal experiences with the Tombs.

"That doesn't answer the question at hand," Isaac said, his voice resolute and grim. "The Day is full of nonsense and that puts us all at risk."

"Everyone was raised on one End or the other," Jono said. "We didn't question why we did the things we did any more than they. Look at everyone at Windom and you tell me that they aren't just eating what they're fed. The Dark may be more logical, but that doesn't make us wise by default. We live in a city that by all rights should be a barren wasteland. We survive in the cold when nature would have us dead. We know that we're surrounded by unnatural things."

"So we should give these angel stories a chance to be true even though they defy everything science verifiably knows about how the universe works?"

"Stories aren't science. The Day chooses to live in all types of weird ways. People choose to live the life that they want. There has to be something of value in it, right?"

"But they are not equal," Isaac said.

Keiko stood up. "Look, I love the Dark End, but let's get calibrated here. The Day has life pretty welded. They can grow food in the dirt just by tossing seeds at it. They lounge around all wake with their friends, eating and drinking and laughing it up."

Isaac sneered. "If the Day folk were left to themselves, they'd be living the exact same way they were thousands of years ago. Living fossils preserved for all to see. They don't believe in progress."

"That's my point!" Jono replied. "We do. We *believe* in progress, but guess what? Everyone dies anyway. At some point, the value of all this tech is subjective. People don't believe in things without a reason. Are you really going to tell me there's absolutely nothing the Day could possibly do better than us? That there's nothing we could ever learn from them? More importantly, what is broken about us that we don't even know why we've never asked that question?"

Isaac banged the back of his head against the stone bench. "The Dark has infinitely more answers than they do!"

"Answers to what questions? We don't know what the pox is, and before you even think of saying I'm giving abysmal hexes a chance, I'm not, but there *are* gaps that shouldn't be there. What does it make us if we just accept the 'truth' we're told?"

"Efficient."

"It makes us exposed. No system is perfect. By staying locked in our Dark Ender bubble we are obscuring the truth. If we can't find the flaws in our own system, then we won't be ready when someone else does. *That* is what the pox is. Our blindness manifested."

Keiko nodded. "I click you, Jono. Think of it this way, Ohm. We're experts because we focus on a specialty, but that means there are some things we're choosing not to focus on. We have gaps that can be exploited by our enemy."

Isaac huffed. "Sure, we're not perfect. But it all depends on your goals. If you want to survive exploring the stars, well then, I'd take the Dark any wake. If you want to sleep all hours, eat until you're bloated, dance and sing, then the Day is all yours."

Keiko smiled. "That does sound like they're living the good life."

"Only until until some new virus wipes out your whole civilization," replied Isaac.

"So what is it that we're living for?" Jono asked. "Happiness or progress?"

"Does it have to be one or the other?" asked Keiko.

"It has to be both. It has to be everything."

They savored the silences and let ideas swirl in their minds. The city burst with life all around them as Saint Newton's two bell towers loomed above, its stone walls holding no opinions of their own.

"They're broken."

In the alley behind them, a familiar voice mumbled from above and they turned to face it.

Natharen Vault crouched on the lip of a window. The lost boy that they had found alone in the ruins of Lailet Dem had made the whole city his new home. The boy had taken to hiding in the nooks of the metropolis and only appearing on the surprising occasion to gawk at them and yammer madly. He was wrapped in a thick-collared coat that hung past his feet like a cape. The top hat he wore made him look like a child dressed up in his father's clothes.

"The *stars* are broken." Natharen shook his head as looked up.

"We haven't seen you in weeks!" Keiko walked below the boy who then looked curiously down at her.

Natharen pulled an apple from his pocket and took a bite as he gazed curiously at the three cadets. The mysterious boy ignored them on most encounters, but this time he lingered.

"I checked in with Chivalry House," Keiko said. "They say you almost never go to their school and they barely see you even stop by to eat. Your bed is always impeccably made, though. Are you even sleeping there? You should really try making new friends, you know. I bet there are a lot of kids like you."

"There is no one like anyone else," Natharen replied. "We are different. Impossibly unique and irreplaceable."

"Okay. But a few friends your own age could be nice, right?"

Jono stepped forward. "Maybe we should try a different tactic. Hey, Natharen, are you coming to the Ohm's Hollow's Eve party?" Even as Jono asked he didn't expect the boy to reply. "It's next week at Isaac's parents' house up on North Crustling Street. But you know that, don't you? You watch us all the time, even if we can't see you. Why don't you join us instead of stalking around the city?"

Natharen surveyed the familiar faces as though he were seeing them for the first time. "I cordially invite you all, to the end of the Mummer's Ball, where devils will sing, the chimes will ring, and the stars will come quickly to fall . . ."

"You never make a click of sense, do you, kid?" Isaac said.

Natharen stood, about to leave, but he paused and looked back. "I heard you talk of angels and wings and sillier things. It's all wrong, like a song, in someone else's dream."

"See?" Isaac said to Keiko. "Even your crazy orphan friend agrees with me." Isaac turned back to Natharen. "I guess you're smarter than you let on."

But the boy had already disappeared.

Chapter Twelve

Pondering the Pox

"What do you remember about how it started?"

Professor Fourier stared out over the star-filled distance while dim machine lights blinked across the small room where he and his young pupil worked.

Isaac sat at a desk beside him. He rubbed his eyes after hours of puzzling through equations. They finally had a moment to rest as the computer calculated their complex hypothesis.

Isaac's wakes blended together between school work, training with team Firewall, the mentorship with the squires, and every other second spent pondering the pox.

Isaac yawned. "You saw the interviews we all did after it happened. It's all there."

Fourier nodded. "I did. They collected your testimonies when you got back from the Day, to keep the experience fresh in your minds. I want to know what you think about it now. You've had time to process what happened.

I know that you are cautious about making assumptions. Thus I expect your interview did not include every thought you weren't ready to share. You know that leaping to conclusions, often based on emotional reactions, can be dangerous. I know you fought on the battlefield at the Keeper with your fellow cadets and you rightly refuse to trust the decisions of us foolish adults. So tell me, Mister Ohm, what do *you* know about the pox?"

Isaac looked into Fourier's blue eyes. He wasn't like most adults. He was a true skeptic.

"Not much," Isaac said.

"The first step in gaining knowledge is identifying what you do not know."

"That's a tall order," Isaac said. "We don't really know what the pox is in the first place. We don't know how it works. We don't know what causes it. We don't know if it is a natural phenomenon or created by machines or magic. We don't know how it really started, beyond all that mythology the Tombs were shouting about."

"What evidence do we have?"

"We do know the Tombs are liars, so trusting their explanation is a false start. We have variable eye witness accounts of the pox at ninety-three events since that wake at Lailet Dem. The instruments at the Pathaganon have tracked one-hundred-and-seventy-two pox-like spatial events in near-Earth space since the system was operational four weeks after zero wake. We've looked over the location patterns, across the globe, and across our orbit of Sol. There's nothing conclusive, no location pattern to predict where it will hit next. The rate is frequent but sporadic. We don't know if it is accelerating or declining."

"I know what our systems know, Isaac," Fourier coached him. "What I need to know is in your head. What ideas are in your mind about the pox that won't be in anyone else's that is studying it? Perspective is crucial in formulating innovative hypotheses."

"The scope of our systems *is* the point," Isaac replied. "The Pathaganon can track comets orbiting Sol across the Kuiper belt and plot their trajectories for thousands of years. Our systems can see far beyond our planet, so why is it that we are only aware of the pox happening close to Earth?"

Fourier smiled. "Continue that thought."

Isaac paused for a moment. This was important and his answer needed to be careful. "I don't know what causes it, but I do know that it was released."

"Released? So it is a phenomenon driven by an external trigger then?"

"Perhaps unlocked is a better word," Isaac replied. "The pox cannot be random in space and time. It is bound to this planet for some reason. There is a trigger on Earth activating the outbreaks. Either this trigger has a limited range of activation, which keeps the pox close to us, or . . ."

"Or what?"

"Or the *target* is close. The target may be on the planet."

"Do you think someone is controlling it? Aiming the pox?"

"If they are, then their aim isn't very good. Only seven of all outbreaks had any contact of significance."

"Unless the contact isn't the target," replied Fourier.

"What do you mean?"

"Fear. The Tombs would want to maximize the world's terror by making it random, unpredictable. The Tombs are out there, stalking us in plain sight."

Isaac chewed on the idea, but it didn't quite fit. "Would they choose fear over destruction? They tried to get both Ends to kill each other. Right now the pox is a boogey man more than a terrorist threat. If they truly controlled the pox, why not simple aim it at Eies and eliminate the Empress? A dead Empress would cause more of a panic than random appearances. The Day is a clutter of republics. They would all splinter. She's the only one keeping this world stable on both Ends. If the Tombs aren't really out to kill us all, then they are hiding their intentions pretty well."

Fourier shook his head. "Maybe it is uncontrolled."

Isaac slouched in his chair. "But the pox shouldn't be bound to our orbit. It can't be completely random, otherwise we'd be seeing it across the whole star system."

"We are missing something," Fourier said.

They sat quietly, letting the gentle clicks of machines and blinking of lights of the small office contrast the wide panorama of the night world outside the window. They let the silence sink in, and their minds reflected against other times, other places. The world around them was full of mystery and wonder and yet, for some reason, there wasn't documentation to explain what the pox was.

"Jono," Isaac muttered.

"Cadet Wyer?" Fourier asked. "What about him?"

"He was researching Eve's Dale our first year at Windom. I saw him get scolded for it once in the library, and it always stuck with me. We don't like looking at the blemishes in our selves. Even Professor Wishe, who is a hollow, was compelled to shun what happened to that town. The Day used it to make irrational claims that the Empress was using pit magic, and our whole End used their blame as a reason to hate the Day. We wanted to have it as an excuse to feel like victims, but we never asked what really happened. That impulse to ignore the unpleasant things of our past—we couldn't even explore the idea that the Empress, or even someone else here in the Dark, did something wrong."

Fourier pondered that for a moment. "*We flail as martyrs in our grand parades, while the emptiness dines and the memory fades.*" It was a quote Isaac had heard before, but he couldn't quite place the source. "But we have looked at the available data on Eve's Dale. There is no sign of a clear trigger of the event, whether you take the Empress' side of the story or the Day's accusations that she was using abysmal magic."

"If the pox does transcend space and time, couldn't the trigger have been anywhere? Or any when?" Isaac frowned. There was so much that was still unknown.

"What I know, Professor, is there *was* an outbreak then. It happened once before Lailet Dem and it was contained to one town. One place in space and time, quite pointed, and then it was gone. Now we have an unpredictable but reoccurring series of events. That trigger went off back at Eve's Dale, and now it is going off repeatedly. There is a cable that ties the two together, and the finger on the trigger is twitching more now than it was then."

"How do we find our trigger?"

"We look for connection between the two. We look wherever others don't want to look," Isaac replied. He was beginning to understand Jono's point. "Our pride is hiding the facts right in front of us. We turned our back on the warning sign at Eve's Dale. We didn't act. We didn't know. *We* are the problem."

Fourier grinned morosely. "Got any ideas on how we fix ourselves?"

Isaac sighed. "Question everything?"

"I was hoping for something a little more specific."

Chapter Thirteen

A Song of Illusion

"All the King's men, oh, traveling far!
They search for lost lovers, in valley and star!"

Nicklus Knox sung as though a wild pungrus was turning itself inside out. "Creatures of summer and winter take heed, for all must know of the Shadow's misdeed!"

Three teachers stared blankly at the young man upon the stage at Saint Newton's. The curtains were wide open and a mess of unfinished set pieces were being prepared by the crew.

Professor Moss tapped his notebook, a grimace on his face. "I have you listed as trying out for the role of the First Heart Guard, and yet, Mister Knox, you are singing the lines from the role of the Herald?"

"Yes . . . that's what I meant to sign up for," Nick said, trying to save face.

A student in the back of the auditorium giggled but was quickly quieted. Another teacher coughed.

"Should I start over, or . . .?" Nick shifted awkwardly from side to side.

"No, I think we have everything we need," Professor Moss said. "Thank you, cadet. Who is next?"

Nick stomped off of the stage as Roger Hyland cautiously followed.

Behind the half built set, David Kepler was preparing a blank panel for digital painting. Isaac sat on a box of supplies; he wore a king's outfit with a red satin jacket and puffs of white silk protruding from slits in the shoulders. His crown was a pristine artifact his father borrowed from the Eies historeum. If he weren't an ayleen, he could have passed for Day Ender royalty.

"This whole set is really coming together!" Isaac said. "Are those Sand Worms?"

"Yeah," David said. "There's a scene in the background where the army crosses the Sandy Sea."

Isaac pointed to the canvas backdrop. "What's that going to be?"

"We leave it blank for the start of the show. I'll paint it live for each performance, so it's unique each time."

"Sounds like a lot of work just to repeat the piece."

"That's the point. It's art. It's all about creating the illusion that you're witnessing a unique living moment. And you're one to talk about too much work. Mentor to the Day, apprentice at the Pathaganon, and now actor? Are there even enough hours in each wake?"

Isaac shrugged. "I'm stuck on a puzzle and looking for new perspective. Maybe something in this odd Day Ender show will spark an idea."

"That's very open-minded of you."

"I'm desperate." Isaac kicked his feet in the air, letting his heels clunk against his supply box of a throne. "Hey, are we all still going to Oscar's for the Giftmas morning parade?"

"The whole clan will be there. That is, if Uly and Rex don't hijack a float and get the family banned from the district."

"Yeah, the district mayor was pretty mad last year."

"I heard his husband's hair was growing scales for three months."

"Aren't your brother and sister around here?"

David looked worried. "You saw them? They must be up to trouble. Listen . . ."

There was some clanking up in the rafters.

"Next!" a teacher called from the front of the stage.

"That's me." Isaac hopped off the box.

"Break a hinge," David shouted after him.

Isaac approached the stage with his head held high and an air of royal elegance embodied in his fancy costume. He cleared his throat and launched into King Heart's dying sonnet. Even Moss had a hard time not looking enthralled.

Isaac waved his golden scepter and clasped his heart as his voice bellowed through the cathedral.

"Yet here I lie before the grave!

My kingdom left to heartless Fates.

Will my gardens grow without me?

What future waits, I cannot see.

Will the pit consume us like a hood?

Will my intentions be understood?

I gave my people all I could,

Did I cast my shadow for good?"

Isaac sang the last note with delicate power. He rested his head with a final gasp of air and then dropped. The King was dead. The audience of professors erupted in applause. After a moment, Isaac stood, bowed, and then left the stage while the teachers still clapped.

On the edge of the stage, Oscar was waiting for Isaac, wearing a nervous smile. Oscar also wore a king's costume, but his looked patched together with scraps of cloth. His red jacket looked like oil stained brick, and his crown was cardboard painted yellow. Bits of shiny blue metal were glued on as appalling representations of gemstones.

"You're trying out for the King too?" Isaac asked.

Oscar shrugged. "I figured I'd try for the top. If they don't like it, they may still give me a smaller part. Or maybe even King understudy."

"You'll do great, mate." Isaac patted his shoulder but couldn't keep down a proud smile.

Oscar cautiously waddled onto the stage with a patchy red cape waving behind him. He adjusted his yellow crown. Oscar closed his eyes to calm his nerves, but then he stumbled on his own cape and nearly fell over. Oscar launched into the song, his voice cracking but full of heart. He took long breaks between some of the lines.

The teachers looked at each other, confused. They couldn't tell if he was trying to be impactful or if he had forgotten the lines.

Oscar waved his arms for the big finish.

"I gave my people all I could,

Did I cast my Shadow for good?"

Oscar ended with a proud smile across his face. He glanced at Isaac, but the ayleen looked worried.

"Look out!" Isaac yelled.

Oscar spun around just as an enormous pink balloon expanded from behind the castle. It inflated into the shape of a cat, its pink belly stretching as it floated upward. It got stuck between the canvas backdrop and the castle tower, but it kept expanding until it burst with a thunderous echo that rattled through the cathedral. The shockwave tipped the castle's tower over, which knocked against the castle wall. The whole set wobbled and then toppled down to thud against the stage, inches away from Oscar's stubby tail. He screamed as he leapt out of the way.

"Rex! Uly!" David yelled, waving digital paint at the air. "Show yourselves, you little space rats!"

A pebble plunked into a pond, causing a school of orange dragon fish to scatter. The water rippled, its peaks sparkled in Dawn's sun.

"This is real, you know," Professor Wishe said, her voice soft and kind.

"We're in the code world," Jono said, peering into the pond, watching the fish slowly return from their hiding spots under rocks and lily pads.

"We are, but we are also using a channel in the Empress' Eyes. We can manipulate the world as we perceive it, but that is the real burning sun out there, and this hill is as real as if we were at Dawn ourselves."

In the distance, Jono spotted a couple having a picnic.

"We aren't alone then."

Wishe smiled pleasantly at the sight. "They look like they're having a peaceful time. I've wondered, Jono, how does it make you feel to be helping the students from the Day? I'm sure they're very grateful for your friendship."

Jono shrugged. "They seem to be doing okay, mostly. Both Ends are so different from each other. I'm not surprised they feel confused about how we do things in the Dark. And we all need to get to know each other better, or we may go to war again."

"That's a logical answer, but not a feeling."

"I feel . . ." Jonothon sighed. "Stressed. Responsible. I feel like it's the right thing to do, so I have to do it, but really I just want to be left alone and hide in a cave."

"How do you feel about Suriana?"

"I . . . I don't know."

They sat in silence for a moment, letting the Dawn's light warm them.

"Let's move on, shall we?" Wishe's hollow form floated up then over the pond. "I want to spend some time this wake in meditation. How does that sound?"

Jono shrugged.

"Wonderful. We'll start by closing our eyes."

"Why don't we turn the sun off?" Jono replied.

Wishe frowned. "I want you to feel this world and choose to focus on senses other than your sight."

Jono tucked one leg under the other as he sat. Wishe shut her eyes and rolled her head back; Jono tried his best to mimic the pose. The coded hillside felt warm with the light, even though his skin wasn't really feeling it.

"Close your eyes, yes, even here in your mind. Breathe slowly, just like you were taught to do when you were young. In through the nose, out through the mouth."

Jono breathed slowly.

The world around them filled with the sounds of distant life. A bird chirped in a faraway tree. A brook babbled nearby.

"Be calm and allow your mind to observe yourself. How does your body feel?"

Jono felt a weight on his shoulders. His neck was tense and his legs sore. "I feel heavy. Powerless. There's too much of everything." He probed deeper into himself. "Unanswered questions. I'm drowning in them."

"What are they about?"

"Everything." Jono's face strained as he tried to relax. "Polari. The academy. The Tombs. Life. The whole universe. Angels. Stories. I don't know what is real."

Jono paused to let Wishe comment, but when she didn't say anything, he continued. "I met a man out in the frozen woods. He says he is Edgar No Eyes, or Niles, I don't know. It's impossible, but there's something familiar about him. It's like crazy old Edgar No Eyes is younger and alive. But I saw him die."

Wishe let the comment hang in the air. "Let your mind relax and see what's in front of it. Don't judge or explain, just let your worries have their say."

Jono let his mind go. He envisioned a crowd of students in the halls of Windom. They were chatting and shouting but silent in his mind.

"Observe the world as it truly is," Wishe said, her voice now distant, barely audible. "A storm of notions, and below that are the containers for these notions. People, things, places, ideas. If you strip away the meaning we put on them then they are simply what they are, notions moving through a sea of time."

The students faded in and out. They were pieces in a vast puzzle of rock carved by ancient machines into a school, or a city full of countless other stories playing out all at once.

"Look deeper," Wishe whispered, "and you will find that matter is merely energy folded over itself. We're all matter built upon infinite layers of ourselves. We look down from the crest of our tower at an endless sea of our being. Most wakes we only see the hull and not the mechanix below. What do you see when you look at the world?"

Jono breathed in. "I see people. They're so caught up in the surface, like they're lost in a fog but can't sink below or rise above it. I'm surrounded by people that don't know where they are and never question what's happening around them. Before the Keeper, people thought the other End of the world was evil. They hated magic and didn't question it. Just like the Day despised mechanix. But now everyone finds new things to not question. We study the other End's culture, but we don't ask *why*. We spend all our time wondering about who likes who or how to impress our teachers. We're in the middle of a game inside a game, and no one is looking past the next turn."

The sounds of the world faded around them as Jono lingered in limbo.

"Have you heard of the Angels' Masquerade?" Wishe asked.

"My mom read it to me when I was little. There's a girl in a cloud castle who is alone, and she finds happiness in an imaginary world."

"Stories have a way of becoming more than just words the instant they are read. They live in our minds, just like the information from our senses. The stories are transformed in our minds, and they seep into our societies. We are a collection of stories, observed and imagined. Psychologists have studied the process of how the mind willfully plays tricks on itself. Just like when you stare at a stone wall and your mind makes shapes out of the tiny bumps, so too does the mind make meaning out of stories. We can see a tree and know what defines it, but we also add meaning and stories to the data our skin, eyes, and ears send us. The tree becomes a reminder of a first kiss beneath the willow branches. Being around it makes our bodies feel the benefits of that memory."

"So nothing is truly real? It's all an illusion," Jono said.

Wishe let a warm wind breeze through the code world before replying. "Is the illusion real? Even if it's different than what we think it is?"

"It's like we're blind," Jono said, his eyes still shut tight. "There is a world around us, but we don't see it for what it is. We miss things."

"Just like the girl and her angelic self in the parable, it is *we* who create our own world. What we choose to see and choose to ignore. As the story goes, a child is conflicted between her inner self and with the world she wants to see. In psychological terms, an Angels' Masquerade refers to the level of internal projection a person invests in their worldview. Everyone does it to some extent, and in many ways, we are who we are because of the projections of value we put on the world."

"We're all liars, then," Jono said.

"Just because something isn't literally true, doesn't mean it's without value. However, when a person's masquerade conflicts with the world around them, it can cause incredible harm both physically and mentally."

"Like the Tombs," Jono said. "They see the world as an evil place that needs to be destroyed."

"If we're all liars, then who are we to say they are wrong?" Wishe said, challenging him with the idea.

That thought cut into Jono's gut. He was certain there was a real answer, something to prove the Tombs were wrong, but he couldn't craft a reply that wasn't built on some type of belief as well.

Across the distant hills of space and time, a gong sounded.

"Our time is up," Wishe said. "How do you feel?"

"Good," Jono said, opening his eyes then frowning. "That's a lie. I'm tormented. I'm not ready. I need to have an answer."

"Take your time," Wishe replied as she stood then floated to stand beside Jono, "but be careful. Delving too deep into your mind can be a dangerous maze within a maze. Every layer you go deeper, the harder it is to find your way out. I've been your tether thus far."

"I know my way around the code world."

"You do," Wishe conceded. "Much better than most. But everyone lies to themselves about something. Confidence is a powerful thing, but doubt can keep you alive. Some patients lose themselves in the world they build in their minds, especially those suffering from emotional pains. It's the Angels' Masquerade in literal practice. Extracting such a mind is not easy. The damage can be permanent."

"I won't go any deeper," Jono replied with a calm smile. "I just want to sit here and think."

"It is peaceful here." Wishe smiled. "If you need me, all you have to do is call out. I'm only a whisper away."

Jono nodded and waited until Wishe's already ethereal body disappeared.

He looked around the Dawn. If he was in one part of the Eyes of Eies, there could be access to more of what the Empress could see. He couldn't sit idly by. He needed to know what was happening with the Tombs, and this could be his only chance.

Jono caught a sliver of a star twinkling away from the Dawn's horizon. With a wave of his arms, the patch of earth flew toward the tiny star. Through the crack in the star, he heard voices whispering. He pulled himself up to the star and looked through it like a window.

He had a view into the throne room of the Crown. The Empress sat on her throne of black cables as the image of three terralunans hovered in front of her.

"It has been an appropriate amount of time," snarled a gray-skinned terralunan, whose face was hidden under the hood of a purple cloak. "We must see for ourselves."

"I do not think that is wise," the Empress replied.

"We have been far more lenient than the contract required. Make this so. You do not want to test us, Empress."

The Empress rose swiftly and glared at the three cloaked figures. "You have no idea what I know or what I am capable of. You may sit on your pebble like a throne, but we both know how your lives teeter on oblivion. No one trusts you, and the noose you have fitted around your own necks is growing tight. Do not test me, sir."

"There is no conflict in our hearts," said the terralunan. "But this must be done. We need to see for ourselves how well this process is transpiring. Security is far stronger here than on your planet. With this gift, we will return to you what your heart desires most."

"In time," added another

"Yes, in time."

The Empress did not move, and in that lack of motion Jono saw true struggle. "Now," she said. "And I will institute my own security of which you will not question."

The three terralunans bowed. "Your needs will be met, so long as our requirements are fulfilled as well."

The Empress sat again. "Then it is agreed. Good wake."

The terralunans disappeared, leaving the Empress alone in her throne room. She held a stern look, but in the corners of her veiled eyes Jono saw worry.

Jono left the code world wondering what the rulers of land and space plotted while the rest of the world carried on below them.

Chapter Fourteen

The Tales that Dead Men Tell

Cid surveyed the maze of wrinkles presented to him by the mirror on the wall of his apartment. He wiped a smudge of grease off his forehead.

"You look great, Uncle," Keiko said from across the room as she polished a metal breastplate. Jono was nearby, working on his costume.

Cid squinted. "I look haggard and old, but it's sweet of you to say. How much do you know about Professor Ism?"

Keiko shrugged. She put down her work and came to stand in front of Cid, adjusting his crooked bowtie for him. "I've only had Professor Thoags for codeistics. He's more of a mech code specialist."

"Professor Ism is brilliant at theoretical codeistics," Jono said as he cut a large piece of blue cloth while Forge tugged at the edges. "I think she's also helping Professor Helios with some project at the Pathaganon."

"I don't think my uncle is worried about her teaching skills," Keiko grinned.

"Ah, right." Jono had to think a moment. "She's about the nicest teacher at Windom. She won the student's Teacher Appreciation Award my second year."

"She can't stop talking about *you*, Wyer," Cid said as he tried to remain still during Keiko's continued primping. "A mathometry prodigy, she says." Cid checked his teeth in the mirror. "The best codeist she's ever taught."

Jono's cheeks flushed. He turned from Cid and Keiko. "She's just being nice."

Cid paused. "Is she a *polite* nice or a *genuine* nice?"

Jono shrugged.

"You could do worse than polite nice," Keiko said.

"At least with polite she may go easy on me. The rust on my dating skills is getting . . . rusty."

"You'll be fine!" Keiko said. "Just be friendly, and if you can't think of anything to say, ask her a question about herself."

Cid pulled his niece into his arms and kissed her forehead. "How did I get so lucky to have you in my life? You have your mother's spark in your eyes. She was a brilliant codeist. Did I ever tell you that?"

"No," Keiko said, giving Jono a look of knowing embarrassment. "That bit is new."

"My sister could write the stars with code." Cid boasted as he released Keiko from his embrace then wrapped an arm around her. "When we were about your age she would make the most elaborate code worlds and share them across the Line. Epic adventures all over time and space! Do you remember when I would read you stories like that?"

"About Captain Nevers and the Star Hydra?"

"You were so scared the Hydra was going to eat the Earth and poop us out."

"That *was* terrifying for a kid."

"Ayame must have made hundreds of little code adventures back in those wakes. There may even been some fragments that survived the Great Line Crash, but that was twenty five years ago. That was all before she met your father and got infected with his passion for biochemix archeology. It's a funny thing, time. Like it was only three blinks ago that I was tagging along with their expeditions, a little baby girl strapped to her chest. And now . . ." Cid looked at the clock. "Now, I'm late. Where did I put my mask?"

"Here it is." Jono handed Cid an ornate mask that only covered the eyes and forehead. It was a black and red monstrous face with horns that covered his ears and curled over his head.

Cid placed the mask over his face. "How do I look?"

"Elegant and terrifying," Keiko said.

"Are you sure you two are okay taking Forge with you?" Cid asked.

"He's part of our costume," Keiko said. "Aren't you, Forgypoo?"

Forge barked his approval.

"Don't wait up." Cid winked at them.

✪

Greenhouse clouds clung to the penthouse tower like a thick fog. Gray mist rolled in with a ghastly life of its own as eerie growls and howls echoed through the smoky veil. A wizard, a knight, and a one-foot tall furry dragon entered through arched trees and stepped onto a grassy lawn decorated in dangling webs and zombified hands reaching out of the grass.

Jono scratched his chin beneath the long white wizard's beard that was strapped to his face.

"What vile creatures does Isaac have lurking here, I wonder?" Jono said as he waved his wizard's staff before him. "Nothing more ferocious than you, right, Forge?"

Forge flapped his artificial wings and floated over the grasping hands.

"Let them come!" Keiko roared, waving her fake sword lit with fiery lights. "My spellblade has yet to taste the sweet dessert of monster flesh!"

"Boo!" Isaac leapt out from the bushes beside the massive front front door. He wore large claws over his hands and his body was wrapped in slimy weeds. His green, scaly body was painted white and gray to make him look like a pale corpse.

"What are you supposed to be?" Jono asked while Forge growled from between his legs.

Isaac gasped. "Don't tell me you've never seen Bog of the Twisps? It's a Hollow's Eve classic! When a mysterious fungus infects a cemetery in the Twisps, *the dead rise once more*!"

Jono shrugged. Isaac shook his head in pity and wrapped an arm around his shoulder.

"Simply tragic, mate. After you've said your hellos, find me and I'll take you to the theater room. You have to, at least, see the opening scene. It is cinematic history! Oscar's already around somewhere and David's family stopped by as well. I'll warn you, David is the ghost of some famous painter, Ichabod Stock, but no one else knows who that is, so just pretend like you're familiar with him, okay?"

Keiko and Jono nodded. In ten seconds, they'd both blinked through the Line to research Stock's famous dancing layers style and his most famous painting, the Vortex of Saint Mariah's Eyes.

Beyond the ghastly decorated door, the inside the penthouse was a wide room with clear walls showing off a stunning view of the city. Guests mingled in the living room and across a balcony that wrapped around the tower. Projections washed over the walls, with zombies marching and shadowy dragons chomping down on the guests. The projections shifted the scene; one moment they were inside a dank cavern and the next it morphed into a decrepit mountaintop castle.

Eloise Ohm stood on the base of a marble statue in the center of the room and tapped on her glass to get everyone's attention. She was dressed in a business suit, but half of her body was painted to look burned and peeling.

"Thank you! Thank you all for coming," Eloise shouted. "I would love to take all the credit for this fantastic set up, but that blame lies with the creative and disturbing vision of my husband, Osfred!"

Isaac's father waved to the crowd. His werewolf costume of tattered shorts and shirt with large tuffs of gray fur poking out held equal amounts of quality and fatherly cliché.

"To our dear friends from the Day," Osfred said as he raised his glass, "you may be thinking to yourself that this Hollow's Eve custom of ours is strange, silly, and at times inexcusably juvenile. You are right on every count, but have fun all the same!"

The crowd cheered and clapped.

Behind Jono, Doctor Stone arrived, barely squeezing through the door in a white toga wrapped around his metal body. He wore a ring of oak leaves crowning his brow with the tiny Zunn Mu resting on his head with a crown of her own.

The crowd was full of odd costumes. One woman in a red devil costume walked by, holding a leash on another woman dressed like an angel. A man came cloaked in black with gold chains around his wrists and ankles. His face was a pale blue, and he held a scythe with the name Suneater carved into its flimsy blade.

"I am the Lord of the Infinite Abyss!" the man bellowed. "Bow before the fallen angel, Attrayer!"

The crowd hollered and clapped as this mythologically accurate portrayal as Attrayer pranced around the party, sprinkling stardust that popped green and purple around him.

"I recall that Hollow's Eve was a much tamer event in Polari," Aquinas said as he met Jono a table covered in appetizers. The tumnkin was dressed in his official Fellowship robes. "I used to hole up in the cabin and avoid such sacrilege, but now that I'm the Fellowship's World Peace council representative and Eies' only fateriarch, I have an obligation to be social at these. . . cultural events."

"It's a hard life," Jono joked. "Invited to all the fancy parties and having to pretend like you enjoy it."

Aquinas nodded without noticing the sarcasm in Jono's voice.

Aquinas sipped a cup of punch as he gave wary stares to passing guests. "Truly, Jonothon, all these devils and monsters and corrupted angels make me nervous. It's not wise to goad the real powers that be with such flagrant disrespect."

Despite Aquinas's caution, the rest of the guests wildly enjoyed themselves. Osfred danced with Forge hopping around him on his hind legs and even Doctor Stone shook his metal parts on the dance floor.

Jono watched the crowd from his seat in the corner. They all looked so happy, chatting and drinking and smiling at each other. In that moment there were no Tombs to fight and no pox to cower from.

A glimmer of light caught his eye, as Suriana stepped through the door dressed in a shining white gown with feathered wings. She was a radiant star in a sea of darkness.

Riley peered out from behind her in a mech costume made out of painted cardboard. Murphy Wumples completed the trio in a nasty zombie sand worm costume with a long tail that dragged on the floor. Jono waved, and Suri beamed at him. The others looked relieved to know someone at the party.

"Ibn Sheik Suriana, you are as transcendent as ever." Aquinas took off his hat and bowed.

Suri curtsied back at him. "Thank you, fateriarch Aquinas. Isn't Hollow's Eve such a delightful custom?"

"Delightful is one word for it." Aquinas forced a smile. "If you'll excuse me, I need to save Chancellor Viscariot from what looks like a Sphinx that seems to be indulging her drink too much."

"I love your mech suit, Riley," Jono said. "Really looks authentic!"

"I made it myself," Riley said proudly. "Also, Keiko helped. See these loose wires? I've gone haywire and I'm on a rampage! If we were in the Day, this would be the scariest costume by far!"

Riley stomped around in a circle.

"Hollow's Eve is such a peculiar wake," Suriana said as she got a look at the other guests and their costumes. "How did this start?"

Jono waved his wizard-robed arms for them to come closer, "Gather round and I'll tell you the tale that dead things tell. Long, long ago, before aliens and dryads and scaldios appeared on Earth, when humans were slowly evolving, there were terrible plagues and famines that nearly eradicated our species before we'd even left the planet! Back then, they didn't know a lot about the world, so they were afraid that all the dead humans would come back to life one wake out of the year as hollow ghosts with unfinished business in the world!

"On Hollow's Eve, we prepare to meet the dead by learning about the people in our past that did amazing things so their legacies can be built upon by the people that are still living."

"Plus we just try to scare each other!" Keiko said as she pounced onto Jono's back. The two tumbled over each other laughing.

"Yeah, there's that," Jono said once he'd righted himself. "But while a lot of people have fun with scary monsters and such, it's just in the spirit of Hollow's Eve to dress as someone in the past or characters in stories. As a kid, I dressed up as Illius a few years in a row. David over there is a famous painter. I think he painted the murals inside Saint Newton's cathedral hundreds of years ago. Look, there's Oscar in a completely unscary costume."

Oscar walked up, wearing the same king's costume he wore to the opera tryouts. "I'm King Heart from the Ides of Decsomber." Oscar waved his cardboard-tube scepter at Murphy.

"It's brilliant. You would be a fantastic King Heart," Suri said, giving him a curtsy.

"What are you supposed to be?" Oscar waved his scepter at Murphy.

"It's the scariest thing I could think of," Murphy said defensively. "In Al Jebra, sand worms lurk beneath the ground, sleeping for centuries. But the wake when Attrayer returns from the Pit, they will stir from their death-like sleep and swallow cities whole!"

Oscar nodded his royal approval. "Sounds scary. You want to go on the ride?"

"What ride?" Riley and Murphy asked in unison.

"That." Oscar pointed to a line of people that went out on to the balcony. Just then a green dragon rollercoaster car whisked by with its passengers screaming in delight.

The three left Jono and Suri alone by the punch bowl. The two of them smiled at each other as Jono served Suri a cup of punch.

As Jono was pouring, he spotted a shadowy figure crawl along the ground. The shadow surrounded the woman in the devil's costume, creeping silently behind her. David's younger sister Ulysses screamed from beneath the black cloak, and the woman yelped in fright. Her bubbly drink flung into the air and splashed Uly's twin Rex in the face.

Suri leaned against Jono. "You and Keiko are nice to dress as Day Enders for Hollow's Eve."

Jono shrugged. "I've been mistaken for a wizard before. I figured I might as well embrace my fate."

"The beard is very becoming on you," Suri said with a tug on the unrealistic hair.

Jono stroked his beard. "Thanks. It's nice not having to shave one wake a year and just let it all grow out."

"All this after only after one wake?" Suri replied coyly.

"It's a condition passed down in my family for generations." Jono shrugged like it was nothing. "It comes from an ancient witch's curse. Poor old lady was jealous of the Wyer family's world famous good looks so she cast this blight on us."

"That sounds like a horrible ordeal. It does explain how you are barren of any physical feature that is even remotely attractive. So tragic."

"I appreciate your sympathy," Jono sneered as he held out his pointed hat. "I'm taking donations to help ease the burden of Ugly Witch Curse for children across the Dark End."

"I'd love to ease their suffering. In fact, in the Day, we have an ancient technique that may very well cure them."

"Is that so? And what could you possibly have in the Day that could cure such a terrible affliction?"

"We've kept it secret for centuries, but seeing as we are all friendly Ends now, I suppose I could share a secret or—"

The building began to rattle and shake around them. Lights flickered as the punchbowl wobbled off the table and shattered in a super nova of pink juice and glass.

Outside, the dragon roller coaster screeched to a halt as it gripped to the rails.

"It's the pox!" someone screamed.

"Get to cover!" yelled another.

Aquinas darted underneath a table as the building shook and was quickly joined by the terrified crowd. He dug through his cloak, looking for his staff as he mumbled a verse from the Biblios. "'And thus the earth did tremble as the gates of the Pit cracked open to unleash the wasteful legions of Oblivion upon the innocent!'"

Aquinas pulled out his staff, its crystal glowing brightly. He held it up, its bright light seemed to distract and calm the people around the room.

After a few moments, the shaking stopped. Aside from the mess of food and juice on the floor, everyone was alright.

Osfred stared at Aquinas' staff. "What was that? The light was mesmerizing."

"Everything's fine," Eloise said. "It was just an earthquake. The Line is ticking all about it. Our buildings are very secure. Unfortunately, punchbowls are not so well designed." She snapped her fingers, and skinny bots darted from the walls to clean up the mess.

Osfred raised his glass as he crawled out from below the table. "I told you that we throw the most exciting parties!"

✿

Late into the sleep hours, people were cleaning up after the earthquake and sobering themselves from Hollow's Eve parties. A few overly imbibed individuals cheered out of their windows that they successfully survived the end of the world.

As Keiko, Jono, Isaac and Forge made their way back to Windom, they stopped at a crowd that had gathered in Starfall Square.

"What's going on here?" Isaac pushed through the crowd to get a look.

A gleeful Edgar Niles had climbed onto the statue of the Angel Ariam. He stood on the open stone book held in the statue's hands as he waved and yelled at those around him.

"The coming of the pox has been foretold, I tell you!" Edgar shouted. "I told it to you centuries ago, in a past life, when my form was strong and handsome and people would listen! I have died and returned to remind you that the pox is unrelenting. It is a curse, making the world go mad in payment for our sins! It is the abyss above us, hungry for the thriving life we hold so precious. If we open our hearts to the sirens of Oblivion, if we dare to peek into that chasm, the Pit will swallow us whole! Verily, I told you this all was coming, as is written in The Old Book!"

The crowd roared with laughter at the sight of the gangly madman. A voice shouted from the gathering audience. "If you are an angel, prove it! Show us your power!"

"You should know your Biblios better, sir," Edgar replied. "*I* am Athuliandros." Edgar spread his arms wide and nearly lost his balance. "The humblest of angels! A herald! A storyteller! A word weaver! The first angel to awaken and a harbinger of the things to come! Millennia ago, I wrote of my crusade to the Gates of the Veil at Lailet Dem and how all must follow the Narrow Path back to our creators. I warned you then that the pox would test you!"

Jono, Keiko, Isaac, and Forge pushed through the crowd to get a better view.

Edgar struggled to maintain his balance while he flipped through the pages of his biblios. "The Neo Testament of Athuliandros, chapter seventeen, verse three: '*And lo, did the spirit of the angel that resided within me whisper many things, visions of the future that awaits the world along the Narrow Path. Terrible catastrophes will begin to be witnessed. The people will fear the loud cracking in the sky and the burning of flesh. A growing scar would shatter across the earth in waves and in spots, and the people would know the coming of the fallen angel when fear returns to their hearts.'* There you have it!" Edgar smiled, confident in his case. "The fear of the pox that shakes the world this wake, written by my hand in ages past!"

"Reading stories doesn't prove anything," shouted someone in the crowd.

"You want proof?" Edgar said with a mad grin. "Proof is coming! The other angels, they have powers far beyond me. When the angel Shiva awakens, her power will shake the earth! Her power can protect you from all that you fear."

"The only thing we fear is the pox!"

"Then you should rest easy, my sister." Edgar smiled wide. "Rest knowing that once Shiva is awakened, she will raise her hand, and *lo*! She will hold the pox still and banish it from the sight of the world."

"I'll believe that when I see it!"

"You will! You will! All will see it! All will believe it!"

Amidst the crowd, a city guard bot transformed from a bench beside the fountain. It approached Edgar as non-aggressively as it could.

"Sir, would you please come with me?" the guard said in its robotic voice. "Your doctors inform us that you have not returned for checkups since you got your new arm and leg installed. They just want to make sure everything is working properly."

"You must not peer too deeply into the body of an angel!" Edgar replied, fear and uncertainty cracking his voice. "I am pure! I am the perfected human state! You cannot probe into the workings of your makers!"

"Mister Niles, please," the stone bench robot replied. "We have hot food and a soft bed waiting for you."

Edgar tried to ignore the guard and turned back to the crowd. "All will know the truth and the might of the angels! We will bring peace unto the world! As the others awaken they will bring unity to this fractured sphere!"

"Edgar, please don't struggle." The city guard's booster jets on its feet flared and it floated over to the raving man. "I'm just going to carry you somewhere safe, where you can rest."

Edgar's frail body was no match for the guard's mechanical strength.

"Have faith my brothers and sisters!" Edgar shouted as he was lifted into the air and carried off into the distance. "Sleep peacefully knowing that the Age of Angels is upon you!"

As the spectacle disappeared, the crowd dispersed and went back to their parties.

Isaac pointed at them. "You see this? Crazy is dangerous. Even here in the heart of the Dark, you would think we wouldn't let mad stories infect our ability to reason. Even here, crowds gather around a crazy man claiming to be a super powered immortal that can see the future!"

Jono shrugged. "People like drama."

"*A scar will shatter across the earth . . .*" Keiko mumbled.

"It's insane," Isaac said with a dismissive wave of his hand. "That could be anything. A psychological scar, an earthquake, a biological infestation? Nature has always been trying to kill us off in imaginative ways. Plagues and meteors and famine. You can't justify a prophecy that everyone knows would happen! And a loud cracking in the sky?" Isaac laughed. "Like ancient people never got scared of thunder and lightning before?"

"Why does the world keep treating mythology like it's real history?" Jono said as he stared sadly at the frail man carried up and between the buildings and greenhouse clouds.

"I don't know, mate," Isaac said as he put his arm over Jono's shoulder. "The world is a crazy place."

Keiko sighed. "Poor, crazy Edgar No Eyes."

Chapter Fifteen

The Shadowy Brooch

Freya tossed a pebble over the edge of the globall sphere. It was lost in the shadows deep in the cavern.

"I'm starting to have second thoughts," she said.

Keiko grabbed her shoulder. "About how your life has been wasted not playing globall until now?"

The pebble finally clattered against the distant ground. Freya winced. "More like how I don't want to die without the sun on my skin."

"You'll have plenty of time to choose exactly how you'd like to die. Look around us. There are hundreds of gargoyles just itching to swoop down and catch a falling player."

"Catch a falling Dark Ender, maybe."

"They're bots! They do what they are programmed to do. Trust me."

Freya frowned at the exuberance of Keiko's insistent friendship.

"That too is asking for a well of faith."

"Alright, Roariors!" their coach called out. "Let's play!"

The players took their positions on opposite sides of the globe. A siren blasted and the round began. Keiko's half of the Roariors made quick work claiming their starting territory on the globe. In the first round, their team had secured three towers, but Baisly Ming's side won two of their own, unlocking an ice gun and grappling glove.

In the next round, Freya deactivated one of Baisly's towers, causing the grappling glove to shut down just as Wendy Var was swinging for the Star Tower. She flailed in the air for a moment before a gargoyle swung her into its stony arms.

Keiko cheered. "That's the type of sieging action we need from the rest of you clunkers!"

A smile of pride slipped onto Freya's unsuspecting face just before a blast of ice hit her in the shoulder, freezing her to the ground.

Baisly rushed over, blasting ice as Freya did her best to avoid getting covered. "Looks like the new sieger's going to be out!"

Another blast froze her free hand to the field. Freya flared the fire on her hair. A wave of flame rippled over her body and her hand began to burn. The ice melted just enough for her to break free. Freya rolled out of the way just as another ice blast landed behind her. She waved, and a wall of pyrefire erupted between them. The next ice blast melted into a spray of mist before it could get close to her.

"Hey!" Baisly yelled. "No spells, burnt brain!"

Freya picked herself up. "Pyrefire's not a spell. It's magically infused in my DNA. There is no casting involved."

"Time out!" Baisly snarled. "What do the rules say about magic anyway?"

Keiko frowned. "We can't use installed buffs, so any type of magic is out."

"See! That's cheating. All powers need to be unlocked from towers. You can't use your flame against the ice gun." Baisly pointed the gun at her. "So take your blast like a soldier."

"I'm not going to *be* a soldier," Freya replied. "I'll be dubbed a *knight,* and no knight yields to their enemy."

The floating globe deactivated. It floated down to its pedestal, and the machine inside it when silent.

"Great work, baby knight. You broke it," Baisly grumbled.

"This is gizmos," Keiko said. "We still have the globe reserved for an hour."

Across the stadium, a cloaked figure waved at them.

"Who's that?" Freya asked.

Keiko's eyes turned green. "It's Helios. I haven't seen her all year."

"What does she want?"

A message pinged in Keiko's brain. "Something big. Roariors take a break. Come on, Freya, let's see what's ticking."

A fleshy hand grabbed the edge of the roof, and a metal wire followed by wrapping itself around a stone statue of a ponderous woman looking silently out at the city below.

Commander Grail pulled himself onto the rooftop with Jonothon hanging from his wires above him.

"Tower climbing is a dangerous sport," Jono said. "Especially with your fleshy arms."

"Not everyone has spy wires to swing them around, Wyer," Grail said. "I need to work these arms along with the rest of my fleshy muscles. It's not easy walking around with power gear arms all wake."

"They would make climbing easier."

Grail nodded as he caught his breath. "Machines do help, but natural climbing is worth the effort. To feel the burn of your muscles and the sweat of exertion. We are chemical machines, Wyer, and exercise keeps us operating effectively."

Jono's wires swung him up to the next building ledge. Tower climbing paths were marked all over the city. With a quick blink from the Line, their eyes projected green guides that steered them up uneven stone blocks and handgrips up towering brick walls. In the earlier eons of the city, people would climb on their own, following the path their eyes could find.

Jono and Grail had started on a moderate path in the dank caves of the East Trench and they had already climbed past the greenhouse clouds. The trail kept them going all the way up the East side of the city to a viewpoint at the top of the city's mountain range.

"If you wanted a nice view, Commander, you could always just look out the windows in Windom."

"Where's the effort in that? The greatest treasures in this world are the ones we earn with our greatest efforts. Ease wipes the gleam off the most beautiful things. Come on, we are almost there."

Jono stowed his wires and followed the commander, climbing with his hands and feet. His fingers ached as they inched their way upward, but each meter felt like he was overcoming a great challenge.

"Have you been watching Edgar rant around the city? With him and the Fellowship sermons, we're drowning in angel stories," Jono said as they climbed between two buildings in a narrow alley. "People are starting to think angels are going to save us from the pox."

Grail grabbed the edges of two close rooftops and lifted himself up. "Dark Enders will need a little more than a young version of Edgar No Eyes to convince them the supernatural is real. Still . . . people are attracted to the dramatic, so they are listening to the conversation. Once that novelty wears off, we will hopefully have more interesting cultural exchanges with the Day. They have a rich history of art, philosophy, and naturalism. We would benefit from considering those things a byte deeper than we currently do."

"It was the Tombs that really started it," Jono said. "Before that poem in the sewers, people didn't take

Aquinas' sermons seriously. Then after the earthquake, more people are paying attention. Whatever is going on, the Tombs *are* part of it."

"If that is true, what is it that you think we should do?"

Jono lifted himself up another ledge. "Anything we try is risky. How do you shut down the Tombs, end the Pox, and keep peace between both Ends? We don't even know what they're trying to do. I think we wait and see and be prepared for it to all go bad."

"Your family lived a path of the angels. Is that an interest you still pursue?"

Jono surveyed the cityscape and took a deep breathe. He'd almost forgotten how his personal life was open knowledge for Grail. "Children don't choose the beliefs of their parents. How's Raina?"

"Professor Helios is doing fine. Thanks for asking." Grail was silent for a moment, and—perhaps for the first time—it seemed like he didn't know what to say next. "Do you have someone special in your own life?"

Jono shook his head. "Not special like that."

"Really?" Grail frowned. "That is odd. I hear your name come up frequently in reports on in-class messages being passed between students."

Jono tried not to look too interested. "Oh? By who?"

"Confidentiality, Wyer. It's the burden of my station."

Jono huffed out a short breath. *Confidentiality, at least when it doesn't concern my privacy.* "And I thought you believed that an informed people were a responsible people."

"The truth is evident if you have the eyes to see it. If I give it to you, you will know the shape but not the subtleties of it. You must discover it on your own to truly understand it. Speaking of your self-discovery, how are your introspection sessions with Professor Wishe going?"

Jono shrugged and gazed out at the vast glowing city. He wasn't sure why Grail was asking him—he could go to Wishe for that information, or just spy on the sessions if he had the desire to do so. "The world is insane."

"Hah!" Grail laughed as he landed beside Jono. "Now that you've accepted this fact, you can make some real progress."

Jono dangled from the bottom of a balcony with his wires holding him up. "What's going on with the Tombs?"

Grail sat on the lip of the rooftop. "Why? Do you have new intel to share?"

"Why do you always deflect my questions about them?" Jono took a seat next to him. He felt so small next to the massive commander, but Grail's tone made him feel almost like a peer, a friend. "I should be helping you."

"You should be *living*. The Tombs are the problem of six million of the most highly trained professionals with the largest resources in history at their disposal. I know you want to help, Wyer, but the best way you can do that is resolve the turmoil within you. Truly know yourself and know what you believe in. Trust me. You will be stronger in the future by building your identity upon a solid foundation."

Jono sighed. "How did you do it?"

"Focus on the fundamentals. There is a natural structure to life, but it can be hard to understand it while in the middle of all this chaos. Cut out that which does not matter and fight for what does."

"How do you know what matters?"

"You already know the answer to that. You just have to let yourself believe it."

"Stopping the Tombs matters."

"That's one place to start. Here, I have something that may help." Grail pinned a small black medallion to Jono's shirt. The oily center of the medallion looked like an intricate carving of ghastly creatures that moved on its own.

"What is it?"

"Do you want to be part of history?"

Jono squinted at him. "That strictly depends."

"You're right to be skeptical. History is marked by great leaps as well as terrible tragedies. So, let me rephrase the question. Do you want to help us defy the Tombs?"

"Absolutely."

"It is risky."

"I know those risks. I've taken them before."

"Good. How do the Tombs operate?"

Jono thought for a moment. "They trick people into being afraid and vulnerable."

"And how do we combat that?"

Jono thought for a moment. "We need to do things by surprise ourselves."

"Exactly. Let's inspire the world. Make them hopeful again. Are you ready to be surprised?"

Jono smiled. "Let's do it."

Grail snapped his fingers, and the oily center of the medallion burst into a cloak of shadow that wrapped around Jono's body. One moment Jono was sitting next to Grail on the roof top, and the next, the living shadow swept him over the edge.

Chapter Sixteen

Journey of the Ragnarok

Brick walls and stone bridges flashed past Jono as he struggled against the hold of the charging shadow. The black cloak leapt and plunged down through the city, sliding along buildings, swooping under bridges, and flying through the dark crannies of the city.

Jono tried to hold on to something, but the inside of the fel cloak was like floating on a cloud in a windy storm. From the outside, the cloak was a sleek black that melted into its surroundings like a shadow. From the inside, Jono could see the wide city through its shaded veil. A guidance system hovered in front of his face; it tracked his progress toward a yellow dot in the distance.

The shadow swept under elevated rail lines as a train rushed over them, and then slid along a spiral staircase down twenty floors. The fel cloak soared through a narrow alley and whipped around a corner as it disappeared into a crack in the mountainside.

Jono held his breath. His body just barely fit through the crack, and now he slid through a series of secret tunnels in the rock. The tunnel was pitch black, and at times he didn't know which way was up or down.

A speck of light rose in the distance. Jono burst into an open room. The fel cloak delicately placed him on his feet.

Jono wobbled as he regained his equilibrium.

"I just rode on a fel cloak," he said in a gasp.

"So did I," Isaac said, stepping out of the shadows. "Where are we?"

Jono looked around the room. Thirty nine students filled the dimly lit chamber. It didn't take Jono long to realize they were the nineteen Day exchange students and the twenty Dark End mentors.

"Why all of us?" Keiko said.

"Maybe the Tombs don't like what we've been up to," Nicklus said, his arms crossed and his chin held high. "They're going to punish us for socializing with the Day."

"We've been kidnapped!" Ammer shouted, his head lifted toward the stone ceiling. "You Dark Enders better not be holding us for ransom. The Sage will burn this city to the ground if you don't release me!"

"Does anyone have any clue as to what is going on?" Suri asked, moving to Ammer's side to offer comfort.

"It's a surprise!" Jono said with more than a hint of excitement. "I was climbing the city with Commander Grail when he sent me here. Fel cloaks are the fastest way to get around undetected. We're here so that any Tombs spies won't know where we are."

"Is something bad going to happen?" Riley asked.

Isaac went to one of the walls and examined it. "This is some kind of protected bunker."

Keiko's eyes switched to periwinkle blue. "The walls are lined with solid lead. I can't see through it, which means people on the outside can't see in. They're hiding something here."

"Yes, we are." The voice came from Raina Helios as a door in the wall slid open. The former Windom professor smirked at the crowd of students. "Want to see what it is?"

Behind Helios, the room opened into an enormous cavern with landing lights and flight deck equipment. A black ship in the shape of a dragon sat in the middle of the hanger. Three humming engines glowed blue on each of its four arms and two hind legs. Massive wings folded over its back. Technicians ran around its base, doing checks on the metal beast's tail.

"This is the secret we've been planning with the Day for two years. It is my pleasure to introduce you to the Ragnarok!"

The huge dragon ship flared its engines, its jaw creasing as if in a smile.

Helios waved them on. "Follow me, cadets. We are short on time and need to hit atmo before the announcement goes out to the world."

The cadets approached the behemoth in awe. But the squires lingered in the back in a terrified trance. Helios stopped, cleared her throat, and then waited for the startled squires to follow.

"What is this monster for?" Murphy asked.

"With those engines I bet it will have more than enough thrust!" Keiko cheered.

"Thrust for what?" Jono asked.

Keiko spun around, ecstatic. "Space!"

"Don't spoil the surprise, Kirin," Helios said as they approached the Ragnarok's side. Beneath its belly opened a platform that lifted them into the cabin. They climbed through the belly of the ship and found seats unfolding from the floor and walls.

Helios handed each of them a green pill. "Everyone take one of these and strap in."

"What's the pill for?" Nick asked skeptically.

"Gravity force nausea," Keiko said with smile. "This is going to be one burn'em ride!"

"I can't believe we are doing this," Riley said, strapping himself into one of the seats.

"Why us?" Ammer asked. "And what about the Terraloonies? Aren't they going to shoot us down?"

"Or worse." Jonothon looked at Keiko. She was the only other student that had faced the obsidian Chimera. They both knew the terrible power of the beasts that guarded the barrier to space. "They wouldn't be sending us to fight against a guardian, would they?"

"That's it. Lock it down!" Helios shut the door behind them and strapped herself in.

The Ragnarok began to shake, and the mech turned slowly around. Massive hull-bay doors cranked open from the side of the mountain, the glistening starry shroud greeting them.

The dragon ship stepped toward the gate, pawing at the edge. The bridge of the ship filled the dragon's skull as the captain peered over the edge of the cliffs below the Crown castle. Leagues of jagged mountaintops sparkled in the distance.

The Ragnarok snorted exhaust then leapt forward. Half of the students screamed as they were swept downward, while the other half held their breath. The beast's wings spread open and locked into place, the engines on its joints flared, and they swooped upward and rocketed toward the stars.

Across the planet, people were fixed to their screens. The Sage of Ages and the Empress of Eies stood side by side on the balcony of the throne room in the Crown castle. The dot that was the Ragnarok soared up behind them.

"This wake is another milestone in restoring peace and fulfilling our destiny to be a part of the galaxy," the Sage read from his script.

"Just as we must build a new path for the generations that follow us, so too must these new generations embark on a journey of discovery together," the Empress said. "This year, we have done more than begin a student exchange program to nurture the leaders of a peaceful tomorrow."

The Sage pointed his staff at the stars. "We have sent these brave young friends on an unprecedented path to show the world, and all those under Sol, that we are ready to return to the stars once more!

"While the blockade of Earth remains in place, the Lords of Terralunis have permitted a generous first step in our process to rejoin our families beyond. Students of both Ends will visit Earth's moon, to learn about the culture and history of the Terralunans and continue the peaceful path of progress that leads us back to our birthright. This is the first time a child of Earth will have set foot on the moon in over three hundred years!"

"And all of the world will be a part of it. You will watch our valiant adventurers through their journey, and together, we will reclaim our destiny."

The Empress gave a chilling yet welcomed smile. "Thank you."

"May the angels watch over them."

The Ragnarok shook and hummed as it flew higher and higher into the sky. Screens on the wall displayed the outside world: White-capped mountains melted together until they seemed like one flat surface. The Earth began to bend below them. The Dark End became a dull blue haze with the specks of city lights glowing against the darkness of their End and the depths of space beyond. The gases of the atmosphere rushed and burned around them until silence swept over the ship as they left the grasp of their home planet.

The ship tilted and the engines flared again. A hint of color crept over the edge of the world as they shifted direction. The light of the Day's sun glided over the horizon. Turquoise oceans gleamed in contrast against the Dark's vast, icy tundra.

Jonothon stared in awe.

Keiko leaned over his shoulder. "We need to travel more."

Jono nodded in silent reverence. The planet was spectacular, an island of life in an infinite abyss.

"There are the ruins of the Keeper," Isaac said, pointing down at the planet. "Dawn is so different from up here."

"I can see Caer Midus," Suri called out, and the students swiped their screens to find where she was looking. Golden castles glistened against the mountainside as a tiny yellow line.

As the ship flew further away from the planet, distant metal objects orbited in the space around them.

"Burning stars!" Nick screamed as a glowing tail of snakes passed on his screen. "What was that?"

Jono leaned to see out of the windows display just as a fiery paw passed the camera. On the starboard side flew the Obsidian Chimera. Its lion face stared coldly forward. Its paw burned with hot white fire as its tail of snakes dangled behind it.

"Look over here!" Murphy squealed.

On the port side flew another guardian, the Ruby Sphinx. Gleaming gems burning red against the cusp of space festooned her golden skin.

"It's all part of the plan," Helios said. "We are going to their house, so we'll have an escort."

Chapter Seventeen

The Space Between

Floating was more difficult than it seemed. Once they broke through the atmosphere and the roaring of the gases that blanketed the Earth quieted, everyone unlocked their seat belts to test the weightlessness. The seats slid shut into the hull around them to give them room.

Students bumped into each other and bounced off the walls. A cluster of students hung together, unable to get enough room to themselves.

"I'm in space," Isaac gasped. "Real, honest space."

Keiko squealed and grabbed Jono by the shoulders, spinning him around as they floated. "Can you believe it?"

Riley held onto the wall tightly to evade the clutter of ricocheting students.

"Come float, Riley," Suriana said, beckoning her with an outstretched hand. "Push off gently with your legs and float over."

She nodded and pushed off. Nearby, Keiko grabbed Isaac by the jacket and they swung around each other before releasing and flying into opposite walls. Their antics disrupted Riley's trajectory, and she found herself bouncing off the floor and ceiling with her hands wrapped around her head.

Jono could maintain perfect control of his floating by shooting out a few spy wires to hold him in place. He showed off by walking across the floor, spy wires from his ankles holding him down as everyone else floated helplessly.

"I got you, Riley." Jono scooped her into his arms and guided her into a familiar, upright position.

Isaac bounded toward David, but he'd erected a pixel bubble. As Isaac bounced off the barrier and spun over himself, he asked, "How do pixel fields work in space?"

"The pixels cling together microscopically," David said. "Watch this." A pixel bubble expanded and sent David floating in the opposite direction. "My own little space craft."

"Welded!" Isaac said. "I need to research a chemix version of that."

"Let's keep new chemix tests to Earth, Mister Ohm," said Professor Helios. "We haven't tested the interior of the Ragnarok to deal with filtering a stray Orphean drought."

"Or a stink bomb," Oscar said with a smirk.

"I make one little chemix mix up years ago and you never stop reminding me. Mistakes are a critical part of the learning process," Isaac grumbled.

"Not when you're mistakes can blow us out into the pit of space, Ohm," Nick said, relaxing on the ceiling as if it were the floor.

Oscar opened a pack of jelly stars he kept in his pocket for emergencies and placed them floating in a line, but Nick launched off the ceiling, swooping in to gobble them up.

"Those are mine!" Oscar said.

"Watch out!" Keiko called as Nick crashed into Suri, as they both crashed toward the wall. Nick grabbed onto the ceiling as Suri braced for collision. She held her hands up, but stopped abruptly before hitting the wall. She looked down to see a metal wire wrapped around her waist.

"I've got you," Jono said.

"My hero." Suri smiled. "You've got quite the control with those things."

"I've had a lot of practice."

"Swing me!" Suri said, beaming.

Jono waved his hand and the wire from his arm swung Suriana in a circle around the cabin.

"Do me next!" Oscar shouted.

Jono grabbed Oscar with another spy wire and pulled him across the room.

"I have an idea," Jono said. "And I'm volunteering you three." More wires from Jono's arms grabbed David, Keiko, and Isaac. He moved to the center of the cabin, where wires from his shoulders locked him to the ceiling, and wires from his ankles locked him to the floor. He spun in a circle, and his five riders swung around him in a circle.

The ship shook as the engines shifted, and Jono's spinning circle broke free. They floated together, their momentum keeping them spinning. Jono sent out another wire to stop himself, but his riders swung around him, heading for a crash. David summoned his pixel bubbles to catch the two groups just before they crashed into each other.

Suri giggled as she clapped with excitement. "That is brilliant! Okay, next time, Jono, you should use your wires to shoot me as fast as you can, like a sling shot, while David catches us on the other end!"

"I like how this girl thinks," Keiko said.

For the next hour, they all played in zero gravity together with no thought of borders or past wars. They were simply children playing in a new and wondrous world.

"The seats will be coming back out," Professor Helios said. "Everyone strap in again for docking."

"Where are we going?" Isaac asked. "We can't be at the moon yet, can we?"

"Our first stop is the Einstein IV space station," Helios replied. "It's time you all had a lesson in space travel."

An enormous rotating space station orbited Earth, its three interlocking wheels spinning around a single axle. The Ragnarok approached the station among a speckling of ships and star craft that flew in and out of docking stations. It reversed its engines to slow its approach to one end of the axle. The ship's six claws grasped the station gently, but still the passengers shook as it stopped. The belly of the ship aligned with the station door and the floor of the cabin opened up to a docking portal, which appeared to be a translucent green membrane.

"Single file, everyone," Helios instructed, giving a clear field-trip vibe to the excitement pulsing through each of the students. "When you go through the portal, it is going to feel strange. First you will pass through a gelatinous membrane. This holds in the cleaning gas, which is thicker than the gasses we are floating in now. Do this one at a time."

David was the closest to the portal. He touched the transparent membrane. "It's almost like touching water, but it sticks to itself and not to me."

"Don't worry about holding your breath," Helios said. "It's oxygenated and perfectly safe."

One by one they floated into the membrane, through the cleaning gases, and into the station's brightly lit holding room.

It almost felt like swimming. Jono imagined them all as fish swimming from a fish bowl to a large aquarium, only this was a tank of air, not water.

Doors of different sizes covered every surface of the cube-shaped holding room. Bright white light filled the space. Nearly everything was off-white with a blue tint.

"Time to get sterilized," Helios said. "Pick a door that fits your size. Inside there are two compartments, one to decontaminate you, the other to decontaminate your clothes, jewelry, tech—anything not grown into your body."

"See you on the other side." Suri waved and disappeared behind a door. The blue tint on the door turned red.

Jono found a door his size with a green light. The emblem on the door was a circle with a banner in the middle which read, C.O.S.S: Coalition of Solar Space. He knew people lived on other planets and on stations like this one, but he'd never heard of the C.O.S.S.

The decontamination room was snug but left enough room to get undressed. Jono's clothes and the memory watch he kept in his pocket slipped into a waiting tube. The room's lights shifted to a dull purple, and a warm mist sprayed from the walls. It tingled all over his body, like a sauna—warm and relaxing. The misty air filled his lungs. Another wave of cooler mist cleansed the first wave. Then the mist sucked back into the walls and a bell tone told him his clothes were ready.

He dressed and stepped through the door on the other side and into the enormous axle of the space station. It was bright with more blue-tinted surfaces. The tunnel was lined with rooms between the major corridors to the three rings.

Isaac pointed at the windows to the wheel corridors. "The rotation creates centrifugal forces to simulate gravity."

"Why would I want gravity in space?" Keiko laughed. "I just escaped that infernal chain."

"Spending too much time without it would make your muscles atrophy, and you'd become a husk of flailing flesh and bone that couldn't survive a return to the planet," Isaac replied.

"You and your logical consequences," Keiko scoffed.

"Everyone follow me," Helios said, "and stick to the right side. In space it is impolite to go floating about in all directions."

Oscar floated past them in the middle of the tunnel. He smiled sheepishly.

"Case in point," Helios said with dry finality. "When you land, Mister Bohrs, float back over here and stay in line. This is a momentous occasion. The station cameras are already watching us, and so is everyone under Sol. Let's try to make a good first impression."

Helios led them down to the second wheel corridor. They went through a series of rooms where the feeling of gravity slowly increased. By the time they reached the edge of the wheel, it was almost as if they were back on Earth.

The second wheel—or as the large sign on the wall introduced it, Athena's Round—was so large it was hard to tell that it curved from the inside. The walls were a dark brown metal with comfortable teal couches and soft red carpet. Jono had imaged the whole station would be like the sterile holding bay, but all the decorations made it almost seem comfortable.

Seated on a small teal chair with purple polka dots was a gray-skinned man reading from a holographic screen. Upon noticing them, he shut the reader, which collapsed into a thin metal wand. The man stood.

"Raina, it's pleasant to finally see you in the flesh."

"Likewise," Helios replied. "Cadets, this is the C.O.S.S Undersecretary to Earth, Mister Asmodeus Fleeth. He will be preparing you for your visit to Terralunis."

"He's a terraloonie," Knox whispered.

Fleeth pretended not to hear it and bowed deeply to them. "It is my great honor to help facilitate this historical occasion. If you will follow me, we will begin the briefing on your tour."

The briefing room reminded Jono of a classroom, with large wrap-around screens and rows of desks. Fleeth waved his wand which began a presentation behind him.

"As you have noticed, we are aboard the Coalition of Solar Space's Einstein IV space station in orbit around your home planet, Earth. This station is home to fifteen thousand permanent residents and houses an average twelve-thousand transient passengers every wake. These transients come from across the colonized planets, moons, and space stations in the Sol system. Wakely life aboard the E4, as we call it, includes various sports facilities, like our system renowned Globall field, a netball court, and the gravity shifting swimming pool. The E4 offers the pinnacle of spacely comfort and service."

"What about the burning sun above the Day?" Jono said. "That must be a huge station."

"That is the most protected place under Sol." Fleeth's tone grew serious. "No one visits that. It is sacred . . . to us all. Even to those that don't know it."

"Why?" Jono asked.

Fleeth took a deep breath. "That is not for me to say. Returning to my presentation . . . you will spend the following wake preparing for your tour of Terralunis by studying our pristine cultural lineage and societal norms. You will be embarking on the tour the following wake. By way of introduction, Terralunan culture is an ancient and proud tradition that has existed in its pure form since its origination eons ago. Unlike the changing cultures of the colonists that stretch across Solar gravity, or the Dark and Day Ends of the Earth, the haven of Terralunis has protected a refined heritage of ancient humanity honored in the halls of the moon."

Nick raised his hand, and Fleeth pointed his wand at him.

"If you are all pure humanity, why are you all gray?" Nick asked.

Fleeth clasped his wand with both hands to restrain his venomous stare. "It is impolite to ask questions that would only lead to emotional disagreements. This is an excellent example of what you must *abstain* from when you arrive on the moon. Is that noted everyone? Excellent."

Fleeth waved his wand at the screens, and a map of the Terralunan moon appeared. "Now if we can get back to your lesson . . . I'm sure you will all need the extra time for additional research so that you can ask insightful and informed questions on your tour."

The largest observation cafeteria on Einstein IV was a domed atrium on Poseidon's Round. Screens covered the walls, serving as digital windows to the space outside the station. They could see the rest of the station, and as they rotated, Earth loomed above them.

The students huddled together at one table while strange varieties of people sat all around them. One green, rocky creature took half a table for itself and ate a deep fried goat, bones and all. At another table sat a group of thin, pink people with purple hair the texture of seaweed. They wrapped their arms around each other while one had a finger in a bowl at one end of their chain. The soupy food went up through their transparent skin and passed through the group as they whispered to each other and glanced at the Earthkin.

"Where do you think they're from?" Jono asked.

Isaac snapped a picture with his goggles then compared them to images on the Line. "They are ristosharns. They're primarily settled on some of Saturn's moons, but a small colony lives on Earth in a city beneath the liquid seas. They rarely come to the surface and keep to themselves in an isolated culture and economy."

"There's a sea colony in the Day?" Riley asked.

"There are tons of them," Suriana replied. "But I don't think I've seen any ristosharns before. Maybe we should visit them sometime."

"Dryads aren't so keen on going underwater," Riley said, continuing to stare at their strange eating method. When the group collectively shot her a glance, she looked down at her own food.

David nodded toward a new group that sat down at a nearby table. "Look. Humans."

Isaac scanned them. "Their coats are common uniforms for factory workers on Mars. And over there, that yeton has a blue badge. That means it works in a prison on Europa."

"What *is* that person?" Suri pointed to a blue creature with collection of tentacles below its waist, a pointed head, and four arms. "I've never seen anyone like it."

Isaac scanned it. "That's a quotos. The Line says they live primarily on Neptune and in the Kuiper Belt. They need to wear a suit to protect them from the Earth-like gravity."

"Is it male or female?"

Isaac's face scrunched with a combination confusion and interest. "Both."

"Hey, you!" The voice was deep and came from a beast of a female tuskan in a thick leather spacesuit. "You're Earthkin, ain't ya?"

She stomped over, making the students feel like a group of ants about to be squashed. She came to stand next to their table, lowering her snout to sniff them.

"I ain't never thought the wake would come." She licked her chops and smiled. "Can I take a picture with y'all?" She held out a silver orb that looked like a marble in the palm of her hand. The device opened into a bot, which whizzed into the air and began circling the Earthkins, looking for the best angle.

When none of the shocked students answered, Jono said, "Um, sure."

The tuskan lay down, as her large body spanned the length of the table.

"Okay," the tuskan said. "Smile and say, 'We're from Earth!'"

"We're from Earth!" they all said in unified discomfort. The hovering robot flashed several times, taking a slew of pictures from slightly different angles.

"Perfect!" the tuskan said with a chuckle. "This is going on my OneLife page. All of the Hildas are going to be jealous! Thanks! And congrats on finally making it back into space. We miss you crazy two Enders."

Chapter Eighteen

The Cosmodermis

Every one of them was covered in plastic wrap. Or at least it looked and felt like it. The material was clear and produced a squeak when rubbed together. Keiko's bionetic eyes were set to microscopic vision as she scanned over the vast landscape of Isaac's arm.

Swarms of tiny pixels swam through the material of the suit, constantly repairing its layers while they recycled breathable air into the thin space inside the suit.

"Hey Jono, didn't you have to wear a mask like this when you were a kid?" Keiko asked.

"That was just a beat up old miner's mask. I wish I had something as nice as this."

Asmodius Fleeth gave Helios a discouraged glance. As they traveled in the Ragnarok toward the moon, everyone was preparing to survive the sterile environment for the week-long tour.

Isaac pointed out that Freya's normally floating strands of fiery hair were pressed against her skull, making her appear as though she had a bald, glowing head.

"Don't you dare laugh," Freya snarled.

Isaac snickered. "I have no idea what you're talking about."

Freya glared and floated away.

"Look at this!" Oscar called out. "All you have to do is think *food* and it activates. Just open your mouth!" Oscar snickered as he demonstrated. With his wide mouth open, a tube of orange mush tunneled through the clear suit and shot into his mouth like a fruit smoothie shooting through a straw. "Delicious!"

"How . . . how do we use the bathroom?" Riley asked.

Fleeth pointed to a floating map with small squares glowing blue. "We have special facilities designated for the cleansing and expulsion for all none terralunan species. Your cosmodermis suits are designed to keep all extra-lunan material from contact. The cleansing rooms are the only place you can be outside of your suit. Please consult your schedule for your designated time in the cleansing facilities."

"But what if I *really* need to go?"

"Your suits are capable of processing any . . . incidental materials, but I doubt your trousers are designed to conceal the stain of evidence. I suggest you hold it. Any other questions?"

Isaac breathed deeply in and watched the translucent suit stretch around him. A breeze of air poured from the suit across his face and into his mouth. "Fascinating! How long can the suit self-sustain?"

"While on your trip to Terralunis, your suits will be recharged with all the energy and materials they need through the connection from your boots to the floor of our city," Asmodeus Fleeth explained with a condescending sneer. "As long as you stand for more than ten minutes per wake, you will be kept in perfect health. That shouldn't be a challenge, should it?"

"What if we get lost in space?" Keiko asked. "Left to float in the endless void?"

Fleeth sighed. "A cosmodermis suit can maintain healthy biological functions, depending on body size and level of strenuous activity, from forty-eight to seventy-six hours. I do trust that while you are guests in our home, none of you will behave in a manner that would warrant being shot out of an airlock. Or am I mistaken?"

"Don't these things come with jet packs?" Nick asked, turning around to try to get a look at his own back.

"You won't be *needing* jet packs," Fleeth said. "The majority of your stay will be within the city to learn about our culture and present a more sympathetic view of Terralunis to the rest of the Solar system. Each of you will be paired with a terralunan host to guide you through your education of our pristine society. Your schedules are all loaded into your cosmodermis suits and will appear as projections floating in front of you when activated.

"You will stay with your host in their cabin. You will join them for meals and participate in their jobs to assist in making Terralunis the paradise you will behold. We have struck a delicate bargain with the cold space around us, and as such, every job is critical to the health of our whole. We expect only the utmost respect for your hosts' jobs, regardless of whether it is waste recycler or meteor defense, am I clear?"

Everyone nodded, but they secretly hoped for a host as welded as meteor defense.

"Good. You will report to my office every wake for short interviews about your experience. These will accompany the footage that will be broadcast the following wake. Please do not attempt to deviate from your schedules or make any unhelpful statements while being recorded. The terralunan ruling council will be reviewing all the video prior to release so compose yourself with the grace and eloquence that we were promised. And remember, everyone under Sol will be watching."

The Ragnarok continued across the gap of space toward the moon, with the Chimera and Sphinx right beside it. As the glowing gray sphere neared, they could see that it was wrapped in rings of lights and glowing domes. The entire moon was covered in one massive city, shining against dusty gray fields between white tunnels and domes. Towers protruded from every hemisphere with glowing spheres at each peak.

As their ship approached the domes, tiny rock fragments collided with a force field around the moon.

The invisible shield flared purple as it obliterated the invading pebbles.

"I guess that makes it hard for anyone to sneak in," Keiko said.

"Or out," replied Jono.

The ship flew through illuminated purple rings that guided them through the energy field surrounding the moon. They followed a path of ships moving over the city in organized lanes. The Ragnarok stuck out against sleek white crafts that looked like flattened eggs. The guardians led them to an enormous dome that seemed to be part of some centralized complex.

"We are going to the Chronishaft," Fleeth said. "It is the heart of our city that cuts right through the center of the moon and out the other side."

The Chimera and Sphinx floated just outside a circular opening in the dome as they landed in the center of a stark white room. The Ragnarok fumed and settled in as the door shut behind them and the room began to fill with treated air. The airlock's door opened on the interior side and the ship lumbered into a sprawling hanger bay.

The Ragnarok's belly doors opened and Fleeth took a deep breath in.

"Nothing like the sweet smell of home," Fleeth said with a smile. "Miss Helios, if you will instruct the children to follow me. It is time they found out what they are here for."

Chapter Nineteen

The People of the Moon

O ut of the long tunnel windows, beyond the
white city, and past the purple-sparking
force field, Earth still lingered above them.
It was distant and small in a deep sea of black.

"Stop gawking and keep up," Nick insisted as Suri and
Jono were caught up in the wonder the view.

The white tunnels were lined with open windows. Each
section ended with a gate and a pair of potted plants. On
the walls hung old paintings from Earth's history.
Ancient royalty posed in unmoving oils and acrylics. The
stillness and finality of it mesmerized the students who'd
lived with moving art their whole lives.

A purple moss lined each side of the floor as well as a
stripe along the ceiling.

"You didn't think we'd have any plants here, did you?"
Fleeth said. "Moonmoss is a delicate creation specifically
designed to recirculate air optimized for terralunan
physiology. During your time with us, you will be

surprised at how inaccurate Earthkin stereotypes are. Here on Terralunis we have the most advanced agriculture under Sol."

"They still need soil from the Day to grow anything," Ammer whispered to Suri and Riley. "You can't grow anything on this rock without *us*."

David waved his hand in front of one of the plants, and the leaves moved without him touching them.

Oscar looked at him, surprised.

"My pixels can seep out through the suit. Double protection, just to be safe," David said.

"Good thinking," Isaac said. "I would have perfected chemix bubbles by now if I had only known we were coming!"

"You two should be careful about using our installs here," Oscar said. "They may get mad and shoot you into space."

"Then I guess we'll have forty-eight hours for you to figure out how save us, Bohrsy," Isaac said as he waved his fingers over the chemix kits installed in his wrists.

The students passed rows of hallways with other terralunans, or 'tills', that stopped and stared coldly. A child scooted behind an adult's legs and began to cry at the sight of the strange, colorful people invading his home.

"If you look out the window to your left, you can see the fourth defense tower activating." Fleeth pointed to a tower that glowed with purple power. "Whenever we have incoming debris, our defenses will either shoot a small rocket that will push it out of a collision course or we will simply blow it to pieces."

The tower fired and after a few seconds a distant rock exploded into a dust cloud that floated in the opposite direction.

"As you can see, we are not to be trifled with. Now, if you will follow me, we are almost at the Well. This is a gathering room where you will be paired with your terralunan custodian."

"What do you mean 'custodian?'" Nick asked.

"While I'm sure it appears to you that I do nothing but guide children on tours every wake, my position is actually quite important for the stability of our entire star system. Volunteers from every walk of life on terralunis have been so kind as to donate their recreation hours to house you and educated you on our culture. When we arrive, you will be paired up with them. We will meet up again for supper in the grand hall."

They stopped at a round door.

"We are staying with these people?" Murphy asked. "I didn't know I'd be staying with strangers."

"None of us knew we'd be here at all," Nick grumbled.

Fleeth leaned down to face Murphy. "I can assure you, child, you are safer here than anywhere on that little planet of yours. You will all experience what life is like here. Some of you will be housed in the tunnels with our operational neighborhoods. Others will be in the defense barracks, and a few will be housed in the governance hive. Do not expect to spend much time playing with each other while you are visiting Terralunis. We have made an exceptional allowance for you to learn about us, not cast spells at walls or whatever it is that you do."

"Do your people not spend time with each other?" Suriana asked.

"All social groups are organized by aptitude, social need, and hierarchy. It is inefficient to have these groups intermingle in most situations." Fleeth scowled at the annoying question. "Segregation is a central part of Terralunan culture and a key to our successful survival over the millennia."

Fleeth led them into the Well room, which appeared to be a small auditorium. At the center was a pool filled with translucent blue water. Around the room, terralunan men and woman gathered, all wearing thick purple robes. Everyone looked human, except for their pale gray skin. They all tried to smile pleasantly, but their sternness was evident in the awkward creases on their faces.

One till approached the group. "How do you do, Ms. Keiko Kirin?"

"You know me already?" Keiko asked.

"Oh, yes," replied the woman. "We terralunans believe in the value of preparedness. Especially for an encounter such as this."

"Too bad they don't believe in preparing us," Isaac whispered to Jono.

"My name is Wanda the Eighteenth," the till said. "If you will follow me, Keiko, I'll show you to our quarters in the bakery dome."

"Baking?" Keiko scrunched her face in confusion. "I thought I'd be paired with a mechanix expert."

"Oh, we don't bother with things you are good at down on the Prior lands. Up here, we hope to illuminate your mind with something new. Is that sufficient justification?"

Keiko shrugged. "I've never met a crescent roll I didn't like. Let's bake!"

As the cadets and squires paired up with tills, Jono couldn't help but notice the hidden scowls on their faces when they didn't think their partners were looking. He had the distinct impression that *volunteering* had a different meaning than it did on Earth.

The room eventually cleared out, except for Jonothon and one old man who slept snoring on a bench. "Excuse me," Jono said carefully, "I think you may be my custodian."

The old man snorted in his sleep, and the noise startled him awake. He shook his bald, gray head and cracked open a pair of yellow eyes.

"Don't mind me, lad. I'm just resting my eyes." He smiled, and Jono couldn't see the same scowl he'd noticed in the others. The man lifted his arm and said, "Here, help me up."

He must have been the oldest of the lot. His back was hunched and he used a wooden cane to help keep him steady. The crooked stick was out of place in the sleek metal halls embroidered with luminous panels. The old till man rested a hand on Jono's shoulder as he shakily moved foward.

"You wouldn't mind helping an old man move about, would you?"

"Not at all, sir."

"Sir? How formal! I'm Pascal the whatever-ith. And here I thought all you Earthkins were brash young things, eager to find new rules just so you could break them!" Pascal laughed. "Don't go letting an old man down now. I stayed alive for three hundred and three years to see this wake. You've got a mountain of prejudice to live up to!"

"I'll try not to disappoint." Jono smiled. Pascal was already deflecting his own assumptions. "I'm Jonothon Wyer. I'm from the Twilight Ring on Earth, in a small mining town called Polari."

"I know quite a great deal about you, Mister Wyer. You don't think we Terralunans let strangers into our homes for the first time in centuries without doing a bit of homework, do you?"

"What about the other people from the Coalition of Solar Space?" Jono asked. "Don't you ever let them on the moon?"

"Oh, C.O.S.S, shmoss!" Pascal shook his cane. "They have no authority over us, although they like to pretend to, and we simply don't have the energy to constantly correct them."

They had strolled down the hall as the last of the pairs dissipated into separate corridors leading throughout the city.

"I suppose you'll be wanting a tour of our defense

cannons and guardian factories like the rest of them?"

Jono sturdied the wobbly old man. He didn't walk like he was able to go all over the moon.

"You're the local," Jono replied. "What's your favorite place here?"

"Hah!" Pascal waved his finger at Jono's face. "You are a smart lad to consult your elders. And for it you will be rewarded." Pascal shuffled away. "This way. Keep up! We don't want those other yokels following us!"

They wound through halls beneath the moon's surface until they were far from the active quarters. After endless tunnels that turned to gray walls with dim mauve lights, Pascal led him to a large round door.

Pascal chuckled and looked at Jono, eager for the surprise. The door rolled open to reveal a room bursting with plant life. Vines climbed gray moonrock walls, and massive leaves glistened with dew. Flowers glowed in every color imaginable. The ceiling and the far wall were both transparent, giving a perfect view of a tiny blue speck: the old dead sun, Sol.

Jono gasped. "This is amazing!"

"Of course it is. It flourishes thanks to the careful hand of the sourest old geezer this rock ever birthed. He has no patience for any of the stuffy brains that run this pebble, but he's a genius with these plants. It's probably the only reason the Vesagarchs keep him around at all, I'd wager."

"That's you, right?" Jono grinned.

"I knew you were a smart one." Pascal plucked an

orange ball from a tree branch. "See these?" He took a bite and nectar exploded from the fruit. "I'd hold my moonterangs against any fruit you've got down there! A tart sweetness so balanced it makes the stars weep from jealousy!"

Jono admired the man's passion for his craft. He clearly didn't fit in with all the other snarling and serious folk who called this place home. He was different, an outcast among these bland people. Even though he didn't belong, he made a small place on that dictatorial globe where he could be himself.

"Down here is where I live." Pascal led him to a glorified utility closet. "It's not much, but since I keep lying about how delicate my garden is, they let me stay here and I get to avoid the doldrums of the regular housing quarters."

The bedroom had no windows, but a tapestry on the wall added some color to the stark hole. Garden tools and supplies cluttered the space, with a set of purple robes hanging on an open rack. Above a desk covered in knickknacks was a wide shelf with blue sleeping mat and a blanket on it.

"That will be your bunk for the next few wakes. It will be nice to have an extra pair of hands in the garden. The squaddots are about to be ripening and I have a terror of a time plucking them."

"You don't have bots to harvest them for you?" Jono asked.

"You are not a gardener, Wyer, but have you ever

plucked a perfectly ripe fruit from a tree? The delicate bond between the mother limb and sweet child is just so that when you gasp it, it's as though the mother is giving her most precious gift away, never too soon, nor too late, and pop! That sound! If there is anything more precious in life, I do not know it."

On the desk sat a photo frame. It rotated through pictures of plants and a few Pascal self-shots with a bushel of fruit over his shoulder. Then came the image of a much younger terralunan boy.

"Who is that?" Jono asked as he picked up the frame and flipped through more of the pictures.

"That would be my ward."

"Is that like your son?"

"In a manner of speaking, yes. I raised him from a young age."

Jono froze on an image of the young boy standing by a pool of water on the moon's surface. The boy was smiling, but his yellow eyes looked like a tiger's on the hunt. A fleshy scar curved across his bare chest. Jono flipped through the pictures, and as the boy got older, more scars appeared over his arms and legs.

"He was a clumsy one," Pascal chuckled. "Always getting hurt in one way or another. I could never leave an open burner around him and stars forbid gardening shears. He almost put an eye out more than once!"

An eerie gaze began to form in the boy's eyes as the pictures continued and scars spread over his body like a rash.

That was when Jonothon spotted a tiny lightning cross, surrounded by a circle, written in ink on the boy's wrist: the symbol of the dead sun and mark of the Tombs. He wasn't a clumsy boy, he was doing it to himself. He was building a pattern. He was carving a testimony of destruction.

Jono gasped. "That's Vincent Chaucer."

The old man scowled. "No, his name was Praxis the Thirty Seventh. My poor ward was lost to us nearly one hundred years ago. An accident with a moon thresher, and . . ." Pascal became quiet. "I did say he was a clumsy child. Six of his generation were lost when the machine broke. We terralunans pride ourselves on our strict adherence to process, but even we can make mistakes."

Jono stared into those golden eyes and knew the truth. The boy looked no older than nineteen, but considering how old Pascal was, terralunans must have aged slower than humans. There was no denying it. That was the man that Commander Grail had known as Vincent Chaucer while at Windom. He'd grown up to become a terrorist and a murderer. He probably used the five other deaths to cover his escape from the moon, adding another life to take his place in the debris. Six innocent people, just so he could escape.

But *why*?

Was it something about living on the moon that was so horrible? Or was he born a psychopath just looking for people to hurt?

The old man's eyes glistened on the verge of tears. Jono

couldn't bring himself to tell Pascal the monster his ward had become.

Jono set the frame on the desk. "It's got to be hard to get a good rest in this cramped room."

"I rarely use it," Pascal said, his tone turning chipper once more. "Most wakes I lay on the grass." The ancient man smiled through the waves of wrinkles on his face. "It's there that I wake up to Earthrise, and that is when I dream."

"There is no way this is a coincidence."

Jono sat around a table surrounded by the vast darkness in the code realm of their private team chat. He'd scoured the wireless link to be certain no one else could be spying on them.

"Someone set this up," Isaac said. "Do you think Grail knew about it and that's really why we are here in the first place? To gather intel on Chaucer that we can use to track him down?"

"The Empress is in on this, I'm sure of it," Keiko said. "Who else would be able to set this up? Or do the tills know what you've done over the past few years? Maybe they want to get in on your good side."

"What if the Tombs orchestrated this themselves?" Oscar said.

They all became silent.

"The Tombs seem to have a finger in every pie," Oscar

continued, "and they really like clunking with people's heads. Maybe they want you to know more about Chaucer."

"But why?" Jono asked.

"To make you scared?" Oscar suggested.

"Or to convert you?" Isaac said.

"That would almost be bigger than the Empress converting to the Tombs," Keiko said.

"I'm the last person under Sol that's converting to their madness, you can bet your life on that," Jono said.

"We have," Keiko said, her tone a mix of joking and familiarity.

"Multiple times," Isaac said. "So, Firewall, what's our plan? My custodian is taking me to the archives next wake. Do we know what job Chaucer was born into? They might have records about him."

"Only that he was using a moon thresher when he killed those other people. What job is that? Tunnel construction?" Jono said. "Who do we know that was assigned to that?"

"Isn't Kain in that group?" Isaac asked.

"No, Ammer is in construction," Oscar said. "I passed them in the hall. Kain is in child indoctrination."

"There's no way we are convincing Ammer to spy for us," Isaac said. "He's a squeaky hinge, that one."

Jono agreed. "I'll keep looking in Pascal's room for more information."

"I'll, um, look around the bakery, I guess," Keiko said. "Everyone loves a bakery, right? Chaucer could be a secret donut fanatic."

"My custodian, Gortimer the Twelfth, said he's taking me to the birthing chambers in a few wakes," Oscar said. "There could be something about how Chaucer was born in there."

"It's a good place to start," Keiko said. "Be careful and don't draw any attention to yourself."

"Until then, keep acting like everything is normal," Jono said.

Isaac sneered. "For as normal as being on the moon gets."

Chapter Twenty

The Baths of Eternity

arissa spooned clumps of white mush onto plates with a forced smile that wasn't fooling anyone as Asmodeus Fleeth's voice calmly narrated over the scene.

"The students have taken to their new roles in Terralunan society with a grace that should make their native lands proud. Everyone needs to eat and here in the operations cantina, a Day End student learns about the noble service that is food preparation."

Rows of gray-skinned workers, and the occasional hungry Earthkin student, lined up and filled their tray with shiny red fruits, a steaming protein brick covered in brown sauce, and a lump of white grain mush.

"Everyone on Terralunis is celebrated for their wake's work with a pleasant respite to sit and mingle among their peers. Harmony is a prime virtue on our humble home. Fit the right person to the right task and everyone is happy."

The video flashed to a shot of Nick and Ammer squabbling and shoving shoulders into each other back on Einstein IV. It then cut to Nick and Ammer sitting across from each other in the cantina. They were both smiling, and Ammer even let Nick have half of his protein brick, who shoved it through the mouth of his cosmodermis in one bite.

"Even an earthkin with a quick temper can find a calmer sense of being under the influence of Terralunan culture. We hope they bring the lessons of harmony back to the planet with them, don't you?"

"How did they get the footage?" Nick scowled at the screen. "I didn't know they were filming! And I was smiling at the girl behind you."

Ammer shoved him from behind. "I wasn't even smiling. I was trying not to throw up! The only reason I gave you that steaming brick was because it tasted like rotten worm bile."

"Lunch is the one thing this rock has going for it. You Day Enders have sand for taste buds," Nick said. "And I was only sitting next to you because you were the only non-loony in the room."

"Boys." Suriana leaned in. "We are watching ourselves being broadcast to the entire Sol system in a historically momentous event. Let's try to enjoy it for a moment."

The boys shrugged and turned back to the screen. They'd been gathered in a viewing room to catch the video broadcast.

The video continued to document their first wake on the moon. Keiko was surrounded by till females, baking rack after rack of butter loaf bread for the governing sects. Isaac stood in the center of a vast library of servers, near the heart of the moon. David watched as a doctor monitored a terralunan while she exercised.

"Everything is optimized to provide Terralunan citizens with a long, healthy, and productive life," Fleeth's voice reminded viewers. "The whole is better for the contributions of each member of society, like a perfect puzzle, all put together."

Elise stood on the moon's surface as the Earth, split between both Ends, hovered far above.

"I love it here," said the video Elise.

"I was being sarcastic!" the real Elise snarled. "Did you see how they cut that? I was working with the gray dirt cleanup crew, combing the dust to make it look pretty. It was awful."

Kain nodded. "Do you get the feeling we're helping the tills look good more than they're helping us learn?"

"Nobody under Sol likes the loonies," Nick said, "and we're puppets here trying to make them look good. Maybe instead, they should try to be less burn'em tyrants for a change?"

"Look, Jono. There you are!" Suri pointed at the screen.

On the screen, Jono was helping pluck moonterangs in the garden. The different angles of the garden made it look much larger than it actually was.

"Across the planets, stations, and ships, a healthy diet is

critical to a sustainable bio system. Here on Terralunis, our agricultural system is unparalleled across Sol's orbit."

"Do I really look that pale?" Jono asked.

They cut to an interview shot with Suriana. The girls from the Day squealed while Suri attempted to contain her pride.

Suri sat with purple drapes behind her. "The Terralunans have been incredibly gracious hosts. My custodian works in the school for the young tills, ranging three to eight years old. It was a side of Terralunans I had never seen, and probably never even thought of before. The teachers there were smart and caring, and honestly, I was surprised at how fun they can be!"

The video cut to a scene where Suri sat in a circle with young tills, playing games and clapping hands as they sang nursery rhymes.

"Looks like you're famous, Suri," Jono said. "The whole system knows that face now."

Suri laughed. "I will try not to let it get to my head."

Keiko leaned over to them. "It's only a matter of time before you're doing interview across the stars!"

Jono grinned. "I hear Ganymede is lovely this time of year."

Suri frowned. "Too icy for my tastes. Deep down I am just a simple Day girl with a need for bright lights and warm baths."

"The fire resorts on Titan should be perfect for you then," Isaac said. "I read that you can see the fire shows from a naturally jetted tub on a mountain top."

"Only if my Titan fans insist," Suri said. "It is all for the fans."

The two heads of the wolf fighting over a goat bone would have been more terrifying if the beast wasn't a baby. The small fenrir was pudgy at eight months out of the nursing pod.

"I told you I'd show you something you've never seen before," Pascal said as Jonothon leaned against a clear wall that separated them from the guardian in training. "Old Jemmy, the breeder, owed me a favor for a few moonmelons I grew special for him. Here's where we raise our baby monsters to keep all you Earthkin so scared."

The miniature beast rolled around, its two heads yapping and snapping at each other in the most adorable way possible.

"It's worked so far," Jono said, "but you probably don't want to show how cute they are at this age. It may dispel the terror."

"Quite right. Fear is a delicate recipe." Pascal chuckled. "But even as a whelp, that fenrir could rip you in four pieces and still have two paws left to play a piano."

The fenrir's two heads panted happily with a bloodstained muzzle.

"Have they ever broken loose?" Jono asked.

Pascal shrugged. "They are all gene-gineered to serve the lords of Terralunis. They physically cannot harm any of us or take any action that could result in the slightest scratch on our perfect gray skin."

"Do you always keep them alone?"

"They have a wireless link to other guardians, and to central command." Pascal tapped his forehead. "They're never alone up here."

A ping hit the back part of Jonothon's brain.

I've found something, Wyer. Oscar's voice was full of nervous excitement as it hit Jono's mind.

Where are you? Jono thought back.

In the birthing chambers with Gortimer, Oscar replied. *There is a door that looks important. What should I do?*

Can you get in safely using your illusion pixels?

I think so. Oscar's voice trembled with false confidence.

"Let's see what other breed Jemmy is cooking up, eh?" Pascal leaned on Jono's shoulder. "I hear he bred a chimera with djinnghul! That must be a fright even as a whelp!"

Jono smiled. "Just point the way."

Only go if you can do it without being caught. Don't take excessive risks. Jono thought.

Oscar paused for a moment. *I can do this. Trust me, Wyer. I'm a professional.*

The birthing chamber was a wide chasm in the heart of

the moon where translucent green pods hung from thick red vines over bubbling turquoise pools. Across the cavern stood a golden gate that led into a dark tunnel.

"I thought you said Terralunans were human?" Oscar asked as he avoided touching what looked like dangling red roots. "I didn't know humans came from squishy eggs."

"How did you think we replicated?" Gortimer sneered. "Through pregnancy? Disgusting! And inefficient to say the least! It's a farce of folk that call themselves human. They steal our name on Earth for what's left of an archaic sentiment that makes a mess of everything. We are pure human genetic designs. Humanity in its most elegant form."

Oscar swallowed as a gray body stirred inside its sack.

"Yep. Elegant."

Gortimer barely looked at him as he held a sensor up to each pod to monitor the children's health and development. "As I was saying, the pod compounds must be delicately adjusted as the fetus develops into its role. Each profession is reared with its own genetic template and developmental formula."

Oscar mustered his courage, and with one step backward, he left a hollow image of himself as the pixels covered his body and mimicked his surroundings to make him effectively invisible.

Gortimer continued to ramble on about the delicate nature of Terralunan embryonic pods while Oscar stepped carefully away. The golden gate was already cracked open just enough for Oscar to slip through.

I've ditched the till and I'm heading down a dark tunnel, Oscar thought to his team mates. *It's long and still dark, oh! There's a light ahead.*

We don't need the narration, Isaac thought from the council chambers. *Just link what you see to the group. We'll have it all streaming through Team Think.*

Right, sorry. Just nervous. I mean . . . yeah, nervous.

Oscar followed the light to a massive marble chamber. Dim turquoise light glowed from the rows of rectangular panels that lined the floor and walls. At the far end of the chamber, one panel hovered with three pillars surrounding it.

Oscar investigated each of the glowing panels.

There's a liquid in them. They're like bathtubs but sealed shut. Oscar tapped the clear cover. Through the murky goo, he could see a humanoid body. *There are tills trapped inside! They're old. I thought the birthing chamber was only for babies.*

Look around, Jono thought. *Is there anywhere that could have records?*

I can't hack a console, Wyer. Only you have those installs.

The gate wasn't locked. Maybe this isn't either.

Oscar searched the room, but it was nothing but marble baths and glowing ooze. *No mechanix. It's no use. I need to get back before Gortimer notices.*

Plaque! The thought came from Keiko a little louder than it needed to be.

What?

Go back to that last bath and look at the bottom, Keiko

thought. *There, you see it? That metal rectangle.*

I see a dark little box. Oh, there's writing on it. It says 'Shonvax'.

What does that mean?

Do Tills have their own language? I never thought they would.

Go look at more of them.

Oscar ran down the hall to the center, reading the plaques. *Mirgram. Haslick. Grosinyn. Forcrab. Walthar. Oh, there's a number.* Oscar noticed a small dial on the corner of the box. *Lorlax and the number twenty six.*

It's a name, Jono thought. *These baths are for specific people. Chaucer was Praxis thirty seven.*

Oscar touched the numbers as they scrolled up. Each time, a new image appeared in front of the person's face. *They all look the same to me. Is that good? I should really be getting back.*

One last thing, Isaac thought. *The bath that is up right in the back of the room. We need to know what name is on that one.*

Oscar scurried past the rows of baths until he arrived at the steps in front of the monument. The plaque had been ripped off of the marble. Only the last letter remained: *n.*

Praxis doesn't end with an 'n', so who is this? Jono thought.

Oscar scrolled through the numbers. Each number lit up, except one.

It skips thirty seven. What's that mean?

Oscar waited for a response, but none came.

He peered at the monument but couldn't see much through the murky turquoise liquid, only the figure of the gray person floating in there. On the side of the marble bath was a small timer.

That's new, Oscar thought.

The numbers were counting down, but in numbers Oscar had never seen before.

Team, are you getting this?

There was no answer.

The golden gate behind him creaked open. A burly till guard looked across the room, but all he saw was a marble pillar where Oscar had been standing. The guard walked down the hall, and Oscar mimicked the guard's appearance.

He ran out of the room, past all the baths. The other guards were still standing by the door to the baths as Gortimer babbled to the hollow version of Oscar, who hadn't moved from the birthing pod.

The hollow Oscar disappeared and for an instant, Gortimer noticed something was amiss.

"Where did you go?"

"I'm right here," Oscar said, trying to hide his gasping for breath.

Gortimer squinted at him. "I thought you were . . ." he looked to his left. "No matter. What do you think about my idea?"

Oscar had a frozen smile on his face. He had no idea what Gortimer was talking about.

"Brilliant," Oscar said through his smile.

Gortimer beamed back at him.

"Marvelous! I'll get your pod prepped for you!" He activated one of the pods, which slid open. "Think of the fame you'll have, being the only non-Terralunan to experience a birthing pod!"

Oscar looked at the ooze seeping over the cusp of the open pod. His fake smile tilted downward.

"Hooray . . ."

The rest of their attempts at finding information about Vincent Chaucer were less than inspiring. Isaac was able to find the job listings of Praxis the Thirty Seventh and an official log about the moon thresher accident, but nothing in the report seemed useful. Keiko learned that he was fond of lemon jelly donuts from the oldest woman in the bakery with a shockingly good memory. Jono tried to steer Pascal into conversations about Praxis, but every time the old till changed the subject.

Soon their time on the moon ran out. The Earthkin found themselves huddled in the docking bay as the last of the cameras floated away.

Fleeth had just finished his rehearsed speech about their trip being a step toward a brighter future. But once the cameras left, his wide smile faded, and his exhaustion was apparent in his slumped shoulders and exasperated sighs.

"That's that," Fleeth moaned. "You children . . ." He shook his head. "It's over now. Enjoy your silly planet."

"What's that supposed to mean, moon man?" Nick snarled. "I've had enough of being your puppet! When we get back the Empress and the Sage are going to know all about your little spin show."

Fleeth stared back at him blankly. "I have no idea what you mean."

"Don't you? You've probably been experimenting on us this whole time. Are we going back to Earth with a plague? It that it?"

"Knox, calm down," Elise said, putting a hand on his shoulder.

"We're going home," Kane said.

"No, we've been tricked here and I want to know the truth. These space suits probably don't even do anything. How about I use my fire bombs to wreck your little PR stunt?"

Fleeth grinned. "You couldn't tear it with all the firebombs on Earth."

"Oh yeah?" Nick said, warming the bombs on his shoulders.

"Do it," Fleeth said with a toothy grin.

"I'm going to!"

"No, you're not."

"I'm going to burst right through and taste the sweet space of freedom!"

Elise took a step back. "Stop it, Knox!"

"Do it!" Fleeth snarled.

The firebomb shot from Nick's shoulder. For an instant it stretched the cosmodermis and almost looked like it would break free, but then it burst in a flash of fire. A cloud of smoke filled the suit. Nick fell to his knees, coughing violently as the nano filters began cleaning the air.

Fleeth exploded with laughter.

"That is the best experience I have ever had with an Earthkin! This is going in my diary! Farewell, children. You will not be missed."

Jono, Keiko, Isaac, and Oscar sat at a round table in the middle of the endless black code world. The light from a single candle illuminated their faces.

"So, what did we learn?" Jono asked.

Keiko was quick to reply. "Chaucer is a Terralunan. Maybe one of the only ones to escape the moon and live on Earth. That's rare if not unique. He must have been found in some records or tracked in the Eies of Eyes."

"And he was able to fake his death and get off of the moon," Isaac said. "That's not easy. It's got to count for something."

"How did he do it? Did he have any help from the Tombs?"

"Were the Tombs even around that long ago?" Keiko asked.

"He had their mark," Isaac said. "Even in that old picture Jono saw, he had the mark. It doesn't mean the Tombs were an organized group yet, but it's definitely evidence to support the hypothesis."

"Maybe he did it himself and he just knows how to be really sneaky," Oscar said. "You're pretty sneaky, Jono. I bet you could figure it out."

"But why did he join Windom after he got to Earth?"

"Maybe he thought that the Empress would protect him from the loonies?" Isaac suggested.

"Okay, but how did he stay hidden after he faked his death in front of Grail all those years ago?"

"It seems like he has a pattern of faking his death." Oscar looked around the table. "Will he try to do it again?"

Jono sighed. "Maybe. We still have more questions than we have answers. Let's think on it and gather again once we're home. Good work, Firewall."

They smiled at his praise.

"Go team," Keiko said with a single fist held high.

Jono opened his eyes to the depths of space out the Ragnarok's window screen.

The ship rocketed through space, heading directly back to Earth. A vast sea of stars filled the void around them.

Exhaustion overwhelmed the novelty of being in zero gravity. They ached from the week in space eating weird things and suffering under the tills strict culture. Half of them tried to sleep through the rest of the journey, while the others distracted themselves with class work, videos, or games.

Nick sat in the back of the ship, ignoring Elisa and Kain's attempts to make him laugh, still fuming in silence.

"You'd think he'd be happy to head back to Earth," Keiko whispered.

"I don't think Knox is happy about anything, ever,"

Jono whispered back.

He and Keiko shared a long smile.

In a burst of fire and air, the back of the ship exploded, tearing the metal hull open. All sound was instantly sucked out of the cabin. Red emergency lights flashed over the last two rows of seats that were pulled loose from the floor and floated untethered into space. Oscar, Nick, and others clung to their chairs helplessly.

The cabin filled with red light as klaxons blared unheard alerts to the crew.

The cameras following the outside of the Ragnarok caught the left rear leg engine exploding and tearing off of the mech-dragon's body. Debris and gases spread across the empty space as the ship spun, uncontrolled.

Emergency cosmodermis suits sprung from each of the chairs. The students gasped as the clear material wrapped around them. They gazed up in horror as loose chairs floated through the gnarled opening in the hull and out into the vacuum of stars.

On screens across the Sol system, a smiling glass mask sparkled from beneath a black hood. Those who knew the yellow eyes of Vincent Chaucer recognized him immediately. He slowly clapped his gray, scarred hands.

"Bravo. A thrilling end to such exquisite cinéma vérité," Chaucer said dryly. "You didn't think the Tombs would miss out on the festivities, did you?"

Across the system, people stared silently at the horror on the screen.

"You can try to stop us, but first you'll need to know who we are. I'll give you a clue. Look to your left and look to your right. And now look in the mirror. You all have the same seed of destruction within you, and that seed is growing. All of you are Tombs. Some of you just don't know it yet."

Chapter Twenty-One

Brink of the Abyss

odies strapped to chairs floated into space toward the splintered trail of debris. Metal scraps hovered behind them as the Ragnarok's engines flickered then died like snuffed candles.

Cadets and squires screamed in silent, helpless horror. The last three rows were torn from their hinges, smashing against each other as they were sucked into space. Helios yelled muffled orders over the com system. In those seconds of madness, they gawked at each other, helplessly watching their friends float away.

Outside the hull, Nick kicked and waved his arms, but space didn't heed his attempts to swim through it. He looked to the ship's metal scales as they gleamed in the light of the distant Day's sun. He looked over at Kain and Elise with the crushing conclusion that this would be how they died.

David sent his field pixels as fast as he could, but without an atmosphere for the nanobots to swim in, they struggled to keep any shape. He tried to cover the gap in the hull, but the field was too weak against the vacuum of space, and the momentum of Paegor Bron's helpless stone body smashed right through his pixel field.

Everyone struggled to break free from their harnesses, desperate to help, but only Keiko was strong enough to tear off her safety straps. She scrambled to free David, Isaac, and Jono as they floated toward the hull breach.

Isaac spun upside down as he hastily created an elixir that would seal the gap. The three of them slammed against the hull, right next to the opening. Isaac threw a white capsule that exploded when it touched the metal frame of Freya's floating seat. It burst into a web that flailed and stuck to whatever it touched. Ammer, Freya, and Murphy were caught in the web. Isaac grinned sadly as he kept floating away.

David's field pixels flew into space, linking to each other in order to stay in control of their movement. He grabbed as many floating chairs as he could, but the pixels weren't strong enough to pull them back in. They dangled in space like balloons tied to string.

Jono crawled out of the breach, his wires grabbing onto the Ragnarok's scaly metal skin and carrying him securely across the ship's back. David's pixels had stopped the students' escape, but more were floating further away. Jono extended his wires, sending himself as far out as he could. He grabbed one student at a time and pulled them back inside.

Elise and Kain made it back into the ship holding each

other. Nick's cosmodermis was smeared with floating tears as a wire gripped his ankle and sent him back to the ship. He passed Jono, shock on his face before he struck Isaac's web. Jono caught and pulled in two more, then four, then eight students. They floated farther and farther away from the ship with each passing moment.

Suriana, finally freed, grabbed the gnarled metal at the edge of the breach and helped Isaac, David, and Keiko pull the returning students back in as quick as they could. She took a locket from her belt, tried to whisper through the cosmodermis and opened the clasp. A flurry of pink wisps burst into the shape of a hand, but quickly faded into a helpless cloud in the emptiness.

Jono noticed the faint pink dust float past him. He looked back to see Suri pointing desperately behind him. He turned to where she was pointing and saw Riley floating the furthest away from the ship.

Inside, Keiko waved and pointed to get Helios to adjust the angle of the Ragnarok's tail. Helios aimed it toward Riley as the dryad sped helplessly away.

Jono's wires crawled and spun him head over feet along the back of the ship and down its tail. He dangled at the end of his wires with other wires flailing and reaching into space. As he reached the tip of the tail, one long wire from his ankle gripped the furthest part of the ship while his arms and wires stretched toward the terrified girl. But his wires had extended as far as they could, and with one swipe they grabbed a leaf from her hair . . . and tore it off.

Riley spun in a forlorn circle against a backdrop of

blackness. She reached out to Jono, to his wires, but she was too far and Jono's wires too short. The grip at the end of his wire clamped as helplessly as Riley's desperate fingers.

Jono mouthed the words *Cut Strap*.

Riley nodded. She looked around, but couldn't find anything sharp to cut it with. She had no bionetic installs to save her. No magic to cast. No spy wires or firebombs or clouds of pixels. A barky limb that had sprouted on her elbow, however, was pointy and rough. She jabbed it against the thin cloth of her harness. She was floating further away, but it was working. She banged and shoved against the harness until her branch was bleeding with sap. The strap finally tore and she slipped out of the harnesses' death grip.

She positioned herself to launch toward the ship, her silent gasps for breath a chorus reverberating through her own body. When she pushed off the seat, she expected to fly straight toward the ship, but the seat spun as she kicked, sending her on an askew vector. Nerves shot and adrenaline surging through her, Riley felt a final moment of panic as one of Jono's wires snaked through empty space toward her.

Her wooden finger touched the tip of the wire. It clamped tight, yanking her in and then wrapping around her hand, arm, and then, as Jono reeled her in, the rest of his wires wrapped around her body and pulled her close to his chest. She clung to him as they stared out at the emptiness of space, the wide planet above and the shattered wreckage around them. They hung on the edge of the endless nothing in shock, but alive.

Spots of light filled a sea of darkness. They flickered and waved, an orange candle flame illuminating solemn faces. The streets of Eies were lined with candles for those few moments when every light in the city went out. Even though no lives were lost on the sabotaged Ragnarok, the message from the Tombs was clear: *Fear us, for we can kill you at any time.*

This was the world's reply. A moment of peace shared across the globe, from the stone and metal streets of Eies to the cobbled paths and golden towers of Caer Midus. People locked arms and sang a gentle tune of solidarity.

Dvaniur Grail watched the screen in front of him flick from one vigil to the next. "Were we wrong? Again?"

He sat on a couch at his home in Eies, with the city darkened beyond his floor-to-ceiling windows. After the moment of silence, the lights of the city turned on. Across Earth, the vigilant people sang *We Will Carry On* in unison.

Rania Helios touched his shoulder. "They are alive and the world is more united than ever."

Grail didn't move. "I thought of all places, even here, that they would be safe in space."

"Breaching the blockade is more than we could have hoped for. The Empress and the Sage agreed that we needed to give that to them."

"We were reckless, Raina. We put those children on the center stage. How did we not think it dared the Tombs to retaliate?"

"Life is a dare, Dvan, you know that," Helios said. "This dark earth around us dared us to freeze and die, the pox dares us to cower, and the Tombs dare us to fear them. *We* dare to inspire our home to dream of something more than submission. It's who we are. It's who every one of those cadets and squires are. They survived out there in space, and they fought to rescue each other."

"Wyer knew the risks, but the others?"

"We're all at risk, Dvan. Here against the pox, the greatest risk is to try nothing at all. They enrolled in the Windom academy for a reason. The squires left their warm lands and easy lives to make a statement, to defy those monsters that keep our future hostage. They chose this too."

Grail despised the feeling of helplessness, but the Tombs were always one step ahead. "What next? Hunting down the Tombs is not going fast enough."

"I spoke with Wyer's team before the debriefing," Helios said. "They took the opportunity on Terralunis to get intel on Chaucer's true origin, without any guidance from us."

Grail allowed a proud smile for a moment. "They have always done what they could. If we didn't include them, you can bet your stars Wyer would have found a way to get involved."

"It's not much, but what they collected is a start." Helios stared out the windows at the city below them. "Our enemies are leaving clues in every corner, but we can't seem to connect them. The Ragnarok was my project, and now I'm shut out during the investigation."

"We will catch whoever planted the bomb, and with it, a trail to Chaucer," Grail said. "An old colleague of mine is on the investigatory team. It appears a small pipe in the sixth leg engine was manufactured with a pixel material beneath the sheathing. We didn't catch it on the scanners because of the dormant pixels bonded with the sheathing. Once the engines activated, the pixels were powered and began forming into a bomb. They were ready for the remote detonation ever since you left the launching bay."

"Meaning they waited until we were on our return approach before setting it off," Helios said. "Someone in the Crown knew about the sheathing and how to sneak in pixels to make the bomb and hide the transmitter. It's only a matter of time before we catch them."

"Let's hope we do, before we lose what we cannot replace."

A flicker of rainbow light flashed from the center of the quartz crystal that hung from a chain around her neck, but Cassindra Viscariot couldn't bear to answer its call. The Sage or Aquinas would demand answers she didn't have. She curled her legs against her chest and leaned against a willow tree in the Quartzden Grotto. She hid herself away in the garden's thick bushes, yearning to be rid of the weight of the dark world around her.

She desperately needed to be alone, but even here the pervasive hum of the city clawed at her mind. Over these months, the cold and the noise had infected her. Her skin felt perpetually tainted by the oily veneer that hung in the air. If only she were back beneath the sun, the warmth would cleanse her spirit. It was this fetid city that barred the whispers from giving her comfort, and yet, she did not return to the Day, because a terrible thought had leeched itself to her heart. Perhaps she was wrong. Perhaps she didn't deserve solace.

It was all her fault.

Those children could have died out in space and she was the one who'd sent them there. Her heart felt still and cold, and for the first time in her life she doubted. Had she truly heard the whispers of angels? Or was it her own zeal that thrust innocent children into the target of their enemy? Where were the whispers now that she needed then? If there truly were angels hiding in the world, how could they stay silent at her desperation?

Viscariot clenched her eyes shut. Her mind screamed and begged the angels to grant her clarity, but no whispers replied. A tear escaped from her closed eye.

"Why won't you answer me?" she sobbed to the plants.

"Whisper louder," replied a gravelly voice from behind a bush.

Chapter Twenty-One

Viscariot flinched in surprise. "Who is there?"

A ragged man groaned as he stood up amongst the brush. He wore a thick blanket buckled around his neck like a cloak. His wild black hair nearly obscured a maniacal smile. Edgar Niles, the mad man of Eies who believed himself possessed by an angel, stood before her in all his unwashed glory. Her first sight of the disheveled, blasphemous man inspired the idea of giving up the faith altogether. She felt violated for being overheard in her moment of weakness. Her face morphed into a snarl.

"What are you doing there?" she demanded.

Edgar shrugged as he approached her. "Was sleeping. But you, my muddled friend, sounded like you could use a word from the wise."

Edgar sat down next to her, and despite leaning away from him, he waved his gaunt fingers in front of her face. "Your dilemma is clear as mud. You need to whisper louder. You are so quiet, you can't hear yourself think." Edgar stomped his feet and pounded his fists against the dirt. "BE LOUD! See? You need to shout otherwise they can't hear you."

Edgar crooked his head with a proud grin as though he'd shared a treasured secret.

Viscariot recoiled as his noxious breath lingered between them.

"Thank you?" she muttered.

Edgar's expression turned serious as he grabbed her by the shoulders. "I have an *angel* inside of my brain!" He sniffed her. "There's one in you too, eh?" He sniffed at the willow tree then leaned his ear against the bark. "Angels waltzing on the atoms of everything. I feel them, all around us, inside and out. Listening. Watching. Who's watching?"

He looked around with worry, as though unseen, spying eyes were watching them and then spun back to glare into her eyes.

"We're the same, you and I. Two cogs in a clock, eh? Clicking and ticking, while the world pretends that the veil they see is real! But we know the difference, don't we? Just a masquerade of atoms and photons, painting lies for our eyes, but we? Dearest friend, mates to the end, we see through the veil to the paradise beyond, eh?"

Viscariot rallied her senses and clenched the wand on her belt. This spectacle of insanity could turn violent at any moment. "Listen to me, friend, you need to—"

"Shh!" Edgar smashed his index finger against her lips to silence her. "Let go of who you aren't and realize who you are. Whisper loudly, but in silence, for the minions of the Abysmal King are listening. He cannot be trusted. Do not let him sway you. I'll lead their prying eyes away."

Edgar jumped to his feet and sprinted through the willow leaves, waving his arms and shouting in tongues. He ran through the garden and burst out its doors, disappearing into the city.

Viscariot gasped at his madness, but then realized her hand was no longer shaking and her tears had dried on her checks. She no longer felt the urge to weep or doubt.

He'd jolted her back to who she truly was, confident in the path set before her. Surely, he was not who he said he was, but even so, the angels spoke through the most inexplicable voices.

She smiled and pulled the glowing crystal around her neck to her chest. The Sage and Aquinas would need her to see them through this shaded path. Hadn't all of the children survived? The boy had even acted bravely, rescuing many of the others. Wasn't that a clear sign that this path was ordained to succeed? That the boy was destined to be a herald of peace for the world?

Her vision of the path was all so clear to her again. They'd skirted the edge of tragedy, and the angels had seen them through! There would be more trials to come, more threats from their enemies, and even though she didn't know where this path would lead her, she knew, to the core of her being, that it was what the angels compelled for her.

She only needed to shut her eyes to distraction and doubt, and follow the Narrow Path wherever it led.

The passengers of the Ragnarok sat in a circle among a grassy field in the code world as Professor Wishe hovered in the circle's center.

"I'm sick of this," Nick said, tearing up handfuls of grass. "We were on the front lines of this war, and now we're locked in this school like a cage. I should be out there shoving a firebomb down a Tombs throat!"

The rest of them sat in silence.

Nick tossed a clump of grass and dirt aside then slammed his fist into the ground. "That's all I have to say."

"Thank you for sharing," Wishe said. "Remember, all thoughts are welcome. No one should be judged for how they feel."

They'd been going around for what felt like hours, each student taking their turn to talk about their feelings in the aftermath of the Ragnarok incident. Mostly they didn't know what to think or otherwise couldn't put those feelings into words.

"Riley," Wishe said, turning ever so slowly toward the young dryad, "do you have any feelings you would like to share."

Riley looked around the circle. "I . . . I'm glad I met you all," she said, hanging her head low, "but . . . but I miss the Day. I don't think I ever should have come here." She hid her head in her hands while Freya, sitting beside her, patted her back with soothing strokes and motherly shushes.

Suriana stood. "I know it is not my turn, but I have something to say." She paused until Wishe gave her a nod. "We are here to share our feelings? Well, I feel like we have given the Tombs more than they asked for. When we came from Day, we didn't know what we would find in the Dark. Would we be hated? Would we get sick from the lack of the sun? Would we be murdered by magic haters? We were *brave* to come here, and now, those cowardly Tombs plant one little bomb and everyone acts like they control the universe. They don't! They don't control this city or the world. They don't control our lives. *We* do. There will always be monsters that want to hurt us. There will always be things to be afraid of, but we? We *are* brave.

"We have done what no one thought possible. We made friends with the other End. We have been to the moon. We are the first earthkin in generations to do that. Don't let those monsters take that away from us. I refuse to let them win. I refuse to be afraid. We are stronger than them, the Dark and Day together."

Suri took her time as she spoke to meet gazes with every other student in the circle. Tears welled in her eyes, and she saw plenty of others verging on the same. But she held her head high and straightened her, digging her heels into the ground.

"I see it in every one of you. You will find your strength. You will live on and do important things and be important to a lot of people. We will survive. Whether you feel that now, remember that I believe it and believe in each of you."

There was no applause, no sign of praise, but in those yearning eyes she knew the seeds of courage were planted.

Cid waved his hand at a board covered in diagrams of mech parts. The diagrams moved on their own, and wrapped around a sketch of a feli'yin knight.

"I know machines may be frightening, but with them, you can be strong," Cid said. "You can be armored. You can even fly. That is the power of technology. To give you the ability to do things you cannot on your own. To make us all more powerful, safer."

His students were silent and barely paying attention.

"I want each of you to strap into one of the mech suits to feel what mechanix can do for you." Cid smiled, trying to give the class the confidence they lacked. "Try one part at a time and test how it works. The arm units can help you lift up the table. A leg unit could leap to the ceiling with ease."

The class moved into groups with slow reluctance, each trying the various pieces of disassembled mech parts.

Riley struggled to strap on an arm suit, but after it got caught on a hair leaf, she started to cry. "I can't do this," Riley cried. "I don't care anymore."

Cid kneeled down and adjusted the arm gears. He lifted the mech arm gently. "Here. This piece just needs to be adjusted slightly. There, see? It fits. Try that."

Riley swallowed her tears and moved the mech arm. The metal and lights worked. She lifted up the edge of a table, surprised to see it move so easily.

"Do you want to know why I got into mech engineering?" Cid sat down next to her. "I got in an accident. A hover jet malfunctioned when I was a little older than you. Crushed my legs right off."

Riley looked at him with horror then at his legs.

"I had to wear mech legs for eight months while new legs grew back from green tubes." Cid smiled at her. "Hardship is a part of life, but it doesn't need to cripple us. It can make you stronger. It can make you wiser. It can protect you from terrible things that come from the outside. And see," Cid said, pulling up his pant leg. "No mech parts needed. There're things that can help, and with the right equipment, we can get through anything. Even the stuff giving us trouble up here." He tapped a finger against his forehead.

Riley stared at him with wide eyes still full of fear. But there was also a sliver of hope. Her mouth twitched at the feeble hint of a smile.

Green and red lights flashed across Keiko's face. "Three on your left, Ohm!"

Tortogres burst out from the trees and leapt onto Isaac' lizard-shaped mech, slamming it into a stream. Water erupted around the dark metal machine and the shelled beast that clawed at it, a cloud of fine mist sparkling in the brilliant light above them. Oscar's mole mech blasted a hole through the shell of another tortogre that crashed through leafy trees lining the banks as Jono's wolf mech clawed Isaac free.

Keiko's lion mech smashed the final tortogre into the ground. The three massive shelled beasts lay dead as the four mechs collected themselves, their pilots panting for breath. They stood in a lush, narrow ravine under a high sun. Keiko looked at the timer on the right of her mech's heads-up-display. They were already twenty minutes into their mission and they hadn't even reached the mountain bridge yet. Disgraceful.

"Click it together, Firewall," Keiko commanded. "Get your pistons oiled and follow me."

She knew it was too late for them to cut off the crystal resupply convoy. By now the reinforcements had made it safely past the walls surrounding their target, the Day's Clarion Point citadel.

She scowled at the team behind her but said nothing. Everything is harder the longer you wait to do what is needed. If only her team would get clicked, they could have picked them off and had an easy time of storming the battlements. Now, desperate times demanded gizmoed solutions.

"Change of blueprint," she said. "We turn off the ravine and head west toward the tunnels then cut right into the heart of the citadel."

"But the tunnels are enchanted. We can't see them through the trees," Oscar said.

"Plus, there are sixty mage knights with fully powered crystal towers," Jono added.

Every word out of their mouths made Keiko more annoyed. "We have one disenchanting shot left from the troll wizard's staff we took back when we landed, and yes, before you say it, I know that will alert the citadel's defense charms. That's why we're going to pull an Echo Charlie Dos pattern and—"

"Is that the one where we charge in a line?" Oscar asked.

"No, it's when we split up," Jono said, "but those other tunnels are too small for our mechs to get through and still fight."

Keiko banged her head against the back of her harness. "That's why we tuck and burn. We'll be going too fast through the tunnels for them to catch us in a spell. We'll be inside before they know it. Once we're in, we target the wisp powder storage and blow the whole castle to pieces!"

The comms lay in silence for a moment while they marched through the final zone of the ravine.

"I don't think that's going to work," Jono said.

Isaac sighed as though he couldn't be bothered to care. "Stars! Can we just lock on Kirin's plan and get this over with?"

"That's welded, Ohm. Way to contribute," Keiko grumbled.

"It's *your* plan, Kirin," Isaac snapped back. "You make it welded. I'm just along for the ride."

"Just follow orders this time and all of you stay clicked. I don't want the Firewall's scores to be on the Wall of Shame this month."

As the four mechs marched onward, splashing along the stream, bright rays of light cut sporadically through the thick canopy above them. The Day's Titan's Teeth Province was known for its vast mines filled with wisp powder, which they purified and distributed all across the Day to fill wands and power crystals. One strategic collapse of the supply chain would leave the Day vulnerable for weeks. All they had to do was get a spark into the citadel's refinery at just the right spot.

Keiko's mind raced through every possibility that could go wrong. They didn't know what sort of reinforcements awaited them in the citadel. If it was tortogres, she could use her gas blasts and then unleash her squid bots. If it was a sundrake brigade, they'd be lunch. Their best hope was in catching a phalanx of mage knights by surprise.

"Do you think the squires are going to take mech pilot training?" Oscar asked.

"Why wouldn't they?" Isaac asked.

Keiko moaned. "How is that relevant to our mission, Bohrs?"

"Look at who we're fighting," Jono cut in. "Don't you think it would be harsh to make squires kill simulated mage knights?"

"Maybe they could reprogram the sim to replace the Day with invading aliens or something?" Oscar said.

"As an alien, I'm offended," Isaac said. "And you should be too, Bohrs. We can't change every bit of training just to make the squires feel snuggly warm."

"It's a bit gizmos that we still have sims like this in the first place," Jono said.

"This is all for them!" Keiko growled. "Don't you clunkers get it? Those squires are part of the Firewall now, but that doesn't mean there aren't knights out there that still want to kill us all. Or even kill them for being traitors for coming to the Dark End. If we're going to be ready to protect our team from the Tombs then we better be oiled to take on foes on either End. Same goes for the squires. Now, if you cogs are done squeaking," her mech pointed to the end of the stream that seemed to appear out of a crack in the mountainside, "can we please invade the enemy base and slaughter us some knights now?"

"Sorry," the rest of the team replied in unison.

They stared at the rock wall for a long moment and nothing happened.

"Who has the disenchantment wand?" Oscar asked.

Jono's mech pulled the golden wand off from Oscar's mech's back. "You did." He then pointed the wand at the wall—he reached his fleshy hand out of the mech to touch the wand, ready to cast the spell.

"We get one shot at this," Keiko said. "Above us are dozens of knights and beasts that want our heads to decorate their walls. The instant that illusion is broken, they're all going to know about it. We split up down all four tunnels and meet in the city near the fountain. Ohm and Bohrs, you focus on taking out the stockpiles of wisp powder. Remember, we need a chain reaction to get down into the refinery. Wyer, you take the rear. Both of us will hit their crystal defenses as soon as you touch sunlight. Let's show them what soldiers are made of!"

Jono touched that wand. "Kylops Avidya!"

The wand cast a beam of rainbow light that distorted the mountainside, morphing it into a stone tunnel that curved up into the mountain.

Keiko charged first with the team right behind her. The four mechs tucked their arms and guns close to their metal frames as they blasted up a maze of tunnels. The roar of their engines echoed through the shattering tunnel walls that scrapped against their mechs. Blasts of red, purple, and orange magic bolts flew past them

Keiko's mech burst through an angelic fountain in the central square of the citadel. She was surrounded by mage knights that turned toward her in surprise. She unleashed a storm of gas bombs and squidbots as the three other mechs popped up from below in different areas around the courtyard. The sudden barrage ignited a nearby stack of barrels containing unrefined wisp powder, which exploded, flinging knights into the stone walls.

A blast of blue light cut through Oscar's mech, severing its leg. The molemech stumbled to the ground as Oscar shot back as best as he could. "I'm down! Help!" He used maneuvering rockets to thrust his mech out of the way of another blue beam.

Keiko pointed at a set of blue crystals that lined the fort's defensive wall. "The crystal pillars! Take them out!"

Isaac turned his mech's cannons on the crystals, blasting them with explosive rounds. But more blue beams cut through the smoke from the explosions, detonating his missiles before they could hit their mark. Isaac's lizard mech lunged backward.

"They're not going down!" Isaac said as he dodged out of the way of another beam.

Jono's mech leapt onto the battlements. Its saw arm cut one of the crystals' mountings, toppling it over the edge. The crystal crashed to the ground and shattered. Keiko caught Jono looking back down at his team just as another crystal shot a beam directly through the center of his mech. Static filled Keiko's ears as Jono's mech stumbled back, falling off of the battlements and smashing a crater in the cobblestone below.

"Jono!" Keiko screamed.

Keiko's mech engines roared as she charged over the battlements, cutting and tearing crystal cannons from their spires and kicking them as far as her mechanical legs could punt. She dodged beams and pummeled through a phalanx of knights as they cast spells that tore into her metal hide.

A group of robed mages swarmed around Oscar, unleashing waves of fire spells. Thick black smoke billowed from his mech as Oscar's screams went silent.

Isaac sprang up in time to smash a tortogre away from pummeling Keiko with an enormous ax. His lizard-mech reached down to help her up, but then its arm fell limp as a sparking blue blade poked out from the mech's chest and tore its way upward, severing its metal head.

Keiko blasted the knight just as another tortogre slammed against her back and pinned her down long enough for the army of pixie vines to wrap around her metal joints.

"Tricks on you, burnt brains," Keiko growled. She flicked on the mech's self-destruct just as a knight swung his sword down on her head. The mech detonated into a trillion fragments of burning metal. Shrapnel cut down swaths of knights, and the tortogre was turned to a smoking husk. The citadel quaked and a tower beside the blast crumbled and fell.

The image on her screen disappeared. Keiko yelled and smashed her fists against her padded harness.

The door to her pod opened into a hall inside of Windom lined with mech simulators. Keiko tore off her harness and was already yelling before her team had crawled out of their mechs.

"What the still-burning stars was that?" Keiko took stiff breaths through flaring nostrils. "That was the worse run I've seen in weeks! That formation was bilge. We didn't even set off a spark in their alchemy factory before they slaughtered us!"

"Don't blame me. My molemech's ankle thruster was damaged right at the start," Oscar said as he climbed out of his pod.

"And I had a gear latency drain," Isaac said. "I told you we should have spent our launch points on repairs instead of weaponry."

"Ammo wins battles!" Keiko yelled. "Besides, you two should have caught both of those in the manual pre-check. In real life, mechs will get damaged. If you don't take care of them, you're smelting your own coffin."

"There it is. The lesson of the wake." Oscar looked around satisfied. "Next time, we'll check better. Who wants to ask the squires if they're up for a game in the den?"

Keiko clenched her hands into fists. "Are you serious? If that was real, every last one of you would be dead. I can't be there to keep you alive every waking second! I can't watch over everyone by myself! We're the Firewall, remember? Our team is supposed to be built for something. How can we trust each other when the next fight comes knocking and we I can't even trust you to take training seriously?"

"It was just a game, Kirin. We'll do better next time," Oscar said.

"Next time, it's going to be real, and you're going to get a crystal shard through your skull, Bohrs," Keiko snapped back. "Don't you get that?"

"You saw my scores," Oscar replied. "There's no way I'm going to be assigned to a mech division once we graduate. It's not like we're even going to be a squad once we get out of Windom. I bet I'll work in supply management. I can't wait to pick out the chair for my desk. I've always imagined red cushions. Anyway, Ohm will do research, and Jono is clicked into Cloaks. I'll probably never even leave the city again."

"Bohrs is clicked on that," Isaac said. "They'll split up the Firewall long before we graduate. Honestly, Kirin, out of all of us, this training is only going to be useful for you. We're all just doing it because the class is required."

"Is that how you're ticking? All of you?" Keiko scowled at her friends. "Let's just throw away the only team that's actually fought against the Tombs? Let's just abandon each other because our academy plans to split us up, so what's the point?"

Jono leaned in to try to grab her attention. "It does make sense for us to focus on our specialties. I will fight the Tombs, but I should be code cracking and that is something I need to do alone. This was all a waste of time. If I have to fail in mechnaut class in order to stop the Tombs, then that's worth it."

"You are all wrong. I don't care two squirts about careers or grades," Keiko growled. "We don't need to be a team so we can capture flags or score bonuses. When the pox hits and this city starts to crumble, who else is going to get us through the chaos? When the Tombs rain down fire on us, who's going to pull their plugs? The squires are our responsibility now and they're lost cogs here in the Dark! The Firewall is a team, out there, in the real world, whether you like or not."

"You're wrong, Kirin," Isaac said. "We have to plan for a life beyond people trying to kill us. What happens after we live through the Tombs? What are you going to do?"

Keiko smashed her fist against the mech door, the sound echoing through the cavernous hallway. Her enforced skeleton left a dent. "The Ragnarok was just the beginning. There's a war coming and nothing matters but knowing who you can trust to see you through it. I refuse to let you clunkers shut down so quickly."

The light of floating screens bathed Isaac's face in blue, red, and green. Above him was the image of a sunny wheat field with a smattering of pox spotted across the sky like a school of fish swimming in and out of existence. The scene ended then looped to the beginning to start again.

"What are you?" he whispered in the empty room.

Doctor Lamb appeared on the screen and pointed out an overlay of data on the image of the pox. Her hair was pulled back in a tousled pony tail and her eyes were bright despite the dark bags beneath them.

"They were so close," Fourier said as he entered the room with two cups filled with siltbean tea.

Isaac frowned at the smiling faces of the crew of P.E.P. seventeen. "They were wrong. Their hypothesis didn't predict the pox would hit on their way back to Shimmerlake."

The screen flashed at the moment of chaos. The metal caravan was pulled into the air between two massive poxes. The camera was whisked from Doctor Lamb's hand and flew out of the window to watch as the gravitational pull of the pox sucked in the research team. Green burns spotted the field and left chunks of metal and basilisk tail flailing as they fell through a crisp sky.

"Those poor, brave minds." Fourier mourned at the sight of the crew's final moments.

"What does that means for their research?" Isaac asked.

"From what I hear, the Academy of Atomology is rejecting Quantum Elasticity in favor of Erratic Neutrino Combustion, which . . ." Fourier sighed as he sat down, "in my mind, is a path toward embracing unpredictability."

"That's not an answer we can live with."

"The Day is holding out hoping that QE can still explain it, but that may just be to save Shimmerlake University's reputation."

Isaac scratched his head. The purple dye was starting to grow out from his head tendrils and show his orange roots again. "We're never going to solve this if we keep putting pride in front of evidence."

"We need new perspectives, new ideas." Fourier paused. Though Isaac stared at the displays, he seemed to be looking past them, far off. "Are you sure you are ready to be here?"

Isaac nodded. "Sometimes a little data observation is just what the brain needs. Clarity of context and a sense of purpose."

Isaac checked the pox data, his hand shaking.

"It's okay to take time away," Fourier said. "When the body undergoes a traumatic experience, it can leave an imprint that can take some time to fade."

Isaac dropped his hand and stared at the desk.

"It's helpless, being in space." Isaac sighed. "I need to be better prepared, to plan for things others forgot. I trusted the Empress and once again, she didn't see this coming."

"Trust should be earned, but be careful that you aren't blaming the world for not seeing the future." Fourier sat next to him and looked over the data. "That is a standard no one can meet. There must be some consideration for intent and effort."

"I don't blame the Empress," Isaac replied. "But dead is dead and I intend to keep on living."

Chapter Twenty-Two

A Tale of Empty Truth

*T*he screen in front of the stage at Saint Newton's rolled over a list of the cast members for the Ides of Decsomber with the crowd of would-be actors spotting the seats. Isaac frowned at the list, but when he turned around Oscar was beaming. "You did it, mate."

Oscar's jaw hung loose. "I'm the King?" He stood and raised both hands in the air. "I'm the King!"

"You?" Nick said from a few seats away. "You could barely belch out the words!"

Oscar chuckled. "It's because I'm so jolly all the time."

Murphy Wumples tapped Oscar on the shoulder. "I'm your understudy for the King. We should practice our lines together."

"Pay good attention," Oscar said with a laugh. "When all this fame gets to my head, you're the one that's going to have to fill in."

"I'm Maria," Elise squealed. "I got the lead!"

Kain hugged her. "Congrats, sis."

"Look, you're the Shadow, Kain."

Kain giggled and waved his arms. "Fear my endless nothing, ye fragile mortals!"

"Suriana is Draca," Isaac said. "Is that fair? She's the one putting the whole thing on."

Elise shoved him. "Nobody knows this story like she does. The theater department would be insane to not have her in this. I bet they even made her do it."

Nick nodded. "She's the only one in this production with her head on straight, among other things perfectly placed," he said as a thin smiled spread across his face.

Elise administered another harsh shove. "Watch your mouth. She's better than your grubby eyes deserve."

Nick rubbed his head. "Ow! I was just noticing the obvious." When the cast list got to the second understudy for the King's trumpeter, Nick scowled and stomped away.

The crowd dispersed, leaving Roger Hyland alone to stare at the cast list.

"I'm the Herald," Roger said with pride, but no one was around to congratulate him.

Far from the crowds of eager thespians, David sat backstage, preparing the digital canvases for his paints. Each time he would paint a different yet still fitting backdrop, but the pattern of the music and scenes would be the same.

"I can feel you watching me," David said.

Suriana stepped from behind a red curtain. "Sorry, I didn't mean to lurk. I saw you paint music in Al Jebra, but I never really understood how it worked."

David shrugged. "In the Dark, we would just go on the Line and learn all about it. There are about a billion training games on it."

Suriana sat next to him and curled her legs under her skirt. "We Day Enders aren't much for Line games. We prefer to sit in person and learn from the master. So, master of painted songs, how does it really work?"

David forced a smile. "See how I'm waving this brush? Right now it is set to have a particular instrument tied to a particular range of colors at this particular place in the opera. I'm setting the canvas to know that at this moment these shades of teal will play an oboe using the notes of the music, but the sound the oboe makes depends on how I move my fingers. Pointing or clenching, tense or loose, it all changes the music."

Suri stared at the canvas as he demonstrated. "That's the technology of it. What about the art? How does it make you feel?"

"When I perform, I'll have a brush on each finger. It gets complicated, but once I get into it?" David sat back and let his eyes close. He waved his hand; an oboe, clarinet, and flute began to play as his fingers danced in front of the canvas. "Like I'm a god weaving life into existence. I have this connection with it. I feel it move, and there it is. It's real and alive in that moment, and everyone in the audience can feel it too. It's like being in a lucid dream, where you can control everything and make the world transform into the most beautiful place. Anyone that cares to watch, that stops and lets themselves join you in that dream, they feel exactly as you feel. There's no need for clumsy words. It's just a trick of light and vibrations, but still . . . it's a truth you share. You and the audience both know it, through and through, but there isn't quite a way to describe it unless you live it."

Suriana's eyes glistened. "Is that how it is for you at a performance? While we are singing our lines, you're in that trance?"

"Most times," David replied. "Sometimes my nerves take over and it's more forced than it should be. Also, if I haven't practiced the songs enough. It all has to become so memorized that it's second nature. It's at that point that my mind and body and the music perfectly align. If I can get there, then it's not about the music as it was written. It becomes about the living music. I can add little flourishes or change the tone to be quieter or more intense. It all comes alive and breathes and screams and cries and it will only live that way once. It lives to sing its story and be heard in that one moment, that one chance, and then . . . then it's over. And I hope I get to bring something new to life again."

A tear crested Suri's eye. She hugged him before he knew what she was doing. "Thank you, David. This is why we like talking to people instead of programs. You have a gift in you that should be treasured. This is what you can give the world. It's something I always wish I had." She released him from her hug.

David blushed. "It takes practice. I've been painting since I could move. Sometimes, it takes over and nothing else matters. The whole world disappears and all there is to life is the color and song."

"I was the one that convinced the Sage of Ages to do this student exchange," Suriana said. "And this is exactly why."

"So you can learn how to paint music?"

Suri smiled. "No. So we could learn that we are not so different. This feeling, how painting music moves you so deeply? This is what I wanted to share with the Dark End. It is how watching the Ides of Decsomber made me feel. We cannot let those feelings stay bottled up. If we share them, our spirits are free and the world is made better."

David replied with a sad smile. "The Dark and Day have been on the edge of war for thousands of years. Do you think a little song and dance will work to change that?"

Suriana shrugged. "I've only been alive for fifteen years of it. What else can I do but try?"

Keiko found Jono sitting in the darkness with his eyes shut. He didn't move, except for his gentle breathing. Keiko leaned in and blew air against his face. His nose twitched. She blew again and the hair on his forehead brushed against his eye.

Jono blinked his eyes open.

"What are you doing?"

"That's exactly what I came looking for you to ask." Keiko sat next to him and looked around the cramped space. "This is the same secret tunnel we found together where you snuck your wires into Grail's computer when we were looking for Attrayer's Key all those years ago."

Jono nodded. "Time flies."

"So what are you looking for this time?" Keiko asked.

"Clues," Jono replied. "Everyone is keeping us out of the hunt for the Tombs, but we know them better than most. We've seen them in person. We know how they think. We need to be ready. We missed the sabotage. We are lucky that it's not what the Tombs wanted, but we can't be so sure next time."

"You keep saying we, but all I see is your obsession." When Jono turned his head away from her, she continued. "What? Are you saying that blowing up a space ship wasn't them trying to kill us?"

"The Tombs don't want us dead. Not like that. It was too close. They could have killed us all, but they want something else."

"Half of the planet is thanking the angels that no one died, but you give credit to the people that put the bomb on board?"

Jono frowned. "Keiko, there are no angels. The Tombs have always been playing a game with us. They wanted us to be afraid so they unleashed the pox. It worked. They were sending a message with the bomb, but they want us to read it a certain way. They want us to think of them as all-powerful emissaries of this great god from the depth of space capable of taking or sparing a life any time or any place."

"But why? If none of it's real, what's their plan?"

Jono sighed. "I don't know. Maybe . . . they want us to do it."

"To do what?"

"They want us to kill ourselves. That would be their form of justice. They think it would prove something."

"The world is more at peace now than it has been in millennia. If that's their plan, they're clunkers at it."

Jono laughed. "I hope so."

"We missed you at the mentor meeting."

Jono grimaced. "I forgot that was this wake."

"Did you? If we need to build a peace, then I thought the plan to be friends with the Day was the way to do it. Build a unified front against our common enemy."

"It doesn't matter if they're all dead."

"But they're not dead. They're alive, in part thanks to you."

"And when I'm not around?"

"You want to be alone. I get that, but Jono, you can't act like you have to save the world alone. If you do that, you're going to fail. At the very least, the Firewall is with you. Let us help."

"I would, believe me. The problem is I have no idea what to do. That's what scares me."

A wave of blue fire cut through a thicket of gnarled trees then spread into a jagged claw. The blue claw tore through a mech drone just as it leaped from behind a boulder. A singed white tunic with the symbol of a circle and jagged cross fluttered to the forest floor as the drone rained down in shattered pieces.

"Excellent form, Squire Faisal," Solinser Moss said with a venomous sneer. "You'll make a knight sooner than most."

Sweat trickled down Freya's red forehead as she caught her breath. "I will make those dungpits suffer. The Tombs will regret the wake they didn't kill me."

Around her, the other squires cast a fury of spells in all directions, destroying the old wizard bots now dressed with the Tombs' symbol on their robes.

Ice, poison, lava, and arcane fire exploded from their wands, cutting down drones charging at them. The anger, fear, and vengeance poured out of them.

"Channel your fury into your spells," Moss yelled over the roars of magic. "The Tombs were laughing as you dangled helpless in the abyss, but will they still laugh when you meet them in battle?"

Freya yelled as tears streaked from her eyes.

Moss raised his hand and the spells ceased. At once, the squires fell to their knees, exhausted and shaking. Tears swam with sweat as their exposed emotions drained them of all pretenses.

A few squires crawled to their feet, but Freya remained on the ground, gritting her teeth and trying to swallow her sobs. She pounded against the dirt with a clenched fist.

Moss rested a hand on her shoulder and kneeled beside her.

"I know how helpless you must have felt. I too have felt the sting of powerlessness, but heed my words, young squire. Your might and magic will never leave you powerless again. Harness your passion for justice. Use it to make you powerful, and some wake, the Tombs will feel the righteous might of your spellblade on their throat."

Freya looked up at him. The exhaustion had burned away all anger and ferocity, leaving behind only the tearful eyes of a scared fifteen year old.

"Are you certain we should be doing this?" Maergann watched the city rush by out of the window of their jet car.

"The city guards are thousands of bots hidden all around us, but this is beyond the jurisdiction of the city. This is military business," Ramsus said. "And as the resident soldier on point for the Peace Council, that means it's my call. This needs to be done without a show. The higher ups will decide what gets disclosed to the public and when."

Maergann frowned. She was naturally inclined to doubt everything that Ramsus said. "Doesn't bringing me with you on this field trip put your little government secrecy at risk? Who's to say I do not believe in transparency and will let the world know what you are doing?"

Ramsus gave her an exaggerated pouty look. "That's cute. You think I don't do my homework. We completed a review of your entire life long before you came to Eies, Sir Brigid."

"How is that not an invasion of my privacy?"

Ramsus shrugged. "Ask your Day lords. They approved it. You've been on our recruitment short list for the past two years. You already have three-tier approval for admission in our corp."

"What if I like what I do?"

"You are a rank twelve swordspell knight with the job of guarding one child. That, darling, is overkill. I'm a soldier. You are a knight. We do what is needed to protect the lands we love, and sometimes that means leaving behind some of those loved ones. That's not always easy to know, but we never take a risk without a thorough assessment of the facts."

Chapter Twenty-Two

"Is that what this is, an opportunity to assess some facts?"

"I'm hoping seeing the level of depravity we're up against will convince you to join."

The flying car arrived at a grease-stained street in the middle towers of the mech district.

Ramsus's bionetic eyes scanned the street. Inside the thirty second floor sat a man on a chair with his legs propped up on a cushion. On a screen in front of him was a globall match between the Quarington Quasars and the Eden City Ice Kings.

"That unassuming bilge is our Tombs, Cedric Pummel."

Maergann pulled an enchanted visor over her eyes, allowing her to spy into the building. "He looks like a normal Dark Ender to me. Are you certain he's the right person?"

"He's the one. We've built up a mountain of evidence against him thanks to our little spy bots. He was the protective chemix technician at Thanadu Chemix that made the infected pipe in the Ragnarok. It may look like he was working on his own, but the pixels he used were very specialized. He got them from somewhere, but he's not going there again. We need to bag this clunker and see who stirs when they hear the news."

"There's an alarm system around the apartment." Maergann pointed to glowing blue light in her mirror.

Ramsus smiled. "Of course there is. Since the window is open, it's probably the security model that detects any activity crossing the barrier besides himself."

"How do we proceed?"

"Quick and quiet." Ramsus held up a tiny mouse bot. "Little Sparky here will take out his alarms then stick him with a tranquilizer and some pixels that will prevent him from wiping his memory. I won't make that mistake again."

He let the mouse go. They watched from the street as it scurried through the pipes into the alarm box. The mouse bot released its tail, which slithered through the apartment like a snake. It crept up the back of Cedric's chair and poked him in the neck. He swatted at the tail as if it were a bug but otherwise didn't seem to care about it.

"You Dark Enders are crafty," Maergann said. "Disgusting, but crafty."

"Let's rocket." Ramsus leaped toward the room, the jets on his boots carrying him over gaps between buildings.

Maergann spoke several words to cast a spell, granting her a set of ethereal wings to fly her into the window.

They both landed on a tattered rug just as Cedric Pummel was losing consciousness.

"What are you doing?" Cedric mumbled. "Alarm?" He lifted his arm, but he was already too drowsy. He stared at them in horror and gasped.

"I didn't do it!"

"You didn't do what?" Ramsus looked at him, surprised. "You're just having a scary dream, aren't you?"

Cedric's guise of fright turned to a sinister smile. "You and your false city will burn once the King of the Pit rises!"

Ramsus slapped a fel cloak brooch on Pummel's chest. "You keep telling yourself that. In the meantime, have a fun trip to prison."

The fel cloak swallowed Cedric up in a wave of shadow and whisked him silently out of the window.

Maergann shivered at the sight. "I cannot believe I am on the side using the fel."

"Better get used to it. Fel tech is as brilliant as it is frightening."

"All children in the Day grow up fearing fel demons will attack them during sleeps. It's a hard image to let go of."

"Darlin', you're about to be introduced to a whole new world of demons."

The apartment was an absolute mess. The kitchen was filled with broken dish bots filling the sink with rotting food. Clothes were scattered along the bedroom floor, and bland photo galleries hung on the walls with Cedric smiling alongside people that looked out of place.

"Is this normal?" Maergann said.

"You haven't been to many Dark Ender apartments, have you? Remind me to give you a tour of mine sometime." Ramsus winked.

"I doubt it would offer any educational value."

"You don't know what you're missing."

"I know what these photos are missing," she said as she peered at a wall of framed images. "Any connection. No one in these photos actually looks like they're aware of

Cedric beside them."

Ramsus looked over the images. "They're all fakes. He just did a poor job of editing himself into these photos."

"How long has Cedric Pummel been living this illusion without your Empress' eyes seeing through it, I wonder?"

Ramsus scanned through the layers of the room with his enhanced vision. "He moved to Eies over fifteen years ago. He could have come from anywhere before that, even the Day." He plucked one of the frames off the wall and turned it over in his hands. "Unfortunately, our records of the outer reaches of the Dark End can be tenuous at best."

Maergann frowned at everything the Dark was that the Day wasn't. "The Dark is so impersonal. I can see a spy living here in anonymity with ease, but in the Day? In a wake, he'd have nosey neighbors bringing casseroles over and inviting him out for picnics. We'd spot a fraud quicker than your bots could infect someone."

Ramsus smiled as he let the frame drop to the floor. "Spies prepare for their assignment. I'd be careful of depending on cultural inclinations for security."

"Are you saying this is the Dark's method of infiltrating the Day?"

Ramsus mimed zipping his mouth closed.

"Fair enough. What is next? We tear this place apart looking for clues?"

"I found one." Ramsus motioned to a doorway, which they went through to find a bedroom. "There is a shielded spot on the wall there. He's hiding something."

While Maergann moved straight for the wall to look for a mechanism or hidden panel, Ramsus took a moment to scan the room further.

"It's just a wall," she said, lifting more frames off the wall.

Clutter covered the room; the bed had probably never been made, and discarded food containers and dirty clothes blanketed the floor. But there was a disruption to the pattern of filth: a small area of cleared space next to the bed. Ramsus kneeled down and felt under the bed-frame until he found a switch.

"We Dark Enders aren't so straightforward as to put a switch on the wall we're hiding something behind," Ramsus said as he flicked the switch.

Maergann startled as the wall stared to move. It pushed the bed against the other wall and opened up an entire other room. Turquoise lights illuminated the Tomb's symbol painted in dried blood.

"This is a deep well of depravity," Maergann admitted.

"Put these on." Ramsus handed her a pair of bracelets that, when she put them on, covered her hands in tracking gloves.

Ramsus picked up a leather-bound paper book. "Why would anyone print on paper?" Ramsus said.

"The world lives on waves of code," Maergann said. "Paper is for secrets."

Ramsus looked over the book. Its cover had the same Tombs symbol embossed on it. "The Abysmal Biblios? Is this like that book you all read in the Day?" He held it out for her.

She took it, her eyebrows raised. "The Biblios?"

"I've never read it."

"You Dark Enders are so uncultured. Every Day student learns its teachings, even if they don't believe its words." Maergann flipped through the pages. "These are the same stories about the Father, Mother, and the angels, but it is telling them all wrong."

"All wrong? Or from another perspective?" Ramsus asked. "History is written by the victors, but that doesn't stop the losers from writing their version."

"Cedric marked several passages here. '*Verily did I behold within the mirror a visage of eternal truth, that the Lord of the Pit had carved his mark into my heart as a gift of thanks. For then did I witness the majesty of Oblivion and tasted the sourness of the world's illusions. His eyes were my eyes. His thoughts were my thoughts. My heart was his, and it was as empty as the realm of the Abyss. Here I knew my purpose. All of the world must be forced to see the Empty Truth and cower at its divine elegance. All will know our Master's grace, that He hath saved us from that shackles of matter and life, to join Him in the Eternal Pit.*'"

"What a cheerful message," Ramsus said, scratching the back of his head. "It's surprising we aren't all converted."

Maergann shut the book, feeling violated at the idea of the Tombs perverting the tales of her holy text. "If they worship Oblivion so much, why don't they just incinerate themselves and get there faster?"

"That's not how fanaticism works," Ramsus said. "The whole point is to get as many people as possible to buy into your gizmos view. You all get to feel superior to people outside of your bubble, but that ego turns to hate and fear, and soon you need to convert or eradicate anything that doesn't feed on your crazy. It's a drug addiction that grows, and eventually, it leads to death."

"Then let it be theirs."

"Wise words, darlin'. Them before us."

Chapter Twenty-Three

The Merry Lad of Giftmas

now frosted the city in perfectly planned patches. Giftmas lights illuminated thirty floors of shops along Copernicus Plaza as white flakes fluttered down from the greenhouse clouds. Gold and silver chains of bells lined windows. The city smelled of pine and peppermint. Children stared through frosted windows, bundled in thick coats as they sipped spiced crapple cider from any of the cideries that offered their wares on every corner.

The Giftmas break had brought everyone to the shops. Riley and Murphy traded bites from a cupcake sampler they'd bought at Yessler's Stellar Bakery. Commander Grail and Professor Helios savored the view of the city from a bench in a quiet park in between shops. Even Professor Moss accompanied some squires with unprecedented enjoyment on their faces. As Moss sipped a spiced crapple cider and watched the squires pop in an out of shops, a group of disgruntled cadets flung a ring of lights around his head and dropped a star to crown his branchy hair. The cadets cackled with joy as they ran away through the crowd. Moss scowled at the petulance of the entire of the Dark End as a shopper took a picture of the most miserable Giftmas tree in history.

Samuel, the bard bot, perched on a spaceship-shaped fountain in the center of the plaza. He waved at Jonothon, Keiko, and Isaac as they passed by. His floppy Giftmas hat had a spot or two of oil and its red color had faded, but the cheerfulness and heart he put into his songs from long ago only made his tarnished appearance all the more endearing.

After he finished his rendition of Old Good King Wassailus, Samuel waved to the crowd. "We have with us this wake a special guest from the Day that would like to share a heartfelt Giftmas message."

Aquinas stepped onto the lip of the fountain and opened his arms wide. "Thank you all, and Merry Giftmas! As part of all the jolly merriment, it is this time of year that we all pause and take stock in the gifts of life that surround us. Friends, family, and of course, the legacy of the Lad of Giftmas, Saint Nicholas Claus. With that in mind, I would like to read the story of the birth of the Lad."

"What is this, street preaching now?" Isaac shook his head.

Aquinas flipped open his personal biblios then cleared his throat. "The Book of Claus, chapter six verse three. *'And Lo, it was then on Giftmas wake that those Wise Believers, having traveled so far for so long, did arrive at the humble stables of bed of grain. Kings and queens, sages and philosophers, oil mongers, and muscow herders all did come to bear witness to his birth. From out of the humble nursery was the child presented to his flock. He was the Lad of Giftmas, and to every traveler his spirit did lighten their weary souls and heal the aches of their bodies. Even the seven angels did descend upon the stables as stars falling from the heavens. Each Angel kissed the Lad's brow and bestowed upon him their gifts: one of merriment, others of wisdom, charity, immortality, bravery, and for the last gift, the Lad did raise his hand and speak to the Angel Miraphael through the ether. It was His wish to share these gifts with the world, and so did Miraphel bless him with her spirit. His actions would be hers. His gifts would be blessed so that he may spread the good whispers to all the world!"*

Aquinas closed the book. "Even to this wake, may your gifts be blessed with the spirit of harmony, hope, and joy. May you spread that spirit with gifts of kindness and service during Giftmas and all wakes of the year."

Aquinas bowed, and the crowd clapped politely as Sam resumed his post and jolly tunes.

Keiko chuckled. "The Lad of Giftmas was an angel? That's news to me."

"I'm looking it up on the Line," Jono said. In a blink he had the information he was looking for. "About three centuries ago, Giftmas was more popular than all the angel holidays combined, so the Fellowship created a new version of the Lad that they say is actually a discovery of his previously forgotten origin. It's all angelic, and it made them a ton of money selling angel related Giftmas Lad stuff in the Day."

"Can't they just leave a good thing alone?" Isaac said with a sigh. "Now even Giftmas isn't safe from the angels! They need to take over everything. What's next? Angels invented ice cream? Get your holy blessing angel cookies! Only our brand of toilet cleaner is angels certified for no spiritual residue! Leaves your bumper clean physically and spiritually!"

From out of the crowed, Edgar Niles emerged wearing a sandwich board around him that read *Merry Giftmas! The Angels are Listening!*

Isaac gasped. "Not him, too."

Edgar stopped at every table in the plaza, handing out pamphlets about the angels. Edgar waved at Aquinas, who warily waved back before he shrunk into the crowd.

"A most enlightened reading, Fellow Aquinas!" Edgar yelled over the crowd. "I was there, floating above the manger. I know it like it was yesterwake. The Lad, what a sweet child. The stables, though, are always depicted as clean and tidy, but animals are messy things. There's just no way around the smells." Edgar frowned as he leaned down to face a young boy curled behind his parent's knee.

"And what do you ask for from the Lad this year?" Edgar smiled, a mad look in his eyes.

"A rocket," the boy whispered back.

"A rocket? Splendid! Pray hard to the Angels, my son, and they'll get your message delivered for sure. The angels hear prayers better at Giftmas, and I hear yours loud and clear!" Edgar stood up and leaned toward the boy's father.

"Rocket," he whispered with a knowing wink. "Here, have a sticker and remember my words from the Neo Testament: *Give unto others what you would have, and receive from others what they would desire.*"

Isaac scowled at the ragged man. "Are you listening to yourself? That doesn't even make sense. Why don't they give me what I want and I give them what they want? Then we're all happy."

Edgar laughed at Isaac. "Because it's Giftmas! You're thinking too much. Don't question the words of the angels, boy. Just embrace the *feeling* of the words! It's much better that way."

Isaac waited for Edgar to move along before he spoke again. "All these stories. Sermons, fables, jolly lads, and angels? You know who else is gizmos about stories? The Tombs. It's the same clunkered minds, and it's destroying the world. Mark me, we're navigating a sea of madness."

"Speaking of gizmos," Keiko said, "I need you two to help me. I signed us all up to manage the Snow Fall Ball decorations this year."

"You can't just go and sign up other people for work," Isaac said. "That's forced labor. Basically slavery."

Keiko sneered. "Do you want me to tell Evanine Fluff the whole dance is barren of decorations because one clunkered ayleen didn't want to help?"

"Evanine?" Isaac gulped. "Fine, I'll help. Stars!"

"That's the Giftmas spirit!" Keiko said.

"Actually, on that topic, I have something for you." Jono reached into his pocket, but he couldn't find what he was looking for. He looked through each pocket of his coat. "It's here somewhere."

"While you're searching, guess who has a date to the ball?" Keiko said.

"It's not Oscar is it?" Jono said. He clasped the small metal box he was looking for and held it in his hand, still in his pocket. "He kept saying he was going to have a date before me."

"No, burnt brain. Me!" Keiko smiled. "David asked me. I don't think I'll still fit into that old dress, so I'm going have to get something new. With pockets. And a tool belt."

Jono left the box in his pocket. "Isn't he at the opera that wake?"

"Yeah, and I'm helping organize the whole ball, so it's not like either of us will have much time. But he can stop by right when the Ball starts. Also the opera ends with plenty of time for him to get back for the last dance."

"Oh?" Jono tried to sound supportive, but it felt like his stomach had dropped out of his body. "First and last dance at least then? That's good enough, I guess."

Keiko shrugged. "I'm sure I'll be spending the whole time keeping people from spiking the punch or getting into fights. Remember last year when Diego Vega and his boyfriend at the time sent out elf bots to deliver presents, but sprayed people with dye?"

Isaac laughed. "That was the best part of the dance! Roger Hyland had purple skin for weeks!"

"It wasn't funny, and it is not happening at *my* dance, you hear me?" Keiko slapped Jono's leg. "Oh, what did you have for me?"

"For you? What? No, nothing," Jono stuttered. "I mean, I left it in my bunk. It's nothing. I'll bring it by later."

"Alright," she said, giving him a questioning look. "I'm going to the décor shop to order things for the ball. You coming?"

Jono shook his head. "No. I need to do some Giftmas shopping of my own."

Keiko grinned. "I see, clever boy. Don't buy me anything too inexpensive. What about you, Ohm?"

"Oh, I will definitely get you something too inexpensive," Isaac replied.

Keiko kicked snow at him. "Come on. You can help choose the picture themes."

Isaac shrugged. "I suppose someone needs to keep you from picking something wildly inappropriate."

"That's the spirit. Later, Jono."

They waved then disappeared into the crowd.

Jono sat on a nearby bench, alone, listening to Samuel's song about a couple staying inside and keeping warm while snow fell outside their window. He pulled the box from his pocket and pushed a rose engraving on its lid, transforming the box into a mechanical rose. Inscribed upon its leaves were the words *Dance with Me*.

Jono squinted at the rose glistening in green and red Giftmas lights before he turned it back into a box. After stowing it in his pocket, he stood and lost himself in the crowd of jolly Giftmas shoppers.

"Get down!" Oscar slammed into Jono then threw him into a snowy bank just as a volley of snowballs flew over their heads.

Jono spat out a wad of snow. "What the burning stars are you doing?"

"Its war, mate!" Oscar said, peering over the snow bank, a snowball in his hand. "Capricorn Corridor versus Ares Aisle and they're winning."

The square in front of Saint Newton's had been transformed into a battlefield of snowy barriers and piles of compacted ammunition.

A shout came from across the square.

"Now!" Bastion Bittle and Clive Van der Scant led a brave assault on the Ares base, but were repelled in a storm of snowy spheres.

"Where's Isaac?" Jono asked.

"He never showed, just like you were late," Oscar said.

"I didn't know this was happening."

"I left a note. And we had the corridor meeting last week, remember?"

Jono shook his head.

"Fine." Oscar shoved some snowballs into Jono's hands. "You can share my stockpile, but we're down by almost half from Ares."

Nicklus Knox and the thirty cadets from Ares Aisle stood right in front of them. "So glad you could join us."

Jono and Oscar ducked toward the barrier, but the barrage was relentless. Snow piles covered their bodies curled up on the ground.

"Ow! We give up!" Oscar yelled.

"Hey, Twig." Nick stood over Jono with an armful of snow. He dropped it all at once, covering Jono's face. His self-satisfied laughs came to an abrupt stop when he said, "What's that?"

Jono looked to see that the rose had fallen from his pocket and sprung to life.

Nick picked it up and read the inscription. "'Dance with me?'" Nick snorted. "Oh, Twiggums, you shouldn't have."

Jono scrambled to his feet and snatched at the mechanical flower. "It's not for you."

"Good, 'cause I already got a date, and high standards. Guess who's going to the Ball with the pretty sunny princess?"

Jono froze in shock. "You asked Suriana?"

"Who else would I be talking about?" Nick snapped. "Do you think I walk around the Dark being happy for someone else?"

"But she's *in* the opera."

How was it that Jono was the only one that thought the opera precluded students from the dance?

"Not the whole time, bilge for brains!" Nick said. "The Ball goes until the new wake. Plenty of time for action!"

"Knox, you're the single worst representative the Dark could offer to the Day," Jono said in shocked seriousness.

Nick's grin turned to a stern frown, and he shoved Jono, causing him to slip and fall on the icy ground.

Jono's face flushed red with embarrassment as Nick and his Ares buddies shared a laugh at his fall. Oscar offered Jono a hand to help him up, but Jono pushed the offered assistance aside and tried to stand on his own.

"You're jealous!" Nick said, his finger pointed at Jono. "Why don't you grow up and get a date, oh high and mighty Twig! Not surprising, though. Twigs always snap under pressure." Nick and his friends turned to leave. "Have fun all alone by yourself, clunker."

The window made Nick, Suriana, Keiko, David, and Oscar look like water paintings wavering in the colored bath of stained glass. Every row in Saint Newton's Cathedral was packed with parishioners. There were even crowds standing in the back.

At the pulpit, Aquinas wore a somber black robe and spoke slowly about the fears that plagued Earth's ancestors. Together, the crowd took comfort in sharing their fears and hopes. In that hall, their trembling hands took strength in holding each other's in a row. They weren't alone, and the warmth of the fateriarch's words lifted their spirits. Jono sat on the steps outside and could hear Aquinas' voice through the cathedral's open doors. He liked how the orange light glowed through round windows. The clouds grew thin and let the stars creep through.

"The pox is unrelenting," Aquinas said. "It is a curse for a world gone mad. It is the payment for our sins. The Abyss out there is hungry for what we have, the light, the life, and if we open our hearts to doubt, if we dare peek over the chasm, the Pit will swallow us whole!"

Jono shook his head, wondering why he waited for his friends outside at all.

"You're not going in?"

Jono turned to find Kirstin Orbit standing beside him. She was dressed in a formal gown from the Day. Jono hadn't seen her since she the cadets had left for the Day's own exchange program. Her red hair was tied back in twisted rings like he'd seen other Day Enders wear it.

"There's nothing in there for me," Jono said. "I see you're back from the Day. Things not work out?"

Kirstin sat down next to him. "No, things are going fine. Great, actually. I like it over there. They're happier than we are. It's simpler there. I may stay longer than the year."

"Kirstin Orbit, first ever knight from the Dark End," Jono joked.

Kirstin grinned. "Maybe. This world is changing so fast. Who knows what's going to happen next."

"So, what brought you back?"

"Life is short and I'm not going to miss out on a Giftmas with my family." She stopped. In that moment it was almost as though she'd forgotten her father had died at the battle of the Keeper. "At least the family I have left. Something's better than nothing, right?"

Jono nodded but remained silent.

Kirstin sneered. "Out with it, Wyer. Don't treat me like some delicate mushrup. If you don't think so, say it."

Jono shrugged. "It doesn't matter."

"Don't be a coward," Kirstin said. "A brave guy like you says what's on his mind."

Being called a coward, even in Kirstin's playful tone, hit Jono in a soft spot of his heart. Was that what his classmates thought of him? Did they have any clue about everything he had done to save them? To save the world? How could they leave him alone when they knew they were the only family he had left?

"I'm trying to be polite by waiting out here. Being cowardly is what they're doing in there. I was raised on angel stories. That's all they are. Stories can't save us."

"Maybe not." Kirstin shrugged. "But what's so wrong with taking a moment to feel a little hope? So what if it's a story that gives it to you?"

"The same thing that was wrong with feeling like the Dark could do no wrong and the Day could do no right. Blind faith leads to bad ends."

Jono turned away from her, but he could still see the way she scooted a bit closer to him. They both knew what the other had lost.

"I'm sorry about Polari, but can't we take the good from this and leave the rest?"

"The pox could pop up at any moment and swallow the Earth whole. The stakes are too high to stake your hopes on fiction. You have to pick a side. Truth or lies."

"Be careful with that, Wyer," Kirstin said as she slid off the steps. "Ultimatums are what got us into the mess in the past. The truth is always more complicated than that, and so is goodness."

Jono looked up and found a kind smile on Kirstin's face, but it only made him feel more indignant. "There has to be an answer to all of this. And if there is, doesn't being *correct* about it matter?"

"Maybe there is no answer," Kirstin replied, her hands held up to either side. "What then? Perhaps the only choice is between being sad and alone or happy among friends."

The orange light of the cathedral hall that had spilled into the street disappeared when Kirsten shut the door behind her.

Jono knew it was a stone tunnel without touching it. A chill ran from his hands up his arms, cutting through his layers of clothing. Something compelled him through the hazy darkness toward the murmur of a crowd in a distant room. He ran through foggy halls until he arrived at a set of double doors. A red bow had been tied around them, and when he reached out, the bow untied itself and the doors swung open.

A brilliant light filled the tunnel. The Windom ballroom was decorated as though it were a hundred different living rooms on Giftmas morning. Brightly adorned Giftmas trees stood by each fireplace with laughing families of Windom cadets. A great buffet sat on tables lining the back wall, the smells of classic Griftmas delights tantalizing Jono's senses.

The ballroom was bursting with joy. Everyone smiled as they opened presents. People hugged and joked with each other. Uly was riding a mechanical dragon while chasing Rex around the hall. Isaac's parents were proudly piling more gifts in front of their tree. Keiko and Cid were playing fetch with Forge's wrapped bone.

It was perfect.

The instant Jonothon stepped into the ballroom, that all went away. The room turned cold and blue. Tattered banners hung limp from above. The buffet was rotten, and the Giftmas trees had lost their pine needles. Only empty boxes and torn paper remained of the presents.

Jono stepped cautiously through the barren room. Someone else was there, watching him from out of sight. The smell of burning lingered in the air. Marks contorted the rugs and floor, twisting them into one. The more he looked, the more the marks appeared everywhere. It was the pox. It must have come and everyone fled the city.

A screech forced Jono to spin around. A young girl in a red sweater ran away, between stacks of dead Giftmas trees.

"Wait!" Jono called as he ran after her.

It was impossible, but she was the girl from the park in Polari. She ran past mountains of empty presents and ducked under tables of rotten food. With every turn she was slowly changing. Her straight brown hair became bobbing blond curls.

Jono ran as fast as he could, but his legs felt like mush.

The girl appeared from behind an empty fireplace with black hair tied into two pig tails with pink bows. When Jono finally caught up to her at the center of the room, her hair was in a blond braid with a white dove clasp.

Jono opened his mouth to speak, but no words came out.

As the girl turned around, her hair unraveled from the braid. Its color turned black with a metallic sheen. She glowed an eerie blue. As her metal hair wavered in a ghostly wind, he realized her face was covered in a mirrored mask, the Tombs symbol carved into it. Jono saw fragments of his own jagged face reflected back at him. Her gray eyes stared accusingly as she lifted a finger in his direction.

"It's not my fault," Jono whispered. "I couldn't save you. No one could."

Ker pop.

Chapter Twenty-Three

He heard it behind him but didn't dare move to see it.

Ker pow.

The room crumbled as the girl pointed, her hair turned white and floated in the pale blue light.

KER POP! KER POW!

The pox arrived in colossal chomps and bites. Whole sections of the city ripped apart and swirled into the air. Nowhere was safe, and there was no point in running.

KER POP! KER POW! KER POP! KER POW!

Gargantuan green spheres popped all around him as it ate the room in mammoth bites. The ceiling crumbled, falling in massive chunks of metal and stone.

"I'm sorry," Jono said, dropping to his knees.

The pox expanded, devouring everything in the city, the Dark End, and all across the Day. It ate away at the planet, leaving only crumbs of dirt floating in starry space. There was no more Earth, no more Eies, and no more Windom. Jono stood on the last chunk of stony ground as the girl with the mirrored face silently pointed at him.

This is your fault, she said without words.

And then the pox swallowed them both up, along with all the stars, and there was nothing left in the universe for all eternity.

Chapter Twenty-Four
A Hole at the Ball

An ivory dove burst from a star at the top of the tree in a brilliant flash of light. Its six wings spread out as it fluttered across the banquet hall.

"Careful with those!" Keiko's voice echoed in the wide hall. She rode atop her mechanical tortoise, Wallace, shouting instructions and scrutinizing others' decorative choices.

Jono sat in the corner with Forge sleeping on his lap, watching the festivities around him grow ever more surreal.

"They're not supposed to go off until the new wake!"

"Sorry!" Oscar said from across the hall.

Oscar was already dressed in his King's outfit, the same ragged one he wore for his rehearsal. Jono got the feeling Oscar was still at the hall avoiding the terrifying fate of potentially forgetting his lines. But there wasn't anything he could do to help him. Weren't they all avoiding something terrifying in one way or another, helpless to their fates? There was nothing he could do for any of them.

The six-winged dove circled the room, sprinkling white sparkles down on a crew of students busy decorating for the Snowfall Ball.

As Jono watched everyone's bustle to set the scene for a Merry Giftmas Eve, he felt like he was stuck in another world, watching this one from the outside looking in. They were like robotic drones, only seeing the bright light in front of them but ignoring the possibility that the pox or the Tombs could attack at any moment. His hand twitched as he pet Forge. All they wanted to do was escape from the world on impending doom, and still, Jono couldn't let go of the fact that none of them were safe.

Keiko tossed Jono a plastic cup embossed with the image of a castle and swords. "Don't you love it? I think these little touches will make the Day feel more at home during Giftmas in the Dark End."

Jono shrugged.

Keiko had the Giftmas Eve Snow Fall Ball coming together with absolute efficiency. Pine trees lined the walls and volunteers were putting on the final ornaments. Red and green banners hung between each window on the city-facing wall with fake snow clinging to their trimming. The hall's fireplaces roared and spread ample warmth.

The academy's gargoyles were hanging final red and green drapes across the ceiling, but Jono couldn't help but focus on the starry sight beyond the glass roof. The moon hung over him like a threat. *Chaucer is coming*, it whispered. *Even we are helpless to stop him.*

"I bet large gatherings like this would be perfect targets for the Tombs," Jono said.

"I'm sure the city guard is stepping up their patrols," Keiko said. "It doesn't help to worry so much, Jono."

"The Empress's Eyes are watching everything in the city," Oscar said as he walked by with an arm full of tinsel. "She must have upped her number of secret cameras all over the planet in the past few years, especially in Eies. If there's any threat, she's going to find it before we ever could."

"Or we are all about to die and there is nothing we can do to stop it," Isaac said, stopping by to sneak a tree-shaped cookie from a nearby table. "Might as well have a little cheer, then. It is Giftmas time."

Everyone else was busy hanging up decorations, but Jono just sat there, feeling like an anchor, the only thing tethering the whole affair to reality. He couldn't muster the effort to help. He could barely keep himself from lashing out at his friends.

Forge panted and nudged his head against Jono's leg whenever he stopped scratching it.

"How's the pox research going, Isaac?" Jono asked when Isaac stopped by for another cookie. "Is there anything we can use to predict where it's going to hit next?"

Isaac shrugged and took a bite of the present-shaped cookie. "Professor Fourier thinks some of the research teams across the globe are close to cracking the pattern and isolating on a trigger, but I'm not convinced. For now, the Pathaganon is closed for Giftmas." Isaac returned to painting a decorative banner with green dots, careful in his application as if it were a complex chemix mixture. "We set up the automatic systems to run some more analysis while we are away. It's calculating predictions across thousands of models with trillions of factors, so we'll just have to wait for the results. Careful with those, Oscar! Not so close to the yellow ones. They have a chemix half-life set to burst precisely at the end of the wake. Mixing them would set them off."

Jono shook his head. "What if we can't wait? There's something ticking the adults aren't telling us."

"It is possible," Keiko said, hopping off her mount. "Wallace, could you bring Riley over there more tinsel banners?"

"Happy to oblige," the mechanical tortoise replied as it lumbered away with boxes of decorations on its back.

"Oh, there's Marissa." Oscar pointed. "She's my date for the Ball."

Oscar smiled and waved with his whole arm in a wide arch.

Jono frowned. How was it possible that *he* was the only one without a date? How did that jolly lump convince the squire that hated the Dark the most to join him for the Ball? Maybe she only agreed because he was going to be in the opera all evening. Was she the reason that Oscar was staying late? Perhaps he didn't have stage fright at all.

What if there wasn't a problem with any of them.

A chilling thought, that maybe he was, in fact, the coward. What if he could never be anything more than the sickly, lonely boy he thought he'd left behind.

"We need to wrap this up in time for everyone to get dressed," Keiko said, "and we still haven't brought in the bot-tables for the food. So stop goofing off."

"Who are you going to the ball with, Keiko?" Riley asked.

"David Kepler. He's Paegor's mentor."

"Oh. He's cute!" Riley said with a giggle.

"I'm meeting him here after his performance at the opera," Keiko added. "He's light painting the backgrounds live. I saw him practicing two wakes ago. He's very talented."

"Why aren't you going?" Riley asked.

"I promised I'd help host the ball this year. How about you? Is there any special person you're meeting?"

Riley's barky skin blushed, and she shook her head.

"Don't worry. You'll have plenty of people to dance with once the ball starts. It's fun. Trust me."

"How're those chemix shows coming along, Isaac?"

"Just about done," Isaac said. "I should get going. I don't want Evanine to see me before I'm ready."

"You think a tuxedo will make that purple hair dye look more suave?" Keiko said.

Isaac straightened himself and smirked. "Let's just say I'll have some tricks up my sleeve."

"You better not burst a stink bomb on your date." Keiko scowled at him. "Girls hate that."

"Especially girls covered in fur," Riley added.

"Don't worry," Isaac said. "It's all going to go perfectly welded. You'll see."

Jono glared at the spectacle around him. It was a mammoth testament to ignoring the threat around them. How could they all be so blind? The world was on the brink of chaos and all they wanted to do was worry about who's dating who and what they're going to wear to the ball. What about the people that had their lives torn apart by the pox? There were still refugees in need of help. And what about the Tombs? They were certainly plotting an attack.

Everything made Jonothon's head hurt. He couldn't be wrong. Not this time, not after everything he'd done. No one bothered looking at the bigger picture. Everyone else was caught up in this fantasy world where they embraced the illusion of safety around them. It was all so naïve.

Worse, it was going to get them killed.

"I can't do this," Jono muttered. "I don't belong here."

"What?" Keiko said as she helped Oscar finish rolling up the banners. She dropped her end of the banner and marched over to Jono with a yearning in her eyes. "Of course you belong here."

Jono shrugged then stood to leave. Forge hopped off his lap and looked inquisitively up at him.

Keiko charged after him.

"Jono stop."

Jono grimaced as Keiko grabbed his shoulders and turned him around. Her touch felt like daggers and he didn't know why. Her eyes pierced into his, searching for something he didn't have to give. She slid her hands up his neck to cup his face. His blood felt like ice, and he stopped breathing. In that moment, the noisy world around them faded to silence. There was no Ball. There were no Tombs. There was only the two of them facing each other, an island in the infinite universe.

"Jono," Keiko whispered firmly. "No matter what happens, no matter where we are or what we're doing, you are *family*. You always belong."

Her brown eyes searched his. That loving stare cut into his heart more deeply than he realized possible. An impulse in him wanted to reject it, to push her away. He wanted to feel bad, angry, forgotten, lost and alone, but in those silent eyes he saw a truth that made his terrified stomach turn.

She loved him.

But the world could be ignored for only so long. The squeals and shouts around them crept back into his senses. Their private island faded into the chaotic world they shared with a sea of joyful faces and terrified hearts. The conflict tore at him. He couldn't bear it. He couldn't be a part of that world. His eyes began to sting. "I need to go."

"Okay." Keiko released him. "I'll be here."

Chapter Twenty-Four

"I know."

He meant to say far more than his gravelly voice could muster.

Johan Fourier was late.

He was lost in a crowd of last minute Giftmas shoppers, but even more lost in thought. There was something nagging at his mind, and when something nagged at him, he had a hard time letting it go. Walking around the city helped. There was something about the distractions that bounced around the city at Giftmas time that helped him ignore the world and sink deep into his thoughts.

"There's something I'm missing," Fourier mumbled.

A pleasant shopkeeper overheard him and waved. "Missing a little something for the spouse?" the portly man said with grin. "We have the most unique gifts certain to surprise and delight!"

Fourier was silent until he realized the shopkeeper was talking to him. "Oh no, it's something at work. Not present related."

"Presents can be the solution to work problems as well, my friend!"

Fourier forced a smile. "Thanks, I'll remember that."

He turned up the collar on his coat and continued down the street.

Giftmas had seized the city in its familiar adornments that danced in his periphery like street signs keeping his mind focused—a tactic he'd used for years. Whenever he was at a loss for ideas, he would sink himself in the middle of activity to stimulate his subconscious. He'd been stuck in his doctoral thesis for a month before his epiphany about Treacle's Equation came while in the middle of a grudgon mud rave in the Twisps that his Pathaganon roommate dragged him to.

The liveliness of the city made him feel at ease, allowing him to merely navigate through it in silent thought. A multitude of noises blended into a gentle hum. Lights and the chill of the snow made the warmth of his coat all the more comforting. The poverty of the city reminded him to . . .

Wait, what?

A curious sight caught the corner of his vision and pulled him out of his pondering the pox.

There was no poverty in Eies.

Fourier stepped backward and leaned around the alleyway corner. There, in a dimly lit alley on the edge of a crack between towers that looked down through hundreds of city floor was a small, clumsily constructed hut made from an Eies Explorer's banner and some sticks that must have been stolen from a tree in one of the many city parks. Within that hovel, Natharen Vault ate a slice of carrot cake and read from a hovering screen. He shook his head and laughed to himself.

"She'll never learn, but it works for her," Nartharen said. "That's why she's loved, I supposed."

Fourier cleared his throat as he stepped into the alley. "Pardon me, young man. But are you alone on Giftmas Eve?"

Natharen didn't bother to look at him. "You're never alone when you're haunted by ghosts."

Fourier tried to make sense of that but decided to abandon the attempt. "I suppose you're right. Wouldn't you like to join me for a hot meal? I'm headed to a party, and you would be more than welcome at the Empress' academy."

"Wouldn't you prefer an answer to a meal?" Natharen replied.

"An answer to what?"

"To the pox."

Fourier paused. It was a strangely direct question, given his work, but surely the world over would like the same answers. He put on a smile and light tone to hide his true curiosity. "Why? Do you have some?"

Natharen looked him straight in the eyes. "Your work is close, Johan, but you're all wrong. You see the data for what it *is*, but you don't see it for what it *isn't*."

Fourier recoiled. "How do you know who I am? My work is very secret."

"I know you by watching which choices you choose," Natharen replied plainly. "And you are many things, but a revealer of truth? That's what I'm counting on."

Fourier stepped cautiously toward the hut. "What do you know about the pox?"

"I'm following it, same as you." Natharen's gaze held an eerie quality, like he was seeing something in Fourier he himself wasn't aware of. "We are hunters on the prowl for an elusive prey. We follow clue after clue as our prey stalks us in return. I know that I'm missing pieces."

Fourier sat down next to the hut. His rear landed on a soft patch of snow that cushioned the cobblestone path. "The problem is that our pox data, as much as we have been collecting, is still limited. There are too many holes and we don't know the difference between what's missing from what just isn't there."

Natharen's eyes lit up. "That's it, exactly. It's not the clues, it's the holes. The holes are the path. Follow the holes!"

"Why the holes?" Fourier looked under the banner, but the boy had disappeared. "How did he do that?"

Fourier stood, now alone in the alley with the distant sounds of merriment filling the air.

"Holes? What does that have to do with the pox, unless . . ." He gasped. "Holes! Burning stars. It's the holes!"

Fourier sent Issac a ping across the Line. *Meet me at the lab. There is something we need to test. This could be the key to everything. Isaac, the target isn't about the attacks. It's the holes! The holes will lead us to the trigger!*

Fourier held his hat to his head and he ran madly through the streets to the nearest tram station. Just as he turned a corner, he collided with a short man thick with muscle. Johan thudded onto the ground and winced.

The man smiled beneath his wide-brimmed hat as he reached to help Johan up. Strands of blond hair hung down around his face.

"Pardon me," the man said with an eager grin. A tuft of blond hair poked out from his chin, and as the man reached an arm out, Fourier recognized the face of Eljin Tombs. "But would you grant a stranger some directions? You see, I'm on my way to an opera."

"Giftmas is a stunning time of year," the Sage said with a polite smile. His long, leafy hair rolled over the shoulder of his regal suit.

The bells of Saint Newton's rang out over the city. People from across the globe gathered for the performance and to see the leaders of both Ends in person. The crowds were adorned in ornate gowns and suits with tails. They wore top hats and carried light umbrellas to guard against the gentle snow. They all wore intricately-styled masks with thin screens over each eye.

The snow and lights made the city feel warm and welcoming despite the chill. Small bots kept the sidewalks clear of moisture but allowed piles of the icy frosting to line the cathedral's stone edges for the desired seasonal affect.

Viscariot arrived with Aquinas, both dressed in elegant

attire. As he passed, the Sage gave her a concerned look, but she replied with a confident smile that seemed to say *Trust to the path, and all will be well.*

Osfred and Eloise Ohm lingered on the sidelines of the main path to the cathedral, watching the crowds arrive. Osfred's facial spines were curled upward from his lip. They both smiled pleasantly as dignitaries arrived.

"The one there in the brown overcoat, that's Leshvin Penrose, Headmaster of Saint Snarls in the Day," Eloise pointed out.

"An excellent institution," Osfred replied. "Should our Isaac tour the Day, that is the only school that would be acceptable."

"Oh, look!" Eloise tapped her husband on the shoulder as a black carriage floated up to the gates. The side of the carriage melted into a shadow of metal, revealing the Empress sitting inside. The crowd whispered and gawked.

The Sage was the only one to approach, his leafy hair wrapped in a blue bow. The Empress extended her arm, and the Sage took it gently. They both smiled, knowing that cameras were watching them.

"It is most excellent to see you here, Madame," the Sage said. "This will be good for our people, seeing us so at ease."

"It was a wise idea to host this performance."

"Speaking of the opera," the Sage said, "I was given this peculiar mask, but I confess the ways of an opera in the Dark End confound me."

The Empress rested a hand on his arm. "The mask is meant to immerse you in the experience. It enhances the illusions of the stage and helps you remove yourself from the world's distractions and truly feel immersed in the performance."

She placed her own mask to her face. Her violet eyes were radiant beneath the black and red mask.

"In the Day, we enjoy a play on a grassy field with the wind and light all part of the show. I am intrigued to see how the Dark interprets the arts of the stage."

"Then I trust you will be pleasantly surprised," the Empress replied with a genuine grin. "Let us hope the watching world will find this event as inspiring."

"Trust me, my lady, The Ides of Decsomber will not leave a dry eye on the globe."

Keiko had lost her head. Literally.

As the picture hovered over them, her headless body stood confused in a shimmering blue gown while David looked shocked at an open Giftmas present with Keiko's severed head stuffed in the tissue. Her eyes were shut with her tongue sticking out the side of her mouth, looking as convincingly dead as a severed head ever was.

The gag pictures were loved by most of the guests at the ball.

Isaac and Evanine had a more formal image of them awkwardly holding hands in front of a Giftmas tree displayed on the wall.

Keiko frowned. "It doesn't make sense."

David looked up at the banner with her. "*A Giftmas to Remember*'? It's not particularly clever, but it makes sense. But that's what we get when decisions are made by committee."

"No. It's something that's been bugging me for a while. I was thinking about the Tombs."

David clapped his hands. "The Tombs? My favorite subject for a Giftmas Eve date. Should I get some provisions? It sounds like this may be an involved discussion."

Keiko waved him away, and David returned shortly with two large cups of pink dragon heart juice and a plate of snacks.

"Thanks for indulging me," Keiko said, taking her drink. "Here's the thing. How can the Tombs even sneak into Eies without the Empress seeing them? I thought her eyes were everywhere?"

David shoved a tiny cucumber sandwich into his mouth and thought about the question. "Do you really think even the Empress, constantly plugged into the largest computer under Sol, can catch every suspicious person everywhere in the Dark End? There's bound to be holes."

"So you agree that the eyes are limited?"

"Of course," David said. "The world is an enormous place. I always thought the idea that her eyes could see everything everywhere at all times was just a story to scare kids into not stealing cookies when their parents weren't looking. Stars, it worked for me. I was terrified she'd throw me into orbit for snickerdoodle theft." He circled his heart and raised his hand. "Those all-seeing eyes have kept me an honest man to this wake."

"An honest man? Now who's being bland?"

"We all can't live up to the infamy that is Keiko Kirin."

"Thank you for acknowledging my prowess. Now back to the point. If there are holes, then someone must have a map of holes in the eyes . . ."

"Here's an idea. The eyes could be moving," David said. "They could patrol around in certain paths or even at random. That way they could cover one hundred percent of the map."

"But not one hundred percent of the time," Keiko said. "The Empress would have to know that. She'd have a schedule and a map of when and where holes appeared. What if the Tombs got ahold of it? They could sneak around the city, or the world for that matter, undetected."

"If I was the city guard that would be the first place I would set a trap," David said with a frown. "It's too tempting for the Tombs to not try to steal access to the map of the Eyes, if it exists. I'm sure they watch every access point and just wait for anything unusual. But the Tombs would know that."

"What if there's a Tombs inside the city guard?"

"It's possible. Talmage was a spy and no one caught her."

"But she wasn't giving out top-secret information that

could change at a moment's notice. It's a lot easier to be a spy if you don't do anything unusual."

"So how did they do it?"

"If I knew that, I'd be the Chief of the City Guard."

Keiko frowned.

"On that happy note, the opera is starting soon," David said. "Do you want a quick dance?"

Keiko grabbed his hand. "Absolutely."

On a stage in the middle of the ballroom, a band of bots played a slow Giftmas balad. David wrapped an arm around Keiko's waist and just as they were about to begin to sway to the rhythm, Professor Curia Ism approached them looking worried and gorgeous in her cream-colored gown.

"Kirin, you've done a marvelous job with the Ball. I love all the Day décor. Nice touch."

Keiko stepped away from David. "Thanks. Is there something I can help you with?"

"Actually, yes, I'm looking for someone, and since you'd been here setting up all wake . . ."

"Cid? I thought he was coming to the ball with you."

"Oh?" Ism replied uncomfortably. "No, your uncle asked, but it was a week after Hollow's Eve and I had already said yes to Professor Fourier. You haven't seen him, have you?"

Keiko shook her head. "Not a ping."

"It's so unlike him." Ism stood over Keiko and David, pondering something when she seemed to realize she'd interupted them. "Sorry to intrude."

"Not a problem. I can't stay long actually," David said. "Curtain call is in forty minutes."

Keiko smiled and yanked him closer. "Then start shaking those hips, Kepler. We got some dancing to do!"

Cedric Pummel was laughing so hard that tears burst from his eyes. He set down his pale ale and grabbed his heart.

"You two are the best mates on the planet," Cedric gasped between breaths.

Ramsus and Maergann sat across from him in a rowdy corner of the Burly Belch.

"Cedric, my boy, you're a wealth of wisdom." Ramsus lifted his stein, and Cedric clinked his glass.

Maergann glared at the two new best friends, but said nothing.

Cedric leaned back in his chair and sipped his beer. "Ram, you have no idea how nice it is to have an open ear. You too, Maery, dear. Everyone else in this dump of a city is so stuck in their little bitsy lives that they can't feel the filth below the hull."

"Not you, though, pal," Ramsus said with a wide grin. "You got this whole farce figured out!"

"Oh, it's not me." Cedric raised a hand and bowed his head. "I'm just another automaton that had his eyes switched on. It's the Tombs that flipped the switch."

"Is that so?" Ramsus sank into his role as confidante. His tone was compassionate and open, like they'd been best friends their entire lives. "They sound welded. How long have you been with them anyway?"

"Years, mate. They pinged me about three years after I graduated from D'Arrow."

"You were stationed in Kipsee Hills after that, right?"

"Yeah, you remember. I was doing garrison work out there, and then one wake, one little ping set me on the path to discover the truth."

"And what truth is that?"

"That we are bred in sin," Cedric replied. "We are damned in the womb. We carry the stain of our forbearers, and nothing we can do will wash it out. The truth is all *this*, these comfy chairs and tasty beers, these pleasures are the lies that damn us. And we deserve it, every bit."

"Deserve what?" asked Maergann.

Cedric chuckled. "The sorrow. The hurt. You know that feeling that you get like there is a stab in your heart, the clenching of stomach?"

"Like when you know you've done something wrong?"

"Only *wrong* to this mad farce. Those pangs? They are the whispers the Abyss speaks in. It sings of truth, that we are vile things and only through fire will we be cleansed."

"So why don't the Tombs just kill us all and be done with it?" Maergann said.

"You don't get it, dear. The Tombs are so much smarter than that. See, it doesn't matter who lives or dies when we are all headed off the same cliff. No, what matters is that you accept it, that when the Abyssmal King rises, you bow willingly, that you embrace the hell that you deserve."

"Is that what's so wrong with us, then? We refuse to submit?"

Cedric shook his head. "You make towers of pride to yourselves. You flit across the Line, flinging thoughts around like children under Sol. You wave spells at your problems as though you are special. Powerful. You are *not*. You are all dirt. Worse, dirt that refuses to accept what it is. You defy Oblivion, but not for long. It is a hungry god, and the Pit is stirring."

Maergann fumed. "The Pit offers only oblivion, and you prefer that to light and life?"

Cedric smirked. "Listen to this Day Ender, eh, Ram? No problem singing to six angels, but they get all clunkered at the feet of the one true angel. Your whispers are wrong, Maery. Attrayer is a god and the others are ants. You'll see."

"How exactly will we see?" Ramsus asked.

"Do you think the pox is Miraphel's artistic calling card? Or that Gaiander the nurturer will make plants and fishies grow with it? No, that power is the sole domain of the Abyssmal King Attrayer, fearful-is-his-name. With just the right push, the Tombs will bring you all to believe. Before we are done, you will beg for Oblivion's sweet embrace. Better still, we'll make missionaries out of you yet."

Cedric giggled and then took another sip of beer.

Ramsus stood up. "You sold me. Time to send in our applications. You got a recruiter we could talk to about signing up?"

"Wise call, my friend, but no, they ping you when you are ready," Cedric said, wagging his finger at Ramsus. "Just start doing good works for the one true King and they'll be watching, trust me. They know how to find you."

Ramsus forced a smile. "I guess we're off then. Hey, Ced, you up for a pizza party and bit of terrorism next Bluewake?"

Cedrid raised his glass. "You know it, buddy!"

As Ramsus and Maergann disappeared down an ever-darkening hallway, Cedric waved at his dear friends.

"You two stay sparkin'! See you on the other side of the pox!"

The code world faded from their sight as Ramsus and Maergann found themselves surrounded by a narrow stone hall deep in the gut of the mountain. Behind a clear panel, Cedric was strapped into a chair, his arms and legs bound with a humming machine clenched around his skull like a claw. He rested peacefully in the manufactured dream.

"It pains me to see that monster so happy," Maergan said, "when all I want to do is rip his intestines out through his throat."

"You missed your calling, Sir Brigid," Ramsus said. "You should have been a poet."

"Does this trickery not sting at your conscious?" Maergann asked. "It's like shaking hands with a devil."

Rasmus frowned, but he understood what she was saying. "There's no utility in emotional revenge."

Maergann fingered the hilt of her spellblade. Being inside such a narrow vein in the mountain made her uncomfortable. "Perhaps, but there is plenty of satisfaction in it."

Ramsus grinned as his eyes flared with a red rage. "Oh, we will get our satisfaction, set your stars on that. But when it comes, it won't be with a single spy, but with battalions."

Chapter Twenty-Five

The Ticking Bomb

*T*he bells of the banquet hall rang as more people arrived for the Snowfall Ball. Delicate flakes of artificial snow fell around them, only to burst into soft clouds once they hit the ground. Couples lined up in rows to get their pictures taken by the festive scenes in each corner of the room. With each scene change, they kissed under mistletoe, pretended to be skiing down treacherous mountains or fighting off snow monsters. The hall echoed with laughter. A crackling fire roared in the fireplaces below a mechanical clock that was wrapped in a pine wreath.

It couldn't have been more perfect.

Jono looked down through the frosted glass ceiling above the hall, his heart aching at the sight, but he didn't know why. They were all so small and puffed up in glistening gowns and tuxedos. They were dancing dolls with painted smiles and not a thought in their hollow heads.

A voice came from behind him. "Keiko said I might

find you up here."

He turned to find Suriana dressed in a beautiful white gown with golden beads along its sash. Winged emblems decorated the chest and shoulder. Her radiance illuminated the city. She was a star, descended from above. Everything about her was heartbreakingly perfect. Her emerald eyes stared achingly through him—all his weakness, all his fear must have been written on his face.

Jono couldn't breathe. Green eyes. The color of the pox. His anguish was conquered by the chilling vision of what the pox would do to her, to all of them. The pox destroyed beautiful things with no regard for their majesty. He would give anything to stop that from happening. Even if they all hated or forgot him, he would never let that happen. Jono released a breath and noticed that she held a small present wrapped in brown paper and tied with a teal bow. He struggled for words. The dress. It was her costume. Why was she wearing it now?

"Aren't you going to be late for the opera?" Jono asked.

"You noticed the dress?" Suri smiled with a wave of her hips. "Do you like it? I wish I could just stay at the ball with everyone, but I'm so glad to be able to share the Ides of Decsomber with the Dark."

Jono nodded and hoped she didn't notice that his eyes were red. She didn't mention it and instead held out the package. "I know its Giftmas Eve, but everything is going to be so busy, and I didn't want to wait. You can open it now if you like."

Jono took the package in confused silence and tore

open the paper to find a leather-bound copy of the Realms of Illius.

"Riley couldn't stop saying how much you liked it." Suri smiled. "It's the missing book. I thought you may like to be reminded of how you grew up."

"Illius . . ." Jono looked down at it, tracing its spine with his index finger. "I used to like this. I used to look up to him."

Suriana smiled.

Jono scowled, a strange pain stabbing in his gut. His youth was the last thing he wanted to remember. He wasn't the person he'd always dreamed of being. He didn't need to be haunted by his life of failure any more than he already was. He held out the book to give it back. "I'm really not into fairy tales anymore."

Suri froze, her mouth gaping.

"It's . . . it's a gift. I spent weeks looking for it. An actual printed version was a rare find," she replied, on the edge of tears. "I was trying to be nice."

"Nice?" Jono turned from her and scowled at the dance below them. "There's a real threat that could kill us all at any moment. Being *nice* isn't going to stop the pox or the Tombs. Neither is dancing or singing."

"We need something to bring us together, I was only…"

Jono's hands were shaking uncontrollably. "Why did you even come here? Just trying to be nice to us soulless Dark Enders?"

"I know terrible things have happened, on both Ends," Suri said, her words choked with tears, "but you need to have faith that it *will* get better. The angels have power over the pox. They will stop it, and we can all live in peace once they—"

"What are they waiting for?" Jono snapped. "What kind of super-powered angel would let all this happen? Why don't they save us *now*? Why didn't they stop the battle at the Keeper? Or Jason Wheat from dying? Why didn't they stop the pox from destroying *Polari*?" He turned toward her once more, his face red and his hands balled into fists, shaking. "More innocent children will die if *we* don't do something. If *we* don't stop it. I can't let that happen, and all this meaningless revere and ritual isn't helping. It's not because the angels evil or blind or sleeping, it's because they're *not real!* The Tombs, though? They're real. They're trying to kill us all, and we're here dating and dancing and acting like burn'em children while the world crumbles! I'm sorry. I just don't have any time for it."

Suri gasped. "Polari?"

"The pox took it. Tore it into a rubble of metal and bones. I've *seen* their faces. I *watched* it happen. They're gone. All of them. And I can't let—"

"I didn't . . . Jono, I didn't know."

Snow fell like ash from the heavens as the murmurs of revelry below sounded to him like the whispers of devils.

"This mentor thing isn't enough. Everything we've been doing here, making friends and learning about each other? It's good for the cameras, but it's not going to save any lives. The angels can't save us, only *we* can save us. Suri, I'm sorry, but if you came here to save the world through friendship and angel stories, then you're part of the problem."

Suri's eyes swelled with tears.

"I didn't come here for any of that," Suri gasped between sobs. "I came here for *you*!"

She yanked the gold chain from around her neck and threw it at his feet. At the bottom of the thin chain dangled an old blue button that had been scratched and chewed and beaten from generations of wear. It was a button from a lifetime ago, from the jacket Jono had worn most of his childhood—the tattered hand-me-down coat he wore when he first met Suriana. The wooden button had barely made a sound hitting the stone rooftop, but as the shock overwhelmed him, it might as well have been an explosion.

Jono realized what it meant and the horrible thing he'd just done. All his false confidence sank to the bottom of his stomach, churning there in disgust. She'd carried that button with her ever since they met at Caer Midus when he was eleven. They barely knew each other, but she'd held onto it.

Jono opened his mouth to apologize, to beg forgiveness, to scream that he was sorry, but nothing came out.

The image of her swollen, tearful eyes burned through him, and lingered in the dark even as she fled from the roof and disappeared through misty clouds.

Jonothon crumbled. He scooped up the button. The thin gold chain was threaded in and out of the button's holes. He brushed his thumb over the old scratches on the blue button, almost like it was carved on purpose.

That long ago wake, when the fel shades attacked and the button broke off, all he wanted to do was to *save* to her. To impress her. To be worthy of the first new friendship that had found him.

And now he needed to save them all, but he couldn't even save himself.

He thought about that sad boy struggling up the hill in Polari, dreaming of a being a hero. He felt like he was rotting inside, that he'd betrayed a promise he made to that lonely boy. Here he was, with friends, power, health, and he was destroying it all himself.

It wasn't the pox or the Tombs; he pushed his friends away. Everyone that was trying to help him. Everyone that cared for him. His parents and sister had barely heard from him the year before the pox hit Polari. Jonothon looked at his gnarled reflection in the frosted pane of glass that looked down at the dance hall. Everyone looked so happy. Their lives glowed with joy and hope. That icy window crowned his head like the prison of his old breather mask. For everything that had changed, he was still that lonely, broken boy.

"I'm doing it again," Jono mumbled to the eleven-year-old boy in the reflection. "It's just like in Polari. I'm pushing everyone away. I'm going to lose them all."

Go. A soft voice in his head replied. *You can go be with them.*

"How can I be with them if I can't save them?"

Being a hero is not the only way for people to like you. Your friends love you for who you are.

"They look so happy." Jono's whispers cracked through his tears. "Not a worry in them."

You should be happy too.

"Their lives are in danger and they're dancing!"

Is life worth saving if it is not worth enjoying?

"Lies can make people happy. The world was happier when they hated the other End. Now they're all confused. They want their hatred back."

You can't save the world alone. You need them because you need to be happy.

"I can't let them die. I don't know what to do."

Look inside and see the truth for yourself . . .

Another voice entered the conversation, snarling with hatred. "You don't know what to do?"

Nicklus Knox stood above him on the rooftop, his arm cannons flaring with hot orange fire.

"What's wrong with the soggy Twig now?" Nick yelled. "You miss your mommy? You hate the world so much that you got to ruin things for everyone else? That it?"

"Go burn yourself, Knox!" Jono growled through his tears.

Chapter Twenty-Five

"What did you tell her?" Nick's shoulder cannons flared with his anger.

"Who?"

"Suriana."

A wry grin cross Jono's face. "What, did I ruin your date?"

"I asked her to the dance but she never said yes," Nick growled back. "She said she was going to ask someone else, but I guess it wasn't you, soggy eyes. Now, she's running down the hall crying, and lo, who do I find at the end of the trail? What kind of sick monster makes a girl cry before her big show? What kind of self-righteous clunker can't stand other people having a good time?"

"Burn off! You don't know anything!"

"I know what you are, you pathetic, sick loser!"

"You're a scared bully, just like the Tombs."

"I'm nothing like them!" Nick yelled. "You're the loser that pretends you can save the world. Well, you can't, 'cause the world is broken. It's not fair, and stupid little twigs like you can keep crying over their family while everyone around them dies too. You're not going save anyone, Twig. It's idiots like you that are going to end it for us all."

"At least I didn't help the Tombs release the pox."

Jono turned to leave, but a blast of fire shot against his back and slammed him to the ground.

"Say that again," Nick roared.

Jono struggled to his feet. "I didn't make you follow a traitor. That was your choice."

"I'm not a traitor. You're a disease, Wyer! You ruin everything you touch!" Nick's arm cannons exploded in a volley of fire bombs.

Jono wrapped his wires in front of him to shield against the barrage, but the fire bombs exploded, flinging him through the glass rooftop, shattering it above screaming dancers below. He felt weightless amongst the falling shards. Out of the corner of his vision, he caught the glimmer of Keiko's blue dress.

Then his wires shot out instinctively. They grabbed the window frame and with a single thought, they flung Jono back onto the roof.

A swift wire from his shoulder caught a firebomb in the air and tossed it back at Nick. It exploded between them, knocking both of them back. Jono's wires curled into a circle and rolled him onto his feet.

Nick shook melting snow from his hair as he stood. "You should've never come to the academy. Everything was welded until you showed up!"

Nick shot another barrage of fire bombs, but Jono's wires bounced and flung them in harmless trajectories, causing them to light up the sky like fireworks.

The crowd in the ballroom below cheered when Jono twirled around and redirected a bomb that seared Nick's hair.

A nearby billboard with Jason Wheat's smiling face asking for respect for the Day's values exploded as Jono swung himself though the gap with bombs burst all around him.

Nick stepped through the open hole, his bionetic cannons glowing orange as they charged with his rage. He looked around, but couldn't see his target. Jono swung up from his hiding place below the lip of the roof. A wire wrapped around Nick's legs, and as Jono pulled himself over the top of the sign, he twisted Nick around and flung him back onto the rooftop. A torrent of wires punched and grabbed Nick while a storm of fire bombs shot back at Jono.

First a wire grabbed an open hand then another pinned a leg, and in a breath, Jono had Nick pinned down in a jungle of wires.

"You burnt brain!" Jono yelled. "You're not good enough for her. She's trying to keep the world from war! War is all you're good at. Destroying everything around you! You don't understand that we need to change or the Tombs are going to kill us all!"

Nick struggled, flat on his back. His cannons flared. "Not if I kill you first!"

Nick's body became a salvo of igniting bombs. The blast echoed through the elevated streets and sent Jono flying helplessly off the roof. City lights pulsed as his limp body soared over rows of rooftops. Listless wires flailed in the air behind him.

Jono crashed through a tiled chimney and slid limply onto the roof below. His head thudded against a stone terrace, and the world turned to nothing.

Chapter Twenty-Six

Whispers toward Oblivion

*W*yer...

The voice was soft and reassuring, and yet he recoiled from her kindness.

Wyer...

His eyes cracked open. He was looking down on his body, curled up on the rooftop. His jacket still smoldered.

I told you I would be here when you needed me.

"You came inside my mind?"

Only because your need was so desperate.

Jono looked around. The city glistened and the shadows against brick walls pulsed with life.

Professor Wishe glided down from above.

"We're in the code world," Jono said.

"Your mind needs to deal with the trauma it is undergoing." Wishe's words were soft, nonthreatening.

"This therapy version of the code world, it can't lie, can it?"

"It is a reflection of the truth. No falsehood can persist here. You can see through any illusions that mask the world."

Jono nodded. "I need the truth."

"You know the truth. You just need to acknowledge it."

"Beneath it all, even the code, the stories, angels and Tombs, dances and school and lies and fear. I need to get beyond all of it. I need to see reality for what it is."

"Introspection is the key to outer knowledge. But the layers of the innermost mind are not the same as the world itself."

Jono stood up and started running. He leaped from rooftop to rooftop, and with a wave of his hands, the world began to shrink into stepping stones. The city became a puddle of clouds as his hands reached up and tore down the skyline as though it were a canvas curtain.

"It's an illusion," Jono said in a gasp. "All of it! The school, the people that live here, the Dark and Day. Even light itself. Photons dancing on photoreceptors, painting a masquerade in the brain. All life is a trick."

"Even tricks can be true," Wishe said, floating alongside Jono.

"Is that all our lives are, a series of comforting tricks? A drug of dreams through Line games and hollow hearts? I *don't* believe that. There's something more, some deeper truth, and if I could just see it without all these lies, then all of these problems would fade. We would be free."

Behind the think canvas of stars, a grassy hill of Twilight appeared.

"Where is it?" Jono said with emotionless determination.

"Where is what?" Wishe asked.

Below the hill, Polari twinkled in a chorus backing distant stars. Secret planets revolved around those distant beacons of light. Hidden lives churned on those invisible specks, just like the life replanting trees in the park and repairing the streets around Groandring Elementary. The town was real and healing and moving beyond the horror of its past.

"Not here." Jono scowled. "Deeper."

He turned around, searching the ground.

"What are you looking for, Jonothon?"

"I'm not afraid anymore," Jono replied without looking at her. "I just need to know. I need to face it."

Jono turned away from Polari. He shrank down past the blades of grass that grew like towers. The blades blocked out the sky. He was running where pebbles were boulders. Mushrups loomed over him like mountains, and insects lorded over the world like distant moons, simultaneously enormous and specks lost in space.

Jono crashed through the world of stone and rock as everything shrank further still.

Wishe looked around them as she raced behind him.

"I can't keep up, Jono!"

The world morphed in a surreal mix of the microscopic and the psychedelic. Tentacles of a single-celled organism dominated the universe with the might of a kuthulan god. Battalions of chemicals clashed in an endless war. Bonds clenched and shattered. Light slowed as Jono raced beside the mark of photons streaming in all directions.

Chapter Twenty-Six

Emotions contorted against matter like an ocean of kaleidoscopes.

You are diving through the depths of your psyche! Where are you going? Wishe called from behind him.

"To the heart of everything."

Wishe clasped her hand to her heart as she realized his intent. He was stripping away all the structure and illusions of the world. He was tearing through the lies his eyes and brain concocted together, magnified by the sight of the code world, beyond the falsehoods of the material and into the heart of existence itself.

Jono, I don't know the horrors awaiting you, but there are places even I cannot follow. Down this pit lurks a realm in the mind that is untouchable. While you are tied to the code world, you can see everything outside of you, and the deeper you go, you see the chaos within! The conflict of inputs can trigger mental dangers that are unpredictable. I don't know what form it will take or what it will promise, but you risk losing yourself if you continue!

Through the chaos of matter and energy, Jono shrunk deeper still. Wishe's pale green light dimmed behind him. Its hollow trail stretched and faded until he was in a lightless world. Onward he ran, deeper and deeper, down and down. If there was ever a road to the doorstep of the angels, to the heart of existence, he was on it.

Wishe's words of warning echoed like forgotten memories that scratched at his mind, desperate to be remembered.

No, Wyer. Your mind could be lost forever.

Matter sparked in and out of existence, a quantum storm of light amongst the infinite darkness. Shades of shadow flapped harsh wings in the jagged pitch-black forest where nothingness cut into matter.

Empty whispers moaned at him.

You are going to fail!

It wasn't Wishe anymore. Even as he ignored its silent screams, he knew the monster's name; it was his own shame.

Fail again! Fail again!

Like harpies in the abyss, echoed one, ten, a thousand, all taunting him.

You are weak!

You are lost!

A perversion of his own voice, shrill and spiteful.

I dare you to keep going! You aren't strong enough! Thorny woods of matter cut at him. The world grew colder the deeper he went.

I never wanted to dance with you in the first place! screamed a vile version of Suriana. A vision of her flashed in the nothingness, just long enough to show the bitter temptress. *I hate you, Jono! You are nothing to me! I am special and you are only worth toying with!*

You want to dance? You're a joke, Jono! A devilish Keiko cackled. *I was only using you to get into Windom because you are so pathetic! You have no family! I just wanted to see you squirm!*

You don't need them. Oscar's voice was heartless, and he chomped on something crunchy and sloppy. *Ignore the wenches and enjoy the feast. Feast on their bones! Feast on their flesh!*

Take what you want! Isaac commanded. *You are powerful now. You don't need permission! It can all be yours if you don't let them stop you!*

Does that make you angry, boyo? Eljin laughed at him. *You feel the burning inside you, eating you away? I dare you to use it! Stop me! Kill me! I know that's what you want! Try it!*

Jono kept pushing through loss and heartache, through love and pride, past fear and hatred.

You deserve this! Aquinas bemoaned. *You rejected the angels, and now you are helpless! They will make you pay for your heresy! They will laugh as you burn in the pain that you unleashed!*

Did you think there wouldn't be pain? Chaucer's voice cackled at him. The sound of bones crunching grew from a distant rumble into a storm. *The pox was just the beginning! My army of the dead grows, and all of your friends will be joining it! They will rise and drown your world in a sea of bones! The false innocent will be slaughtered! Grab him, my army! Hold him down! Tear his body to pieces!*

Where were you, Jono? It was his mother now, crying through the emptiness. *We needed you and you didn't save us!*

You're a fraud, Twig! Nick snarled. *Everything you pretended to be was a lie! You're no hero! You're a coward that led your family and friends to their graves!*

In the darkness, Commander Grail's voice moaned in pain. *Wyer . . . What did you do? We needed you and you betrayed us all! We are all dying . . . you've . . . killed us . . .*

Voices screamed. The darkness grew colder. The heat in his own body faded. He wasn't moving anymore. He was freezing. Ice covered his feet and it was growing. Inside the jagged shards of that ice, his reflection smiled devilishly back at him. His mirrored face cracked.

I knew you'd come. The icy devil smiled. *The world out there is no place for you.*

"I need to know the truth," Jono demanded. "Is there anything more than a world full of lies?"

This is all there is.

The ice began to vibrate.

Here is the peace you seek. Oblivion is the only truth. The rest is only pain. Only in the void can we achieve tranquility.

The ice climbed up Jono's legs, clawing over his chest.

"Even *you* are lying," Jono said, "you're hiding something. What is it?"

Stay with me, the devilish Jonothon said. *We are the same. We are one. Cold and empty and alone.*

"I'm nothing like you!" Jono smashed at the ice, and the quiet hum grew louder.

Jono spun around in the nothingness. He was frozen upside down. He smashed and clawed, and with every hit, the ice vibrated more. The noise became a song, a distance choir humming across the eons.

"What are you hiding?" Jono yelled.

Only the truth, the mirrored devil said. *See for yourself. Listen to their song and know the truth of the universe!*

With a mighty blow, Jono shattered the ice. He cut through the final tapestry of fleeting electrons and came to the center of everything that ever was, is, or will be. Jono found himself standing on the cliff of Oblivion, on the lip of an infinite crag that roared of silence. In front of him stretched the chasm of existence.

There were no angels dancing on atoms.

The heart of god was empty. Jono felt as hollow as the center of the abyss whose sirens sung an empty ballad with the absence of sound. This was the truth everyone else was afraid to see.

Come home. Return to the void. Be one with nothing.

Jono peered over the edge. He felt the urge to jump, to abandon all material existence. Oblivion swarmed in front of him with an eternal hunger for something to fill it. It was a seductive call—no pain, no regret, no fear, no angels, no warm, welcoming arms of a benevolent god.

Jono gasped at the great revelation as he teetered on the edge.

"There's nothing."

Chapter Twenty-Seven
One Last Wishe

*T*he song of Oblivion was as sweet as it was terrible, a truth so stark and undeniable that one's being is forever changed having heard it. Its call was the only truth.

And yet . . . something remained.

Jono gaped at the infinite emptiness, and yet he hadn't come all that way to be lost in it. He'd brought something else to Oblivion . . . himself.

He'd come with a purpose, to know the truth of the universe so he could do *good* in the world. He came to look at the harshest reality and to save the people he loved. He couldn't stop now.

A glimmer caught his eye. A sliver of light reached even here to the edge of nothing. It drew his gaze away from the pit. The spark's simple life darted and grew, building on itself, summoning forces that reached for others like it.

He closed his eyes to the endless nothing. He took a breath and turned around. With his back now toward the cliff of Oblivion, he could see the other side of this infinite truth bursting with a light as bold and relentless as the cliff was devoid.

He fell to his knees before the glory of all existence.

Life existed! It defied the void! It was, by the mere virtue of existing, the most amazing thing ever!

Within a single flake of light were the images of every connection it had made. Every birthwake candle it lit, every glow over a student studying, every reflected shimmer off a bead on a wedding dress. Within that speck of light was more life than Jono could ever live, and it had nearly fluttered into the void.

As Jonothon opened his eyes, the vision of all existence across time and space rushed forward like a tsunami over his senses. It nearly pushed him over. He stood on the very edge of existence, his back to the emptiness, looking in on the totality of all that was.

The sight, the feeling, the perspective was transcendent.

Everything was beautiful.

Everything that is, was, or will be, was there, defying Oblivion. The zeal of life refused to be more than nothing.

Chemicals sprouted from atoms. They flowed and swam, mixing and merging, throbbing and growing. Life was birthed and beautifully lost in a chaotic dance.

Popping and stretching. Thriving and exploding. Life

barked and chirped, sang and cried. It roared to the planets, tore at flesh, and gripped at hair as chemicals churned within the body that contained it.

With a single glance, a trail of matter formed in an endless universe rushing away from the edge of the abyss. Particles built themselves into matter, matter building into minerals, plants, insects, birds, lizards, and people. People of every species! Ayleens and grudgons, humans and terralunan. Life overflowed the crucible of creation as people flowed and merged, individuals and collectives building into societies. They built dreams of their own that multiplied and ricocheted off each other only to flourish brighter than before.

A baby caught its first breath a trillion times over. A child went to school and made a friend. People loved and built new creations in the world around them. They explored and imagined. They fell in love with the universe that birthed them and sailed across the countless worlds their imaginations created.

They dreamed and fought. They grew old and died. A zillion funerals. A zillion births. A zillion fresh and growing lives to build and live, different from those before. The cycle of joy and mystery and sorrow and peace was born anew, again and again and again.

It was something.

It was real.

It was painful and true.

In every one of its forms, it was the beautiful and relentless opposition to nothing. It laughed triumphantly against the abyss.

It was.

Jono gasped for breath. Tears drenched his cheeks, and joy burned in his eyes.

Persephone Wishe sat next to him. He'd never seen her with tears of joy. She looked so . . . human.

"I've never been here before," she said. "I've never thought to come. Thank you for sharing this with me."

Jono sobbed. "I've been so wrong," Jono choked through the tears. "So caught up in myself. I'm sorry. I'm so sorry."

Wishe smiled. "You are imperfect, as are we all. As is all of life. Perfection is a static thing, like the abyss. But imperfection? It grows and changes, stretches across the universe. The imperfect *lives*. It tries and fails and tries again. The imperfect is the only path to creation."

"I should have learned from other people's mistakes. Even fiction, we can learn from it. The angels, Illius, all those stories—it's *us*. It's our reflection trying to be shared."

Jono let the wave of images and feelings of life wash over him. It pushed the edge of nothing further away until they were once again surrounded by life—his own life. Jono's friends, his family, the places he'd been and the dreams he imagined.

Keiko played with a mech during their first year at Windom. Isaac showed him the space stations around the Solar system. Oscar laughed with a mass of s'mores stuffed in his cheeks over a campfire. David waved his hands, and gloriously painted art that sung across the horizon. Suriana brought enemies together as friends. His father, mother, and sister giggled with him in a center of torn-open gifts.

Even the pain and tragedies that swam within its tapestry were a defiant cry against the oblivion at his back.

"It's *you*," Jono managed to whisper through the tears. He loved every connection in the tapestry. He could see every story, real and imagined—every life, the happiness, the sadness, the boredom, and the ecstasy. A gazillion minds yearning and creating together and on their own.

This was the temple he'd been looking for. Every story about gods and angels and monsters was weaved into the story of life; the real and the imagined were linked, inseparable.

Jono felt the guilt of losing his family ease. He let go of his insecurity and his desires. Life existed. It was the greatest triumph imaginable, and he didn't have to do anything at all!

Wishe stood beside him with a gentle smile on her face.

"Thank you," she said. "This was your journey, your exploration, and your discovery. I'm humbled you allowed me to witness this. Life is very special. And we need to—"

Wishe stopped.

The collage of life melted away, and they were standing on the rooftop in Eies, directly above Jono's body. Cars flew above, and Keiko and Isaac clambered across rooftops toward him.

Wishe grabbed him by the shoulders. "The current view of the city is an interpretation of the Eyes system the Empress uses to watch over the world. It's a real thing, with windows into material space. It sees everywhere. In the air, in our bodies, and no one notices unless there's a problem."

"Professor!" Jono cried out, the world shuddering around him. "What's wrong?"

"Look."

She pointed to a distant building, the bell towers of Saint Newton's cathedral. Across the distant dream of his beautiful city, a splinter of red cracked down through the Crown's tower.

"Just as light creates an illusion for our eyes, there is something in the code creating an illusion for the Eyes of Eies. Look again."

The spark of red flickered against the world.

"False code is masquerading as though it were the true code world. What is it concealing?"

Wishe shifted the entire city with a swipe of her hand, and the panel of reality turned to reveal a tormented infection of red code. The true code world was crumbling around them, and an illusion was taking its place. Violent red vines burst from buildings and stars. They slashed through bridges and streets, tearing into the world then mimicking the data it infected.

Wishe wrapped Jono in her arms as six ethereal wings burst from her back. The red vines lashed out at them just as she leapt into the air and took flight.

"We are still in the network in Eies, but so deep that most of the systems don't monitor it. We have to go down again, not up. It's corrupting every system above us!"

The code world was at war all around them. Red claws ripped out of the darkness and slashed through buildings.

Jono gasped. "The Angels' Masquerade! That's what the Tombs created. It's a virus in the Line! It's corrupting everything and mimicking the original data. Everything it touches becomes a new host and continues to seed it."

Wishe dodged claws that swiped at them from infected buildings. "I'm trying to warn the Code Guards, but the masquerade has already corrupted the security alarms. It's removing any information about itself to avoid detection."

The vines of the masquerade virus chased them across the city. Wishe weaved between vines and claws, but as she flew over then under an arcing tendril, they came to face a towering building with vines blocking their path on either side. A claw cut through the code of the building in front of them, and they had nowhere to go.

"Hold on," Wishe said as she loosened her grasp on Jono, holding out her right hand. From her palm emerged a shield of code. The claw smashed into it then tore away, flecks of red bleeding from its shattered surface.

But more of the infected code closed in, threatening to crush them. Wishe flew forward at a terrifying speed, vines trailing behind her in a tangle, fighting to be the first to reach them. Before she could slam into the building, she pulled up and flew along its façade, Jono's face centimeters away from its surface.

"We have to warn the Empress!" Jono yelled.

"The Ides, Jono! The Empress and the Sage will be watching the performance at Saint Newton's. That's why we saw the crack! It will be the last place that the masquerade will infect to avoid getting spotted by the Empress. It must surround the whole system before it dares to activate and attack her."

"We all have installs! What about us?"

"It could infect their installs. Then it could control us or even kill us instantly. Everyone with installs connected to the Line is at risk!"

"The Tombs could take over the whole city with a single thought," Jono said. "They could make us kill ourselves."

"Only the Empress could shut down the links and purge the infection. That's why they need to isolate and surround her before she is aware. I can't get to her through the Line. You have to go now, Wyer!"

"Download yourself into my brain. It's not safe here."

"I'm doing everything I can to stop this from infecting you. If I stop even for a moment to download myself, you'll be lost." Her voice bellowed and cracked in pain.

Across the city on a rooftop, a golden door opened. Wishe headed straight for it.

"You need to get back into your body and disconnect immediately."

"I won't leave you!"

They landed by the door just as the red vines swept over them.

"Don't distract me, Wyer!" Wishe screamed. "I can already feel the virus winning."

Claws of red ribbons tore through the code landscape and left them on a floating island surround by red devastation. Wishe fought off the attacks, and Jono shrank from the code world and back into his own mind. He pulled Wishe's hand with him.

"We need to escape!" Jono yelled.

"You need to warn them!"

Wishe's ethereal body was everywhere at once. She hacked at the red vines as they swirled over the world.

"Jono!" she cried. It was as though Wishe had traveled the world in an instant and returned to him, exhausted.

"Get out!"

A wave of red swept over the cityscape and crashed on top of them. Wishe created a shield big enough to encase the two of them and the door.

"Take the door! Disconnect from the Line!"

Thunder shook as the corrupted city crumbled around them. The roof below them cracked and broke. Vines lashed out from the cracks and wrapped around Wishe's legs, their red corruption infecting her flowing gown.

Chapter Twenty-Seven

"Come with me!"

"Please, Jono. I . . . it's too . . ."

Her eyes went blank. Jono touched her cheek. The red corruption cracked her body like a stone statue. Wishe's face fell from her head like a mask. Her body shattered and split. Jono grabbed her broken face as he fell through the door, which shut behind him just as red fire consumed the code world.

"Jono!"

His real eyes opened.

Keiko, Oscar, and Isaac's faces hovered above him. They were dressed in thier Snowfall Ball attire and Oscar in his kingly costume.

"Disconnect from the Line!" Jono gasped. "Now!"

Chapter Twenty-Eight

The Saint's Bell Tower

"We disconnected," Isaac said. "What's going on?

"You banged your head pretty good," Keiko said as she inspected Jono.

"Nick got it worse, though." Oscar giggled. "That burnt brain finally got what he deserved. That fight was worth missing the opera. Good show, Wyer."

"Everyone is in danger!" Jono cried out, trying to sit up. But his body felt sluggish, and Keiko kept him pinned to the ground.

"Calm down," Keiko said. "Stay still until we can get someone up here to have a look at you."

Jono struggled for enough breath to speak. "Stay off the Line! It's a virus. This is the Angels' Masquerade they told us about. The code world is a false world hidden in plain sight. They twisted the code. That's how they stayed hidden! The virus is corrupting the Line and any installs connected to it! They'll be able to control anyone with installs. I . . . Wishe. She saved me. She got me out. If not for her, I'd be a husk right now."

"But if everyone else is infected, why hasn't it started taking them over?" Isaac asked.

"The virus copies the real code," Jono said. "It mimics how it normally works, so it can spread undetected."

"It's a virus that does nothing?" Oscar asked. "What's their plan?"

"The Empress. They're after her. She's the only one powerful enough to stop them. They can't trigger the virus until they have her surrounded."

"Sounds like Team Firewall needed to be an actual firewall," Oscar said.

"If the Tombs know that we know their plan, they could activate it any moment," Isaac replied.

Jono shook his head. "They can't risk the Empress catching on before they've corrupted the entire city and all the people in it."

"How do you know all this?" Oscar asked.

"Professor Wishe told me. The Empress is the only one that can stop it, rewrite it somehow, but she—" Jono caught himself and recalled something the Historian had told him many years before. "She can't see where she doesn't look. It's deep inside the system of the Eyes."

"Aren't all the famous people at the opera?" Oscar asked.

"Suriana is there," Jono said in horror.

"Everyone under Sol will be watching it," Keiko asid.

"The Ides of Decsomber," Isaac said. "As poetic a place as any for the Tombs to send a message."

"It's time to suit up." Keiko tore off the bottom of her gown to reveal blue jeans rolled up to her calves and a utility belt around her waist. She looked back at her surprised friends. "What? It's not like you're the only one that gets to be paranoid about a Tombs attack. I just sent out my personal distress signal. It doesn't use the Line frequencies. You there, Wallace?"

The crackly voice of her robotic tortoise spoke across the radio in the center of her belt. "Yes, ma'am. How may I assist you?"

"Get your hull here quick and stock your shell for the apocalypse," Keiko said. "Momma needs to save the world."

Jono got to his feet and surveyed the city. "Isaac, you can get people's attention with your chemix. Oscar, use your illusions. Spread the message as fast as you can. Tell everyone to disconnect from the Line."

"What if they don't believe us?" Isaac asked.

"Make sure they do," Jono said. "We meet at Saint Newton's."

"If we catch the steam rail soon, we can still make the second act," Oscar said.

Jono shook his head. "The rail system may be infected. We need to get there without them stopping us."

Jono looked over at the cloud-covered city to the two bell towers that peaked through the rolling white.

"Oh, Jono," Keiko said, grabbing onto his shoulder. "I know that look in your eyes. Don't do something crazy."

Jono thought of Suriana on the stage at Saint Newton's, at the center of the Tomb's attack. "Crazy is the only plan I got. Go!"

He sent out wires to grab the side of the buildings beside them. After taking a few steps backward—and waving his friends out of the way—he slingshot himself off the roof. His wires darted out, grabbing whatever they could and throwing him further through the city. The wires spread out like arms of an octopus, flailing until they snatched onto walls or windows or rail lines, and then they flung him forward again. Jono swung under bridges and flipped through the air. He tumbled onto a catwalk, rolling until he was on his feet, ran, and then leapt again into the stone and metal jungle.

Oscar's worried face peaked over the edge of the roof.

"I am not doing that."

A boom rang out in front of Isaac as his red potions smashed together and rocketed into the greenhouse clouds. The elixir's red light swirled in water vapor as they coiled and spread out to spell *DANGER – GET OFF THE LINE* across the greenhouse clouds.

"Is that going to work?" Oscar said.

"Does anyone look up any more?" Keiko asked.

"No one's going to say how impressive it is?" Isaac replied.

The three of them looked to the far end of the roof as a large part of the stone lip and red brick lifted itself up and crawled toward them as it shaped itself into a robot.

"The city guard!" Oscar said, relieved. "We'll get them to take us to Saint Newton's and when we show up, the Tombs will wet themselves when they see this army surrounding them." Oscar waved the guard over.

The brick guard picked up his pace, charging forward.

Oscar's wave slowed, and his smile waned.

"Is that an 'I'll save you' charge, or an 'I'm going to crush you' charge?" Keiko asked.

The city guard raised its metal and brick arm. Isaac swiped his wrists together and a burst of air and smoke flung them backward as the guard smashed the rooftop.

They tumbled across the roof and stumbled back to their feet.

"Run!" Isaac yelled.

"Spread out!" Keiko said. "It can't follow all three of us!"

Another mechanical guard rose over the rooftop right in front of Keiko.

"Or not . . ."

Its massive hand closed around her, but she slid below its grip before it could get ahold of her.

A third brick mech stomped its giant foot at Oscar, but its foot passed through the illusion as the real grudgon scampered away.

Isaac flung a green elixir at the first guard's head. It splattered and sizzled in gold and green flames, melting through the guard's metal skull. Unfortunately, it didn't do anything to slow down the mechanical monster.

"Help!" Oscar screamed, trapped between a guard and edge of the building.

Isaac was busy running away in the opposite direction.

"I'm stuck, too!" Keiko peered over the side of the roof.

The guard behind her lunged forward.

She felt a rush of air and the roar of rockets as she was lifted into the air. Wallace flew forward, its bottom shell opened to scoop Keiko into its mechanical frame. Keiko spared no second and used her new mech arms, formerly Wallace's front legs, to smash the guard back the way it came.

She stood triumphantly over the mangled brick and metal body. "Now it's a party!"

Wallace's rocket feet ignited, and they flew over the roof. Keiko grabbed the next guard's arm and used her momentum to swing it away from Isaac and fling it into the last guard, knocking them both off the roof.

"I always though the city mech guards would be tougher than that," Keiko said with a smirk.

"Let's not test them," Isaac said.

Wallace's back shell slid open. Isaac and Oscar clamored into the cargo hold. The engines roared, and they soared over the city.

Keiko laughed. "Time to pummel some Tombs!"

A gentle snowfall filtered the city as Jono inched closer to Saint Newton's across the skyline. Jono swung under a bridge and crashed into the open cabin of a flying car. An old human couple looked back at him, surprised.

"What in the burning stars are you doing, young man?" the old woman exclaimed. "Pilot, land us somewhere safe."

The hollow head of their automated pilot smiled, but a faint crack in the shadow of its grin flashed red.

Jono gasped. "It's spreading."

"What's spreading?" squawked the old man.

"Don't get on the Line! The Tombs infected it! Land as soon as you can!"

"What are you doing?"

Jono stood up. "Improvising."

He leapt from the car just as a delivery train soared past them. Jono's wires grabbed onto the train, and it slung him around. He ran along the side of a building as the train charged through Eies then swung himself on the top of the train just as it darted into a tunnel through a tower.

As the train burst back into the light of the city, Jono leapt and caught another rail heading toward the cathedral. The breaks screeched the moment he grabbed on, sending him flying into the air.

His wires thrashed in all directions, until he snagged onto a railing and swung forward into flying car traffic. A car swerved, and Jono bounced against its hood and smashed against the side of a building. A wire from his back latched onto a metal sconce and flung him onward. Disoriented and losing control, Jono lunged forward, sending his wires out to carry him across the city.

He swung, and was pulled around until he finally tumbled, bruised and exhausted, into a bell tower in Saint Newton's cathedral.

Jono moaned and peeled his cheek away from the cool stone floor.

"Of all the people to stumble by in my hour of triumph." Vincent Chaucer stood beside the massive copper bells. "I'm glad it's you."

Chapter Twenty-Nine

The Ides of Decsomber

*T*he stage was a beautiful rendition of a castle at Twilight. David stood behind the thin castle walls and painted a dim, star-speckled sky that flowed up and around the moon. A distant sliver of Dawn kissed the horizon. Each stroke of his living painting sang like an orchestra, setting the opera's somber mood.

On a balcony above, Suriana stepped through dark blue drapes. She radiated beauty in a flowing white and gold gown, the embodiment of the noble Draca. Hair extensions wrapped a single braid around her shoulders and around her waist.

The tragic love story began its final act. Words faded onto the painted vista of clouds as David waved his brushes behind the stage.

With the Heart King slain, Maria, the mighty knight, believed that the Shadow was free and the world would be lost. The armies of the Summerlands marched against the Empire of Winter. Here, they will meet at the Great Wall of Twilight on Giftmas wake, to unwrap the bitter gift of war.

Yet Draca, the child of Autumn, seeks to end the waking wave of Shadow by appealing to the Ancient gods on that one special wake when they listen to prayers.

But beware the Ides of Decsomber, for they are cold gods this month . . .

Suriana stepped onto the fake stone balcony. She spread her arms and sang mournfully.

> "How were we so blind?
>
> How did we not see?
>
> Hope was here for us to find,
>
> And yet we flee into the sea?
>
> Here I stand,
>
> On the edge of fate,
>
> Unknowing,
>
> Unsure,
>
> If sleeping saviors grant
>
> Any providence for me . . ."

Clomps of metal footsteps echoed from behind the stage. Roger Hyland stepped out wearing knight's armor. He opened a red scroll.

> "Our good King Heart is dead,
>
> The Shadow of our enemy,
>
> Encroaches on our territ'ry!
>
> Are you all honest knights?
>
> Will you all stand and fight?
>
> Blood for blood!"

Across the canvas behind him, an army of painted knights shouted their reply, "Blood for blood!

> "Heart for Heart!"

And knights echoed his song. "Heart for Heart!"

Roger waved his scroll at the audience.

"We will right this world for keeps!

This war ends with us this sleeps!"

The tower set rotated to make Suriana appear inside the alchemist's room. Glowing candles set in a pentagram made it clear that the room was temple to the gods beyond the stars. Three tapestries hung from the walls representing the three factions of gods: the soft, the mighty, and the withered.

Suri cautiously approached a pedestal. As Draca, she feared the price of calling upon the ancient and unpredictable gods. She looked toward the stars and wondered of the fate that had befallen Maria.

"Will I ever see your smile?

Or hold your steady hand?

Love dares to fade, a distant isle.

What if it all had not begun?

I am the darkness,

You're the stars.

All that I wanted,

was to be one.

Our love is brighter

than the sun . . ."

"I've been waiting for you to show your ugly face."

Jono bit into the anti-animancer pill on his bracelet. He

swallowed the pixels inside that would neutralize Chaucer's power to control physical objects.

"You think being an animancer is the only way I know how to control people? How naïve." Chaucer laughed and held up his right hand, which was encased in a massive gauntlet of black steel humming with power. "The masquerade is almost over. Soon we will cripple the Empress, and the world will cower before the Abysmal King!"

Chaucer swung at Jono, his gauntlet buzzing through the air with terrifying speed. Jono ducked, and Chaucer's attack connected with a protruding corner, smashing the stone into rubble. Behind him swept up a wave of fel shades that lined the room and morphed into frightening creatures.

"I know who you really are, Praxis the Thirty Seventh!" Jono said. "I know what you did on Terralunis!"

"What you saw was how a life breaks free from the trappings of history," Chaucer snarled. "The moon was a prison. They keep their secrets locked in lies, but I discovered the truth! The pox is just a herald. The Abyss is stirring and will consume everything!"

Elise Etheredge leapt to the stage in Maria's knight costume.

"Hopeless! Shameless!

This world has turned the sweet to sour!

The Shadow,

Devours,

The war song calls to us this hour!

This world holds no more light!

All my life,

All my heart,

All my mind is in this fight!"

Suriana knelt before the pedestal. She cut a hidden packet on her arm, causing fake blood to spill out and fill the circle carving on the floor around her.

"Can the sleeping hear me?

Do you know my heart's desire?

Do you . . . feel me tremble?

In my doubt, do you find ire?

Will you answer all my prayers,

Or will they fall upon deaf ears?

If you hear it, heed my call!

Burning blood will greet them all!

If you hear it, heed my call!"

Isaac gasped as he peered over the edge of Wallace's shell, the wind whipping against his face and his purple hair tendrils waving vigorously behind him.

Oscar tapped him on the shoulder and pointed.

Brick guards were coming to life on every building they passed, leaping over the rooftops after them.

"They're still after us!" Isaac yelled to Keiko.

"The whole city is infected!" Oscar said. "It's trying to stop us!"

They soared under a bridge just as the bridge itself lifted up, making people tumble down its back. Huge stone arms smashed into Wallace and sent them rolling down a cobblestone street. Isaac and Oscar slid out of the shell and landed into a pile of snow. They all groaned as Keiko struggled to stand inside her tortoise armor.

The bridge roared at them, transforming into a thrashing mech of metal and stone. Two other city guards awoke from the street; lamp posts lifted from the ground and turned into flaming arms.

"We're surrounded!" Oscar yelled.

The bridge mech swung its massive arms downward. Keiko held up Wallace's mech arms to brace for impact, but both of the bridge's arms were slammed to the side by a pair of metal arms.

"Commander!" Keiko said in a gasp.

Grail reached out to lift her up. "Kirin! Good gears, what is happening?"

"Look out!"

The bridge mech swung back and knocked Grail into the window of a nearby cupcake shop. Wallace's engines roared, and Keiko flew out of the way.

A lamppost arm wrapped around Isaac and lifted him into the air. His wrists collided, and an orange ball inflated. It fell onto the guard's foot and burst into bubbling acid that dissolved the lamppost's base. The light in its lamp head flickered and popped as Isaac slid free. The other lamppost swung down just as a wave of swaggering flame cut between them.

Raina Helios stood in front of Oscar as vines of fire swam out of her mechanical arms.

Isaac smiled as a glowing red potion floated between his palms. "Let's tear up this town!"

Helios' fire vines wrapped around the mech as Isaac bombarded it with acid elixirs.

Keiko grabbed the other lamppost mech as Wallace head butted it.

"A little help here." Grail had both of the bridge mech's arms in either hand. Keiko flew over and grabbed one of the arms.

"Give me a clear shot!" Helios yelled.

Keiko and Grail pulled the arms apart as Helios unleashed a mammoth beast of fire that charged at the bridge and clamped onto its head. The fire beast raged against the guard bot, heating its metal head until it glowed red then melted, its arms thudding lifeless against the street.

"We saw your warning," Helios said.

"No one looks up, huh?" Oscar said with a grin.

Keiko shot him a smirk.

"What the burning stars is going on?" Helios asked.

"The Tombs corrupted the Line with a virus," Isaac said. "They've taken over the city guard."

Helios glared. "Is that possible?"

Before they could answer, Grail asked, "Where's Wyer?"

"He went to Saint Newton's," Keiko said. "The Empress is there for the opera. She's the only one that can stop it."

"We need to get there," Helios replied. "Now."

"The virus is infecting the whole city," Isaac said. "No trams are heading to the cathedral anymore. The masquerade virus knows we're on to it, and it's doing everything it can to stop us."

"Wallace can fly the three of us," Keiko said, "but your weights would be too much."

"Don't worry about us," Grail said, as Helios wrapped her arms around his neck. His massive arms shifted and engines flared from his palms. "We need to make it to the Empress before it's too late!"

A stone pillar shattered against the might of Chaucer's fist.

"You aren't a prophet, you're a murder!" Jono yelled as he dodged a fel shade's tentacle. "We're going to stop your virus!"

"Oh, will you?' Chaucer sneered. "You think that's the only masquerade we are toying with? Reality is the true masquerade and the pox is the revelation!"

A felbeast leapt at Jono just as two of his wires swung with a thin blade of blue electric fire. The fel morphed in half to avoid the attack. One half slithered onto the bell tower's ceiling, but the other was caught in the blade's sparks and turned to dust.

"You don't control the pox!"

"I don't need to," Chaucer said. "I don't need to control the tempest when the winds howl and rain falls. All I need to do is get you to stand in its path."

The bell tower shook.

For a moment Jono caught a distinct aroma of burning air seared by a pocket of nothingness.

"You see? The pot is stirred and now it begins to boil!"

Jono wrapped Chaucer's ankles in wires and flung him across the room. "And your face begins to bruise!"

KER POP

It was small but undeniable. The smell of burnt dust waved in the air. Holes appeared in the walls, revealing the city outside.

KER POW

How could the pox come here of all place? Now of all times? It couldn't be a coincidence, but Chaucer admitted he didn't control it.

A crocodile fel shade lunged at Jono and slammed him against the wall, its shadowy teeth cutting through his coat. It was all his wires could do to keep it from tearing his flesh apart.

KER POP KER POW

Jono's electric wire wrapped around the fel and cut it into sparking dust. He leapt onto Chaucer's back and slammed him to the ground.

"It's over!" Jono yelled.

A blast caught Jono in the side and flung him out of the bell tower. He grabbed onto the stone pillars with a wire and pulled himself up just in time to see Eljin standing in the open hatch of the bell tower's floor, the limp body of Professor Fourier slung over his shoulder. Eljin smiled triumphantly, his gun pointed at Jono.

"Boyo, you have a habit of being in all the wrong places."

Eljin shot again, but Jono's wires released their grasp, and he fell from the bell tower into the dark, snowing sky.

"There it is!" Keiko shouted as the clouds opened up

around Saint Newton's towers.

Candles lined the walls around the courtyard. As they approached, glowing eyes within the stone switched on. The buildings, streets, and lampposts around the cathedral transformed into more guards.

"This isn't going to be easy," Isaac said.

"I count two guards for each of us, Ohm," Commander Grail shouted over the wind and snow.

"More must be coming," Helios said. "Hit them hard and fast. We need to get inside."

"Everyone ready?" Grail asked.

Keiko in her Wallace armor swept down to pummel the first guard as Isaac leaped out with acid elixirs flying at the guards at their sides. Oscar tumbled to the snowy ground as he sent a squad of soldier illusions charging forward. Grail smashed a guard's lamppost gun as Helios's fire cannon tore through its lump of a stone head.

One of Grail's arms shifted into a fiery blade. He spun and cut a brick mech in half.

Above them, strange pops made the snowy air glow green.

"What is that light?" asked Helios.

"It can't be!" Keiko said.

More city guards landed between them and the cathedral doors as green stars twinkled right above the ground. A tiny bite disappeared from the doors. Another cut into the bell tower. In miniscule cuts and bites, the pox began to feast on Eise.

Grail growled. "We are out of time."

The stage shook and bells rang from above. A chorus of warriors sang out as they battled the forces of Shadow.

"Too late!

The Shadow wins!

We are too late!

All our sins come to reap now,

The sad fate we have sown!"

Elise called from the lower battlements of the castle. In Maria's bloody armor, she lifted her sword over her armies.

"Give me one moment!

Give me just one more swing of your ax!

Give me one more spell!

Show me the spirit our enemy lacks!

For Draca, I'll fight on!

One moment to make her sacrifice count!

For your kin, lift your blade high!

For your loves, our vict'ry is nigh!

For the gods that cry for our vow,

Don't give up on me now!

Though I know you're weary and sore,

Though your bodies are broken and weak!

We fight on as Draca implores,

Fight for the world,

One moment more!"

Suriana reached out from her pedestal on the balcony. Her fake blood poured down Draca's white gown.

"Hear me, Maria!

The old gods are the Shadow itself,

Their jealously feeds it!

Their loneliness fills it with shame!

T'was doubt that revealed their false claim.

Curiosity discovered their flaw!

We only need lay down our arms!

They feed on our fury,

In their sleep,

They feast on our fear.

They dine on our vengeance,

Set your heart,

To love most sincere.

Lay down all your worries,

Lay down all your rage.

The Shadow's but a mirror,

Don't let bloodlust set the stage!

Cease this war,

Follow a path that I shall miss!

The time for peace has come,

And although my life is done,

Remember once, we could be one,

Our love's still brighter than the sun—"

KER POP KER POW

KER POP KER POW

Suriana's singing turned into a scream. The pox burst around the stage in flashes of green.

KER POW

One large, glowing pox floated in the backdrop. It swallowed the canvas sky and half of the castle's tower. The balcony began to crumble around her. Suri grabbed the edge as the set tilted toward the roaring pox. The tower's roof fell, followed by the pedestal, and then the rest of the set collapsed into the pox.

Suriana screamed as the castle's balcony flipped over. She fell toward the green ball of burning light just as wires wrapped around her waist and pulled her into Jonothon's arms.

Her eyes were full of shock and terror.

Jono swung them from the rafters to the back of the stage. The crew, including David, crowded around them.

"Suri! I'm so, so sorry!" Jono said.

"Jono!" Suri gasped. "The pox is . . .where did . . .how did. . ."

"The Tombs brought the pox here. I don't know how," Jono said. "You need to get everyone out of here."

"The Tombs are here?" David asked.

"We don't run from evil," Suriana said as she stood and drew a wand from her gown. "We fight it."

"Look out!" Kain shoved Jono out of the way as a snake-shaped fel shade dropped from the rafters. David created a pixel wall in time for the fel to pound against it. More fel swooped down around them.

Kain stepped forward, but the gnarling shadows slammed him into a nearby wall—the black matter cut and suffocated him as he struggled helplessly.

"Vulcan's Spit!" A shot of fire lashed out from Suri's wand and seared through the fel's back.

Kain fell to the floor, gasping as Elise fought off swirling fel shade with a power gauntlet she wore under her costume.

Roger Hyland swung a fake sword at a fel, but the beast darted around each swing.

The rest of the cast clamored for an exit amongst the chaos.

"The Empress," Jono said. "I need to warn her. This is all a distraction!"

David slammed his fists against the ground and split the hordes of fel in two with his pixel walls. He groaned as his pixel walls created a tunnel in the descending waves of shadow.

"Go!" David grunted with effort. "I'll block them!"

Jono ran to the front of the stage as Suri pulled a seed from a pouch in her gown.

"Catch!" Suri tossed the seed to Elise and the moment she caught it, the seed burst from her hand. It expanded into a wooden dome over Kain, Elise, and David just as David collapsed and his pixel walls disappeared. The wooded dome sheltered them as a wave of fel shades fell on them. The hull of the shell sparked with fire as the fel touched it. The beasts of black shadow screamed and writhed away.

"I'll hold them off." Suri slammed the hilt of her wand onto the stage. "Ifrit's Gate!"

A wall of flame roared from the wand and cut off the

fel from their attack. Hundreds gnashing mouths roared as they searched for a way around.

The crowd across the cathedral was screaming, some rushing for the door while others looked for any way to help.

The Empress rose from her balcony seat when Jono came out from behind the stage.

"Wyer?" the Empress called. "What is this?"

"A virus hiding in the Line!" Jono yelled back. "It's infected everything. You need to cleanse it now before it's too late!"

"What about the pox?" Aquinas said from his seat in the front row, pointing at the growing spots of green burning air.

The Empress rolled her head backward, and her eyes turned black. Her metal hair fanned out in a flash as an invisible energy emanated from her body, shaking the windows and stone with her silent power.

"Empress?" the Sage said, standing from his seat and taking a step back. He held his staff in front of him, as if to protect himself.

She convulsed as she stood silent and frozen. Her body was still as the crowd watched her. The pox burst around them, growing and ravenous, shaking the cathedral. One burst of pox bit a hole in the wall, while a larger pox devoured half of the roof. Stone and metal screamed as it rained down on the crowd. Dust and stone fell onto the Empress but tumbled away without touching her.

In the cloud of dust that surrounded her, a dark field in

the shape of two wings spread out to shield her. Matter flowed around her body, rippling over the void wings that wrapped around her. The pox cowered in her countenance, and the crumbling debris held still in the air at her power.

"It cannot be," Aquinas gasped. "*Wings beyond the eyes of the watchful. How ye manifest thy glory in the corners of the world.*"

Jono imagined her mind racing over infinite wells of code all over the world, hunting and purifying the infections. He had no idea how long she would take or how long she would be vulnerable as she raced to save the world's data and all the lives connected to it.

"Wings from the beyond?" Viscariot stood up from the crowd. "I've seen you before . . ."

A scream rang out from the bell tower above. They all looked up to see a body fall limply from the tower and thud in the middle of an aisle.

Jono gasped at the sight of the vest and striped shirt. A top hat wafted down and landed next to the man's blank stare.

Chapter Thirty

The Angels' Masquerade

"Welcome, friends, to the bitter end of the Angels' masquerade!" Chaucer's voice boomed from the above. "But of course, you've been here all along!"

Jono looked up from the stage. Chaucer stood on the edge of the collapsed ceiling, staring down with a maddening smile. Eager fel shades clamored alongside him.

"An angel off to save the code world and leave the fleshy one to rust?" Chaucer said. "Is that what you see before you? You embed a world of lies into your minds so deep that you think it is real. What is code if not the lie you prance in front of your own sense? You give the shadow of life to dead things, and I ask you, when you glare into your own mirror, what truth will you see? Will you see friends and an angel inside of you? Or will you embrace your one true nature—that you are stained with life and will only find salvation in the loving arms of Oblivion! Come, for the Abyss is hungry. And you are fat with the lies of matter. Witness your angel, Ariam the wise, as she soars along the Line to save the wool that blinds you all!"

Chaucer pointed at Fourier's limp body in the center aisle. Those few who dared approach retreated at his mere gesture. "This man tried to understand the pox. He tried to stop it. A professor of science? This is what the Tombs will do to your greatest minds!"

Chaucer rode a throne of gnashing fel beasts down the wall. Beyond him, the holes in the cathedral showed a city where the pox burst through buildings and bridges. Eies was under siege.

"You do not understand the pox, because you do not understand the world. *You* are the plague and the pox is purity! Deep in your hearts, you know this to be true. You struggle against your fear because you know how weak you really are. Fragile creatures clinging to a masquerade of lies and decay!"

Edgar Niles crawled over to Fourier's body on the floor. His weathered face grew full of terror. "They cut his heart out!"

Chaucer smiled. "It's a funny thing, the heart. We give it a role in our emotions. We sing ballads of our love, but love is a delusion. We are puppets in a chemical machine. Meat puppets, all of you! Soon you will meet the only truth that matters."

As though on cue, another burst of the pox flared in the center of the aisle. A patron was sucked wordlessly into its abyss. The roar of screams echoed and shook the cathedral.

"You do this to yourselves! You bring the fallen angel's mark down upon you. You!" Chaucer pointed at Viscariot. "The Peacemaker? You yearn for greatness, but you don't even know what you are, do you? Worm in a corpse? Savior of the world? There is power in you. Power to stop me. Who would deny your destiny? Kill me!"

"Stop this!" Viscariot screamed. "If I have any power, it's bringing those together who *can* stop you." She looked around, hoping for the bravery of men and women to stand with her. But as the pox ripped holes in the world around them, the citizens of Eise scattered.

Chaucer smiled. "*Who's* the liar now?"

Cassindra Viscariot gasped as the vacant seats beside her tore into a flash of pox. She clung to the back of her pew as the hot green fumes pulled her closer.

Aquinas leapt over several rows of pews and grabbed her arm. "Hold on!"

The Sage pointed his staff at Chaucer. "Chains of Icarus, seize that monster!"

Golden light darted from the crystals on his staff, but it never reached Chaucer. The light seemed to writhe in pain then scatter into dust. A scrawny old woman stepped from the cowering crowd, laughing. She took off her face as though it were a mask, and her body convulsed and transformed into that of a bulky man with a red beard. The Tombs named Morse stood in her place, opening his coat to reveal a black crystal that seethed with power.

"I bet you didn't think any of these still existed did you, Sage?" Morse said. "It's my little souvenir from Lailet Dem. What good are your spells around a void crystal?"

The Sage wasted no time leaping from the balcony, using his staff to hook its edge and swing him to the ground. He landed in front of Morse with a thud and rose with towering dignity. "There is more than one way to defeat you!"

"Defeat us?" Chaucer laughed. "You *are* us!"

Several people darted from the cowering audience and grabbed the Sage from behind.

"What is the meaning of this?" the Sage said as he struggled to free himself. "Release me!"

Every fifth person rose from the crowd, blank looks on their faces. Mothers, husbands, daughters, sons, all exchanged their opera masks for silver ones with the Tombs symbol cut into the metal.

A dryad grabbed his spouses's arm. "Flensa, what are you doing?"

In unison, the standing crowd chanted. "We welcome the kiss of the Abyssmal King, Attrayer!" Painful screams joined their chants as the masks burned the scar of the Tombs across their faces.

"Bring us to the void!" Their voices echoed through the acuostic hall. "Our only home is Oblivion."

Freya stood up from the crowd, her red skin burning with rage. She leaped over the pews and flung herself at Morse in a wave of flame that set the floor on fire. Morse growled and with a heavy blow, slammed her head against the wall. He closed the distance between them before Freya could recover and picked her up by her neck.

"Tell me, does a pyrebran's flame go out when it dies?" Morse grinned as his flesh burned against hers. "Let's see if you go bald."

Freya struggled to raise her hand as the crowd around them desperately tried to tackle Morse while they fought off the growing horde of Tombs.

"Got any last spells you want to fail at before you die," Morse said.

"Pyre fire's not a spell." Freya choked out the words as a blast of flame shot from her chest and tore a hole through Morse's coat. The void crystal flew into the air.

Morse released her from his grip to go after the crystal, but the crowd tackled him in the process then held him down.

"Get the crystal!" The Sage yelled. "Destroy it!"

The crystal slid across the floor and under rows of pews.

Ammer scrambled from the crowd and dove under the pews. He stood up triumphantly. "I got it!"

"And I got you," said another Tombs as she pulled him from under the pews by his feet. She grabbed the back of his neck and lifted him into the air. Green oil left her glove and began shrinking around Ammer's throat. She snatched the void crystal from his hand as he struggled to breathe. "Enjoy your cat's eye scarf. You're all so much fun to play with."

Around them, the newly revealed Tombs fought to pin the soldiers and mage knights in the audience. From the balconies to the mezzanine and floor, fights raged among friends and family.

"Embrace the pox and bear witness to the mark of Attrayer!" Chaucer bellowed.

Magic and mechanix clashed in the chaos of soldier against soldier, knight against knight. The Tombs were ready, but the defenders of Dark and Day still had greater numbers.

"Slay the deniers and offer yourselves!" Chaucer shouted. "Every sacrifice is a beacon to summon the Abyssmal King! Look as the pox grows! Watch as your deaths welcome the loving arms of Oblivion!" A purple dust joined the cloud of cathedral debris, seeping into the air like a rolling fog.

"What's happening?" Freya said. "I can't move!"

Morse broke free of the frozen people around him. "That's more like it."

"Sit," Chaucer commanded from his shadowy throne that clung to the wall. The crowd obeyed, helpless to the power of his animancer pixels. Chaucer's fel throne descended. When it reached the floor, he stood and walked among the crowd.

"How does it feel to know you deniers are helpless?" Chaucer said as bursts of pox spotted the room. "How does it feel to know you have lost everything you love?"

The cathedral's thick door smashed open, revealing Grail and his metal fists. Splinters of wood flew through the air, some sucked into the spots of pox.

"How does it feel to fight someone immune to your tricks?" Commander Grail and the others stood in the archway.

Keiko charged the cannons on Wallace's arms. Isaac held a handful of elixirs, ready to throw. An army of illusions popped up around Oscar. And Professor Helios's arms glowed with wild fire.

Above them, the pox ate through one of the bell towers. Metal and stone crashed in front of them. Keiko managed to fling herself between the collapsed tower and the crowd.

"The whole thing's coming down!" Keiko yelled.

Chaucer laughed at the chaos. "Where will you run where the pox cannot find you?"

Animancer pixels forced the audience up, corralling them around the entrance to create a barricade

"Will you crush them all to stop me, Grail?" Chaucer goaded him. "Or will you brave the pox-filled room at all? These hungry specks could expand at any second and bring this stone tomb down on us all." Pox peppered the air. Some flashed in and out of existence. Others lingered, eating holes into wooden pews and stone walls. They pulled like a wind, sucking in the air around them. "I will do anything to stop your rampage," Grail said.

"Prove it! Smash through this wall of fools and come at me! Or should we wait to see what the pox has in store for them? Look at this one! It's growing. If its hunger is not fed, it will become insatiable. It will grow to consume the entire city. The entire world!"

The pox roared and in a swift bite, it tore a hole in the floor, swallowing twenty people, Tombs and not, alike. It pulled at all of them in a hungry gale. Viscariot's hair flowed toward the pox, the green popping fumes singing her white locks. Aquinas held onto her as his loose clothing billowed in the pox's pull.

"The pox is the herald's trumpet!" Chaucer shouted, his arms raised high. "Its song cannot be unheard! Its truth cannot be rewritten! The Pit hungers for all matter! And the King of the Abyss comes . . . for you!"

He pointed at Chancellor Viscariot. The pox bubbled and burst.

KER-POP! KER-POW! Viscariot's face grew cold and full of terror. *KER-POP!*

The great supporting pillars of Saint Newton's collapsed around them. Grail rushed to prop up two of the massive pillars before they could crush the crowd. It was all he could do to keep them alive.

"Don't do this Vincent!" Grail shouted. "This is madness!"

"How little you know, Dvan. I am doing nothing. This is the fruit they planted. This is the harvest they hath sown!" Spittle flew from Chaucer's mouth and his eyes opened as wide. "They do this to themselves!"

Aquinas struggled to hold Viscariot back, but his feet and grip were slipping. More pox surrounded her, feeding off of each other, growing until green, fiery oblivion surrounded her in a sphere of hungry, burning air.

"No!" Aquinas cried out.Viscariot's screams stopped as though her voice was plucked from her throat. Then she stood still, as if all fear had left her. A golden glow burst from her pale skin and ignited across her platinum hair. Her mauve eyes turned to gold, and her outstretched hands held off the abyssal maw.

"Stop," she said calmly in the storm raging around her, and the writhing green pox did as she commanded.

She clenched her hand into a fist and the fiery sphere imploded in a burst of burning air. The pull of its gravity reversed in a blast that knocked everyone in the hall backward.

Chaucer had no words, no more threats. He seemed both satisfied and stunned.

In the instant of shock, Grail leaned the pillars against each other, pushed himself through the crowd, and, in a single leap, grabbed Chaucer by the throat and pinned him to the floor. His metal fingers separated from his hand and drilled into the floor.

Chaucer's looked up with yellow eyes at Viscariot, who still flared with golden power. A gold tear crawled down her cheek.

The Sage of Ages gasped at the sight. "Such power has not been seen in the world since the angels slept. It is the kiss of Shiva!" Viscariot waved both hands and the pox disappeared in a green flash.

"I remember," Viscariot whispered with a power in her frail voice that shook what remained of the cathedral.

She stood still and seemed to observe something no one else could see. A smile followed her gasp; she wept and cheered then turned toward the balcony in sudden realization.

"You!" Viscariot pointed at the Empress. "You knew."

The Empress' eyes returned to normal. Her hair fell to her side. She replied only with kind eyes and silence.

"You didn't wake me?" Viscariot cried. "I, who has suffered through mortal pain and fears?"

"How could I?" the Empress replied with sorrowful tranquility. "Only you could remember who you were when you were ready."

"And him?" Viscariot pointed to the cowering Edgar Niles who still lay next to Johan Fourier's body. "I remember his spirit as well. It glows in my soul's eye. That ragged man is one of us. He spoke the truth to your city, and you . . ."

"Protected him the best that I could," the Empress replied. "I have watched over him just as I watched over you. The Eyes of Eies have guided you here."

"I'm not crazy?" Edgar laughed and felt his own face to make sure that he was real. "I really am an angel! Huzzah!"

"Empress," Jono called up to her from the floor, "what about the virus?"

The Empress held up her hand. "The Line has been cleansed of the dormant viruses, but any code that was touched by the virus in its activated form could not be saved."

"Then Professor Wishe . . . ?"

The Empress' eyes were sore with sorrow. "I failed her. She was infected. If any sliver of virus still existed, it could kill anyone connected to the Line. All of it had to be destroyed."

"The lives of all your connected souls. It is you that has saved both Ends countless times!" Viscariot beamed through her golden tears. "Sister, I remember. I've known you for eons. Survivor of the ages. Partner of the design. You were there at the gates of the veil. You have always been watching and waiting for us to awaken!"

Viscariot's eyes glowed hot and gold.

"I know who I am now. I know my purpose." Viscariot scowled at Chaucer. "To purify."

Out from the palm of Viscariot's hand grew a white mist. It spilled onto the floor and slithered to cover Chaucer as his cloud of pixels fought back in retaliation.

Chaucer yelled as pixels poured from his flesh. His installs were forcibly disengaged from inside his body. His animancer pixels obeyed a new master and leapt out of his pores.

The cloud of pixels condensed into a singular heap then crushed together and thudded, dead on the floor.

Chaucer collapsed.

With Chaucer's pixels gone, the hordes of controlled citizens shook themselves out of their malaise and turned against the remaining Tombs, shackling them with enchanted chairs and mechanical snares.

Viscariot looked up at the cathedral with a smile of triumphant pride. Around her glowed an aura, hot and white, against the crumbling stone pillars. With the Tombs subdued, the crowd gazed upon her in awe. She shook her right shoulder, and one golden feathered wing appeared with two smaller wings protruding below it. Her left shoulder followed. Six translucent wings illuminated the cathedral with their golden light.

"Rise, all children of Earth. You have nothing to fear now," Viscariot said, her voice a booming force of power. "We three Angels are woken! Our righteous rule will rise again, and all of you . . . will know the peace you deserve!"

Chapter Thirty-One

The Spirit of Giftmas

ells rang across the city, and the news flooded the world and beyond. In homes, bars, space stations, and camping grounds, everyone was transfixed by the images of the waking of an angel.

Cheryl Chongwas stuttered in shock behind her news desk. "It is now confirmed that the masquerading virus has been purged from the Line. The leader of the Tombs is in custody in Eies and, miraculously, the Empress herself has confirmed that she and two others are the first of seven angels, the same beings from the stories. What this means for the future of the Solar system remains to be seen, but people are jubilant in the streets across the Dark and the Day on this most surprising Giftmas wake."

"Cassindra Viscariot, president of the Peace Committee, has been identified by Fellowship scholars as the living embodiment of the angel Shiva. Shiva has long been the patron angel of the Day, represented by the six-winged dove, and is said to bring with her peace into the world."

"The third awakened angel is a man of unknown origin, but we have learned his name is Edgar Niles, referencing the very same Niles in legends that hosted the angel, Athuliandros. Tom, I am lost for words."

"I don't think you are alone, Cheryl. I expect the world will be reevaluating a lot in the coming wakes."

"If all this is true, then there are four other angels out there, waiting to wake up, to realize who they are or come out of hiding."

Paintings of the four sleeping angels scrolled across the screen. They were scenes from the biblios of an angel raising plants out of piles of ashes, an angel pulling a rainbow from above to give color to a dreary village, an angel meditating on a mountain top, and finally an angel of black space with stars reflecting from obsidian skin as evil, hungry eyes gazed down at the paradise of Earth.

Tom read off a list of names as the pictures appeared. "Gaiander the nurturer, Miraphel the artful, Thagnon the stalwart, and Attrayer the fallen."

"There's going to be a lot of folks that return to the shrines and start looking for clues for those three good angels," Cheryl said.

"It could be anyone," Tom added.

Cheryl gave Tom a playful look. "I can assure you, it's not me."

"Don't be so certain." Tom chuckled as the world and beyond pondered his words. "Keep your eyes open for the miraculous, folks! The pox has met its match, and I can't believe I'm saying this, but there *are* angels among us."

Trumpets sounded and choirs sang with snowflakes falling on the Giftmas Wake parade. Soldiers marched in red and blue uniforms with tall hats on their heads and yellow buttons on their chests. They spun toy rifles in the air and broke into an absurd dance of joy every other block. The city guard bots had all been cleansed of the Masquerade virus, and they marched behind the soldiers with floppy red Giftmas hats on their heads.

Music filled the narrow streets of Eies as crowds lined the sidewalks and peered from balconies and windows. Hollow hearts filled the skies and shared the sights and sounds across the star system.

For the first time ever, the mechanized Eies dance troupe was joined by dancers from the Day dressed in fairy costumes. Together they frolicked in each other's arms, kicking up piles of snow and spinning in the air with their mouth open to catch the falling flakes.

Colorful floats rolled down the lane. Each celebrated a different region of Earth. The Snow Cone float had hills of fake snow where penguins slid and flipped around an icy half-pipe. The Caer Midus float was surrounded by fake trees and tumnkins playing pan flutes, arm-in-arm, beneath a bright blue balloon. An Aires float lit up the street with mirrored towers that glowed pink, orange, and lavender.

Samuel, the bard bot, stood on top of a float with a simple wooden frame meant to be the stables where the Lad of Giftmas was born. The bot proudly sang *Hark, The Herald Angels Sing* as actors dressed as the seven angels blessed the child with special powers. The Lad, now a young man, burst from the cradle. He wore a fake white beard despite his eternal youth, which symbolized the wisdom of his years. The Lad of Giftmas fought off actors dressed as nightmare creatures and tossed presents to the crowd.

Costumed soldier mice and snow spirits ran around the crowds, sipping on spiced crapple cider, dancing and giving hugs to strangers. A group of frostlets carved massive ice sculptures with their magic into scenes of the Lad and the angels.

The central float of the parade was a red throne room resting on a pillow of white clouds. Seven golden chairs with red velvet cushions were set in a circle. The front of the float held seven candles.

On the streets of Eies and from all the watching cities across the Earth and into space, crowds cheered at the sight of the Empress of Eies, now known to be Ariam the Wise, Cassindra Viscariot, Shiva the protector, and a groomed and better dressed Edgar Niles, known as Athuliandros the missionary.

Students followed the float, performing an erratic and hastily practiced performance. Freya spun around in circles and shot plumes of fire into the air. Murphy rolled along the ground and danced with his short legs kicking out in rapid bursts.

A marching band joined them, blasts of music that filled the air and airwaves.

Suriana leaned over the balcony of her father's apartment as the parade passed below. Her expression was a mix of awe and disbelief. Alistair hugged her from behind, and the Sage of Ages brought them both hot crapple cider.

"Can you believe this?" Suri said. "It's really happening. The angels are real and they are here. Awoken in the *Dark* of all places."

Alistair nodded. "The biblios advises to expect the unexpected when angels are involved. I have to admit, it does feel a little odd." The Sage quoted, "'*Look ye not for gifts of angels in the halls of Fellows or dens of prayer, for their work lies elsewhere, on the fetid shores of disbelief.*'"

Alistair pondered the words. "Maybe it had to be in the Dark. If angels awoke in the Day, the Dark Enders would call it false, I'm sure. Imagine that. And an angel in the Empress herself? That may be the only thing to convince the Dark to believe at all. In a way, the signs were there. How long has there been an Empress over the Dark, her Eyes of Eies always watching over her people? Perhaps hiding among non-believers is her way of whispering."

"Perhaps," the Sage said. "But be wary of knowing

what the angels plan. It is a ponderous thing, the mind of an immortal. They certainly must see the world in ways we do not."

Alistair turned to the Sage. "You've met the Empress. Or Ariam, if that's who she really is. You've been close to her. After all the harsh words that may have slipped off a Day Ender's tongue, does she harbor any ill will against us? Was the angel inside her even awake when our armies met at the Keeper?"

"All these are mysteries to me," the Sage replied, smiling. "She was reserved. Perhaps guilt in the soul is punishment enough."

"Or by the grace of Shiva, she will stay her hand."

The Sage turned to a plethora of floating mirrors that showed people all over the Day cheering and weeping at the sight of angels on Earth. "She was flawed before, that much I could tell. Brazen and wounded when she met us for war."

"And since then?"

"Earnest in a desire for peace." The Sage pondered the celebration below and the joy across the world. "Perhaps it was at the Keeper that the sleeping angel inside her stirred. Perhaps that wake melted her metal heart. Even the greatest sinners among us have angels whispering wisdom in our hearts. Perhaps she was chosen as a sign for the Day to forgive the old transgressions of the Dark. And through forgiveness, we will be reborn."

Suri curled over the balcony's rail in awe of the cheering crowds. "There will be peace at long last."

Alistair rested his head next to his daughter. "My little peacemaker. What ever will you do now that you've lost your job?"

Suri sighed. "I couldn't be happier to be put out of this work."

"You could always hunt for the sleeping angels! With two Dark Enders now embodied and only one from the Day, we should hope for another back home," Alistair mused as he sipped on his cider. "Where do you imagine the others will be found?"

"I always imagined Miraphel living in the Day, painting colors on rainbows and crowned in flowers," Suri said. "She and Gaiander were always my favorites as a child."

Alistair waved a finger. "Myself, I simply cannot image Gaiander anywhere but the forest gardens of the Midwake Ring. The nurturer yearns for life to grow. Rock and ice just don't seem the right fit. What say you, Sage? Care to prognosticate on the waking of the final four?"

The Sage grinned kindly but shook his head. "I have no predictions for the wakes ahead. The work of angels is beyond me. We are blessed to bear witness to this spectacle. What happens next? I do not know. It is for us to wait and watch, for we are living in an age of miracles."

Atop the celestial float, the Empress smiled warily as the world watched. She leaned toward Viscariot and whispered, "Tell me again, how is this wise?"

Viscariot smiled at the doubt. "Sister, I know you have a cautious spirit. You have watched over us, steering us to this wake, but now your eons of loneliness must end. The world must change, and we must no longer sleep or hide." She gestured to the crowds that cheered around them. "Listen to how they praise us. This is who we truly are. This is who they need us to be."

Confetti fluttered through the air, color mixing with the stark white of snow as the crowds cheered, clapped, and saluted the passing float.

Edgar poked his frazzled face between them. "Look at where we are! Everywhere I wandered, in crags and caves, in gardens and deserts, my mind pulled me onward, to a place where my wandering heart is made at ease." His crooked smile twitched. "I dreamed of places, and so many were wrong. They made me feel wrong, broken, but here? This is right. This is where we are. Where we need to be. I know it."

"Truly stated, brother," Viscariot said. "You are on the Narrow Path and you are not alone. The wakes of ascension are coming, and we will usher them in together."

The Empress tried to swallow her discomfort. "Dreaming is easy, but the mechanix are hard. It's the *how* that troubles me."

"Don't worry yourself about the how," Viscariot said with glowing pride. "Have faith! And cherish the moment when the world begins to be its better self."

"That's right. Just be here in the now." Edgar waved madly with both his fleshy and mechanical arms at the adoring crowds.

Faces of every species looked at them from balconies and bridges, from people huddled together on the sidewalks. In their eyes, the Empress saw a craving for answers, for leaders to guide them to fulfill their dreams. They were eager children, hungry for the future, and she mourned the wake when they would learn that great dreams have great costs.

Across the Earth, statues of the six good angels were dusted off and decorated in pine wreaths and ornamented in red and gold. Shrines that had lain dormant for centuries were freed from the sediment of nature, their shattered roofs repaired, their pillars erected once more. Even across the Dark End, curious new archaeologists followed rumors and ancient records to uncover shrines of times long lost scattered across the land.

The world was enthralled with angels.

Some hoped their newfound faith would ward off the pox. Others hoped to send a message to the awakening angels.

We are on your side. Your will be done.

It was also a signal to the Tombs.

Your wakes are numbered. There are angels coming to bring justice.

The world appeared to stand united for the first time in memory. With the power of the angels, the pox would be defeated and the Tombs would be dismantled. There was nowhere left for them to hide that the whispers of the angels wouldn't find them.

Rows of seven candles decorated the world's refurbished shrines and along window sills of many homes. The light of the three center candles illuminated ruins and brought new life to cobweb-covered halls. The remaining four candles stayed unlit, waiting for the wake to share a new message of awakening, waiting for the wakes of the rule of the pantheon of angels to begin.

News spread swiftly to all space under Sol.

Peoples on space stations, planets, and starships wondered about the happenings back on that distant homeland of Earth. Were the angels real? Were they offering blessings? Were they granting wishes? But most of all, where were the remaining three good angels to be found?

On the Einstein IV station, aliens and magical creatures of every species crowded around the windows looking down at Earth. They watched screens full of celebrations. They saw magic folk weep in the embrace of mechanical arms.

"I thought that was all just fairy tales," a tuskan woman said. The crowd around her nodded in silent agreement. "This is going to change everything."

The tuskan lit the three electric lights that sat in the Earth facing window and let the other four remain unlit, waiting to hear good tiding from the Earth or beyond.

A candle flickered against the dim halls in a corridor on the moon. Asmodeus Fleeth sneered as he clenched two fingers around the wick and put it out. "Stop this nonsense."

Around him, purple-cloaked terralunans cowered in shadows as the planet split between light and darkness floated beyond a thick window.

"It is happening," said a terralunan.

"Should we allow this?" A cloaked terralunan stood behind Fleeth. "The blockade will not hold with this news. They will come."

"They are coming now."

"Their numbers will grow."

"They will want to see the awoken."

"They will want to hunt for the sleeping."

"Our best course is to ally with them. Gather their favor and wait for the trials to come."

"The C.O.S.S. will take advantage."

"Not if we are better positioned," Fleeth said, cutting through their chatter. "And we are."

Cloaked terralunans swirled around him. "Their numbers are greater than ours, and they have hungered to sever our hold on the planet."

"The C.O.S.S. will fracture from the inside out," Fleeth snarled.

"The ministers of the C.O.S.S. will not give up power without a fight."

"A fight is coming."

"They will be the first to fall when the legions of the Abyss return."

"Will we be ready for what must come?"

"We are patient and at the ready." Fleeth glared at the blue planet. "He will be waking soon. And when he does, he will not be alone."

In the flicker of orange candlelight, the marble face almost looked alive. Green veins ran subtly through cold stone. Jono ran his hand over the blank eyes to close them. A red scar on the back of the mask felt sharp and hostile, but the face of Persephone Wishe was serene and still.

"Are you ready?" Keiko asked.

Jono looked up. The face disappeared from his hands as if it had never been there in the first place. It was only a projection from the code his mind.

The rows of chairs were mostly empty as the Giftmas wake mourners had paid their last respect to an urn of ashes and smiling pictures of Johan Fourier. Windom teachers that barely knew him had come and gone. Researchers from the Pathaganon lingered and quietly discussed the man's legacy. The small Fourier family huddled together in awkward, muted sobs. He had no wife or children, but two parents, four grandparents, a brother, and two sisters had lost someone dear to them.

Jono looked around. "Where's Isaac?"

Keiko pointed to the door.

They met their friend outside the small funeral home in a quiet corner of the city. Isaac sat on the street corner with his head propped up by his hands, and they sat next to him.

"He would be proud of you, you know," Keiko said.

Isaac shrugged with a look that showed that he wondered if it was true.

"He was so close to a breakthrough. He sent me a message. I would have met him at the lab, but then you started fighting Knox and . . . His last words were 'The holes will lead us to the trigger.' It could hold the key to everything, but I have no idea what it means. We still don't know how the pox works or even what it is."

"At least these angels will protect us from it now," Keiko replied.

"Will they? Protect all of us?" Isaac swallowed his anger and sighed. "I guess there's nothing left to do but say goodbye."

Isaac stood.

"There is something else," Jono said.

Isaac paused. "What do you mean?"

"Fourier's work isn't over. You were his apprentice." Jono slapped his friend on the back. "The work is yours now. The research lives on."

Isaac's sad face cracked with the hint of a smile.

"You're right, Jono. This isn't over."

"It's over," Maergann said.

The Burly Belch was nearly vacant. While the city streets and homes were full of celebrating communities and loving families, the bartender and owner, Earl, snored behind the counter.

Maergann glanced at the corner where a Windom cadet with firebomb installs moped alone with a honey-ale. Ever since she came to this greasy city, she was constantly assessing threats, even out of lonely cadets on Giftmas wake.

"Only if you want it to be," Ramsus replied from across the table.

Maergann shook her head, barely remembering she'd said anything to illicit a response. "The angels of legends are real and awakening, the Tombs at Saint Newton's were all killed or captured, and our case with Cederic Pummel went cold. The Tombs indeed keep their agents in isolation from each other. So if you are here to still convince me to leave the royal guard, then you have a carrot, I assume?"

Ramsus glanced downward then met her gaze. "A vegetable?" He looked genuinely puzzled.

"It's a term from the Day. Carrots and sticks. Enticing rewards and threats of punishment." Maergann explained. "That look in your mechanical eyes tells me you have a secret you are itching to reveal. Something you believe will persuade me to join your little enterprise."

Ramsus grinned. "You read my mind, proving my point that you're a perfect fit."

Maergann took a gulp of amber liquid from her mug. Patience was a virtue, and if her future path would lead alongside that boorish soldier, she would be wise to not rush into it. She let the room linger with the clash of silence and the hum of elation from the city beyond its walls.

"What is it?"

"A direction." Ramsus pulled a mauve crystal from his pocket and slid it across the table. The crystal was more than about sharing information; it was a gesture of partnership. How else could a soldier properly use a crystal, if not for the magical skills of a knight from the Day?

Maergann gave him a suspicious glance and picked up the crystal. She held it against her palm and let its message cast itself in front of her eyes. It was a vision only she could see, but Ramsus knew what it was and would be watching her expression. She refused to give him the satisfaction of an answer before her words spoke it.

In a fading wisp of light and mist, she saw the image of a crowded train station. The view zoomed in on an old pale man with a long white beard. He stepped into the train just as a flash of red rippled over the city.

The masquerade virus.

In that instant, his beard disappeared and the grinning face of Eljin Tombs was looking back at her.

"The train was departing for Aires," Ramsus said.

"Surely a Tombs is not foolish enough to leave us a trail?"

"The 'old man' disappeared halfway through the flight."

The images faded into the train station in Aires, the orange horizon of Dawn above them melting against the clear windows of the skyscrapers around it.

She looked over the scene. The horde of travelers disembarked until she saw it . . .

"There are two." Maergann released the crystal, and the vision faded from her eyes. "Two identical women left the station from different cars in different directions. Show me more."

Ramsus leaned across the table. "The last ping was six minutes ago. He's in the Day, half-way through a bog in the Diremark. So, Sir Maergann Brigid, honor guard and champion of virtue, are you ready for a hunt?"

Maergann chugged the rest of her beer and slammed the mug onto the table in front of Ramsus's full glass.

"Drink up, soldier. My blade is thirsty for *satisfaction*."

Fathoms below the city, deep in the contorted bowels of the mountain, Vincent Chaucer sat behind a clear wall. Hundreds of locked doors separated him from the world above. There existed no cell on the planet more secure, and yet Chaucer had the pleasant appearance of someone who was exactly where they wanted to be.

Dvaniur Grail stared at him from a plush red chair on the other side of the cell.

"Aren't you going to say something?" Chaucer prodded.

Grail glared at the man who had once been his friend but had transformed into a gleeful murderer. "You're powerless now, Vincent. Is this what you wanted?"

"Powerless? Am I, Dvaniur?" Chaucer chuckled. He sat as relaxed as one could be on his cold stone bench. "You still cannot see what is right in front of you. You still do not grasp the trap I have set into motion. The end of this farce *is* coming. The Angels are waking," Chaucer said in a mocking tone. "The hunt for the rest has already begun. There is unmatched power in them. The world will be unified under their rule, just wait and see. Do you have any idea what *they* will do with that power? Do you?"

"The Empress has maintained stability for millennia," replied Grail. "I trust her to see us through whatever trap you are planning."

Chaucer smiled. "Yes. That is right. The Empress watched over you. Alone. But now more angels wake with new gifts for our little planet." Chaucer leaned his back against the wall. "The Fallen Angel is one of them. He will wake at last, and when he does, this planet will know a fear unlike anything it has endured before. This is not some trivial war or common plague. The Pit is hungry, and when the King of the Abyss rises, he will swallow this soiled existence whole."

"I don't believe that," Grail replied. "We've averted war with the Day. We can stop your pox. We will weather any storm you throw at us."

Chaucer leaned in with a grin of satisfaction. "*You*, perhaps, Dvan. *You* could weather any storm that rages. *You* could survive and conquer the demons that claw from the depths. But them? Listen closely and hear how well their frail hearts weathered the pox. Look deeper at the fallow ground they build their solace upon. Beware what they believe, Dvaniur. Each End was so convinced that the other would use the Keeper to destroy them, and that from a mere rumor of the key of Attrayer. They were so quick to believe such evil existed in anyone that was not like themselves. So quick to believe the worst, and murder was their first reply! You will see, my friend. Just wait and see what they will believe in next."

Chapter Thirty-Two

From a Distant Gaze

Lights filled the East Trench of Eies with orange warmth. Bonfires roared in metal bins with the shapes of snowflakes, a flying sleigh, and reindeer cut through them, casting shadows in shapes around the light. The East Trench was a humble corner of the city, but in the glow of neighbors sharing Giftmas barbeques and friends huddled around bonfires, Jono couldn't imagine anywhere better.

His friends, their families, and all their neighbors filled the snowy street to share a spectacular Giftmas buffet. Candied yams, smoked turkey, and mashed mushrups dashed with spiced crapple sauce and ornamented with schnazberries. Everyone was invited, and the old saying was true: more did make it merrier.

Children squealed as they threw snowballs at each other, and parents scolded a stray collision with the punch bowl. Oscar's younger sister, Esmeralda, led the charge against the west side of the street as she sieged the street with cheers and joy.

Neighbors and friends exchanged gifts wrapped in simple brown paper and tied with colored twine. They drank and joked and made strangers feel like welcome family.

A Giftmas tree stood in front of each doorstop, each covered with ornaments that had been traded between neighbors for generations. No one knew who gave them first, but each stood out with its own story about the people that had lived on that row for generations.

The Kepler family returned to the East Trench from their home in the Nimbus Towers every Giftmas to celebrate with the friends and a family that still lived there.

David's father Percival pointed out a shimmering orange and blue ornament.

"There it is, Fiona! The Bohrs's neighbors have it this year. Uly, look here, this was an ornament my mother received from the mayor of East Trench as an award for putting out a fire seventy-five years ago!"

"Seventy-six years," his wife corrected.

Uly pretended to look interested at her father's story, but when Rex pointed out the were-pup that was curled between Cid Kirin's legs, she bolted into the street to see if it would play with them.

Forge yapped and spun as he chased Uly and Rex for the treats they waved at him.

"Do you have the buns?" Cid asked as he roasted bratwursts on a barbeque in the middle of the street. "And the mustard?"

"Let me check." Keiko dug through the pile of food in Wallace's shell as her mechanical armadillo mimicked her actions in a vain search for mustard.

Oscar's father leaned on Percival's shoulder as they sat on the stoop of the Bohrs's home. "One of these years, old man, you need to invite us up to your fancy parties above the clouds."

Percival patted him on the back. "You want to crash a cloud district party? Take my ticket, please! I'll stay right here, thank you very much. They may know how to make a spectacle up there, but here? Look at this row and you tell me, Reggie, that this right here isn't what Giftmas is about. History! Friends! Family!"

"Freezing our hulls off," Fiona Kepler added.

Zennessa Bohrs raised a glass. "And drinking 'em toasty!"

Keiko kneeled in front of Wallace and held up a small package.

"What is this, ma'am?" Wallace asked.

"Well, it's not mustard," Keiko said. "It's a gift, Wallace. For you."

The bot looked at her inquisitively. "I hardly need compensation for doing my duty."

Keiko giggled. "It's not compensation! It's appreciation. You saved us, and it's Giftmas. Open it."

Wallace tore open the box with his pointy mouth. "New hinge joints! And those thruster upgrades I wanted!"

Keiko wrapped her arms around the mechanical

tortoise's neck. "I love you, buddy."

"Merry Giftmas, Madam Kirin."

"Merry Giftmas, pal."

Jono admired Keiko from a distance with Isaac sitting next to him.

"We survived to see another Giftmas," Isaac said. They clinked glasses of cocoa nog in a toast. "But just barely."

Jono laughed. "I'll take it."

"I heard Knox is still buried in his shame from your fight."

Jono winced. "You'd think he'd be proud. He left enough bruises on me to make people wonder if I'm actually purple with pale spots."

"He won a badge of bruises while we defended the city against an army of Tombs and infected guard bots. The pride of that burnt-brained gunner is more bruised than your skin. Elise told me she actually heard him praying to the angels to keep some Tombs alive for him when he graduates in two years so he can firebomb them into ash."

"So?"

"For a soldier of the Dark, that, my friend, is as desperate as I could imagine."

"He's one broken clunker, but I guess if he wasn't, then I wouldn't have gone deep into the Code World and Wishe would never have spotted the masquerade virus."

Isaac spat out his cocoa nog laughing. "I've got it! For Giftmas, you tell Knox that! He'll claim the victory and tell the whole school how he should get all the credit for the Empress wiping the virus, angels awakening, the fight with the Tombs, the whole list!"

"I don't know what's worse: an angry, depressed Knox or an arrogant, boastful one."

"Two sides of the same bilge, mate."

"Have you heard how our Day friends are enjoying Giftmas in the Dark?"

"They're at the biggest party in the city." Isaac swiped a finger from his temple to the air, and an image hovered in front of them. Murphy and Riley were head-and-shoulders above the massive crowd of partiers. "With the Explorers and every other celebrity in the city."

"Is that Agripa carrying Riley?" Jono asked.

Isaac nodded. "And Shakram Stoli has Murphy standing on his shoulders. I guess it pays to be a guest at Giftmas. I think the squires are going to be welded after all."

"All's well that ends well," Jono said with a smile.

Isaac shook his head at Jono's attempt at poetry.

"Hey, Isaac," David called from across the street. "Come hold my baby sister."

Isaac sneered. "I don't really do *babies*."

"Come on!" David said. "Marabelle likes your scaly face."

Isaac shrugged. "Who am I to deny an infant the majesty of my dashing countenance?"

As they played with the newest member in the Kepler family, Jono realized he felt happier than he had in a very long time. The world was going to be okay. There was a real family filling up that snow-covered street, and he was a part of it. For the first time he could remember, he truly felt as though he wasn't alone.

Dr. Stone waved at him from the block down the road, calling out, "Merry Giftmas!" Stone was visiting one of his many relatives across the city. Zuun Mu, the healthy and hoppy woolly frog, clung to his shoulder, her purple tongue lolling out of her mouth as she looked excitedly around the active street.

Jono caught a glimpse of a ribbon on Stone's chest that made him smile. It had green and white stripe, just like Professor Wishe's hair. Jono adjusted the ribbon attached to his own jacket. Wishe wasn't alone in life either. She was loved by the whole of Windom, and Jono wasn't alone in missing her.

Esmeralda squealed as she raced by in a game of tag with Oscar close behind, his new hat flopping behind his head.

"Embrace the moment!" Oscar laughed.

"What's that?" Keiko asked as she handed Jono a brat in a bun and pointed to a small blue package set between Jonothon's feet.

"One last gift to deliver."

"What's in it?" she asked, taking a seat next to him, a brat of her own in her hand.

"Like you don't already know, Ms. See-through-vision?" Jono grinned.

"I was being polite." Keiko smiled. "It's perfect."

They sat in the glow of red and green lights against snow as the street hummed with joy.

"They're wrong, you know," Jono said.

"The Tombs?" asked Keiko. "That's the understatement of the eon."

Jono gave her a solemn look, and she sat patiently. "I saw oblivion through the Eyes of the Empress. It was overwhelming. Calling me. But they're wrong. Our matter is what makes us wonderful. The trick of energy becoming matter, growing into life . . . it's not an aberration, it's the whole point. Nature builds upon itself. There's the nothing all around us, and yet we live despite it. We exist. We defy oblivion simply by being, yet we're more than that. We learn, we explore, we build and create. We *are* the purpose, we are the consciousness of a universe learning to know itself. Oblivion is our only enemy. All this, the tricks of light, stories of angels? It's all a part of the layers of life, infinitely stacked over space and time."

"Even the pox? Even the Tombs?"

"Even the things that hurt us are amazing in that they exist at all."

Keiko leaned her head against his shoulder. "I'm glad you're feeling better."

"I'm going to *be* better. I won't make those mistakes again. I promise."

"You worry too much, Jono."

"There's no worry anymore." Jono smiled. "Just wonder."

"It's amazing. This city? Our friends? All of this is our family. I just want them to be okay."

"They *exist*. That's all we can ask for."

Forge barked, inviting them to the battle just as he dodged a snowball then charged playfully after his attacker.

Keiko shoved the rest of the brat in her mouth, scooped up a handful of snow, and then entered the fray.

Jono breathed in deeply. The air was crisp and cold and made him feel good to be alive. Around him, everyone seemed to lose themselves in a moment of happiness that hung over the season. Jono clung to the feeling of transcendence, that way of looking at the world he found on the cliffs of oblivion.

No one knew what the coming wakes held, and still, they were alive. They were surrounded by friends, food, and the spirit of a city full of tens of millions of people all embracing a simple wake of joy with the ones they loved.

Jono concluded it was a feeling worth dwelling on. And that was exactly what he determined to do.

It was late in the sleep hours, and the apartments in the Crown were all dim and silent. Exhausted partiers had found their beds and left the city in a quiet peace that contrasted the horror and elation of the past wake. The cheering crowds that had filled the streets had long dispersed. Giftmas dinner parties were long abandoned, leaving celebrants with full bellies and peaceful dreams. Everyone . . . except for her.

Suriana sat alone, silhouetted against the glow of the city beyond her apartment's window. Fresh streaks of tears marked her cheeks. Her trembling fingers grazed the replay button on the postcard in her hands.

The image on the postcard was a shaky view of the fields of Caer Midus as a caravan arrived through its gates. Four white stags pulled a golden carriage. On top sat a young girl in a familiar white and blue gown. Suriana had come to Caer Midus countless times before, but that was the wake when she first met a Dark Ender.

The image glistened over close ups of grassy fields under the sun then to a chubby orange and red bird pecking at a piece of bread that a small finger pushed toward it.

She saw herself again, through the eyes of his memory watch. She was eleven years old, huddled with her group of classmates that had said terrible things about someone different from them.

"You weren't afraid." Jonothon's voice cracked and stuttered in the recording. "You were from the other End of the world, and you were nicer to me than anyone I had ever met before."

The garden in Caer Midus sparkled in light and shadow from vines that created a canopy over marble pillars. She saw herself in the distance, surrounded by young children as she waved a wand at the gamboling images of the story of the Good Wanderer. She sat radiant in a spire of sunlight. That was the stories class she taught. She didn't know he'd seen her there.

"It was such a short time, but I've kept the memory of those wakes at Caer Midus close to me ever since," Jono continued. "You gave me courage. You made me want to be a better person, even if I haven't always acted like it."

The image became a blare of light and darkness as a roar of noise echoed around it. It was recording inside his pocket when the fel shades attacked Caer Midus. The bellow of fel beasts and the clash of flame blades crackled out of the postcard.

"I'm not good with . . . people. I was terrified of the world, and there you were, not fearless, but brave. I wanted to be strong, like you. That's why I went through the shrunken door and came back to the Dark. I wanted to stay with you, to be your friend, but I couldn't. Not like that. I couldn't be a coward any longer. That's not what you would have done. You would have gone to help people if you could. You would have been brave enough. Suri, I am so sorry for how I treated you. You deserve your friends to be so much better. Your kindness meant the world to me, but I was frightened and thought being a hero was the only reason people would like me. Only heroes had friends—that's what the world told me. It's taken this long, but I'm not scared anymore. And in my mind, I . . ."

The image turned to Jonothon's tearful face looking directly at the screen with his bunkroom behind him. He swallowed tears and struggled to go on.

"I know it may not feel this way, but I think I'm more like you then I was before. More open to people that are different. I try to stand up for the Day, like you did for the Dark. I try to understand what others are going through. I like myself more because of that, because of you. I don't have a Giftmas present for you. I don't have anything. In this whole burn'em world, I don't have much, but I owe you an apology and . . . I wrote this for you."

Jono unfolded a thick piece of paper, the page that sat on Suriana's lap.

"It's called 'From Her Distant Gaze.'"

Jonothon cleared his throat.

"The Day is a lonely place,

For the sun.

She gives life to her children,

Yet so far from the warmth they reflect.

She gives joy on wakes splashing in water,

Splendor on wakes as fingers entwine,

Candor on wakes when eyes must see clearly,

Solace on wakes to shine truth through tears.

Ever alone,

She yearns to touch the faces,

Of those that bask in her magic,

But she never moves closer,

Fearful that she would burn them.

The Day is where the sun,

Chooses to be."

Jono folded the piece of paper and put it into an envelope.

"You made me want to be a better person. I'm sorry I

failed you, but I will keep trying. Merry Giftmas, Suriana. I hope you always feel welcome in the Dark."

A tear landed on the screen, and trembling hands hovered over the replay button.

For the first time in as long as she could remember, Suriana didn't worry about her duty to the Day. It wasn't a wish for dating or dancing that she'd kept that tattered button for all those years. It was in the eyes of that lonely Dark Ender that she found the first person in her life as isolated as she was. Her life of duty kept her distant, her eagerness to deserve her position kept her apart from everyone around her. She demanded so much of herself. She wanted to save the world. It was in that lost, pale face that she had finally found a kindred spirit. They were both so desperately lonely, yearning to be known and loved by those around them, and yet were so terribly far from it.

Suriana breathed deeply in the silent glow of the city. She hit the replay button once more and reveled in the feeling of someone seeing through to her true self. In the final moments of Giftmas, she finally got her wish.

Someone knew how she felt.

She wasn't alone.

Chapter Thirty-Three

Sweet Sleeps

"Everything is going to be alright."

The ghost of Beky Wyer brushed the tussled brown hair across her son's brow. The comforter that wrapped around him was tinted purple in the blue twilight, even as a still lit candle fought valiantly to fill the world with light. The bed was far too large for the small eleven-year-old child. Printed words on an open book glittered in the flame's light.

"Do I have to?" Jonothon asked.

His mother smiled down at him. "Everyone needs to sleep, even if the coming wakes will sail you to unknown shores."

"What should I dream about?" Jono asked.

His mother's smile widened, and joy swelled in her eyes. "Oh, the world is so full of wonder, how to choose? How about stomping over mountaintops on the back of an enormous mech? Or soaring through space with stars all around you and nothing holding you back?"

Jonothon pondered the infinite options and came to the following thought: "Maybe I'll dream about being back here."

A lump caught in her throat as she held back tears and avoided looking at the stacks of luggage beside the door. "I hope you do, Jono. Dream of us and the breeze along the field. Dream of my hugs and your father swinging you in circles. Dream of Dahlia's laugh."

"And the bark of the family's new were-pup?" Jono smiled.

"A quiet bark. More a purr, I think. Or a bubbly fish sound." She kissed his forehead.

Outside his wide window, beyond waves of green and below the dim moon light glowing in sky, it was late in the sleeps. But for some reason, the street lights of the quiet town kept shining brightly on.

"Tomorrow's going to be a big wake," his mother said. "Are you ready for this?"

Jono looked at the candle's flame frolicking against the Adventure of Illius. "I don't know."

"That's very wise of you, darling. Knowing is such a difficult thing, but *not* knowing? That's honest and true and in this wide wondrous world, it will give you wisdom when the world has lost its senses."

Jono smiled as she tucked him into bed. "I think I'm ready to find out."

The Empress leaned over Jonothon as he slept in his bunk in twenty nine Capricorn Corridor. No one could see her, and no one was awake to try.

She smiled at the tears of love trickling down his cheeks. His body lay still. His breathing came softly in and softly out. For the first sleep in months, he was truly at peace.

There stood the Empress of the Dark End, leader of millions and angel of wisdom with no place of greater importance to be than beside that young boy, making certain he slept well.

"The vision matrix is more subtle this time," said a gentle voice behind her.

The Empress turned.

She was back in the throne room with an image of Jono hovering in front of her. Her steward, Hobbs, stood beside her in a tidy black suit and red cravat.

"Good." The Empress smiled gently. "Some things shouldn't be analyzed. Just enjoy the dream, Jono."

"It is a sweet gift you bring him," Hobbs said.

"We owe him this in the least," she replied. "If I can't soothe an aching heart, then what kind of angel am I?"

Hobbes nodded in approval.

"Please, monitor the hypnos algorithm to correct against artifacts. I don't want him disturbed until wake."

"As you wish, Empress."

"Thank you, Hobbs."

The Empress sat on her wired throne, alone, watching the boy sleep. The room was a black cave, save for the scattered spots of light from the machines lining the walls, the glow of the hovering screen, and the faint light from Terralunis and the distant stars that crept through the red drapes to the balcony.

"What are you looking for?" she whispered in the darkness.

For a moment, she wondered if the darkness would ever answer, and then, light footsteps came from her balcony and into the room.

Natharen Vault approached the throne of the Dark End as casually as getting in line for a hot fudge sundae.

"The truth," Natharen replied.

"The truth?" The Empress sighed. "How would that be useful?"

Natharen didn't reply, and she was content to fight him over a contest of silence.

"It's always *how* with you, isn't it?" Natharen finally observed.

The Empress stood from her throne and the image of Jono disappeared. She stared at the young-looking boy before her, waiting patiently for him to speak.

"I wake in the middle of a story and don't know where I am. Which version of history am I to believe? Which tales do you remember?" Natharen asked.

The Empress closed her eyes and felt the eons of her memory wash over her. "A history of isolation, responsibility, and a burden too great for one pair of shoulders."

"And which role did I play in all that? Isolation by design? Or by other means?"

"I am but *one* of us. I wasn't meant to be alone," she

said.

"And yet you are the one that remained while all other phantoms faded."

"What are you saying?"

"You have others, angels ascending, quick to wrap the world in their warm white wings. Yet, which is better, stability or change?"

"Change is inevitable."

"Change is for the changers. You, of all of us, know that. What is coming and which road is wisely chosen?"

"I don't have an answer." She stepped closer, reaching out for him, but Natharen stepped backward.

He raised a hand for her to stop.

"I am but one of many pieces on the board," she said.

"You are the lasting peace. I need to choose wisely . . . trust is a window, clear and true, yet mine is cracked all over. Do you know the reason?"

The Empress shook her head.

"Lies can be so pretty, can't they?" Natharen said, pondering the marriage of space and stars.

"They can be more than lies. If they surround you so fully, the lies can be life. They can make all the difference."

"More indeed." Natharen scowled at the idea. "'*Oh, the gods of man, they weep for all, when Babel thrives, all's left is the Fall.*'"

"It was never meant to be perfect, Natharen, or easy." The Empress pleaded with the boy like a concerned mother. "You have to hold on to what faith you can."

"And how solid is your faith, Ariam?"

The Empress took a moment to think. "It is wisely placed. I hope."

"What do you have faith in when the slate is wiped blank? When angels can't remember their calling?" The boy climbed onto the balcony's stone railing. "We are broken, and all this? Momentum has caught us. We are drowning in the current. Are we being put back together? Or being torn apart?"

Natharen waited for her to say something, but sad eyes and silence were her only replies.

"The wick is burning short . . . ." Natharen stepped backward off the railing. His body fell down the length of the central spire and disappeared with a flash of green in the low clouds.

The Empress stepped out onto the balcony and wrapped her arms around herself against the chilling air of the ever-present night. Her watchful eyes hummed in the back of her mind. The eyes called to her like eager children demanding constant attention. Across the whole of her memory, she'd been ready to give the people in the images and sounds the careful analysis they needed, but now that distant choir of data patterns sent shivers down her spine. The eyes sung of spikes and valleys, splinters and shifts in the models of measured behavior that she had maintained to keep her society stable for so many millennia.

The eyes called her to watch over the omens of change, and yet, she shut the signals out. The Empress knew two conflicting truths: first, that she was an agent of stability, and the second, that change was inevitable. A pang of fear stung in her mind, fear of losing control and fear for the loss of the fragile balance of the world.

She looked at the distance universe above her. Those stars, her true companions across eons of time, twinkled on without a care for life or death or the whims and wishes of an angel. It was both cold and comforting.

"I hope you find what you are looking for," the Empress whispered, "before it's too late for us all."

The End.

Look for the next adventure in the
Dark & Day series!

Book 4

The cadets and squires embark on a summer long
adventure in the Day!
Squires struggle to complete quests to become knights!
Pilgrims journey from the Coalition of Solar Space
back to Earth!
The Angels seek to discover their true purpose.
Jonothon gets swept up in an ancient myth,
that just may be the only truly
Impossible Quest!

Coming Soon!

You can help us continue the adventure!

Share Dark & Day with your friends!

Rate and Review Dark & Day on Amazon.com!

Join the Facebook group!

Thank you, and happy reading!